THE SISTERHOOD

Penelope Friday

Bella
BOOKS

2016

Bella Books, Inc.
P.O. Box 10543
Tallahassee, FL 32302

First Bella Books Edition 2016

Editor: Amanda Jean
Cover Designer: Sandy Knowles

ISBN: 978-1-59493-508-4

Dedication

To Nikki and Debby, the sisters I was fortunate enough to have from birth, and to the Sisters I have found in my life since.

Acknowledgments

Many grateful thanks to JL Merrow and to Amanda Jean for their help and support at various points of the editing process of *The Sisterhood*. It would not be half the book it is now without their help, and I know it. You are both brilliant. Particular acknowledgements also need to go to Elizabeth, who could be described as my very own 'big little sister' and on whom Charity's physical looks were based. Please note that Charity is, therefore, very good looking! And, of course, much love to the rest of my family and friends for their support. My parents are wonderful, and my boys more wonderful still. James and Cameron, I love you.

PROLOGUE

"One more push, Madam."

"I can't."

The lady's face was red with exertion and tears stood out in her eyes. A maid patted her head with a damp cloth as the midwife took care of things further down her body. She knew her husband would be waiting downstairs, smoking a cigar as he paced the library, anticipating the news they both so desperately wanted. It was perhaps the only thing the couple had ever agreed upon.

"Just one more push and baby will be here," the midwife said again. It might have been encouraging if she had not spent the last thirty minutes repeating this comforting phrase.

"Aaaah," the lady screamed as the baby finally, *finally*, entered the world.

"Goodness, what a size. No wonder the baby took time coming." The midwife carefully cleaned the worst of the blood and mucus off the baby.

"Well?" the lady asked urgently.

"Congratulations, Mrs Bellingham. A beautiful baby girl. Rebecca has a sister."

Mrs Bellingham turned her head away from the child and cried.

CHAPTER ONE

The simple fact was that Charity Bellingham should have been born a boy.

Charity, not for the first time, was pondering this as she practised her scales on the piano. C major. C minor harmonic. C minor melodic. She had played these enough times that her fingers knew the positions by rote, leaving her able to mull things over as she played. If she had been a boy, perhaps her parents would have loved her. No baby was born knowing they were unwelcome. Charity could never say when the knowledge had come to her that her parents resented her very existence, but she had lived with it long enough to know it for the truth. (C sharp major; all the sharps.) Charity should have been born a boy. Her parents had agreed on very little, but that had been the exception. Indeed, they had only tried for a second child in order to birth a boy, the entail of Charity's father's property being reliant on that one thing. Instead, they had been given Charity—a lanky, active girl, who had all the drawbacks of boyishness without the one thing which would make her acceptable. (D minor harmonic—easy.)

If she had been born a boy, they wouldn't have been thrown out of Forsbury, their old, beautiful house. The entail would have gone to her. If she had been a boy, perhaps her father wouldn't even be dead. She might have been with him just over a year ago, as he had toured their estate, and been able to fetch help immediately when he was thrown from his horse. He wouldn't have lain there alone so many hours, wouldn't have caught that awful chill that had led two days later to his death.

If she had been a boy... (E flat melodic minor.) Charity thumped the notes down, trying to drown out the voice in her head. Her mother looked up from the chair in which she sat sewing, her lips pursed.

"Charity! There can hardly be a need for that volume. It is unladylike."

"Sorry, Mother."

Ah yes, there it was. The fact was that, in all ways save the only one that mattered, Charity was a boy—or at any rate was boyish. Having been born a girl, she had not even had the courtesy to act like one and to pursue girlish interests with the same enthusiasm as her sister. Rebecca, source of this comparison, looked up from her place at her mother's side and gave Charity a sympathetic smile. Becca, like their mother, was sewing a neat line of stitches to embroider a dress. The best that could be said about Charity's sewing was that it was serviceable: two edges she sewed together would stay sewn, but they would win no merit for beauty. She preferred reading to sewing, and outdoor exercise to either.

The room the three ladies sat in was the only 'entertaining' room in the house. Large enough to hold a grand piano, a small selection of books and a comfortable array of chairs, it was small enough that the piano loomed darkly over the space, making it feel cramped and out of proportion. The piano itself was a beautiful object—a dark hardwood grand that took up half of the space in their sitting room. In Forsbury, the piano had had a room to itself, where Charity could spend time alone, unwatched by the critical eye (and ear) of Mrs Bellingham. Another fault to be laid at Charity's door: her mother clearly did not enjoy hearing her play, but as it was her younger daughter's only feminine talent, she felt obliged to nurture it. (G minor harmonic; nearing the end of the morning's exercises. Charity had to practise in the morning. During gloomy November, it became too dark to see the keys by mid-afternoon.) Charity sighed. The relationship her mother had with her was just that—an obligation. Her name said it all. Charity. It was merely charity that gave her a place in the family.

Charity finished B minor melodic and shut the piano lid with a sigh. She would have liked to practise her pieces, but her mother had made it clear that there was only so much of Charity's playing that she could take at one time. Maybe tomorrow she could work on the Purcell. Mrs Bellingham disliked that one less than most of the others, and the silent wave of disapproval was consequently less strong. And the bombastic nature of the music gave Charity a chance to play out the worst of her frustrations without criticism.

"May I go for a walk, please, Mother?" She tried to modulate her voice to the gentle, subdued style Mrs Bellingham preferred.

"No." Mrs Bellingham paused, unusually. "I have something I wish to speak to you girls about."

Charity sat down next to Rebecca, who finished her stitch with great care before putting her embroidery to the side.

"What is it?" The question came from both girls simultaneously.

"It's about the future. Your future." Mrs Bellingham paused, but this time in a deliberately dramatic fashion. "We are going to London."

"We're what?" Charity gasped.

Rebecca simply looked at her mother, dumbstruck.

"It's what your dear father would have wanted." Mrs Bellingham, still dressed in the black mourning clothes she had been wearing for the last year, made the pronouncement with an air of finality. A handkerchief was balled up ostentatiously in one hand, and she dabbed at dry eyes with it. "He would say it was my duty."

"But London, Mother?" Rebecca asked.

Mrs Bellingham's gaze fell fondly on her Rebecca, who was delicate, eager to please and unassumingly pretty. The perfect daughter. "'Give Rebecca her Season', he would have said." Her gaze moved on to Charity. "And Charity, of course," she added, the afterthought clear in her mind.

Charity always was the afterthought. It was so common as not to be worth worrying about.

"When are we going?" Charity asked.

Mrs Bellingham's lips twitched in disapproval, as if she had noticed a worm slithering and sliding in front of her. "Must you be so blunt, Charity?" She paused for a second, in order to make Charity fully aware of her fault. "Next but one Friday, as it happens."

"That soon?" Rebecca's face filled with dismay. "But Mother, how will be ever get everything sorted by then?"

"It already has been sorted," Mrs Bellingham said magisterially. "Our lodgings are arranged. Those of our belongings which we do not choose to accompany us will go into storage. This is no sudden plan. It was always my intention, when the first period of mourning your poor dear father was over, to introduce you into polite society. And I have no doubt at all, Rebecca, that you will be a huge success."

The girls looked at each other. There was no point arguing with their mother; she would do whatever she chose. Perhaps Charity would have challenged her, but a quick shake of the head from Rebecca prevented her. The sisters were dissimilar in almost every way, but they lived cordially side by side in the same house. Indeed, Charity often thought it was impossible for anyone to dislike Becca. Her sister was too gentle, too willing to please, too unassumingly *feminine*, for dislike. It would be like kicking a kitten.

"Yes Mother," Rebecca said obediently.

"Yes Mother," Charity echoed, unable to keep cynicism out of her voice. She did her best with Mrs Bellingham, she truly did, but it was too much to ask that she take her mother's words as gospel. Mrs Bellingham would do what was best for Mrs Bellingham. It was as simple as that.

CHAPTER TWO

It took a surprisingly short period of time to decide what possessions they should take to London with them. Mrs Bellingham took those black dresses in which she looked most imposing, but refused to allow the girls to take any of theirs.

"Your father, God rest his soul, has moved to a higher plane," she said. "And you can hardly go to balls and rout parties in black. Lilac, yes, and white, certainly. And grey, perhaps. An elegant reminder of our terrible loss might be appropriate on some occasions. But black, on you girls, no. I think it is time that you moved back to colours."

"Should we not at least take black gloves?" Rebecca asked tentatively.

Her mother pursed her lips. "Yes, I think that would be appropriate. I would like no one to think that you were in any way forgetful of the duty and love you owe your father. Indeed," she added, "I have no intention of putting aside my mourning. No one knows what I suffered at his death."

The girls exchanged glances. In life, Mr Bellingham had been ever at loggerheads with his wife, but since his death, their mother barely went a day without bemoaning his loss. If Rebecca, like Charity, had the suspicion that a male heir—and thus continued ownership of Forsbury—would have consoled Mrs Bellingham greatly for this bereavement, she at least had the tact to keep it to herself. It fell to Rebecca, therefore, to respond to her mother's comment.

"I'm sure that London society will understand that, Mother."

"I shall make sure they do," her mother retorted, her usual asperity back in full.

And so it was a scant ten days before the ladies were bundled up in warm clothes against the chilly January weather to take their place in the carriage. Most of the possessions had been sent ahead, save for a number of boxes and cases for which there had not been room. Mrs Bellingham had arranged for furnished lodgings, so there was no need for the removal of any furniture. Instead, the larger pieces had been returned to a room at Forsbury. How their mother had talked Cousin Bellingham into storing them for her, Charity did not know. They had hardly been on speaking terms since her cousin had inherited the property. Perhaps, however, he felt that looking after their belongings was a small price to pay for Mrs Bellingham's removal from the village.

The journey was long and arduous, requiring one night's stay in an inn. There was precious little room, and Rebecca and Charity slept together in a bed barely wide enough for one person. Their maid slept on the floor beside them, though Mrs Bellingham managed to find a room for herself alone. But it was not until early evening the following day that they reached London.

It was soon very clear that London life—indeed, London itself—was nothing like anything Charity or Rebecca had experienced before. Charity had envisioned a big town, perhaps something like Birmingham, but nothing could have prepared her for what she found.

As soon as the carriage reached the outskirts of the city, her senses were assailed by the sheer bustle of the place—its largeness, its fullness. It wasn't just the sight of so many people going about their business, nor the cacophony of noise. Charity knew that if she had been blindfolded and her ears stopped, she would still have known she was somewhere new. It smelled different, and the very air seemed permeated by the atmosphere of hustle and determination. Everyone was in a hurry; nothing was ever still. Charity could feel the motion against her skin, even from within the carriage. Beside her, Rebecca looked wan and frightened, her eyes blinking faster than usual. Charity wasn't sure whether the cause was the dirty city air or tears. She reached over and patted her sister's hand. Displays of affection did not come naturally to her, and Rebecca knew it. She turned and smiled waveringly at Charity.

"I didn't quite realise that…" Rebecca broke off after those first few words.

"Big, isn't it?" Charity murmured in response.

Their mother glowered at them. "I'm doing this for your sakes, you know," she snapped. "Heaven knows I don't anticipate getting any pleasure out of it."

"We're very grateful, Mother," Rebecca said hastily.

Charity couldn't quite bring herself to repeat such an obvious untruth. She looked down at her gloved hands and said nothing. Her mother gave an indignant sniff but said no more, and the carriage continued to drive down the large, busy streets. At last, they drew up outside a dingy-looking building.

The lodgings were drab but acceptable. The hangings were old-fashioned and somewhat worn, but the drawing room was large and spacious, and the two sofas were plump and comfortable. If the room designated to be Charity's bedroom was perhaps more usually given up to a maidservant, Mrs Bellingham's and Rebecca's bedrooms were of a decent size. All three were filled with dark, solid furniture clearly chosen for practicality rather than beauty, and as the bags and cases were unloaded from the chaise, the two girls explored their new home.

"Do you think we will like it here?" Rebecca asked.

The quick answer, Charity thought grimly, was *no*—but Becca didn't need to hear that. "When we're used to London," she said instead.

She looked down from her bedroom window, surprised by the amount of noise that penetrated it. The road below was not as crowded as some of the others, but there was a continuous bustle outside and the sounds were so very different from the countryside. No birds could be heard, but horses' hooves on the street clinked and clanked, and carriage wheels made an uneven noise as they jerked over the cobbles. Voices spoke or shouted, the accent harsh and ugly to her ears, and the constant toing and froing of people and vehicles made her feel almost dizzy. Charity turned away and saw Rebecca's pale, anxious face.

"It will be all right, won't it?" her sister asked.

"I hope so," Charity said quietly. "I hope so."

The next morning, Mrs Bellingham rounded up her daughters almost before they had finished their breakfasts.

"Before we do anything else, we must do something about your dresses, girls," she said briskly.

Charity looked down. She was wearing one of her favourite morning gowns, put aside for so long in the country as they wore the black appropriate to their bereavement. The dress was a light apple-green colour that reminded her of spring. "What's wrong with what we have?"

Mrs Bellingham tutted indignantly. "Surely you can see that it isn't suitable? No, it is obvious that you need a whole new wardrobe, and right speedily. I have found the names of some reputable modistes—indeed, the first flight of fashion—and I hope to visit several today."

"Several?" Rebecca repeated faintly.

"Sounds delightful, doesn't it?" Charity murmured to her, sotto voce, and Rebecca fought to conceal a smile.

"Quite. You can hardly be introduced into polite company garbed as you are."

Mrs Bellingham would brook no argument on the subject, and the girls knew better than to try. It seemed a short period before they had entered into the first dress shop, where they were greeted with little enthusiasm by a doleful-looking woman.

"Have you an appointment, Madam?" Mrs Bellingham had not. The woman shook her head sorrowfully as she looked the three incumbents up and down. "I'm afraid Madame Clarabelle is extremely busy. Have you thought to try elsewhere? Perhaps one of the smaller establishments?"

Mrs Bellingham drew herself up. She was several inches shorter than Charity, but she had a presence that Charity knew she did not share. "I was told," she said, almost squawking in indignation, "that this was one of the most reputable modistes in town. If you behave so to all of your customers, I am surprised you have any reputation left at all. Now, are you going to serve us, or are you not?"

It became evident that the answer was "not". Barely knowing how they ended there, Mrs Bellingham and her daughters found themselves back on the street outside the building in a rather short space of time.

"Well!" their mother exclaimed. "Well! If *that* is how we are to be treated, I shall be proud not to have attended."

Rebecca was flushed and tearful; Charity hid her embarrassment behind a layer of silence that allowed her to make no response to her mother. With a frustrated sniff, Mrs Bellingham ushered the children back into the chaise and gave another instruction to the coachman.

It seemed to begin with as if the second attempt was to be more successful than the first. Whether less busy, or more open to new business, Mademoiselle Farellone invited the ladies in without issue, and they were soon sitting comfortably whilst Mrs Bellingham explained her daughters' needs to the dressmaker.

"First season, you understand...Yes, Rebecca is the beauty...A whole new wardrobe...Advice for hats and gloves to match..."

Mademoiselle Farellone nodded, took measurements and made delicate suggestions. Charity was soon bored rigid by the process, but Rebecca looked at herself in mirror after mirror with stars in her eyes.

"This dress? Truly, Mother?" she asked, dressed in a rose-pink confection with a few modest frills.

"Indeed, it suits the little mademoiselle to perfection," the modiste agreed, turning Rebecca this way and that so that she could admire herself on all sides.

"Well…" Mrs Bellingham pursed her lips. "I suppose…" She gave a nod. "And those other two in lilac and white, also." "And Charity?" Rebecca asked.

Charity stood to one side. She had been conscious that the dresses suitable for delicate Rebecca looked foolish on someone as tall as she was; the suggestions by Mademoiselle to this accord had dressed her instead in much plainer garb of dull green, white and primrose yellow, with not a flounce to her name. Although nothing could disguise Charity's height, the simplicity drew attention to her better features: a slim waist and hips, and her pale, unfreckled skin. Charity had not known she could look so elegant.

"The yellow, perhaps," Mrs Bellingham said, superb indifference in her voice. "And the price, please?"

The look in Mademoiselle Farellone's eyes implied that it was the most grotesque of all behaviours to bring up the sordid subject of money. It was nothing, however, to the look in Mrs Bellingham's when she heard the cost of those four elegant gowns. Five minutes later, the family were once more on the pavement outside the shop, with no dresses ordered, but Mrs Bellingham with a face not dissimilar to the colour of a tomato.

"What now?" Charity asked.

Mrs Bellingham gave her a quelling look. "I would have liked to think that I had brought my daughters up better than to ask foolish questions like that in the street."

Rebecca was crying, and Charity reached out and gave her hand a quick squeeze. For herself, it did not matter, but Rebecca had looked very pretty in that pink dress.

But it turned out that Charity had more to worry her than Rebecca did. The ladies returned to their house for lunch. When Mrs Bellingham had regained a normal sort of colour, and had consoled herself by means of a ranting monologue about the profligate rich ladies who had caused dressmakers to think that it was acceptable to charge such outrageously inflated prices, Rebecca asked: "So what should we do about dresses, Mother? We surely cannot go out in society with the few we brought with us."

"Of course not!" Mrs Bellingham's voice was sharp, but no more than usual. She never had liked being questioned. In her view children, even grown-up ones, should be seen and not heard—or, in Charity's case, preferably neither seen nor heard. "Don't talk nonsense, child."

"Then…" Rebecca left the word hanging.

"You will have to make them yourselves," she said briskly. "There are patterns to be followed, lengths of material to be bought at quite reasonable costs. It will do you good to do some work preparing for your launch into society. So far, I have done everything for you, but you girls should pull your weight also."

"Make the dresses?" Charity was so dismayed that the words were out before she had a chance to think. "But Mother, I—" She felt Rebecca lean against her in an attempt to stop her continuing, but Charity couldn't stop herself. "I'm an awful seamstress. I'll be laughed at."

Mrs Bellingham took a long breath, always a preparatory signal for a tirade. "You need hardly tell me that your sewing is beneath contempt. If you were only a little bit more like your sister, things would be better. She has the proper feminine talents: sewing, embroidery, even cooking. You can't clothe or feed a family by means of a piano. If you are laughed at, you must remember that you are reaping what you've sown."

"I'll certainly be wearing what I've sewn," Charity mumbled bitterly.

Her mother ignored this frivolous response. "Time and time again, I've asked you to work on your sewing, but have you listened? You have not. And now we come to this: I am giving you the opportunity of a Season in London, and all you can do is grouse about every little thing. I do not know what I did to deserve such an ungrateful daughter."

Charity bit down hard on the sides of her cheeks to prevent herself responding in kind. Rebecca had been right: she should not have spoken so. She should have known that it would only rile her mother into one of her rants.

"Sorry, Mother."

There was no more to be said. Mrs Bellingham would not change her mind, and any further discussion would just serve to anger her to no good purpose. Charity looked down at the remains of her meal and realised that she felt slightly sick. She pushed the plate away.

After lunch, when Mrs Bellingham had left the girls to their own devices, Rebecca turned to her sister. "I'll help you," she promised, looking up at Charity with much more maternal tenderness than their real mother offered her. "With the dresses, I mean. I don't mind. And your sewing isn't as bad as you claim, you know."

"No. It's worse." But Charity couldn't help smiling a little bit. "You're an angel, Becca. I don't deserve a sister like you."

"Silly." Rebecca brushed off the compliment, blushing a little. "Come, now, let us talk of something else and only worry about those silly dresses when we need to."

CHAPTER THREE

Mrs Bellingham had many faults, but she was at least efficient. Within two days of her declaration that the girls must make all of their dresses, she had ordered several yards of various materials, discovered some patterns which she claimed were suitable and taken Charity and Rebecca to buy the various 'extras' it would not be possible to create for themselves: gloves, stockings and stays. Instead of resting on her laurels at that point, however, it was then time for her next venture.

"I am going out to leave a few cards," Mrs Bellingham announced on the third morning. "My clothes, at least, leave nothing to be ashamed of. You girls can begin the sewing." She fixed a basilisk glare on Charity. "And you, Miss, concentrate. Your sewing is never good, but that does not mean that it needs to be execrable."

"Yes, Mother."

"Who are you visiting?" Rebecca asked, in a clear, if kind, attempt to change the subject.

"Yes. I didn't know you had any friends. In London," Charity amended hastily.

Mrs Bellingham apparently found it preferable to ignore her younger daughter's rudeness on this occasion. Her tone quelling, she said, "I received many letters of condolence on the death of your father. I felt it my sacred duty to reply to each one of them. Many had London addresses, and I am sure they would feel slighted were I not to visit them whilst in town."

Charity groaned inwardly. Translated, her mother's reply meant that she intended to force herself on any and all passing acquaintances she or her deceased husband had ever had, in the hope of being 'taken up' by one or more of them. No, not all, Charity corrected herself—only those with money or position in society. Mrs Bellingham would avoid at all costs anyone of her own or lower status.

"That's nice," Rebecca said.

Charity knew her sister meant it, too. She wished sometimes that she had Rebecca's gift of taking their mother's words at face value. This was, she mused ironically, perhaps the only wish that she and their mother shared. Mrs Bellingham nodded at Rebecca, sent another baleful glare in Charity's direction and left. When it was certain that their mother was no longer in the house, Charity gave a sigh of relief.

"Peace at last!"

"Charity!" protested Rebecca. "Anyway, we have so much sewing to complete."

"Sewing." Charity groaned. "Did you have to mention that dreadful word? Peace…and sewing. Today's joys never end."

Becca giggled. "Charity, you're so silly! Anyway, you know I'll help you. I promised."

"I'm counting on it," Charity assured her.

The making of the dresses was both better and worse than Charity had anticipated. Better, because she and Rebecca came to an agreement that Charity should do the measuring and cutting—a task much better suited to the younger girl, given Rebecca's anxiety around numbers—and, with the maid, form the basic seams and shapes, whilst Becca would work on the complicated embroidery and visible stitching. Worse, though, for the patterns Mrs Bellingham had instructed the girls to follow.

Certain fashion plates had been selected by Mrs Bellingham, almost all with high waists and tight bodices. The dresses played to Rebecca's best features beautifully: her breasts looked plump and womanly, whilst the long skirts skimmed against her hips before falling waterfall-like to the ground. Charity, a full six inches taller and with a much less full bosom, looked ridiculous, however, as if her legs were half a mile long, or like a gentleman had fitted himself out for amusement.

"I look a fool, like your brother dressed up in skirts," she told Rebecca. "Look at me!"

"Oh, Charity, you do not!" Rebecca laughed. She looked at her sister once more, and her mirth subsided. "Though I must confess that it is not the most flattering design for you. I don't know why mother didn't choose different patterns for us both."

"Don't you?" Charity turned to look at herself in the mirror again, feeling helpless and humiliated. Which was, presumably, the effect her mother had intended.

Rebecca bit her lip and smoothed her fingers over the blue figured muslin of her own dress. "Anyway," she said, ignoring her sister's interjection, "I have a couple of ideas for how we could...not change, precisely, but adapt your dresses."

"If you can stop me looking like the biggest freak of nature, I'll be forever in your debt," Charity assured her.

"And anyway," her sister continued teasingly, "it has had one good effect already." Charity turned to stare at Rebecca, raising her eyebrows in disbelief. "I think this is the first time in your life you've ever shown an interest in your clothes!"

Charity directed a playful glare towards Becca, but she couldn't entirely hide her smile. "Miracles do indeed happen."

As the girls had stitched, Mrs Bellingham had continued her attempts to make contacts within the *ton*. Nevertheless, the return calls to the Bellingham household did not so much flood as trickle in. Mrs Bellingham checked through the cards as the maid brought them up, apparently cross-referencing them with her knowledge of the ladies and gentlemen involved.

"Mrs Carbory...hmm. She has a daughter about your age, Rebecca. No sons, but a good background. I believe she attended Lord Firtingale's ball the other evening." Mrs Bellingham put down the cards and picked up the newspaper to rifle through it. "Where was it? Ah yes. 'Mr Frederick Firtingale was seen dancing with Miss C on more than one occasion, as well as with Miss L, Lady K and Miss F'. So she certainly would be worth cultivating."

"Mother, she is not a flower," Charity said impatiently.

"I fail to see your point." Mrs Bellingham picked up another card and gave it a cursory glance. "Mrs Warburton. Oh, no, no, no. Neither style nor breeding. I recall her from my own debut. Plump and clumsy. The surprise was that anyone, even a commoner like Mr Warburton, was prepared to marry her."

It was Rebecca's turn to wince, though unlike her sister she was wise enough not to comment. By the time Mrs Bellingham had looked at all the cards, there were three piles: those who would certainly not be contacted, those that would and those who must be treated with the utmost respect and courtesy. This last pile was very small, and Mrs Bellingham was heard bemoaning the number of calls she had paid that had not been reciprocated.

Nevertheless, there were enough respondents to Mrs Bellingham's calls to mean that when the girls had completed the dresses, they had events to which they could wear them. Charity knew that despite her mother's indignation as to the paucity of invitations, Rebecca was happy to have a more tentative start to their London debut. Her sister was shy and retiring, and although her company manners were perfect, she suffered agonies of anxiety before larger events. Charity, less keen to attend anything bar the picnics and music evenings, anticipated boredom rather than fear at the balls and routs. However, despite her lack of interest in clothing, she was mortified by the knowledge that her dresses, whilst neatly made—Rebecca's stitching was impeccable—looked ugly and inappropriate on her. Rebecca had done her best: her adaptations had dropped the waist a little lower, and she had tried to use the plainer materials for Charity's dresses, which at least made her look slightly more feminine without looking vulgar. But nothing could really make up for a style that seemed deliberately chosen to make Charity look ridiculous.

Now that they had received cards, Mrs Bellingham graciously allowed the girls to accompany her on a round of social visits. While the visits were another form of purgatory to Charity, she knew that Rebecca would enjoy herself, so she kept from complaint. In a situation where well-bred girls were expected to sit and say nothing unless spoken to directly, Charity consoled herself with the thought that at least she wouldn't be obliged to think up subjects for small talk. She knew that the silence would allow Rebecca to lose the worst of her nerves before speaking.

But it was a little over a month after the Bellinghams arrived in London that they attended their first ball. January was over, and the Season was in full swing around them. The maid was kept busy that evening, running between the two girls in an attempt to perfect their hair, dress and accessories. Mrs Bellingham was determined that Charity would not embarrass her publicly by looking shabby or unkempt. Since her dress, whilst appropriate, hung badly on Charity's long, thin frame, poor Annie had her work cut out for her trying to make her younger mistress look elegant. They finally settled on 'not too *in*elegant', and Annie was free to convert Rebecca into the pretty young debutante she really was.

All the hustle and bustle played on Rebecca's nerves, and as they stood together in her bedroom, awaiting their mother's attendance, she moved closer to Charity's side, taking her hand.

"I'm so nervous," she whispered, increasing her grip on Charity's hand to the point that it was actually painful.

"Becca," Charity said, gently detaching her. "You've been to assemblies back home. And there's sure to be some of the people we have met in the park or on our visits."

Foiled of Charity's hand, Rebecca fiddled with her skirt, twitching the folds back and forth. "Yes, but that was not London."

"An undeniable truth," Charity agreed. "But we have met people in town. I'm sure there will be people we know. And anyway, you will take the shine out of most of the ladies. You look beautiful in that dress." She grinned. "It is all thanks to my sewing, you know."

Rebecca laughed, as Charity had hoped she would.

But it was Charity, and not Rebecca, for whom the ball was an unhappy experience. Even had her dress been a perfect fit, and even if she had been personally introduced to every single reveller at the ball, Charity would not have enjoyed the evening. It was not that she did not like to dance, nor that she baulked at conversation. It was simply that it was evident from the moment she entered the room that she did not fit in. Her height was the most noticeable problem: she was taller than every other lady present and the majority of the gentlemen also. Gentlemen, she had discovered from the local revelries she had previously attended, were uncomfortable looking up to meet the gaze of their partner.

Equally, the number of people she recognised and might have been able to speak to were few. Most of the other ladies had friends and acquaintances enough that a tall country cousin with an unflattering dress and a serious expression barely impinged on their notice. The gentlemen followed the all-too-familiar pattern of her previous experiences at balls back home and were disinclined to dance with her thanks to her height, though Rebecca had invitations enough. Charity saw Mrs Bellingham keeping a maternal eye on Rebecca, making sure that her elder daughter did not commit any social solecisms, and ready to introduce her to other matrons when Rebecca stood alone. On the rare occasions her gaze fixed on Charity, she had a steely glare that did not add anything positive to her daughter's evening.

But that was not all. The majority of the chattering was about the *ton* itself: who had met whom, and what they had said; the scandal of Lady X, whose reticule had not matched her dress; the rumours about Mr Y, said to be on the point of an advantageous betrothal.

"I heard," said the lady next to Charity to her friend, "that she might have a fortune of forty-thousand pounds! Fancy that, when he has gambling debts to pay."

"Do you think she realises that he sees her as a pigeon ripe for the plucking?" The other lady giggled.

"With her airs and graces, I don't think she has time to realise anything," the first lady replied.

None of it made any sense to Charity, and even had it done so, it was not the sort of conversation she enjoyed. She moved away, trying to slip through the crowded room to find Rebecca. Mrs Bellingham was seated a little further down with several other dowagers, her usual expression of discontent on her face. Charity halted, unwilling to push her wallflower status upon her mother. Rebecca, she realised as she looked over the heads of the crowd, was dancing. Charity smiled at the seriousness with which Becca was taking the steps. If her partner had hoped to chat, he would be disappointed. Rebecca's entire attention was on the dance.

Further down, there was a lady dressed in blue, who was clearly keeping up a stream of chatter with her partner. The blue dress suited her, Charity thought. She would have been beautiful anyway, but the dress showed off her best features: large blue eyes and the smallest of waists. Charity could have spent a happy time watching her, except as a debutante the expectations were different. All girls were expected to want to dance non-stop. Not dancing was as clear as sign as any that you did not belong.

"Are you enjoying yourself?"

The soft voice made Charity jump, and she turned to look for the speaker.

The new lady was short and on the plump side. She was a few years older than Charity herself but not yet of an age to be considered an old maid. Her dress was pretty but practical: there was no possibility that she would catch a ruffle on a gentleman's cuff, nor did she need a large space to allow her dress the room it wished for.

"Not really," Charity admitted. She realised her mistake immediately. Whilst girls were not supposed to act like country bumpkins, gasping in awe at each new sight, they were expected to show some interest, even if it was couched as languid boredom. "I mean, it's an awful crush, isn't it?" she added, trying to retrieve her position.

Her new acquaintance smiled. "It's not obligatory to keep to the rule book of conversation, you know."

"No," Charity said ruefully, "but it is often so much more comfortable!"

"Do you not dance?"

Charity felt herself blushing. "I do. When I am asked."

The lady's eyes flicked up and then down her, as if assessing her. "Why do you not get asked?"

The question was so simply put that Charity responded with the truthfulness that came most naturally to her. "I think I'm too tall. Oh, sorry," she added, as another debutante tried to squeeze past her.

Unexpectedly, the lady laughed. "That is not a problem I have ever been troubled with, but I take your meaning. My name is Miss Musgrove, by the way. I'm pleased to meet you."

"And I to meet you. I am Miss Charity Bellingham. My sister, Miss Bellingham, is over there."

Charity pointed out Rebecca, who was dancing with a very young gentleman who was giving a similar amount of attention to his steps as Rebecca was to hers. The two ladies watched her dancing for a moment or two.

"She is very pretty," Miss Musgrove said seriously.

"Yes." Charity smiled, always happy to hear Rebecca praised. She ignored the small pang that told her that no one would ever say the same about her. "She certainly is."

Miss Musgrove stood by Charity for a good five minutes more, and Charity began to relax. She felt at last as if she had a friend, or at least a friendly acquaintance. Someone who was willing to stand in silence without filling every second with tedious chatter; someone who had bothered to reach out and speak to a new debutante, even without an introduction from the Master of Ceremonies. She was insensibly consoled, and when, after a little more conversation, Miss Musgrove excused herself to dance with an older gentleman whose dark hair met in a widow's peak on his forehead, Charity missed her.

She missed Miss Musgrove even more as the next half an hour passed without a single person even bothering to speak to her. Charity could see Mrs Bellingham on the other side of the room, nodding her head hard for emphasis as she spoke to another lady of middle age. Rebecca was rarely without a dance partner, and Charity tried hard to dampen down her wistful envy and concentrate on her pleasure for her sister. As if she had caught Charity's thoughts, Rebecca came to join her at the end of the next dance.

"This is fun," Rebecca said happily. Her face was flushed a little pink from the exertion, her smile lighting up her face. "You were right. I was a goose to be so frightened."

Charity firmly pinned a smile on. "Didn't I tell you so?"

She was glad to see Rebecca so oblivious to all the negatives about the ball. It had not been just Charity's own experiences of rejection that had subdued her. With little to do but sit and watch and listen, Charity had had time to notice that their mother had also received her fair share of apparent disapproval. Certain older ladies, with whom Mrs Bellingham did not appear to be acquainted, had nonetheless looked from their mother to her daughters with an expression of displeasure. Charity had not been certain why they looked so grim until she had happened to find herself on a chair quite close to a couple of them.

"I see Eliza Bellingham is as she ever was," one notable matriarch commented.

Charity's eyes had instinctively hunted for her mother. She was speaking to an impressive dowager Charity remembered from walks in the park as having been pointed out as one of society's main figures. The name escaped her mind, but not the tone in her mother's voice as she had spoken of the lady. Glancing sideways at the ladies sitting close to her, she saw that their eyes, too, rested on Mrs Bellingham.

"Pushing, you mean?" another lady asked. She had feathers in her hat, Charity saw: not enough to be vulgar, just to add an extra element to her attire. It was the sort of thing that Rebecca might do and that Charity never thought of.

"Indeed. The fact that it is on behalf of her daughter rather than herself does not excuse her."

"Ill breeding is as ill breeding does," the second replied with a dismissive sniff. "You can marry above your station, but it won't make you any better bred."

"Mind you, the daughter's a pretty thing."

"Insipid." The ladies' eyes drifted to where Rebecca was dancing, her face a study in concentration. "Parochial," the same lady added. "Funny, though. I'm sure I heard the Bellingham woman had two daughters."

It was not easy to try and make yourself invisible when you were Charity's size, but she did her best.

"Oh, she does! The other's a strange sort of thing. Cinderella's ugly sister. Now, where is she...?"

Charity kept her gaze straight ahead, as if she was fascinated by the dancing. Nevertheless, she *felt* the moment that the dowager spotted her. The lady gave a small cry of surprise; Charity could not be shocked by the belatedly lowered voices. Ugly sister? Well, she had been called worse. And after all, it was not entirely inaccurate. Compared to Rebecca, she was plain indeed—though if the story had run true, Charity would have been her mother's favourite. She rolled her eyes at the thought of Mrs Bellingham's reaction to that.

She could only be grateful when the long evening drew to a close.

CHAPTER FOUR

Next morning came the analysis. Mrs Bellingham wished to go over every single element of the ball: what each person had said to Rebecca, whom she had danced with. The minutiae were dissected and assessed in great detail. Charity remembered the way the lady last night had said "Pushing". Whilst she resented deeply the slurs on Rebecca, who was neither insipid nor parochial, Charity thought indignantly, she could not help but acknowledge that the label given to her mother was not entirely unfair. It was evident—more than evident—that this London Season had one purpose for Mrs Bellingham: to find Rebecca a husband. Charity wondered if her mother had considered the fatal flaw in her scheme. Charity could hardly think that a future consisting of Mrs Bellingham and her 'ugly' spinster daughter setting up house together would appeal to her mother. But perhaps she felt that any gentleman who might offer would do for Charity, whereas she was clearly determined that Rebecca should find a husband of wealth or position, if not both.

"And you danced with Mr James." Charity could tell from the quickened interest in Mrs Bellingham's voice that Mr James must be someone of importance. "What did he say? Come, Rebecca, I want every word."

Rebecca looked dismayed, twisting her handkerchief between her fingers. "I hardly know, Mother. We...we did not speak much. I think I bored him."

"Bored him? Of course not. Did he say so? No, you need not answer that. He is too much the gentleman to have said any such thing. You were shy, no doubt, that is all. And anyway, it is bad manners to be too forward in your approach." Rebecca opened her mouth to speak, but Mrs Bellingham continued. "You must not get a bee in your bonnet, imagining slights when none were given. No, no, I feel sure you said everything appropriate."

Rebecca's eyes were lowered. She continued to fiddle with the handkerchief, but she said, "I hope so."

"But you danced. How much of the time did you dance? More than half, I feel sure. And that when you are barely known in London! But not the waltz, I trust?"

Their mother must have known, Charity thought, that neither girl had waltzed. Mrs Bellingham had been firm enough in her warnings (or threats) on the subject that neither of them would have considered doing so, even if any gentleman had been careless enough of their reputation to ask. Indeed, one of the few times Charity had felt her mother's gimlet gaze had been when the strings had started up a tune in three-four time. Charity might feature low on Mrs Bellingham's priority list, but her mother was quick enough to ascertain that Charity was doing nothing that could bring censorship on herself, her mother and her sister. Even if Charity had parental permission to take part in the waltz, however, she felt very doubtful that any gentleman would have requested the dubious pleasure of her company. They had hardly been queuing up for the other dances.

Charity hid a smile, her imagination offering her the ridiculous image of a long line of gentlemen queuing politely to ask her to dance. Her mother's questioning of Rebecca continued, but Charity let the sound wash over her. It was not as if she was required to take part. It was quite pleasant to sit lost in her own thoughts of the ball, which mostly centred on a beautiful lady in blue, dancing like a fairy, and take a few minutes' precious time to herself.

* * *

A week later, a group of debutantes gathered to practise their dance steps at the house belonging to Mrs Scorton, a lady with one daughter and two older sons. Mrs Bellingham was always looking out for gentlemen of marriageable age, and whilst the eldest son was almost certainly out of reach, having recently become betrothed, the younger was nonetheless available. The fact that he had a string of scandals and mistresses in his past (and had been sent down from Oxford after a young lady of good birth had been compromised) was not a concern to the matchmaking mother. Mrs Bellingham insisted that her daughters attend.

"You do realise that not only is Mr Edmund Scorton a very good catch, Lady Jarrow's daughter is going to be at the event? How are you supposed to move in the best circles if you don't take advantage of these opportunities?"

"But are we invited?" Rebecca asked tentatively.

"Of course!" her mother said. Then, "Well, I certainly spoke to Mrs Scorton about it. You know, she has the Plain Jane daughter. Unfortunate to call your daughter Jane and have her live up to all the worst association of the name. Anyway, I said that you both would also attend."

"So we haven't been invited," Charity said.

Rebecca, standing a step behind her big little sister, gave her a warning tap on the wrist. Charity sighed inwardly. She certainly ought to know better than to challenge her mother like this. She would not change Mrs Bellingham's mind and would only make her more determined to stick to her point.

"An oversight," Mrs Bellingham said, giving her daughter a dark glare. "I know Mrs Scorton must have intended to invite you girls. She is certainly expecting you."

Charity could believe that last. Mrs Scorton could hardly have missed Mrs Bellingham's shameless jockeying for an invitation. Original invite or none, the Bellingham girls would be expected. Charity wondered whether her mother realised that her determination for her daughters to take part in as many entertainments as possible was more likely to end in their being ostracised from polite society than welcomed.

Despite this, Charity and Rebecca were welcomed to Mrs Scorton's house with cool politeness by their hostess, and even— in Rebecca's case—greeted cheerfully by a couple of the other girls. Rebecca, whilst not being particularly intelligent or witty, had such an evident air of well-meaning that she disarmed all criticism. To put it simply, she was almost impossible to dislike. Charity knew herself to be in a different class: the girls had little interest in her, but certainly saw her as no threat, so whilst she did not make many friends, she at least did not suffer the rancour that she had feared.

The steps were practised diligently, and for a short while the girls were joined by the famed Mr Edmund Scorton, which made several of them dissolve into embarrassed giggling, whilst he looked them over (Charity thought) as if they were pigs at market. His gaze lingered longest on Rebecca, who was not one of the gigglers, but who practiced sedately under his watchful eye. Perhaps, Charity thought, her mother's plans might come to fruition. Mr Scorton had no time to spare for Charity, of course, but she had not expected him to, nor had she any wish to marry, whether well or badly, so she was left supremely unmoved by the experience. Mr Scorton himself held no fascination for her. He was a short gentleman with what seemed to be a permanent sneer fixed to his lips. Nonetheless, it seemed Charity was alone in her lack of interest. After half an hour or so, his sister Jane begged him to leave, for his presence disturbed the girls' concentration. He shrugged.

"All right, I'm going. Just wanted to look over the new batch of debs, Janie. Always good to know the pretty ones." Not even bothering to lower his voice, he added: "What's that one called?" He jerked his head at Rebecca. "Wouldn't mind saying 'how d'ye do' to her, know what I mean?"

Jane's reply was inaudible, and her brother slouched out again. The practice settled down, but it was clear that Mr Scorton's presence had disturbed the balance. More mistakes were made, and a few squabbles broke out. Jane herself was especially cool to the Bellinghams: clearly her brother's interest in Rebecca had piqued her.

As the party came to an end, Rebecca caught Charity's hand urgently.

"Don't tell Mother. About Mr Edmund Scorton, I mean," she begged in a whisper.

"What, that he spoke highly of you?" Charity asked. "We must mention that he looked in on us, for Mother is sure to find out somehow."

"I know, but...I do not think he was really interested. He did not seem the type to fall in love."

"Love?" Charity asked, startled. Then she collected herself. "Perhaps you're right. I won't tell."

"Thank you," her sister said gratefully.

It took more than a few weeks, nonetheless, before the Bellinghams could claim to have settled down comfortably in London. It took Rebecca and Charity, used to the peace and rural sounds of the country, some time to get used to the very different noise and the bustle surrounding them now. Where once it had been the cockerel's crowing that might disturb their sleep, now it was the hoarse calls of the road sweepers, or the never-ending sound of horses' hooves and carriage wheels on the cobbled roads around their new home. When the first novelty was over, however, and Mrs Bellingham had managed to make a few...not friends, for Mrs Bellingham had no time for those, but 'useful connections', it became evident that in return for the parties, soirees, picnics and outings they had attended, the Bellinghams would have to offer something in return.

It was a difficult situation for Mrs Bellingham. She and the girls clearly did not have the same resources behind them as did their more wealthy and *tonnish* acquaintances. It would have been impossible to hold a ball in their lodgings, even had they the money to do so. Charity had wondered whether Mrs Bellingham would hold an evening party, but it seemed that her mother was too canny to attempt something to which she would not be able to live up to. Instead, Mrs Bellingham chose to have much lower-key but more regular at-home events—a move that not only saved her from having to spend above her means, but also challenged the rhetoric suggesting that she was too forward and laying claims to a higher degree of gentility than was actually true. It was, though Charity did not realise it to begin with, a clever approach to take. Nevertheless, although her mother worked very hard on giving the appearance of simplicity, the events were anything but simple to those most deeply involved, despite being prefaced always by the same five words: "It's just an informal affair."

Charity winced as she heard her mother say the words to a new victim. They were too familiar by now, and whilst Mrs Bellingham claimed to treat everyone the same way, Charity could not help but notice that the only people she did invite to the 'informal' at-home were either rich gentlemen or ladies with well-known links to the former. That wasn't entirely true, of course: there were a few other ladies invited because they would add prestige to any of the at-homes they chose to attend. But it was true enough—and obvious enough—that the very words Mrs Bellingham spoke were a reminder of what was actually meant.

The at-homes themselves were some species of nightmare. If Mrs Bellingham had wanted to torture her younger daughter, these events would have been an excellent choice of punishment. The misery started a couple of hours before the at-home was to take place. Both Rebecca and Charity were prinked and prodded into the most elegant clothes in their wardrobe—though only, for Mrs Bellingham had an eye to the main chance, in dresses that were suitable for such an affair. Indeed, the deliberate attempt to make the choice of clothes and hair look entirely 'natural' and unstudied was one of the things that took the most time. A flower pinned to the dress? Mrs Bellingham might fasten it on and take it off five times before deciding whether it could be considered appropriate. During which time, Charity, feeling much as she had as a small girl, had to try not only not to squirm with impatience, but also to compose her features into a semblance of acquiescence. For the only thing worse than these sessions was when they were accompanied by Mrs Bellingham's worn refrain about how she was only doing what was best for her children and about what an ungrateful child Charity had always been.

Because of the informality of the gatherings, no one knew in advance how many people might attend, which added another layer of anxiety to proceedings. Would today be the day when only one person turned up, leaving the Bellinghams to converse awkwardly, whilst pretending not to be on the lookout for any further invitees? Or on the other hand, would there be enough people that the mean proportions of the room, in comparison with the drawing rooms of richer and more well-connected acquaintances, would become obvious enough to be a source of embarrassment? These worries made Mrs Bellingham even more strict and particular in advance. She never had liked things over which she had little control, and Charity could only be bewildered as to why her mother had chosen this particular method of introducing her daughters to a range of possible suitors and friends.

It was not until Charity mentioned her bewilderment to Rebecca that she found the explanation. Unexpectedly cynical for once, Rebecca had said simply, "It is cheaper. By stressing the informal nature of the event, Mother ensures that no one is expecting high entertainment, and therefore there is no need to buy all the trimmings which might go with something more definite. It allows her to pay off her debts in terms of invitations, whilst also costing as little as is possible. It is really quite clever of her."

"Yes," said Charity, much surprised at her sister's perception. "It is."

"And of course," Rebecca said, reverting much more to type, "it is so kind of her, for she does it all for us, you know."

But to that, Charity had no response.

Today's guests trickled in. Mrs Carbory and her daughter arrived early on. Mrs Bellingham, Charity knew, was torn between pleasure that a lady who was invited to the very best parties would deign to attend such a small affair and annoyance that Miss Carbory was so very attractive. Rebecca was pretty, of course, but Miss Carbory was beautiful and put everyone else in the shade by comparison. Mrs Earl, a plain but smiling dowager, arrived almost on their coattails. Mrs Hollings, a nondescript lady of few talents with whom Rebecca had struck up a half-hearted friendship, arrived twenty minutes later, full of pleasantries and gossip and very little else. She was followed by Mr Lane, a serious-minded young man who, when he could, pontificated on the evils of most modern entertainments and the joy of having a small gathering such as the Bellinghams' own. Charity found him well-meaning but dull. Still, she welcomed him, preferring his conversation to the tedious small talk of the ladies. Charity was not deceived, however: although Mr Lane spoke predominantly to her, she was perceptive enough to note that his gaze lay always on Rebecca. The question was, when—and it was when, and not if—he proposed, would Mrs Bellingham consider it a suitable match? He would certainly be seen by her mother as a good enough husband for Charity, for whom any offer would do, but for Rebecca? Charity was not sure. It was evident that the hope of a brilliant marriage rested solely on Rebecca's shoulders. Would a proposal from a man with but a moderate income, and a position in society very similar to the Bellinghams' own, be considered good enough? Charity did not like to raise the subject with Rebecca, whom she knew had no such expectations from Mr Lane. She would not, of course, speak to her mother about it. But she couldn't help watching, waiting and wondering.

For now, though, Charity's mind lay on a purely practical matter. Mr Lane's presence, she decided with relief, made the number of visitors large enough not to fill Mrs Bellingham with fury for the rest of the evening, but not so many that she and Rebecca would have to stand to make certain there were enough seats. It was not that Charity objected to standing per se, but she was painfully aware of her height at the best of times, and in a crowded room she felt as if she loomed larger than ever.

Mr Edmund Scorton also attended today. He had indeed kept some interest in Rebecca, and Mrs Bellingham was hopeful of an offer. Charity, who had been shocked to the core after seeing him kiss an unwilling housemaid at a luncheon engagement when he thought no one was looking, trusted vehemently that no offer would be forthcoming.

However, the guests were not at an end yet. Just as Mrs Bellingham was giving up on all hope of seeing any more visitors, her man announced the arrival of two more.

"Lord Bulstead. Mr Fotheringay."

Mrs Bellingham turned with a slight frown towards the door. Whilst Lord Bulstead was a welcome guest, Charity—and by the look on her mother's face, her mother also—had never heard of Mr Fotheringay. They entered together, and Lord Bulstead went straight over to Mrs Bellingham with the new gentleman.

"This is my friend, Mr Fotheringay," he said. "Knew you wouldn't mind, ma'am, if I brought him along with me."

Charity watched as her mother tried to compose her features into an expression of welcome. Lord Bulstead's title made him acceptable, even though his age and monetary status meant that he was not a possible suitor for the Bellingham girls. Mr Fotheringay, however, was just a plain old man—quite literally. He looked to be approximately a decade older than Mrs Bellingham, though Charity knew that her mother looked young for her age. Even the fashionable nature of Mr Fotheringay's clothing could not take away from the fact that he was not in the slightest good looking. He was a few inches shorter than Charity herself, with a face which was all jowls and bulging eyes, making him look rather like an ancient and grumpy bullfrog. Worst of all, in Charity's mother's eyes, he had no title. Lord Bulstead was renowned for having friends of all ages and ranks—hence, Charity thought ironically, his willingness to visit the Bellinghams—and Mr Fotheringay did not look as if he were one of the gentleman's more respectable friends. When Fotheringay took a seat near her, Charity discovered that he had also clearly been drinking previously to their meeting: his beery breath was enough to make her feel slightly light-headed. She had never been so grateful to her mother as when Mrs Bellingham called her across to welcome another guest to the room.

Later on, chatting with determined politeness to Mrs Earl— "*Two* eligible sons," her mother had told Charity and Rebecca on the occasion of the lady's first visit—Charity noticed that Rebecca was unfortunate enough to have become caught in Fotheringay's coils. Rebecca looked shy, but Charity was as usual in admiration of her sister's ability to talk even to the least congenial guest. Whilst Charity had not been able to think of a word to say in response to the gentleman's monologue about carriages, Rebecca was not only nodding at appropriate moments but, judging by the fondness with which the gentleman was regarding her, making the right sort of comments as well.

Mr Fotheringay outstayed the rest of the guests. Mr Edmund Scorton, not bothering to conceal a yawn, had left early, and Mr Lane and several of the ladies had followed not long after. However, Mr Fotheringay was only dislodged after a couple of exceedingly broad hints from Mrs Bellingham. She managed to control the worst of her rage until he had left the house, but as soon as the front door closed, her temper broke.

"Lord Bulstead! Really, the cheek of the man," Mrs Bellingham raged. "Turning up here with the scaff and raff of society. Someone he picked up off the street, no doubt, and decided to bring along. As for his friend, Featherleigh, or whatever his name was"—Charity was aware that Mrs Bellingham knew perfectly well Fotheringay's name; it was a matter of principle to appear to forget it—"he should know better, no matter his place in society. Indeed, and so I shall tell both him and Bulstead, Lord or no, when I next see him!"

CHAPTER FIVE

Mrs Bellingham did not carry out her threat to complain to Lord Bulstead of his behaviour. In truth, neither Charity nor Rebecca had ever thought she would: a Lord was a Lord, after all. What they had not anticipated, however, was the mood of sheer delight in which she came home after a visit to Mrs Carbory two days later.

"Well!" she said, settling herself down on the sofa, and fanning herself vigorously. "Well! What a thing!"

Charity rolled her eyes. Rebecca gave her a quick warning glance before saying, "What, Mother?"

"Goodness gracious me, the conversation I have just had with Mrs Carbory," their mother said, her voice full of excitement. "I don't know whether you remember that charming gentleman who came to our last open afternoon the day before yesterday? Mr Fotheringay. Such a distinguished man."

For a second, Charity wondered whether her mother had lost her mind. Charming? Distinguished? Was this really the same gentleman about whom Mrs Bellingham had ranted and raved not two days earlier?

"What about him?" Rebecca asked.

"Mrs Carbory told me that he is...well, flush in the pockets." Mrs Bellingham looked slightly ashamed of herself for the vulgarity. "That is, he is a rich man. An extremely rich man, girls. What a thing!"

"Money." Charity could not keep the distaste out of her voice, and her mother glared at her.

"Yes, Miss, money. Do you really think you can manage so well without it? I would like to see you try!"

"Tell us about Mr Fotheringay, though, Mother, please?" Rebecca implored. Charity knew better than to think that her sister was particularly interested in wealth; her question was intended to distract Mrs Bellingham's attention from Charity.

Their mother put down her fan and leaned forwards, as if imparting a great secret. "Twenty thousand pounds a year!" Her voice was awestruck. "To think of it, girls! Twenty thousand pounds a year, and he at our little soiree!"

Charity thought back to the bitter words that Mrs Bellingham had spoken on the evening after she met Fotheringay. One should really admire her mother for her ability to forget her strictures so thoroughly so quickly.

"Perhaps you should marry him," she suggested drily.

Mrs Bellingham glared sternly at her errant daughter. "No one," she said loftily, "was speaking of marriage. I was merely demonstrating an interest in Lord Bulstead's friend."

"That's more than I was able to do," Charity admitted.

"It was kind of him to visit," Rebecca said hastily. "He did not seem to look down upon us either."

"I should think not!" Mrs Bellingham said, changing her tune a little. She hesitated. "I believe that he gained a good deal of his money from..." her voice sank to a whisper, "trade. But perhaps that is not so important as it was when I was young. Anyway, he should have no reason to despise you girls. You are elegant and well-bred. If we perhaps do not have quite as deep pockets as Mr Fotheringay"—Charity muffled a splutter at this masterful understatement—"then that is no reason for anyone to put themselves above us." She looked sternly at the girls.

"Now, if he comes again, dears, I wish you both to make the greatest effort to make him feel welcome."

Indeed, it was not the only occasion the Bellinghams were to cross paths with Mr Fotheringay. Mrs Bellingham always made a point of speaking to him when they attended events, and Mr Fotheringay came to several more of the Bellingham soirees. It was noticeable, however, that the gentleman was never an attendee at the few elite gatherings that the Bellinghams went to: even with Lord Bulstead as a patron, it seemed that there were some doors not open to him. In other circumstances, Mrs Bellingham's snobbery would have led her to eschew any type of contact with a man of such rank. It was amazing the latitude she was prepared to give a gentleman with the wealth of Mr Fotheringay.

Charity saw it all but was sceptical about the final outcome. The likelihood of her mother remarrying after her first unhappy marriage was surely small, even if the proposal came from a man as loaded with riches as it seemed that Mr Fotheringay was. She suspected instead that Mrs Bellingham's fondness for Mr Fotheringay stemmed from the hope that he might know other men with equally capacious pockets—ones who smelt less of the shop and who might be of an age to be interested in Rebecca, if it so became that Mr Edmund Scorton did not come through with an offer, which seemed likely: he had been much less attentive of late. Charity knew her mother rated her, Charity's, chances of matrimony as slim to none.

It seemed that it was not just within the family that Charity was considered unlikely to marry however. At the next ball she attended, Charity had the misfortune to overhear another conversation. To do her justice, it was difficult not to hear parts of many different conversations between others: the bigger the 'crush' at an event, the better it was considered to be, but it meant that one was rarely more than a metre or two away from three or four groups of chatterers. It could be avoided, to some extent, were one to dance, but then Charity so rarely was.

Today, she was spending her time again watching the lady whom she had admired so very much at the first ball they had attended in London, and who was wearing blue, just as she had on that other occasion. Charity had noticed her at some of the other events also; although she sometimes wore other colours, she had a clear preference for blue and had a number of dresses in different shades. Knowing a little more about the steps of the dance, Charity could now appreciate the young lady's lightness of foot and elegance of manner even more than she had before: she danced like dandelion seeds in the wind, seeming almost to float. It was clear, too, that her sprightly and engaging air warmed those who came into contact with her. There were always smiles on the faces of those around, and she never—whether dancing or not—had any lack of friends and admirers surrounding her. Charity was not surprised. She found herself drawn instinctively to the lady, always looking for her at each event and feeling a warm glow of pleasure when she was present, even though they had never so much as spoken a word to one another.

Charity had not seen Miss Musgrove, the plump young lady of the first ball, again, which she regretted. Their meeting had been one of the few moments of kindliness that she had experienced at these events, and she had thought for a while that she might have come close to making a friend. But Charity could only presume that Miss Musgrove had been out of her usual oeuvre that evening—something which might well have explained her willingness to chat for a few moments with Charity herself.

She was not left to regret this absence for long however. Unexpectedly, she caught her would-be-friend's name on the lips of a debutante who was giggling happily with a few others.

"Miss Musgrove? I believe she's out of town for the moment."

Well, that would explain it, Charity thought. No wonder she hadn't seen her again. Her mind would have drifted, except that another familiar name attracted her notice: her own.

"Didn't I see her talking to that Bellingham girl the other week? Not the pretty one. The other one?" another girl—a ginger-haired girl with striking green eyes—asked.

"The peculiar one? Miss Charity Bellingham?" Charity tried not to be upset about being described as peculiar. It was no more than she had thought of herself, many times, after all.

"Oh, she certainly was."

"But why?"

"Who knows? But I'll tell you something amusing about her."

"About Miss Musgrove?"

"Hardly! Though the subject certainly came up in conversation with her." The first girl took a deep breath, and said with false seriousness, "You may have noticed that Miss Charity Bellingham rarely appears to take part in festivities at balls?"

"She—What?"

Charity knew she should walk away, but somehow she was rooted to the spot. It seemed impossible that she should be the subject of conversation; that anyone should know who she was, let alone know much about her. But a quick glance showed her that Miss Scorton was in the tightly knit group of girls. Miss Scorton had been at many of the smaller events that Charity had attended, and had made clear her dislike and disapproval of the Bellingham family en masse. She had never forgiven Rebecca for catching her brother's interest, though Mr Scorton had snubbed Rebecca publicly at the last ball they attended, turning his attention elsewhere in a way that made his meaning quite clear. Nonetheless, despite it having been Rebecca who had upset her, Miss Scorton disliked Charity even more than her sister, or perhaps merely saw an easier target in her. Presumably she had also disseminated her opinion of them all to her own closest friends.

"She doesn't dance very often," Miss Scorton said lazily, as if she were above the conversation. Far too important to gossip herself, at least publicly, she was willing to facilitate the gossip of others, it seemed.

"Well, hardly! I can't imagine the gentlemen flocking to her side, can you?" said the redhead, knowing herself to be in a different category altogether.

"Ah, but do you know *why* they do not do so?" asked the first.

Miss Scorton made a small snorting noise.

"I can think of several reasons," said the other.

"Oh no, forget any of those," said lady one. "You know, I know Miss Musgrove quite well. Our families, you know," she added vaguely. "So I talk to her at any event at which I see her. And it seems that Miss Charity Bellingham's lack of dancing has nothing to do with herself, her person, at least according to the young lady herself." She shook her head in mock regret. "It's her height."

"Her what?"

"She's too tall!" The girl rocked with laughter. "That's why no one asks her. That's why she doesn't dance! She's just too tall!"

"She truly said that?" asked another young lady in a pink satin dress.

Charity blanched, moving back a step in the hope that no one would see her. She had *liked* Miss Musgrove, and this was the outcome. The one lady she'd met in her entire Season whom she had felt positively towards had taken her words and twisted them to make a joke out of her. Biting her lip, which was quivering in a most unaccustomed manner, Charity wondered how many other people the lady had told about their brief conversation. Was the whole of London laughing at her?

Turning, she stumbled away. She would not cry, she told herself fiercely. She never cried. And she was certainly not going to give those girls the pleasure of having been seen to upset her. Taking a few deep breaths, she raised her chin high and turned back to the throng. What did it matter what a parcel of silly girls said? Nonetheless, one thing was for sure: she would try to make no more friends. Splendid isolation was much to be preferred to this sort of unkindness.

Without her own friends, Charity was forced to rely on Rebecca, and the friends—or friendly acquaintances, it might be more accurate to describe them as—that her sister had made. Despite her shyness, Rebecca somehow understood how to converse with people. She knew what subjects would be welcomed and which would not. She also had a kind word for everyone, which Charity was glad to see appreciated. Charity had wondered whether others might take advantage of her sweet-natured sister, but if they did, Rebecca did not seem to mind. So on those occasions when Mrs Bellingham allowed the girls to go out without her, it was usually to visit one of Rebecca's new acquaintances.

One such was Mrs Hollings, a lady several years Rebecca's senior in age, if in nothing else. Mrs Hollings was of moderate age, moderate height and moderate intelligence. While by no means a stupid women, she had no desire to learn anything new about the world. If she had not needed such knowledge in her previous thirty-five years of life, she seemed to imply, it was clearly not worth knowing. Rebecca got on well with her, though Rebecca got on well with most people. The two ladies discussed the trials involved in trimming a hat successfully, or their favourite flowers in the Botanical Gardens.

Charity was reduced to utter boredom within ten minutes. Although she was fond of flowers, after having once described those she admired most, she felt no need to go over the same ground again and again. She had never trimmed a hat for pleasure in her life, and those she had been obliged to design had been saved from ruin only by Rebecca's skilful fingers. She was unwaveringly grateful to, and admiring of, her sister for this; however, as a conversational subject, it was one to which she had little to add.

From time to time, when the conversation between the two others flagged, Mrs Hollings would look over at Charity, saying archly to Rebecca: "Your sister is very quiet again, Miss Bellingham."

Charity, if her mind had not wandered so far that she was completely oblivious of the conversation going on around her, would blush and apologise.

"I am so sorry. I was just admiring the arrangement on your mantelpiece." Or the flowers, or the piece of embroidery which had been discarded by her hostess on their arrival. After the first couple of occasions when she had been caught wool-gathering whilst in company, she had begged Rebecca to tell her what she might express interest in. Rebecca, who knew her sister well enough to know the boredom she felt during such visits, had provided her with a list.

"Though really, Charity, you could just stay away."

"And stay home with Mother?"

The girls' eyes had met in unspoken accord, and Rebecca had provided suggestions with no further comment. Charity had a strong suspicion that Mrs Hollings believed her half-witted, but that was a difficulty she would just have to accept. However, today's conversation was one in which Charity did not have to feign interest. After they had been provided with tea by Mrs Hollings, and the usual courtesies had been exchanged, Mrs Hollings took the chatter in an unusually personal direction.

"A little birdie told me"—and oh, how Charity disliked that phrase—"that there might be an Interesting Announcement coming in the not-too-distant future." She raised a beautifully groomed eyebrow in Rebecca's direction. Charity, bewildered, looked first at Mrs Hollings and then at her sister, whose pretty face was unusually pink with embarrassment.

"I don't...I mean, there isn't...That is..." Rebecca stumbled through a number of half-sentences without finishing a single one.

"I don't think we know of anything," Charity interjected hastily, attempting to spare her sister's blushes.

"Really?" Mrs Hollings's archness was in full flood. "You mean a certain gentleman—we won't mention his name out loud, not yet—has *not* visited your mama lately?"

"He has," Rebecca admitted, to Charity's surprise and bewilderment, "but...nothing is settled yet, you know."

"I'm sure it will be soon. I don't think...our mysterious 'X'... is a gentleman who wishes to wait too long for his pleasures." She gave a little affected laugh and said in a sing-song voice, "I see wedding bells in your future."

Rebecca blushed and disclaimed, and Mrs Hollings mercifully changed the subject.

When they took their leave, however, Charity turned to her sister. "What did Mrs Hollings mean, earlier?"

Rebecca gave a hunted look around, as if fearing that someone might overhear the conversation. "I...It...Charity, you must have noticed that Mr Fotheringay has visited more and more often?"

Charity stared at her with blank astonishment. "Yes, but you surely don't think that Mother will marry him? When she's so fastidious and he so..." She gave a little shudder of distaste.

Rebecca looked, if anything, more anxious still. "Charity!"

Charity sighed. "I know, I know, it's unkind to speak ill of someone, no matter whom they may be."

"No, Charity, you don't understand." Rebecca drew a deep breath. "He doesn't wish to marry Mother. He wants to marry me."

CHAPTER SIX

For a moment, Charity stood in frozen silence.

"You're teasing me," she said at last.

Rebecca pressed her lips together tightly and shook her head. Charity was finding it hard to breathe. Fotheringay, marry *Rebecca*? No, it could not happen. It must not happen.

"Charity, we can't talk about it here," Rebecca said urgently.

Charity, coming to her senses, looked around. They were in the hustle and bustle of a smart London street. Rebecca was right: it was no place for private conversation.

"All right. Let's get home, and then we need to talk about this."

They made their way back to the house with not a further word spoken between them. Charity was stunned. She was not sure what Rebecca was feeling, but it was clear that she knew more of what was going on than Charity did.

When they got in, they divested themselves of their cloaks, and Charity turned to Rebecca.

"Come to my room." Rebecca obediently followed Charity up the stairs. "We're less likely to be disturbed here than in your room," Charity explained further. "Now…" She sat down heavily on the bed and looked at her sister. "What's going on? You can't marry Fotheringay, of course. But tell me about it."

Rebecca had wrapped her arms around herself as if holding herself together. "Mr Fotheringay has spoken to Mother, and Mother has spoken to me," she said. "We are expecting him to propose to me at any moment."

"But that's preposterous!" Charity exclaimed. "Becca, he's twice your age and more."

"Mother thinks I would do better with an older husband. She says…she says I have no idea of the modern world and I need someone who will be able to guide me." Rebecca looked hopelessly across at Charity. "She considers it the perfect match, she said."

"No! No, no, no, and a thousand times no!" Charity said. Then, more gently, "Becca, I'll support you if you tell Mother that you can't do it. I promise."

Rebecca's eyes filled with tears, and she looked away from Charity, clearly hoping that her sister had not noticed her distress. As if Charity could think of anything save Rebecca's distress.

"I must. I'm not like you, Charity. I'm not brave."

"You are, dear. Braver than me if you really intend to go ahead with this. I couldn't do it myself."

"But if Mother says it's right? And—and she spent so much money bringing us here, just to help us and find us secure homes. How could I defy her now?"

Charity's own eyes prickled a little at this. For of course Rebecca wouldn't, perhaps couldn't, defy Mrs Bellingham. The obedient daughter, she always had done everything that her parents asked of her, genuinely believing that they must know best. To turn around now, and refuse to obey her mother's will, was unthinkable. But at the same time, marriage to Fotheringay was also unthinkable. She looked across at Rebecca and knew she could protest no more.

"If you change your mind, dearest, I will support you," she said quietly. She got up and stood behind her sister, wrapping her arms around her so that Rebecca had a double layer of her own and Charity's arms. "You don't have to face this alone. You don't have to face it at all."

Rebecca turned her head so that she was looking up at her tall sister. "But the trouble is," she said, her voice quivering a little bit, "that I must."

A few days later, in the balmy days of late May, with the Season nearing its end, came one of the minority of events that Charity had actually been looking forward to. Part of her frustration with London lay in the fact that so much took place inside. To be sure, there were always walks in the park and even riding, for those ladies who chose or could afford it. Charity's desire for a horse, however, had met with a stony refusal by Mrs Bellingham on grounds of expense…with the additional comment that she could not trust her daughter to behave impeccably at the best of times, without giving her the opportunity to romp about like some common hoyden on the back of an ill-trained animal. In vain had Charity protested that she would ride the most staid horse Mrs Bellingham could find; in vain had Rebecca tried to persuade their mother to relent (a generous gesture, for Rebecca, though she could ride, did not enjoy the experience). Horses, it seemed, were a luxury and risk Charity could not be allowed to take. For once, when she considered the matter and learned of the costs, Charity could not entirely blame her mother.

However, it meant that a picnic—an entire day's entertainment, away from Mrs Bellingham and away from the dirt and noise of central London—was a treat very much to be anticipated. Even with the knowledge of Rebecca's soon-to-be-agreed betrothal to upset her, Charity was enthusiastic about the event. A few older ladies were coming, of course, to chaperone the group, but only a few, and the group itself was not too large. None of the ladies Charity most disliked were due to attend, so the idea of a day out in the sunshine was a highly welcome one. Rebecca had caught a little of her sister's eagerness and chattered expectantly of flowers and friendship. Charity was glad to see it. Rebecca had been quiet, even by her own standards, of late.

But the picnic, after all Charity's enthusiasm, was not a success. It had been arranged that she and Rebecca would travel to the park with Mrs Carbory and her daughter Catherine, but it was nearly an hour later than arranged when the ladies appeared at the door—time enough for Mrs Bellingham to have furiously called the Carborys all the names under the sun and time enough for Rebecca to have twisted herself into a panic that they had been forgotten. There was no apology or excuse given, and after Rebecca had asked politely whether there was anything wrong and been roundly snubbed, the journey had continued in silence.

The park itself was pretty enough. Large oak trees spread their branches to give shade, whilst sun lovers had plenty of room to revel in the brightness. The party split up into small groups, wandering and chattering and laughing, and Charity thought for a moment or two that the occasion might live up to her expectations. Rebecca was looking cheerful, and the idea that they both had hours before they need return to their mother's bosom was a joyful one.

"How beautiful this is," Charity exclaimed to Miss Watkins as they walked together.

The lady, an unobtrusively handsome woman in her mid-twenties whom Charity suspected felt sorry for her, smiled.

"It is. I love it particularly in autumn, but it is always delightful."

"And such a difference from most of London," Charity added, trying to conceal a sigh.

It had taken her a long time to realise that it was the countryside that she missed most from home. To be able to walk out of her front door and see grass and woods, not dirty, smelly streets. And animals—apart from the array of horses and dogs ranging from sleek, over-fed and over-trained beasts to bone-thin feral creatures snapping at the heels of passers-by, there was barely an animal to be seen in the city. Out here, surrounded by nature, she felt more comfortable in London than on any other occasion. Or she did until she was approached by a familiar figure, one whom she had not thought invited to the picnic—one whom, above all others, she was anxious to avoid.

"Miss Bellingham." Miss Musgrove smiled. "How good it is to see you again."

Charity froze. The audacity of the lady shocked her. To think that she could laugh at Charity behind her back and yet then walk straight up to her and greet her like a friend.

"Good afternoon," she said frostily.

"May I walk with you a little way?"

Miss Musgrove was obviously expecting an affirmative answer. Miss Watkins excused herself, leaving Charity alone to face her nemesis. And Charity could not think of a word to say. Miss Musgrove fell into step with her.

"I confess I prefer outings like this to stuffy ballrooms, would you not agree?" she asked.

If I say yes, will you tell the polite world how I insulted their balls? Charity could not say the words aloud, but with them dancing in her head, she could think of little else to say.

"Excuse me," she managed instead, her voice frosty even to her own ears. "I believe my sister wants me."

She walked away to Rebecca, aware of Miss Musgrove's eyes following her as she went. Perhaps she had been inexcusably rude, but Charity had not been able to help herself. Her heart beating a little faster, she realised that the charm had been taken off the day by the contretemps. Where it had been a sunny, cheerful occasion, it was now grey and gloomy. She looked up to the sky and realised it was quite literally so: the sun had gone in, as if affected by her mood.

"I did not know Miss Musgrove was due to attend," Charity said to Miss Carbory, as they sat together over the luncheon. She had lost her appetite and picked moodily at the feast in front of her.

"It was a lucky chance. She is only recently back from a stay in the country," Miss Carbory said gaily. "Mama met her two days previously and mentioned the picnic to her. Miss Musgrove was, I believe, reluctant to come on such short notice, but Mama was able to persuade her. That was why we were late, you know: we went to check that Miss Musgrove had managed to organise to come."

"I see." Charity mentally added another fault to Miss Musgrove's chart. Not only had the lady mocked her behind her back, not only had she spoiled the picnic with her intrusive presence, but she had also been responsible for the late start—for Rebecca's anxiety—and for Mrs Bellingham's wrath.

"She has so many friends, you know." Miss Carbory chattered on, each sentence digging into Charity as if she were sitting on a thistle. "Everyone likes Miss Musgrove."

Charity bit her lip almost to the bleeding point and said no more. The day was ruined.

But the next day, in its way, was even worse. From the way Mrs Bellingham fussed over Rebecca's clothes, making her try on three different dresses and pair them with her smartest stockings—"But you mustn't look overdressed, Rebecca. Just beautifully natural"—Rebecca and Charity knew what was to come. "Beautifully natural": an ironic turn of phrase given the amount of work needed to appear to be in such a state. Rebecca's hair was curled, straightened and curled again. A small mark on her glove made the pair totally unwearable, leaving Charity and the maid to search through every pair of gloves the girls possessed to find a suitable replacement. The dilemma over jewellery and adornment nearly brought Rebecca to tears, except that she was strictly forbidden to cry because of the detrimental effect it would have on her face.

"You can't have puffy eyes, Rebecca. Not today," Mrs Bellingham said, implying (probably correctly, Charity thought bitterly) that Rebecca might cry all she wanted on any other day without it bothering her mother in the slightest.

Then the girls were sent to wait upstairs, Rebecca forbidden to sit down lest it crease the lilac dress which had been chosen. Charity tried to converse naturally, but it was next to impossible with only one thing on both of their minds, and that something that neither of them felt capable of talking about. Instead, Charity went to the window, hoping that she might see Mr Fotheringay when he arrived, so that Rebecca at least might have that little portion of warning. But the window's view did not overlook the door, and instead she stared at the raindrops sliding down the windowpane and waited.

It seemed forever and it seemed barely a second until they heard the noise denoting a visitor. The two girls looked at each other in silence.

"There's no use my saying anything, is there?" Charity said, trying to keep her voice calm.

"No," replied Rebecca, and Charity could hear the same tone in her sister's voice too.

Finally, the moment arrived.

"Rebecca," called Mrs Bellingham. "Mr Fotheringay has something to say to you."

Rebecca was always pale, but she looked positively white to Charity right now. Charity felt helpless in the tide to prevent what must be to come. She desperately wanted Rebecca to refuse, to turn down the proposal. She suspected that in her heart her sister wanted the same thing. But she knew, and Rebecca knew, that this was not going to happen. When she next saw Rebecca, her sister would be a betrothed woman.

"Coming." But the voice in which Rebecca replied was too quiet for her mother to hear, and the call was repeated.

"*Rebecca*, now!"

Charity squeezed Rebecca's hand and walked with her to the doorway, but she said nothing. There was nothing left to say. Rebecca walked down the stairs as if going to her execution, and Charity, unexpected tears in her eyes, stayed and waited.

CHAPTER SEVEN

With the engagement official, it was time for the details to be arranged. Charity had expected the wedding itself to be the biggest area of contention, but she had mistaken the matter. In a marriage between Rebecca and Mr Fotheringay, it was unexpectedly Charity who was the biggest problem.

"I shall be moving to Bath soon after the wedding," Mrs Bellingham announced to her daughters.

Charity sighed. Another move. Another new city. Another place to feel like a fish out of water and long for the gentle rural town of her childhood. Was this how it was going to be now, following her mother around like an unwanted puppy? She had hoped—indeed, presumed—that they would be returning to Warwickshire. She hadn't had high expectations of happiness, since she and Mrs Bellingham were hardly similar in character, but at least she would be able to get out and ramble in the fresh air and beauty of the Midlands.

Rebecca also looked alarmed at this information. "But Mother, won't you be staying close by?" she faltered. "I thought you would be here, to help me."

That, Charity realised with a bolt of understanding, was precisely why Mrs Bellingham was determined to move away. Never maternal by nature, this was at least a chance for her to off-load responsibility of one of her children onto someone else. But it seemed that Mrs Bellingham had no intention of merely detaching herself from one of the girls.

"Certainly not." Mrs Bellingham pursed her lips. "Far be it from me to interfere, Rebecca. You are to be a married lady, and no one, not even a mother, should intervene in someone else's marriage. No, I feel sure that it is much better for you and Fotheringay to settle down quietly together in town."

"When do we leave?" Charity asked resignedly.

Her mother turned to her. "'We'? Goodness no, Charity. I couldn't possibly have you in Bath. For your own good, you must stay in London."

Charity felt as if she had been unexpectedly pushed off a high cliff. The world seemed to tumble around her, nothing making any sense. She opened her mouth to say something, but no words would come out.

"But Mother, Charity can't live alone," Rebecca said, reaching out a hand to steady Charity as she swayed.

"Certainly not. It is unthinkable. No, there is only one answer. She must stay with you and Mr F," her mother said briskly. Then, toning down the briskness in favour of a more plaintive tone, "I am too unwell to look after Charity as well as myself. Besides, the sort of lodgings I will be able to afford in Bath simply would not be big enough for the two of us. Whereas Fotheringay is rich. It is to be hoped that this modern desire for hot beverages continues. Why, Rebecca, in a few years, he may be worth even more money. He can certainly afford to house your sister."

"Mother, I can't ask him," Becca said, her hands flying to her cheeks. "Please. I...I barely know him."

Charity bit her lip. How could Becca have agreed to marry someone so much her senior? Someone that, in her own words, she 'barely knew'? Mr Fotheringay might—well, he *might*—be all that one could wish as a husband. But how, how could

Rebecca have the courage to go through with the wedding, with the pomp and ceremony of being joined in a lifelong bond to any gentleman she had met only a handful of times? Even if anyone had asked Charity to wed them—which, of course, there had been no hope for; even from the beginning; her mother had known that from the start—she did not think that she could have agreed.

"Nonsense. He is to be your husband, and Charity is your sister. He owes you that much, at least." Mrs Bellingham brushed off Rebecca's concerns as if they were a spider's web she had just walked into. "He can hardly," she added, the words too familiar to hurt Charity, "expect to get all of the pleasures of marriage with none of the responsibility of the unpleasant aspects."

"Please, Mother."

"Oh, very well." Mrs Bellingham stood, smoothing the already immaculate folds of her dress down around her. "If you want something to be done well, do it yourself. If you insist on this contrary attitude, Rebecca, I will have to ask him myself. And don't blame me if he asks you why you have to use your mother as a go-between. No one can say that I don't do the best for my children however."

She bustled out of the room. Rebecca stared after her, the faintest frown between her eyes. "Oh dear. It's so difficult, Charity."

"I'm sorry." Charity realised that what she was really apologising for was her own existence. It was, perhaps, the story of her life.

"It's not that I don't want you," Rebecca said. "It's just…" And then the façade dropped, and Charity saw the fear in her sister's place. "Oh, Charity, I'm so scared."

Charity went to her sister, putting her arms clumsily around her. Rebecca's admission of her worries went straight to Charity's heart. Charity remembered how Rebecca had spoken of love, when Mr Scorton's interest in her had been shown. But instead of contracting the marriage of love she had clearly been dreaming of, her sister was about to be sold to a rich man. It wasn't fair. Oh, it wasn't fair!

"I'm sorry," she whispered again. "I could go away, somehow. I don't know. Be a governess? Someone must want me, surely. I don't want to ruin your life too."

Rebecca held her close for a second. "You never have," she said, letting go and looking up at her big little sister. "Don't ever think that. And I want you, I do. Never doubt that, please, Charity. And anyway"—she produced a wobbly smile—"Mother will sort it out. I'm sure she will."

Charity forced a smile in return. "Yes." Mother would sort it. Of course she would. The alternative was being left with Charity on her hands, and she had no intention of having that. Maybe Mr Fotheringay was to be pitied rather than blamed: little did he know of the family he had just adopted as his own. Charity hesitated. "I hope you'll be happy, Becca."

Rebecca nodded. "Me too," she said, and left the room, leaving Charity looking thoughtfully at the door she closed behind her.

It did not take Mrs Bellingham long to broach the subject with Mr Fotheringay. When something was in her own interests, it was amazing how efficient she could be. Two afternoons later, Charity came downstairs to sit, as she was expected to do, in the drawing room with her mother and sister. The drawing room door was ajar, but just as she reached a hand to push it open, she heard voices from within. Mrs Bellingham's and—oh, that must be Mr Fotheringay.

"I'm really not at all well," she heard her mother say in a trembling, self-pitying tone. "And Rebecca has always been such a dutiful daughter."

"You said. Not sure what it has to do with me, yet."

"Well, you see, you are taking my right hand and stalwart away from me."

Charity knew she should not be eavesdropping, but she guessed the main thrust of the conversation ahead long before Mr Fotheringay did. It was her own future, and she found it hard to walk away.

"You've got the other one, though. Healthy-looking gal. She'll look after you, right and tight."

Charity heard her mother sigh. "I wish it were so easy. Charity has always been a worry to me. Rebecca, bless her soul, has done what she can to lift the burden from her ailing mother, but..."

Lips pressed firmly together, Charity spun on the spot, walking back towards the stairs as quietly as she could. If it were true that eavesdroppers never heard any good of themselves, then perhaps she deserved to overhear her mother's plaintive complaints. Charity wondered what Fotheringay's reaction would be. It might be one thing taking a second helpful young lady like his wife-to-be under his roof, but Charity couldn't help wondering whether Mrs Bellingham had misplayed the situation. After all, who would want a girl of the character her own mother had just attributed to Charity? One last line of her mother's floated up to her as she reached the fifth stair: "And it would be a terrible thing to break the betrothal at this point..."

It was a threat, thought Charity, and one which would probably work. Mr Fotheringay's money might make him acceptable in the polite world, but his background meant that it only just did. If he were to back out of the betrothal... Well, certainly it would be awkward and distressing for the Bellinghams, Rebecca in particular, but as there was no more money for another Season, it would not necessarily do too much harm. They would retire from London, either back to their house in the village, or to Bath, depending on their mother's whim. Whereas Fotheringay would still be in London—he would be not only the gentleman with too few gentlemanly ancestors in his past, but a man who had cast off his betrothed for no good reason. It would affect his standing so very much more.

No, thought Charity grimly, perhaps her mother had judged this just right.

* * *

The wedding, which was set to take place on the sixth of July, just past the final days of the London Season, had as much pomp and ceremony as Mrs Bellingham had been able to cram in. Rebecca's dress had more lace on it than Charity had ever seen in one place, and the mother of the bride was resplendent in purple satin, though still wearing black gloves as a delicate sign of her widowed status. The service stuck to the traditional wording, of course, but the reception afterwards was as modern and up to date as possible. Pink champagne flowed freely, a string quartet played softly until the dancing began and the dancing itself started with a waltz, with Rebecca and her new husband taking the floor.

That last was a sign of Rebecca's new married status. Mrs Bellingham still refused to allow Charity to take part in the waltz, even though she had received the signal from the doyennes of the *ton* that it would be acceptable for her younger daughter to dance. Charity did not mind: it was an excuse as to why she stood hugging the wall whilst the other ladies danced. In such close contact with a gentleman, her height would be more noticeable than ever. She doubted that any man would wish to lead her out. She should have been a boy, she thought for the millionth time.

"Are you enjoying yourself?" Rebecca asked.

Charity took a good look at her sister. She was smiling, but her eyes were scared. "As much as you are, I imagine," she said gently.

An almost-laugh came from Rebecca. "It's that bad?" she said. Then, quickly, "It is an amazing day, isn't it? Mother and Mr Fotheringay have organised it well."

Charity forbore to mention that it was supposed to be Rebecca's day too. She knew, and her sister knew, that it was nothing of the kind. Rather, Rebecca was being sold to the highest bidder. The spectacle was a glossy covering for the truth.

"It's beautiful."

Rebecca nodded. "I'd better go. I think Mother is expecting me to speak to every guest." She reached out tentatively and grasped Charity's wrist. "I don't know if I've said this," she said, "but I'm so glad you're going to be with me. You know, after…"

She trailed off. The honeymoon had been arranged with care equal to that taken with the marriage. Mr Fotheringay had a hunting box, and they were repairing there for six weeks or so, just the pair of them. Charity had no idea what would happen during this time—she suspected Rebecca did not either—but she knew that Becca was dreading it. Just her and her new husband, a man she hardly knew.

"Me too." It was only half a lie: Charity had no wish to live with Mr Fotheringay, but on the other hand, little wish to be with her mother in Bath, especially given how clearly her mother had stated her desire to be rid of Charity. Being with Rebecca would be nice, if only it weren't for *him*. "Becca?" she said as Rebecca turned away. Her sister looked back over her shoulder at Charity, and Charity realised anew how pretty she was. "Be happy."

"Yes." It was only a breath of the word, and Rebecca was gone.

CHAPTER EIGHT

With her older daughter safely married, Mrs Bellingham was deep into organisation for her removal to Bath. She would leave two days after the newly-wed couple returned from Leicestershire, so the rented lodgings were full of boxes and chaos. For once in her life, Charity felt useful: she was an efficient packer, and her mother even unbent enough to praise her on one memorable occasion. Perhaps, Charity thought, Mrs Bellingham felt able to be positive, knowing that very soon she would be rid of both of her daughters. Their mother had never been particularly maternal, even to Rebecca. The fact that Fotheringay was willing to house Charity as well as her sister must have been a godsend.

One thing pleased Charity more than any other: amongst her arrangements, Mrs Bellingham had ordered that Charity's piano, until now in storage at Forsbury, should be sent to Fotheringay's house. Charity had not quite realised how much she depended on the piano and her music for escape until it had not been available. The thought of being reunited with her instrument was a joyful one. The thought of being separated from her mother was also not unpleasant.

The time during which Rebecca and Fotheringay were away, therefore, passed quickly. Mrs Bellingham had decided that they would have a quiet family welcome home before settling down to married life. She had originally intended some sort of soiree to show off her newly married daughter, but the practicalities of such a thing proved to be too complicated—which was to say that it would have involved her staying an extra week in London, when she was more than eager to move on to pastures new.

Consequently, on the evening of Mr and Mrs Fotheringay's return in late August, the sun shining down as if in celebration of the event, they were greeted with an extensive meal but only the company of Mrs Bellingham and Charity. Rebecca, Charity thought, looked tired, but she was usually quiet, so there was little difference there. Mr Fotheringay seemed in health, however, and Mrs Bellingham was unusually effusive, giving Charity little chance to speak to either of the guests and none at all to have private conversations with her sister.

The first opportunity she had to speak openly with her sister was two days later, as Rebecca helped Charity organise the last of her belongings, ready for Mr Fotheringay's servants to remove them from the lodgings and upstairs to her new bedroom in Fotheringay's house. As they sorted out the clothes, Charity asked, "So, did you enjoy your honeymoon?"

"Y-yes," Rebecca said uncertainly. "At least…he showed me round his country estate. It is not like Forsbury, you know. It is not a family house. He bought it when he made his fortune"—both girls were rather uncertain as to precisely how this had been made, though Charity had a vague idea that it was something to do with tea—"just to have somewhere to retreat to in the heat of summer, or…or when it is the hunting season. He says he's considered getting somewhere bigger, but there seems little point as he doesn't intend to use it much. He needs to be in London for business, he says."

"I take it you have no say in the matter?"

"Oh no!" Rebecca looked shocked. "He is so much older, you know, and a man. Besides, I do not think he would like it."

In other words, Charity thought grimly, Mr Fotheringay had married a young girl expecting and intending her to bow to his every whim. Well, it was not an unusual situation, bitterly as she might resent it on Rebecca's behalf.

"I see," she said.

"But we rode around the estate, and he introduced me to everyone. All his tenants, you know," Rebecca said. "And I met... Oh, Charity, there were so many servants! And most of them just stay there, in an empty house, waiting for his return!"

"The indulgences of the rich." Charity forced herself to sound light-hearted. "I daresay you will be accepting this as your due soon. You're a wealthy lady now, you know."

Rebecca looked uncomfortable. "There is so much I am supposed to know," she confessed. "Mr Fotheringay expects me to speak to the housekeeper every morning and arrange...In truth, I do not know what he expects me to arrange, though thankfully Mrs White herself seems to know what to do. In all honesty, I think she is more the lady of the household than I am."

"But he did not marry her." Charity gave her sister a quick smile as she sorted out a pile of petticoats. "And I am certain you are younger and prettier than she, not to mention being better born than either she or Fotheringay."

Rebecca pressed her hands to hot cheeks. "Oh, Charity, you must not say things like that! He would be furious if he heard you."

"Only to you," Charity promised. But there was something in Rebecca's voice when she spoke of Fotheringay which... "You're not afraid of him, are you?" she blurted out.

"Not afraid. It's just that..." Rebecca looked down at her hands, a habit of hers when she was anxious or being scolded. "There is so much to learn, you know, and...and—"

Charity dumped the petticoats down on the bed and went over to her sister. She took one of Rebecca's hands, patting it in a sisterly fashion.

"What? You know you can always tell me anything, Becca."
Rebecca gave a faint smile. "Sometimes I think that you
should have been the older sister and not I. It seems wrong to
burden you with all my worries."

"Well, if it comes to that, I'm forever leaning on you too,"
Charity retorted. "I'd probably still be stitching my first ball
gown if it were not for you."

"Silly!" Rebecca took a deep breath and raised her eyes a
little higher up, which was encouraging. "It's just that I rather
angered him once."

"Oh, that I am sure you could not!" It would be a harsh
person indeed to show much anger towards Rebecca, especially
if that person was her newly-wed husband.

"It was the shooting and hunting, you see."

"He did not take you to either, surely?"

"No. I think he might have considered allowing me to hunt,
but when he saw me ride, he saw that it would not do." Rebecca
could ride, but she preferred horses that Charity privately
termed 'slugs' for their slow, placid ways. Anything less likely to
be a hunter was hard to imagine. "I would only have held him up
and been in the way. It was early, really. The fox hunting season
isn't supposed to start until November, but Mr Fotheringay said
that it didn't matter, just this once."

"Well, that's understandable," Charity said gently. "I take it
he went without you? A little bit unkind, when it was supposed
to be your honeymoon, but—"

"Oh, it was not that." Rebecca drew her hand gently away
from Charity's, twisting it with the other on her lap. "He
brought me home a…a trophy." She blinked hard. "I will not
cry. He says that is silly. But this little fox, Charity, only a cub, I
think. So small, its fur all matted with blood. I could not…I did
not…" She trailed off.

Charity could see it all in her mind's eye. Fotheringay,
bringing home the spoils of the hunt to his new wife, expecting
praise and admiration. Rebecca, looking down at the mangled
body and dissolving into tears at the idea of the pain and
suffering the fox had experienced.

Charity had a faintly guilty suspicion that she might rather enjoy some aspects of hunting, if not the final outcome. She was fond of animals and particularly attached to horses. In her younger days at Forsbury, she had been accused (not entirely without reason) of being more inclined to greet a neighbour's horse than the lady or gentleman riding it. And on the few occasions on which she had had the opportunity to ride full pelt, she had enjoyed every moment. To think of riding *ventre a terre*, surrounded by hounds and like-minded people, was definitely appealing. The kill did not draw her interest; indeed, she would have much preferred not to see an animal die merely for sport, but she had a feeling that she might be prepared to accept that part for the sake of the rest. Rebecca, however, was of a very different temperament, and Charity found it easy to visualise her gentle sister's distress at being triumphantly presented with the broken body of a fox.

"Oh, how horrid for you," she said sympathetically.

"I was a goose to get so upset," Rebecca said hastily. "I know Father hunted sometimes. Most people do. I was just taken by surprise. I had not thought to see—well, you know the rest."

"And Fotheringay was angry," Charity said. Rebecca nodded. "I suppose," Charity continued, feeling her way slowly through uncharted territory, trying to find the right words, "he had meant to please you, and was upset rather than angry."

She had no such conviction, but Rebecca was married to the gentleman now, for better or worse. It was best, Charity told herself, that she be made as happy as she could within the marriage, even if it meant ascribing inaccurate emotions to Mr Fotheringay.

"Yes," agreed Rebecca, in a soft voice. "He told me I must learn, and I will try. That is, I will try not to be such a silly again."

Charity patted her shoulder encouragingly, before turning back to her task. "Well, he will hardly be fox hunting in London, so I think you are safe for the moment! And you must feel for Fotheringay now. He is moving into his own new experiences. You and I will still have each other, but he is changing from a bachelor life to being a married man. It is you who will have to look after him, now!"

Rebecca giggled as she checked the number of morning dresses Charity had brought up. "Now it is you who is being silly. Mr Fotheringay is not concerned. And anyway, it will be strange for us without Mother here."

"Strange, but not necessarily unpleasant," Charity said. "And you, Mrs Fotheringay, will have to be my chaperone. All the time I remain unmarried, you know, Mother will have to live with the fear that I may someday be returned to her care. It is positively your duty to find me a husband!"

"I'll do my best." Rebecca looked uncertainly at her sister, clearly unsure whether Charity was joking or not.

Charity gave her a reassuring smile. "Don't worry, sister dear. I think I was born to be a spinster. Every family requires an old maiden aunt, you know, and I foresee myself filling that role admirably."

Rebecca opened her mouth to say something and then shut it again abruptly. Charity, looking at her, realised that it had been the mention of the word 'aunt': for Charity to fulfil the destiny of which she had spoken, Rebecca would have to have a child. And for that to happen... Well, that was something Rebecca would have to work out for herself, with her husband's assistance.

* * *

It was a curious experience for Charity, though, to see the intimate workings of a marriage. She had only known her parents', and it had hardly been a model for a healthy relationship. They had either fought so that the arguments came thick and fast, or they were no longer on speaking terms with each other, which had been more peaceful but hardly to be desired. One of the few things they had ever agreed about was the unworthiness of their youngest child, and her unforgivable sin of failing to be a son.

Rebecca and Fotheringay's marriage was very different indeed. He gave dictates, and she obeyed them: it was more, Charity thought, of a parent/child relationship than a marriage.

However, it made for a considerably more stable home than any Charity had known before, and outside the instructions he gave, Fotheringay was not a particularly stern husband. As long as Rebecca was where he required her, when he required her to be there, he asked little about the ways in which she spent the rest of her time. Charity did not believe that her sister had deliberately brought this about, but in fact Rebecca bought herself a good deal of freedom by her usual obedience. Rather to her surprise, for a while Charity began to think that the marriage might work quite successfully.

It was true, however, that the two were hardly a match in interests or knowledge, something which became clear that October. The month had come in with gusts and showers of rain, but as the days progressed, the weather became more mixed— neither one thing nor another. It had not the stifling heat of a London summer (that, to Charity's relief, was over), but the days seesawed between warm and fine and rainy and cold. A pelisse or cloak became a necessity outside the house, rather than a garment worn to show off its owner's fashionability.

Meanwhile, the newspapers were full of the war with France and Spain and the latest doings of Napoleon: suspicions were that a sea battle could not be far away, and so it proved. Fotheringay looked up from his perusal of the morning news one breakfast time and commented, "The Navy boys've got their way, then. They were itching for a fight."

"Oh?" Rebecca asked.

Charity could tell that her sister was endeavouring to show an interest despite not knowing what Fotheringay was talking about.

"Napoleon?" Charity asked, to help her out.

Fotheringay shot a disapproving glance at her. "Of course Napoleon. Not himself, of course. He ain't fool enough to get out there in the rough of it. But it's him, all the same. What else would I be talking about?"

Rebecca also looked at Charity, but in gratitude. "You mean there has been a battle?" she asked, dismayed. "What has happened?"

"We thrashed 'em, of course. Load of continental cowards," Fotheringay said robustly. "All due to Lord Nelson, the paper says." He scanned the article that had caught his eye. "Oh, that looks bad." The two ladies looked at him, Charity at least trying not to show her impatience with this unhelpful remark. "Looks like Nelson's number might be up," he explained.

Rebecca caught Charity's eye again in mute appeal.

"Dead?" Charity asked.

"Or dying. 'Course, there are a fair few fatalities. Only to be expected in a skirmish like this. But dammee"—Rebecca winced a little at his bad language—"if that puts paid to Napoleon's little plans to invade us. Can't be done, of course. The English will rout 'em every time. But with Villeneuve…" This time he recognised his wife's bewilderment and deigned to explain, "… the French Vice-Admiral…captured, they won't be trying again in a hurry." He paused. "Pity about Nelson if it's true," he said regretfully. "Good sailor, good tactitioner. But these things happen in war." He took a long drink of his ale and then set it back on the table. "Well, to work. But mark my words, you'll hear nothing but Nelson the next few days."

For once, Mr Fotheringay was prophetic. The battle of Trafalgar was discussed in all houses at all strata of society. The news about Nelson was true, it seemed: the great admiral had been shot in the battle. But those in the know maintained it was the way he would have wished to die, and he was lauded as a hero. By the time Trafalgar had been talked out, both Charity and Rebecca knew as much as most other ladies about the war.

But the different interests and knowledge of Rebecca and Fotheringay concerned Charity a little. Could a marriage really be said to be happy, or even successful (a different thing, by some people's standards) when the parties had barely a thought in common? Her doubts had grown by the end of the month. Rebecca and she had planned a shopping trip for one morning; Charity was in need of some new gloves, and Rebecca had an urgent desire to visit a milliner of her choice. This was to be followed by a quiet afternoon, before Rebecca and Fotheringay went out at night to attend a dinner with some business acquaintances of his.

When Charity descended to the breakfast table that morning, however, it was clear that Rebecca would be going nowhere, and certainly not to the milliner's. She was awake and dressed, but her face showed black circles beneath the eyes, and she rested her head on one hand as if it was too heavy for her body. Instead of her normal greeting, Charity said: "Becca, shouldn't you be in bed?"

Rebecca looked up at her. "We have so many things to do. I will be fine as soon as I have eaten, I'm sure."

"And I'm sure you won't," Charity said briskly. She came round the table to her sister's side. "Come on, Becca, I'm taking you back to bed right now."

"I'm fine," Rebecca insisted, but she was already getting to her feet.

"Then," Charity said, toning down her briskness a little in deference to Rebecca's obvious headache, "you can come and be 'fine' in bed. Come on, dearest," she added, resting a hand underneath Rebecca's forearm. "You know I'm right."

Tears sprang to her sister's eyes. "You're so kind to me, always."

Gently, Charity ushered her upstairs. "Well," she said, "that's nothing to cry about, is it?"

She led Rebecca to her room, where she helped her undress and held back the covers on the bed to allow Rebecca to slide between the sheets. Rebecca did so with a sigh of relief, and as she lay back on the pillows, Charity examined her sister. Clearly she had a high temperature: her forehead burned underneath Charity's hand. For all Charity's brisk, boyish ways, she was an excellent sick nurse.

"Now," she murmured to Rebecca, "try and rest. I will be back in a moment."

Meeting Fotheringay on the stairs, she informed him of his wife's illness. A little frown appeared between his eyebrows.

"That's dashed inconvenient," he complained. "You shouldn't encourage her to lie about. We're supposed to be going out this evening."

"Perhaps if she rests now, she will be better later."

Charity thought it unlikely, but the last thing Rebecca needed right now was Fotheringay striding into her room like a charging bull and demanding that she recover immediately. He continued to grumble, but Charity was past him, requesting water and a damp handkerchief to put on her sister's forehead.

Armed with a range of supplies, she slipped quietly into Rebecca's bedroom. Rebecca had her eyes closed, and sleep would be the best thing for her, so Charity settled into a chair beside the bed. She had been there only a few seconds when Rebecca opened her eyes.

"Charity?"

"I'm here." Charity leaned over her sister.

"Is he angry with me?" Rebecca asked. "I heard you speaking with him."

"Fotheringay? Why would he be angry?" Charity thought back to her conversation with her brother-in-law. He had seemed disgruntled, as if Rebecca was being deliberately awkward by becoming ill. Surely, however, he must have known after these months of living with his wife that Rebecca was anything but obstructive?

"I…" Rebecca looked away. "I wasn't feeling well last night either. And he…" She broke off. "It doesn't matter. I'm just being silly."

Charity patted her sister's hand and then picked up the damp cloth to wipe Rebecca's sweaty brow.

"I told Fotheringay that you would be better left in peace for the moment, dear. So you don't have to worry about him. And anyway"—she smiled—"he would have to get past the dragon guarding your door: me! So stop fretting, and concentrate yourself on getting better."

"Yes, Charity. And…thank you."

Rebecca closed her eyes, and soon Charity knew that she was sleeping. The gentle rise and fall of the sheets bore witness to Rebecca's regular breathing. Looking down at her sister, she was filled with tenderness for her. Rebecca had loved and looked after her in their childhood, when no one else was there to do it. If Charity could return the favour now, it was the least she should do.

The morning passed peacefully into afternoon. Charity had some food brought up to her, and tried to persuade Rebecca to eat a little when she woke, but her sister just shook her head and turned away.

"You must at least drink something," Charity urged her, sliding an arm around her sister and lifting her into a more upright position.

Obediently, Rebecca opened her mouth and took a few sips of water, but Charity could persuade her into nothing more. As the afternoon wore on, Rebecca became hotter and more restless, tossing and turning in the bed and complaining in a most unnatural fashion that she could not get comfortable. When Fotheringay knocked at the door in the early evening, even he was forced to acknowledge that his wife would not be able to accompany him out that night. His suggestion that Charity might come in her place was rejected bluntly by her.

"Rebecca's unwell, and she needs me," she said. "You do not."

Fotheringay puffed out his chest in indignation at this plain speaking. "Remember who pays your bills," he said. "It ain't that sister of yours. She has nothing. You'd be well advised to treat me with respect."

Charity bit her lip to prevent an intemperate reply. Quietly, she said, "I'm looking after your wife. You can hardly fault me for that."

Fotheringay peered round her—he was not tall enough to look over her shoulder—at Rebecca writhing in the sheets.

"You don't seem to be doing much good," he retorted. "She's worse now than she was earlier. Maybe, Miss Charity, she would be better for your absence."

Charity's resolve broke. "It's evening time. Her temperature is rising. Of course she's not well. And if you would only leave me alone to look after her, she'd be doing considerably better. Now, pray excuse me!"

If she did not slam the door in his face, it was only because that would have disturbed Rebecca further. She closed it, nonetheless, with great determination, and further expressed her feelings by making an appalling face at it. She had never particularly liked Fotheringay, but until this moment he had given her no reason for positively disliking him. She exhaled in a quick pant of breath and then turned round. Rebecca was half-sitting up in bed, her hair tangled and her expression anxious.

"Must I get up, Charity? Must I get up?"

"Of course not!" Charity was still angry with her brother-in-law, and her tone was consequently sharper than it might otherwise have been. She felt guilty as she saw the tears collect in Rebecca's eyes. She forced a smile as she walked towards her. "It's fine, Becca. There is nothing for you to worry about. Mr Fotheringay has agreed that bed is the best place for you, and that I can continue to look after you." She bent over her sister and wiped the tears away. "So stop crying, and let your poor old body rest, all right?"

Rebecca reached out a hand and grabbed Charity with a strong grip. "Thank you," she whispered. "Thank you more than I can say."

"Silly!" said Charity affectionately. "Now, whilst you're awake, let me wash your face and brush out your hair. Yes, I know you have a maid to do that, but she isn't here and I am. And anyway, you know you prefer to have me when you're ill."

She cleaned and tidied her sister and then sat with Rebecca until she was confident that Rebecca had fallen asleep for the night. Fotheringay had gone out some time earlier. Charity had heard his exit: it was an unusually bad-tempered display where his valet was criticised for failing to notice a small mark on the collar of his jacket and his footman castigated for not having the umbrella at the ready to shelter him between the front door and the carriage. Rebecca had heard him too. She had said nothing about it, but Charity saw her wince at one particularly loud bellow of disapproval from below. When Rebecca was comfortably asleep, however, Charity crept to the door. Encountering her sister's maid, she gave instructions that if Rebecca woke and asked for Charity, she should be woken up.

At two in the morning, the knock on her door came.

"Please, Miss Bellingham, you said as to come for you if the mistress wanted you."

Charity blinked the sleep from her eyes and threw off her sheets and the lingering remains of her dream. Jenny, Rebecca's maid, stood by the doorway, a candle in one hand.

"Yes. Thank you, Jenny. Just take me to her, and then you can go back to bed and try and get some rest."

The house was hardly at its warmest in the darkest hours of the night. Charity gave a little shiver as she followed the maid down the corridor to Rebecca's room. She could hear her sister crying quietly, and when she went in, she saw a bedraggled heap of dark curls in the flickering light.

"Now then, Becca," she said gently, lifting her sister and cuddling her as if she were a child, "what's the matter?"

"I'm silly," Rebecca cried woefully.

"Well, I know that," teased Charity, "but what's the matter? It's all right, dear. I'm here."

She stayed a couple of hours until Rebecca settled down again, but she never did get more answer as to what was wrong. Charity could only put it down to the melancholy of illness.

The next day, and the next day, passed by in similar fashion. Rebecca seemed to be over the worst of her illness, but having improved to a certain degree, she then did not recover fully. Charity had wondered whether to ask Fotheringay to call a doctor in, but a tentative suggestion had got a response of "Pooh! Nonsense," so she had left it for the present. Rebecca was certainly not dying, nor even severely ill. She was just noticeably unwell, and appeared incapable of improving further.

In truth, Charity herself was not perturbed by spending her time in a sickroom rather than going out and about to events and engagements. She had no objection to most of them, but there were few she really mourned missing, and Rebecca's gratitude was enough to overcome any of her remaining regrets. On the third day, however, Rebecca gave voice to her own concerns.

"I'm sorry." Rebecca still had skin so wan she seemed almost to fade into the sheets on the bed. "I am keeping you from so many things. It is not fair to you."

Charity stroked her hand. "Don't be daft, dear sister," she said, her tone more sympathetic than her words. "You know I like looking after you." Charity had a reputation within her family, not unreasonably, for blunt honesty. It meant at times like this, she could choose to offer a little white lie and still be believed. After all, was it so much of an untruth? The thought of Becca sick and Charity not there to care for her was horrible. "Come, take a sip of water."

Rebecca reached out a hand for the glass, but Charity shook her head with a smile. She put one hand behind Rebecca's head to raise her up a little and held the water to her lips.

"Thank you. I am so much trouble."

"Shh. No more of that." Charity lowered Rebecca back down to the pillow and set the glass on the bedside table. "Now, if I sit here beside you, perhaps you will be able to go to sleep."

Rebecca, indeed, looked almost asleep now. She gave a weak smile to her sister and closed her eyes obediently. Charity picked up the book she kept for these quiet moments and buried herself deep in the novel. Would Pamela prevail? Or was it already too late for the heroine? She gave a little snort of amusement. In novels, the heroine almost always did end up happy; it was only real life which proved different.

Mr Fotheringay had not been in Rebecca's room since early that morning. He'd taken one look at his ailing wife, said "Glad to see your sister's caring for you" and left. Charity resented his attitude towards Rebecca but was grateful for his absence. Living with the man had not been able to reconcile her to her sister's marriage, despite its usual peaceful nature. The age gap, and the lack of interest in Rebecca that Fotheringay showed, made it clear that although they lived in relative harmony, it was by no means an ideal relationship. Nevertheless, she admitted to herself, it must have been difficult for Fotheringay to set up house not only with a young and beautiful wife, but with that wife's "ugly sister". Since the moment she had heard herself described in that fashion, Charity had been unable to forget it. The sting was not in the insult itself, but in the kernel of truth within it. Fotheringay had accepted Charity's presence in his house, and if he only barely stayed on the side of politeness to her, perhaps that was not so surprising. It was his careless disregard for Rebecca that Charity could not forgive.

When Rebecca woke, Charity put the book aside.

"Feeling better?" she asked.

"A little." But Rebecca's face was woebegone as she spoke.

Charity stroked her sister's hair off her sweaty face. "Well, there's no need to sound miserable about it," she said teasingly. "Anyone would think you didn't want to get well."

"I don't."

The words were so softly spoken that for a moment Charity thought that she must have imagined them.

"Becca?"

"I wish I could stay here in this room with you, forever," Rebecca whispered. "Every time I wake up and realise I still feel ill, I am grateful."

Charity's head began to spin. "Dear sister, this is just the illness speaking. It is trying to keep you in its grasp, making everything look bleak. When you're feeling well again, you'll laugh at yourself for the way you felt."

"No." Tears collected in Rebecca's eyes. "I won't. I'm safe here, Charity. *He* doesn't come. It's just you and me, almost like we're children again."

"You're really that unhappy?" Charity asked. "Rebecca?"

A tear slipped down the side of Rebecca's face, and Rebecca wiped it away, blinking a little. "No. Don't listen to me. I'm being silly, you're right. It's just that I'm not well." She tried to raise herself, and Charity slipped another pillow behind her so that she was propped up. "You know what I am. I never had any sense."

"Are you so unhappy?" Charity asked again.

"No," said Rebecca—and burst into tears.

CHAPTER NINE

It was clear to Charity in that moment that there were undercurrents to her sister's marriage of which she had been totally unaware. Rebecca had soon been petted and reassured out of her tears, but the revelation that her illness was actually a relief to Rebecca was quite shocking. Certainly after the first day and night, Rebecca had complained very little about her ill luck in becoming so unwell, but Charity had thought little of that. Rebecca rarely did complain, after all. And even a couple of weeks later, when Rebecca was thoroughly recovered and back to her usual daily tasks and obligations, this new knowledge stayed with Charity, permeating everything she saw and thought about.

What was it that upset her sister so? The idea of being married to Fotheringay, Charity admitted privately to herself, was unpleasant—but then the idea of being married to anyone, and expected to "honour and obey" them, especially without the "love" usually partnered to those words in the wedding vows, was hardly appealing. It was, however, unfortunately one of the few ways in which a lady could assure herself of a stable home. Marriages without love were hardly uncommon, and Rebecca had never thought that Fotheringay loved her.

For a while, Charity played with the idea that Rebecca had fallen in love with someone else. That, certainly, would make her rue her enforced marriage to Fotheringay. However, she was forced to drop that theory very quickly. Rebecca showed little interest in any of the men of their acquaintance, and certainly none for one above another. Further, that explanation would not be consistent with what Rebecca had said. "I wish I could stay in this room with you, forever," were hardly the words of a woman in love. It spoke more of a particular dislike of the marriage she was already in.

Rebecca added no more to what she had confessed. Charity did not press her, knowing from personal experience how one said things when worn down that one would not say in other circumstances and indeed might blush about, or wish unsaid, later. But her mind worried at the problem, and she watched the couple with more jaded eyes.

It was not through anything that Rebecca either said or did, however, that Charity discovered something of what might be bothering her sister. Rebecca had gone out for lunch with a number of other newly married ladies; Charity had been invited out of politeness, but had been quite as anxious to turn down the invitation as the ladies had been for her to do so. She spent the morning playing the piano, quite alone, and revelled in the solitude. Somewhat to her disconcertion, however, Fotheringay was home to lunch, which made for an awkward tête-à-tête between the pair of them. The meal passed mainly in silence, though Charity saw that her brother-in-law was drinking considerably more than could be healthy for him this early in the day. But it was as she got up to leave the room that the encounter became suddenly alarming.

Fotheringay lumbered to his feet behind her. Charity thought that he was about to open the door for her, since the servants had been dismissed to their own mealtime. Instead, though, he grabbed her by one shoulder, spinning her around so that she was facing him.

"I've been wanting a word with you," he said.

Charity, confused but not alarmed, stared at him. "Mr Fotheringay, we had the entire luncheon together. Could you not have spoken to me then?"

"Thought I'd talk to you privately." There was a curious emphasis on the last word, as if privacy was hard to come by. Granted, they had a greater number of servants than in any household Charity had ever been part of, but it was hardly difficult to find a moment or a room in which to speak without their overhearing.

"Pray go on, then," she said. "I am listening."

"See, I've been thinking. You owe me something, Charity, don't you? To stop you being a charity girl all round, eh?" he murmured, his hot, alcoholic breath making Charity lean away from him. "You owe me rent. I keep you, I feed you. If I ask for something in return, that's fair, ain't it?"

"I don't understand."

Fotheringay was drunk, that much was obvious. It was hardly surprising after the amount Charity had seen him put away at the meal. But the request for rent was bewildering. Charity had no money of her own, only the allowance her mother made her, which covered the essentials of dress and fripperies. How could she give something she didn't have?

Fotheringay's hand tightened on the front of her dress; she could feel his fingers through the layers of material. She wanted to pull away, but wasn't sure that the cheap material would take the strain. The idea of her dress fraying, or coming away entirely, leaving her half-undressed in front of this man, was horrifying. Terrible enough as the situation was, she could not bear to be so literally exposed in his presence. Charity raised her hand to his to try to disentangle it, her fingers trembling a little though she did not know why. But his grip was firm.

"Come here. Come an' give your brother a nice kiss," he slurred. "Tha's all I'm asking. A nice kiss, maybe a bit more. You can't be as frigid as that blessed sister of yours, eh?"

With a sudden, sickening realisation, Charity knew what he wanted. What he meant. He was already leaning in towards her, the stench of sweat and brandy assailing her nostrils. For a second, she was paralysed, but then she came to herself.

"No! I won't!" She pulled away—anything was better than this, even finding her dress torn apart in her escape—but the dress was clearly made of sterner stuff than she had realised. His grip didn't loosen. She took a breath. "Mr Fotheringay, if you do not let go of me this second, I will scream until every servant in the house comes to discover the meaning of this. Now, *leave me alone.*"

Whether it was the threat, or sheer surprise at Charity's determined tone, Fotheringay's grasp became unsteady. With a determined yank, Charity was free, and then she was fleeing down the stairs towards the front door as if running for her life. Instinct made her stop a second to find a pair of shoes, but thinking that she heard Fotheringay's step on the stairs, she could do nothing but slip on the first pair she found. Tears she had no memory of shedding were on her cheeks, and her heart beat fast and heavy. She had nowhere to go, no idea save one— that she must get as far away from Fotheringay as possible.

Charity stumbled down the residential street, angry, scared and a little ashamed. She must surely have done something to encourage Fotheringay's advances. Shivering in the cold November air, it was only now that she realised that she had no cloak or pelisse with her. She must look a sight. More tears scalded her face at the thought, and made her eyes too blurry to see properly. She felt her petticoat rip as she tripped on the edge of it and fell headlong to the street.

"Goodness. Can I help?"

Charity looked up at the lady who had spoken. She was descending from a carriage with an air of elegance Charity had never reached. Her eyes were bluest blue and her voice so sweet. Charity's face flamed red with embarrassment.

"I'm sorry. I must be in the way," she said stupidly.

The lady bent down to her. "Victor," she said sharply to the coachman. "Help this lady to her feet."

The coachman jumped down promptly, easing Charity to a standing position once more. "That all right, ma'am?"

Charity wasn't sure whether he was speaking to her or to the other lady. Either way, she could not find the right words.

"Wonderful," her benefactress said, smiling at him.

Charity looked fully into the lady's face for the first time, and her breath caught for another reason. It was the lady in blue whom Charity had watched dancing so many times. She was beautiful. Even more beautiful close up than she had been at a distance. Not merely pretty, like Rebecca, but beautiful.

"I'm sorry," she repeated.

The lady smiled at her. "And I'm Miss Greenaway. Are you really called 'Sorry'? It seems a curious name for a lady. I can see that you are a lady," she added.

Charity, whose face was beginning to regain its normal colour, flushed once more. "I cannot be said to be acting like one," she said. "I apologise. My name is Bellingham. Charity Bellingham."

Miss Greenaway giggled infectiously. "Really? Not 'Sorry' but 'Charity'?" She sobered. "I should apologise. It is unkind to laugh."

Despite herself, Charity's lips began to curve into a smile. "I'm afraid that really is my name."

"Why don't you come in for a minute?" Miss Greenaway suggested. "We are just outside my house. You look as if you are in need of a quiet place to sit."

"I'm fine," Charity said hastily. "Really."

The other lady shook her head. "You really aren't. Come." She reached her hand out to Charity. "I won't bite, I promise." Then, more quietly, "You really don't wish to continue down the street as you are now, you know. I realise something must have happened. But come in, sit down, recover yourself."

Charity took a deep breath. Miss Greenaway was correct; she could not continue to run pell-mell down the streets as she had been doing. "Thank you," she said. "I don't know why you should be so kind, but I'm grateful."

"Victor?" Miss Greenaway turned to the coachman once more. "Please take Miss Bellingham's arm and assist her into the house."

He stepped towards Charity, but although she had allowed him to help her to her feet, the thought of having a man touch her again was repugnant. She saw, in her mind, Mr Fotheringay, and felt his rank breath against her skin once more.

"No!" she said sharply. Then, suddenly aware that she was making the scene she had realised so recently she must not, she added, "Thank you. I'm perfectly able."

Victor nodded his head. "If you say so, ma'am," he said, his voice showing clearly what he thought of young ladies who fell over in the street and then refused help.

"That's fine," Miss Greenaway said. "Come, Miss Bellingham, you cannot refuse to take my arm, at any rate. Victor, please take the coach round. I can manage from here."

"Certainly ma'am."

He turned back toward the coach with the merest disapproving glance at Charity. Miss Greenaway offered her hand, gloved in pale blue, to Charity, and Charity went to take it, but hesitated.

"My hand is all messy." She had no gloves on, and when she had fallen, she had scraped her palms so they were dirty—much like the rest of her, she thought, becoming conscious of the state of her dress. Her left thumb was bleeding, just a little bit.

"So are the gloves," her new friend said gaily. "Come." She took Charity's hand and led her up the steps into the imposing house. "I live here with my mother," she explained as the butler let them in. "Unfortunately, she is an invalid, so I hope you will understand if she is unable to meet you. There is no disrespect intended."

"It's more than I deserve," Charity said. "I don't know why you have been so kind."

"Silly! It's what anyone would do."

But that, thought Charity, was not her experience. She fought off a wave of self-pity impatiently. "I'm very grateful, anyway," she said.

"Come upstairs to my room," the stranger invited. "No, James, I do not need you to lead the way," she added to the butler. "Just down this corridor."

She preceded Charity into a small sitting room, prettily decorated in light colours, with furniture picked out in wheat-brown. It was not big enough for more than two or three people, at most, but the aspect allowed the afternoon sun to flood into the room, and Charity involuntarily smiled at this simple, yet anything but plain, room.

"You like it?" Miss Greenaway asked. "But I can tell from your face you do. Which, of course, gives me the highest opinion of your good taste, since the decoration is my own." Her voice was light and almost teasing. But she sobered almost immediately as her gaze fixed on Charity. "Wouldn't you like to wash your face and hands? I can call a maid to bring some water."

"That would be wonderful. Thank you."

Now she was inside the smart residence, Charity was more than ever aware of her dishabille. A face puffy and tear-streaked. Filthy, blood-stained hands. A ripped petticoat that would insist on showing beneath the hem of her wet and exceedingly dirty dress. Miss Greenaway opened a door that Charity had not noticed, on the side wall.

"It leads to my bedroom," she explained. "Convenient, is it not? But if you would like to come through, I will ask my maid to bring you clean water, and you can…" She hesitated, looking for the right word. "Rearrange yourself, shall we say?"

"You are very kind."

Charity went through the door into Miss Greenaway's elegant bedchamber. It was perhaps four times the size of Charity's own, and once more Charity felt overawed. No wonder the coachman had seemed so disapproving: what had an oversized, grubby woman to do with this sort of beauty? The maid knocked timidly on the second door, which must have led straight out to the corridor.

"Come in."

The maid, to her credit, did not even look, to Charity's surprise, and her tone was as respectful as it might have been for Miss Greenaway herself.

"Fresh water for you, ma'am. And please to be ringing the bell"—the maid indicated a little hand bell by the bedside—"if you need anything else."

Charity looked at the bell with some surprise. Surely its sound would not pierce to the servants' quarters? Or would the maid be standing outside all the while, waiting to do her bidding? It felt like a different world. Charity had noticed immediately the difference between Mr Fotheringay's lifestyle and their own, but this was another step up. She was so out of place here that it was hard to fathom it.

"Thank you," she said at last, realising that the maid was waiting to be dismissed. "It's very kind of you."

The maid blushed, as if being thanked for her job was an embarrassment. "I can put a stitch in that petticoat, ma'am, if you wish?"

"I'd be very grateful."

The maid produced a needle and thread unexpectedly from her pinafore pocket and knelt at Charity's feet. It took not more than a few minutes for her to mend the rent, and Charity could see at once the improvement in her own attire that this attention had effected.

"Thank you," she said again.

"Please ring if you want anything, ma'am," the maid repeated. She dropped a curtsey and within a moment was gone, leaving Charity to do what she could with the rest of her dress to regain some level of decency.

Ten minutes later, clean and somewhat more respectable, she slipped back through the door to where Miss Greenaway sat in the pretty sitting room drinking tea. Miss Greenaway looked up with a radiant smile as Charity entered, and Charity felt a curious sensation within her, as if something had happened to her stomach—or was it her heart?

"I…" She stumbled over her words and began again. "I left the water next door. I wasn't sure whether to call the maid back." There were so many things she might have said, she thought the moment she had finished speaking. What had made her make such a foolish comment? "I'm afraid it's rather dirty."

"It is dirty, but you are not," Miss Greenaway replied lightly. "Which is an improvement all around, if you will forgive me saying so. Now, do you care to talk about it, or should we retain the great English tradition and discuss the weather? Awfully fine for the time of year, is it not?"

"Yes." Charity was not sure whether it was or not: compared to Warwickshire, the temperature had been warm for November, but perhaps it was always thus in London. "I'm very grateful," she added.

Miss Greenaway lifted an eyebrow. "For the fine weather?" She took pity on Charity's discomfiture. "You are welcome. I have always wished to rescue a damsel in distress, and I took the first chance I was given. Now, sit down and have a cup of tea with me, and tell me, don't I know you? I'm sure you look familiar. We must have met. At Almack's, perhaps?"

Charity sat down nervously on the edge of the chair, worried that she would dirty the furniture. For all her efforts, nothing could make her look anything better than a little dishevelled, even with the beautiful stitches the maid had put into her torn petticoat. She doubted she would ever wear the dress again, both because of its damaged state and also for the memories it would always conjure. Mr Fotheringay's hands grasping at her. His brandy-fuelled breath against her skin.

"I've never been to Almack's," she said honestly. "I'm afraid I'm not quite important enough. But I've seen you at other places." She remembered that first occasion, when Miss Greenaway had been a vision in pale blue silk—when Miss Musgrove had fooled her into believing that she had met someone who sympathised with her. "Lady Axondale's ball, near the beginning of the Season. And a few months ago, the picnic." She forced a smile. "The weather has, after all, been fine."

"I thought I would pour it myself," Miss Greenaway said, referring to the tea. She matched the action to the words and filled a tea cup. "I hope you don't mind."

"Not at all." Suddenly Charity was overcome with the fact that she was face to face with the lady she had been admiring from afar. Comprehending the state she must have looked fifteen minutes earlier, she found herself almost tongue-tied. "Thank you," she added, as Miss Greenaway passed the beverage to her.

"My pleasure. Now, tell me." Miss Greenaway leaned forward in her seat. "Am I truly not allowed to ask questions? Must you remain veiled in mystery?"

Charity, who had just lifted the cup to her mouth, choked at this open approach and spilled tea down her already stained dress. "Oh, I'm sorry!" she exclaimed, trying to wipe with her sleeve the droplets that had fallen on the chair.

"I'm the one who should apologise. Forgive me." Miss Greenaway's eyes twinkled merrily. "I am terribly spoilt, you know. Always used to getting my way. It makes me prone to ask the questions I shouldn't. Is this to be the one occasion I must learn my place?"

Charity looked at her, trying to imagine Miss Greenaway caught in the sort of situation that had happened to Charity. She would have found some way, some polite and amusing way, out of the scenario. She would not have needed to make threats, and then to run away.

"It's difficult to explain," she said. "I—I…" She trailed off.

"Shall I tell you a little about me, whilst you drink your tea?" her new friend asked. "I would not like you to think that the confidences are all to be on one side. After all, I am convinced— are not you?—that we are destined to be great friends."

"I'm not sure I'm a suitable friend for someone like you." Charity took a sip of her tea, and then another, noticing all at once how thirsty she was.

Miss Greenaway laughed. "And I'm not sure that I am for you! So we share that, do we not? But now, about me…" She sat back and turned her reticule over and over in her hands. "What should I say? You know, after all, where I live. And I live with my dearest esteemed Mama, Lady Greenaway. Alas," she added, pouting, "the title is not heritable. I am a plain 'miss'."

"I do not think you are plain," Charity said, blushing a little, "even if you are a 'miss'."

"You are well on your way to spoiling me, just like everyone else," Miss Greenaway rebuked, clearly amused. "Mama is, unfortunately, a sad invalid. I am usually chaperoned to events by other people. Lady Carolina Farrell, for example. I expect you know her?"

"By reputation." Charity nodded. "She is a distinguished lady."

"Oh, that too," agreed Miss Greenaway. "My father, God rest him, died four years ago. Mother hardly survived the shock, but I pulled her round. I told her I needed her far too much to allow her to leave me orphaned and alone. It did the trick."

"My father died a couple of years ago too," Charity said. "Though I do not think my mother missed him so much as the house we lived in." She put her hand to her mouth. "I should not have said that."

"There is no room for 'should nots' between us, Miss Bellingham. So, you live with your mother, like I?"

"N-no." Miss Greenaway was treading on dangerous ground here, did she but know it. "I live with my sister and her husband. My mother, too, is..." But Charity stopped. She could not truthfully claim that her mother was an invalid, however much Mother herself would have insisted it. "She is in Bath, taking the waters," she said at last.

Miss Greenaway sipped the last of her tea, and looked at Charity thoughtfully. "And you get on with your sister? I never had a sister. Nor a brother, even." She shook her head sadly. "I expect that is why I am so terribly spoilt, you know."

"Rebecca is lovely." Charity thought of her gentle older sister. "I don't think anyone could dislike her."

"Nor her husband?" Miss Greenaway asked. It was a sharp, incisive question, albeit hidden by the lady's confiding demeanour.

"I..." Charity felt as if someone had unexpectedly lodged a large stone in her gullet. "I..." She looked around the room for anything that might help her. If she had only been the sort of lady who fainted, she thought, this would have been the perfect moment for such an escape. "It was very good of him to allow me to live with him," she said.

"Perhaps." Miss Greenaway changed the subject. "Have you finished your tea? Can I offer you some more? Though," she added, "it will be terribly cold and strong by this time."

"I am fine, thank you."

"It is he who is causing you distress, is it not?" she said conversationally. "The husband."

"Yes," admitted Charity guiltily. "He...said things." She could bring herself to be no more specific.

"Indeed? Well, that is very bad." Miss Greenaway was keeping her tone very light—to reassure her, Charity thought. "Just words?" she added. Was Miss Greenaway a mind reader? Charity thought in panic. How could she tell? Was there something about Charity that made everything clear? "Forgive me," Miss Greenaway said. "It is none of my business. How came you to be outside?"

"I ran away."

"What do you do next, if that is not too impertinent of me?"

"I must go back," Charity whispered, the fact suddenly registering.

Nothing had been solved. Nothing had changed, she recognised, everything flooding back to her. Meeting Miss Greenaway, chatting with her—for a moment or two she had half-forgotten the situation she found herself in. But now, facing it again, she felt a large lump in her throat. For a second or two she thought she might cry, humiliating herself further. Before the tears could fall, however, Miss Greenaway spoke again.

"You must," she said slowly. "But not for long. Surely you could write to your mother? If she knew how much distress you are in, she would help, would she not?"

Charity felt her cheeks warm. How could she explain the cool relationship between herself and Mrs Bellingham to this beautiful lady with a mother she clearly adored, a mother who loved her back with equal fondness?

"I think...that is, I mean...She has a busy life of her own." The stumbling response made Miss Greenaway look at her sharply, and she blushed more deeply still.

"Perhaps she does, but in circumstances like these...?" Miss Greenaway let the question hang, delicately, in the air. When

Charity did not respond, she went on. "Even the coldest parent would warm to her daughter's deep unhappiness. If you explained the circumstances, she could do nothing else but help."

Charity was silent for a moment longer. Perhaps Miss Greenaway spoke correctly. Charity had never needed her mother—not in any practical fashion. This was different. This was an emergency. Perhaps even Mrs Bellingham might be roused to some display of maternity in Charity's hour of need.

"I don't know," she said waveringly.

Miss Greenaway smiled. "But I do. Believe me, no one could turn you down in this state, least of all a mother. Forgive me my outspokenness, but I think usually you are extremely self-possessed. Have you ever truly asked your mother for help?"

Charity could not deny that to some extent she too had been responsible for the coldness between herself and her mother. If Mrs Bellingham had not tried hard to be a loving mother, neither had Charity, certainly in recent years, made any attempts to be a docile and loving daughter. It had been Rebecca who filled that role, and Mrs Bellingham had been considerably kinder to her older daughter.

"Perhaps you are right." For the first time since her escape, she suddenly felt a load lifted, as if a stone which had lodged in her gullet had been dislodged. "Yes. I should write."

"And meantime, I believe I could help, just a little," Miss Greenaway said tentatively, as if trying not to over step Charity's boundaries.

Charity looked up at her acquaintance in surprise at this comment. "You?" she asked, startled. She bit her lip, suddenly realising how impolite she had been. "I mean...I..."

Miss Greenaway laughed. "It is not so strange. From what I have heard from you, it seems as if you are in some trouble at home. I do not ask for details. You really should be praising my restraint! But I believe that you are not..." She cut off suddenly, and Charity stared. "You will permit me to be blunt?"

"Of course," Charity said, honestly bewildered.

"I think that thus far, the circles you have socialised within have been, forgive me, perhaps not of the top echelon. You are clearly a lady, but...not Almack's, you said." A smile danced at

the corner of Miss Greenaway's mouth, and Charity almost
caught her breath at how beautiful her new acquaintance was.
"I, on the other hand, am quite well known. My mother and I
are both rich and well connected," she said simply.

"Indeed." Charity was unsure where this conversation was
leading, but she was willing to follow in Miss Greenaway's
footsteps, wherever it was she led.

"If it were known that you were…a friend of mine, you too
would be very well connected."

For a moment, Charity wondered wildly whether Miss
Greenaway was offering to speak to the patronesses of Almack's,
to get her an entrance ticket. But how could that possibly help
with Charity's situation?

"If you would allow me to convey you back to your house, I
think you might find that your reputation within that building
would improve," Miss Greenaway said delicately. "Persons
unknown and unmentioned might be less inclined to distress
a lady with such important friends, shall we say?" She laughed
gaily. "Ridiculous, of course, that such things matter so much,
but there is no denying that matter they do. Do you see my
point?"

"Ye-es," Charity said slowly.

She thought of Fotheringay, who was undoubtedly rich,
and equally undoubtedly less than a perfect gentleman. It had
been his money, not his connections, which had convinced Mrs
Bellingham that he was a good match for her older daughter.
Nevertheless, he certainly would like to move in more exalted
circles, and would not wish his name to be attached to any
scandal. If Charity were seen with Miss Greenaway, it might
hold Fotheringay at bay until her mother could rescue her.

"Do you like the plan?" Miss Greenaway asked.

"Yes." Charity looked at her protector. "I do not know why
you should go to such trouble for me, but I am more grateful
than I can possibly say."

"Fiddlesticks!" Miss Greenaway shook her head, smiling.
"Why should I not?"

Charity could think of a dozen reasons, but she had no wish
to share them with Miss Greenaway.

"I am exceedingly grateful," she repeated.

"Excellent." Miss Greenaway stood. "Let us make arrangements to take you home," she said, holding out her hand to Charity so that Charity had to stand in order to take it. "You must, of course, also visit me tomorrow to tell me how well our plan unfolded. I should be available for a morning visit, and I hold you entirely responsible for ensuring that you come. Do we have an agreement?"

"We do indeed."

"Then let me go and speak to Victor. Wait here. I will not be long."

Charity watched as Miss Greenaway left the room with her brisk, almost dance-like motion. Part of her found it hard to believe what was happening: the day seemed like a dream. At first, it had been a nightmare, but then she had magically been rescued, and not by a knight in shining armour, but by a lady, beautiful, rich and generous. Could this really be true?

She stared around the room, trying to remember every detail of it. Although Miss Greenaway had given an invitation— or possibly an order!—to Charity to come round the next day, Charity could hardly accept that she would ever see this beautiful room again, ever speak with her heroine. Her eyes took in the light green carpet; the way the sun shone through windows so polished that they seemed barely to exist; the furniture's understated elegance. It was luxury, but luxury which felt no need to shout about its province. Mr Fotheringay's house had expensive furniture too, but it was chosen to demonstrate it. It seemed boastful and brash compared to Miss Greenaway's delicate room.

Miss Greenaway came back.

"That is settled. Victor will bring the coach round. I realised that I did not know where you live. Is it far from here?"

"I hardly know," stammered Charity. Her headlong rush after escaping the house had taken her down roads and paths she remembered little about.

"You poor dear." Miss Greenaway came over to her and put an arm around her waist. "Goodness, aren't you tall?" she said.

"Anyway, you can just give your address to Victor. He will know where to go."

"I don't know how to thank you," Charity said, looking down into Miss Greenaway's guileless blue eyes.

"Nonsense," her acquaintance replied. "I should be thanking you, you know. Your company saved me from the worst sort of ennui this afternoon. I am very grateful."

Charity looked away. She could not think how to reply to the laughing remarks from Miss Greenaway. She had been in the worst position, unsure what to do or where to go, and Miss Greenaway had done so much for her that it was difficult to hear it glossed over so lightly.

"Come," said Miss Greenaway. "We can take you home, and you can come tomorrow to tell me how the evening unfolded."

She led Charity down the stairs to the front door, where the carriage was already waiting. The coachman helped Miss Greenaway in, and then did the same for Charity with equal solemnity.

"Where to, ma'am?"

Charity gave the address, and he gave a dignified nod before climbing up behind the horses. Charity could not tell from his expression whether he was shocked or sanguine about the location to which she had directed him, but she had little time to worry, for Miss Greenaway livened the journey up with her stream of artless chatter. Nonetheless, Charity felt a strong sense of nervousness as the carriage approached the house.

"Now," Miss Greenaway said, "we must make sure that the gentleman of the establishment, if we can call him such, is aware of our presence. It would be a pity to have planned this all for naught."

"Yes." Charity tapped her fingers together over and over, until Miss Greenaway placed her hand over Charity's to stop the jerky gesture. "Sorry."

"You will be fine. Note," she added laughingly, "that I still ask no more questions. You should be impressed, you know. I am not known for my patience. Come, now, let me walk you to the door. And use my first name," she added in an undertone. "I am

Isobelle. Call me that, and your brother can hardly think that we are not well acquainted. Remember, Isobelle." The coachman came around and assisted the two ladies out of the carriage, and then preceded them up the step to the door. The footman opened the door a second or two before they reached it. "And I shall see you again tomorrow, my dear? Lady Greenaway's house. I'm sure your driver will know the direction."

"I shall." Charity glanced into the hall and saw Mr Fotheringay hovering at the bottom of the stairs. She was grimly pleased to notice the discomfort on his face. He must be wondering how well Charity knew this cream of the elite world; why she had not mentioned it previously; what she might or might not have told Miss Greenaway.

"Until then." Miss Greenaway took Charity's hands in hers. "It was such a pleasure to have your company this afternoon. Goodbye, my dear. Or rather, as the French say, au revoir!"

"Goodbye...Isobelle," Charity said, her heart fluttering at this use of Miss Greenaway's Christian name for more reasons than one.

"Sweet dreams. Dream of me!" Isabelle threw back as she left.

Charity stepped into the hall, and the footman shut the door behind her. She looked coolly at Mr Fotheringay, whose face was pale. Walking over to where he stood, she said, "If you will excuse me, I must go to my room to change. My dress has got sadly crumpled and stained in the course of the day. I will see you at dinner?"

"I—Yes, of course." He glanced anxiously at the footman. "Perhaps we could...could have a private word at some point later?"

Charity swept past him, wondering how she had ever been terrified of this pathetic little man, amazed at the difference a few hours had made. "I do not think there will be any need for that. Please excuse me. I would not like to delay my sister's evening meal."

If Charity did not, as Miss Greenaway had instructed, dream of her new friend that night, she did at least spare many thoughts for her during the course of the evening. Rebecca commented at dinner, "Why, Charity, you look so happy."

Charity smiled, as much for the continued concern on her brother-in-law's face as for Rebecca's comment. "I am," she agreed. "I met an old acquaintance today."

"Really?" Rebecca's eyes sparkled with interest. "Who is it?"

Charity considered for a moment before speaking. Rebecca knew, even if her husband did not, that Charity had no previous friendship with Isobelle Greenaway. It would not do for Mr Fotheringay to discover the slightness of their acquaintance. She looked hard at Rebecca as she replied, trying to send an unspoken message.

"You know my 'lady in blue'?" she asked. Rebecca had teased her gently about the mysterious lady who had fascinated Charity so much.

"Charity! You surely have not…" Rebecca broke off, finally realising the warning in Charity's eyes. "You met her again?" she asked. "Now, what was her name, dearest?"

Charity gave her a little smile. "It's not like you to forget a name, Becca. Miss Greenaway."

"Oh!" Rebecca tried to temper her surprise. "I mean, how could I have forgotten?"

"But enough of this," Charity said hastily. "I will tell you later, no doubt. How has your day been? Are your friends all in good health?"

Rebecca, reliable as always, took this hint to change the subject, and the rest of the mealtime passed peacefully. Charity was grateful for a chance to sit quietly and listen to her sister's mundane account of her day. It meant that Fotheringay also began to relax, but Charity had not the energy to concern herself much with him. Surely Miss Greenaway had been right? Surely on this occasion, Mrs Bellingham would do something?

As soon as the meal was over, far from sitting down with Rebecca and explaining about her meeting with Miss Greenaway, Charity sat down in her own room to write to her mother. Miss Greenaway's words still echoed in her mind: *Even the coldest mother must help when you are in so much distress.* She was right. This particular time, Mrs Bellingham must come to the rescue—if not for Charity's sake, for Rebecca's. It could not be right for Charity to stay in a situation where she risked undermining her sister's marriage.

She picked up the quill pen and began to write.

Dear Mother,

Forgive me for writing, but I am in desperate need of your help. I hope that it may be possible for you to allow me to come to you in Bath—if not forever, then for a long visit.

She bit at the top of the quill, wondering what to say of her situation, and how to say it. She must convince her mother of the need for her to stay, yet at the same time she baulked at putting in writing—nay, even saying or thinking about—what precisely had occurred between herself and Mr Fotheringay.

I am experiencing difficulties living here with Mr Fotheringay. He has...

She crossed out the last two words. She could not bring herself to finish the sentence.

I have concerns that my presence here is affecting Rebecca's marriage for the worse, she wrote at last. That was undoubtedly true. But it did not convey the urgency, the desperation, Charity felt.

I need to get away. I cannot live under the same roof as Mr Fotheringay. Please, Mother, I beg you. If not for my sake, for Rebecca's. Let me come and live with you.

Your loving daughter,

Charity

For a moment, she looked hopelessly down at the letter. Her handwriting had never been good, but the scrawl she had produced on this occasion made her look almost illiterate. She considered writing it out again, more neatly, but she could not bear to go through it again. Equally, somewhere inside her she hoped that her mother might see the scribbled note for what it was: sheer desperation. Tears had come to her eyes as she had been writing, and she dashed them away with the back of her hand before they could fall and smudge the letter even more. It was written now. She must just send it and await her mother's reply.

CHAPTER TEN

The next day, Charity woke with a start. There were so many things she needed to do. She must post the letter to her mother, and she must also visit Miss Greenaway again, as she had promised to do the day before. The morning passed slowly; breakfast with Rebecca and Mr Fotheringay seemed interminable. She knew that Rebecca wanted to catch her, to ask more searching questions about her meeting with the lady in blue, but Charity herself was anxious to avoid any such questioning. How could she explain what it had been that had led her to Miss Greenaway's door? And without that explanation, she must seem crazed, perhaps half-witted, wandering the streets of London on her own.

"May I borrow the carriage later, please?" she asked, trying to sound natural.

"Why?" Rebecca began, but unusually she was beaten to a response by Mr Fotheringay.

"To visit Miss Whatever-Her-Name-Was?" he asked gruffly.

Charity was certain that Fotheringay knew precisely what Miss Greenaway's name was; her new friend had made it quite clear that she was Lady Greenaway's daughter. She looked straight across the table at him.

"Miss Greenaway, and her mother, Lady Greenaway. Yes, that's correct," she said coldly.

He looked angry, and Charity looked away quickly, frustrated by the fear she felt. How could she be so scared of him? But then again, how could she not?

"That is perfectly satisfactory," he said. Charity realised, with a lightening of her heart, that what Miss Greenaway had said was true. He was, if not scared, then overawed by Charity's powerful friends. "I'll tell our man to put himself at your service."

"Thank you." Charity rose and left the room before any further conversation could be had.

Nonetheless, a few hours later, when she was standing on Miss Greenaway's doorstep, Charity felt suddenly anxious all over again. It was all very well to intimidate Fotheringay with her talk of Miss and Lady Greenaway, but in truth she was as much daunted by their position in society as he could be. And suddenly the doubts she had pushed down came flooding back to her. Had Miss Greenaway truly meant for her to return today, or had she merely said so to be polite? She fidgeted with her gloves, pulling them straighter on her fingers. The footman opened the door just as she had her hands together, making her look like a supplicant on the point of a desperate request. Which wasn't, she thought bleakly, so far from the truth.

"Is Miss Greenaway in?" she asked.

"May I ask your name, ma'am?" he asked. For an awful moment, Charity thought that she was going to be refused entrance.

"Miss Charity Bellingham."

"Thank you, Miss. Miss Greenaway is indeed in, and Lady Greenaway also." The footman moved aside to allow Charity entrance to the house, but she hesitated.

"Oh, in that case I'm not sure…"

"Miss Greenaway has given explicit instructions that you should be shown into the drawing room, ma'am. Please follow me." He moved away, not even bothering to check whether Charity was following him, and she scuttled after him like an errant schoolboy. Opening the drawing room door, he announced "Miss Bellingham."

Charity entered the room. It was as pretty as Miss Greenaway's little study, though on very different lines. But she had little time to look around: her attention was drawn to Miss Greenaway and her mother. Miss Greenaway stood up to greet her and walked across the room with her hands held out.

"Oh, it is so good to see you again," she said. "May I introduce my mama?"

Charity nodded, struck dumb with shyness. She bobbed an ungainly curtsey to Lady Greenaway. Lady Greenaway was clearly frail. She had lines of pain etched onto her face, and her hands were misshapen and twisted with arthritis. Despite this, she had a beautifully youthful appearance, bearing a great similarity to her daughter. She lay along a chaise longue, set in an alcove underneath the window. But although she was to the side of the room, she somehow still drew immediate attention.

"Forgive me for not standing to greet you," Lady Greenaway said, smiling. Her voice, too, had the same pretty cadence as Miss Greenaway's. "Even with the cane"—she gestured to a dark wooden walking stick leaning against the side of the chaise—"it is not easy for me. But I am delighted to meet you. Belle has been telling me about you. Did your evening go well after you left her?"

"Oh, y-yes." Charity berated herself for her tongue-tiedness. It was not a complaint she often suffered from, but Lady Greenaway's genuinely warm welcome had unnerved her. "Forgive me, my lady, I am not usually so silent," she said, choosing to name the elephant in the room rather than ignore its presence.

Her hostess laughed. "It happens to us all. Won't you sit down and chat with Belle and me? We were getting quite sick of each other before your entrance."

"Mama!" Miss Greenaway chided, but she did not look annoyed. "Please, come. Do sit down."

"It is very kind of you."

"Nonsense! As Mama so impolitely put it, we are glad of the extra company."

She stroked her mother's hand lovingly as she turned to sit back down. Charity took a seat, and the three ladies spoke for a while on general matters. Charity found herself unexpectedly grateful for the hours of interminable boredom she had spent with Rebecca, having just such conversations in house after similar house. It was fascinating to discover that even in the houses of the rich and aristocratic, the same subjects were discussed. Or was it that the Greenaways were being kind, trying to put her at her ease by speaking of things that she might understand? She found she was not certain. Nevertheless, after half an hour of such conversation, Miss Greenaway stopped suddenly.

"Now, Mama," she said firmly, "we have worn you out enough with our idle gossip. Allow me to take Miss Bellingham to my sitting room so that you may have a rest and feel better."

"Or," Lady Greenaway suggested, "so that you and Miss Bellingham can swap secrets that no modern girl would dream of sharing with her mother?"

Miss Greenaway laughed, but did not deny it. Charity was reassured—as she suspected Lady Greenaway had intended her to be—that her own affairs had not been the subject of gossip between the two.

"Rest," Miss Greenaway said instead. "I shall send your maid to you."

"Yes, Mother," Lady Greenaway said meekly. Mother and daughter exchanged a look of such perfect love and understanding that Charity felt suddenly shy and, if truth be told, a little jealous.

Miss Greenaway bore her off determinedly to the pretty room in which they had spoken the day before, stopping only to speak in low tones to a servant. When the girls were both seated, Miss Greenaway spoke.

"It was not just a jest that Mama was tired, I fear," she said. "You must forgive us. We go on as if it were a joke, but she is severely ill. I told her I had made a new friend yesterday—no, I did not say more than that—and she was greatly desirous to meet you. I always indulge her if I can. I hope I did not cause you any discomfort."

"Oh no," Charity said hastily. "She is a lovely lady, and I feel honoured to have been introduced."

Miss Greenaway smiled. "Whether or not that is true, it is beautifully expressed," she said lightly. "Anyway, her maid will take her medicine to her, and she will doze for a while, I hope. Whereas we…Forgive me for asking, but was our plan a success?"

Charity warmed to that "our". The plan had been Miss Greenaway's alone, but it was tactful of her to imply that it had been concocted between the pair of them.

"It was. My brother-in-law is quite in awe of my important friends," she said. "And…" She found it difficult to speak of such intensely personal matters, but Miss Greenaway had earned the right to be told. "…I wrote to my mother last night. I must wait for her reply, but I think—I hope—she will be able to help me."

"Of a certainty she will," Miss Greenaway said.

"Now, with such informalities out of the way—I hope you like my turn of phrase—let us speak of other matters. It strikes me that we have begun at the wrong end of this friendship. I hope you do not object to my calling it a friendship?" Charity blushed and disclaimed. "Let us right this topsy-turvy nature of things and go back to the beginning." She stood and curtsied. "I," she said formally, "am Miss Greenaway. I am delighted to meet you, Miss Bellingham."

Charity, unsure whether she should laugh but falling into line with Miss Greenaway's evident wishes, stood and repeated the gesture. "I am very grateful to meet you, ma'am."

Miss Greenaway tutted as she reseated herself. "Now then, we'll have none of that. I simply cannot be 'ma'am' to anyone. Especially someone whom I feel sure will be a good friend of mine. That is so, is it not?"

"I…I…" Charity stammered, not certain how to respond to this outspoken comment. When she wanted nothing more than to spend more time with Miss Greenaway, how could she possibly answer such a leading question? But surely Miss Greenaway did not, could not, feel the same way about her!

"But of course we are," Miss Greenaway said gently. "It could hardly be otherwise. Now, Miss Bellingham, why do you not sit down? We will start from the beginning, like mere acquaintances."

So for the rest of the visit—another fifteen minutes and no more, for Charity was determined not to overstay her welcome, and had requested the carriage to return half an hour from the moment at which she entered the house—they kept to the mundane topics of every day conversation, Miss Greenaway leading the topics and drawing Charity out on the subject of her interests. She seemed so attentive that Charity began to speak a little more freely, though in truth Charity would have been happy just to sit and listen to Miss Greenaway talk, watching the way she spoke with her hands as well as her voice; watching the array of expressions crossing the other lady's beautiful face. She had felt like this about no one before: the intensity of the emotion was almost painful, and when Miss Greenaway was smiling at her so sweetly, she could almost wish that she wasn't on the point of leaving London. But when, at the end of their time together, Charity got ready to go back to Fotheringay's house, a dark shadow drew over her happiness and she knew that she could not stay where she was.

"Let me know when you have heard from your mother," her new friend said as they parted, holding Charity's hand for a second between her own much smaller ones. "Will you do that?"

"Of course." Charity wondered whether that would be the last occasion on which they met, and again felt that tug of sadness. "And…and thank you."

CHAPTER ELEVEN

Charity did not have too long to wait, after all, for her mother's response. It was a mere two days later that the letter arrived. She snatched it up the moment she saw her mother's handwriting on the envelope, for the first time anxious to hear from her remaining parent. She noticed that it was addressed both to herself and Rebecca, but then if she were going to move to Bath, her sister would need to know the details. A pang of regret washed over her at the thought that she might speak only one more time with Miss Greenaway. Somehow, in the other lady, she had found something that she had not known that she was looking for, without which she would be forever not-quite complete. She would miss Rebecca too, of a certainty, and the thought of living only with her mother was not a particularly attractive one. But of course, Miss Greenaway probably had no thoughts of continuing their acquaintance, and living with Mrs Bellingham was better by far than living in fear of Fotheringay. Sliding the envelope carefully open, she took out the sheets contained within and smoothed the first one out. Mrs Bellingham had written: *My dear daughters,*

I hope that you are both keeping well, and that Charity is behaving correctly. I know I need not ask about you, Rebecca: you have always been well-behaved. I myself am leading a very quiet life in Bath, and cannot possibly have Charity here, as I believe I told you before the wedding. I cannot think what brought you to suggest it, Charity. Besides, however unlikely the possibility of Charity attracting a suitor, she certainly has more chance in London than in Bath. Charity, you must just make more effort to be obliging to your brother-in-law.

Now for my news. You will be glad to hear that taking the waters has had a salubrious effect. I have—

But Charity read no more. She felt suddenly faint, her breath coming out in gasps. It was cruel, *cruel*, to send such a letter. She had known that her mother did not love her, but to dislike her enough to send an epistle like that… For the first time in her life, she had begged her mother to help her, and her mother had rejected her plea.

"Charity?" Rebecca's gentle voice pierced the fog in Charity's mind. She blinked a couple of times and then turned to look at her sister.

"I'm fine. I just felt a little dizzy for a moment. Forgive me. I think I will go and rest in my room."

Rebecca hurried across the room and slipped an arm around Charity's waist. "You do look pale. Is there anything I can do?"

If her mother's disdain had cut Charity to the heart, Rebecca's sympathy nearly destroyed her.

"No, I…must go."

She pulled herself free of her sister's grasp and half-ran towards her room. She knew she was behaving oddly, perhaps unkindly, but she could not bear any company in that moment, least of all Rebecca's. When she reached her chamber, she flung herself face down on the bed and finally let out the emotion she had striven to hide.

When the sobs subsided, she took a few soothing gulps of air, wiped tear-stained cheeks with a shaking hand and began to think. It was clear that she could not turn to her mother for help. Now that she was calm again, she wondered distantly how she could possibly have believed that Mrs Bellingham would come to her rescue. Miss Greenaway's confidence had bolstered Charity's own—but then Miss Greenaway did not know Charity's mother. Charity should have realised that Mrs Bellingham would not suddenly produce the maternal love that hitherto Charity had never experienced from her. It had been foolish of her to expect anything else. No, she would have to cope by herself, just as she always had done, yet this time even more alone than usual, for she could not confide the least hint of this particular problem to Rebecca.

Sitting up suddenly, she raised a startled hand to her mouth. Rebecca. What could she possibly say to Rebecca that would explain that letter from her mother? Becca must be wondering why Mrs Bellingham had felt the need explicitly to say that Charity might not join her in Bath: she must have realised that Charity had requested a move she had been previously outspokenly grateful to avoid.

To her surprise, however, Rebecca asked no such thing. Indeed, Charity would have found her lack of comment extremely confusing and potentially worrying had she any concern left for such a thing, but, caught up in her own issues, she could only be thankful that Rebecca did not ask the obvious question. Of course, she thought that night as she lay in bed, in the few days since Fotheringay had learnt of Charity's association with Miss Greenaway, he had not tried to touch her again. In fact, he barely spoke to her at all, something for which she could only be extremely grateful. But would his awe would wear off in time? Charity shivered at the thought that she might find herself in a similar situation in the future. It was almost too frightening to contemplate.

And would Charity continue to be under Miss Greenaway's protection anyway, she wondered? Her heart sank. It might be that Miss Greenaway, who had clearly believed that their friendship (if thus it could be described) would only be short-lived before Charity moved away, would cease to show an interest in her. After all, who could blame her for that? That Charity had fallen so strongly for Miss Greenaway was one thing: she, after all, was kind, beautiful and talented. But there was no good reason, truly no reason at all, for Miss Greenaway to have any interest in her. In fact, there had been no need in the first place for the lady to have taken such notice of a girl who had quite literally stumbled into her path. Expecting her to continue mentoring Charity forever was surely unreasonable and perhaps even arrogant. Charity bit back a cry of anguish. London without Miss Greenaway—it might seem ridiculous after only two meetings, but it was so—was unbearable to think of. But at the same time, what right had she to force herself upon the lady's notice? She turned over the problem in her mind as she tossed and turned in her bed. What should she do? What *could* she do? Well, Miss Greenaway had asked her to let her know what response Charity received from her mother. That was something. Charity would write to her: that way, she would not look as if she was assuming on Miss Greenaway's good nature, but she would at least have made contact. And surely Miss Greenaway would recognise her at balls, if nothing else. It was not what she longed for, but perhaps it would suffice.

Putting pen to paper the next morning, then, she attempted to compose a missive she hoped would hit the right notes of gratitude and information, without appearing to wish for anything further from Miss Greenaway. Packing away all her tangled emotions for the moment, she tried to keep her language simple and clear.

Dear Miss Greenaway,

I am just writing to thank you for your support and help over the past week. Words cannot express how grateful I am. You were kind enough to suggest that I might tell you when I received my mother's response to my letter to her, which came today. Unfortunately, she is unable to have me with her in Bath; but, since the day I first met you, I have had no further problems with Mr Fotheringay, so I hope and believe that the necessity which drove me to write to her in the first place has passed.

With greatest gratitude and respect,

Charity Bellingham

After folding the letter and then addressing it, Charity went downstairs. It was as well to conclude the business now, so she requested that a footman take the letter round immediately.

Then, following her pattern of many years standing, she went to the piano. If anything could take her thoughts off her troubles, it would be playing through her favourite pieces. And goodness knew, she thought ruefully, that she was in need of the practice. She sat down and played through a couple of her favourite sonatas, and then, finding one that was in need of more in-depth practice, she settled herself to perfecting it.

She hardly knew how long she played, but she was disturbed from her task a while later by the footman's return.

"Miss Greenaway wrote a reply, Miss," he said, offering her a folded sheet.

"Thank you."

He bowed and left. Charity, absently admiring Miss Greenaway's delicate script, opened the letter as fast as she dared. She did not expect to see much writing—an immediate response would hardly lead to flowing passages—but the note was even shorter than she had anticipated.

Dear Miss B,

Come and tell me all about it! Come now—or at latest, tomorrow morning. I will stay in expecting you to call in the morning.

Best wishes,

Miss Greenaway

CHAPTER TWELVE

When Charity paid the expected call to Miss Greenaway's house the next day, she did so with a strange fluttering in her stomach. Until this point, she had always wondered whether Miss Greenaway was just being kind: at the point where Charity's immediate problem was solved, would she fade out of Charity's life with not a second thought? Now, though, it seemed that Miss Greenaway was willing, even pleased, to continue the friendship.

From the first moment Charity had seen her, dancing at the ball, she had thought and dreamt about Miss Greenaway more than she could really explain by any logical process. Miss Greenaway had been a fairy princess, an idol to be adored from a safe distance. It had never occurred to Charity that she would speak to the other lady even once, let alone be on terms of friendship with her. And now that she had met Miss Greenaway and discovered that not only was she beautiful, but kind, warm-hearted and generous to the last degree, Charity barely knew how to cope with her emotions and feelings about her. She felt hot and cold all at once, desperate to meet her again, and unsure about how she would possibly manage to say good morning, let alone hold a conversation. She had thought it a fleeting friendship on their previous meetings; now, though, the possibilities of a stronger bond filled her with both hope and fear. And her jumbled emotions made it difficult for Charity to know whether she was looking forward to the visit, or dreading it.

It seemed strange, too, that the thought of the Greenaways' house was positive. She had only been there twice before, neither time the best of circumstances: it would seem more natural to associate the journey and the house with the chaos and distress in which she had first discovered it. But it felt instead almost like a safe place. If Charity anticipated the meeting with Miss Greenaway with mixed feelings, the house itself still seemed like a refuge. And when she arrived, she felt, and perhaps it was just imagination, that the staff welcomed her in with more warmth than was strictly necessary. The pleasure with which Miss Greenaway greeted her, too, helped Charity get over the worst of her nerves.

"Miss Bellingham!" She came towards Charity, her hands held out to her. Charity felt herself tremble as their fingers touched, and she pulled away after a second, confused and embarrassed by the feeling. Miss Greenaway did not seem to notice however. "It is so lovely to see you again," she continued. "Mama is resting this morning. Her doctor is attending her this afternoon, and she always likes to be at her best when he comes. You might think that this is somewhat at odds with the usual situation in which one calls a doctor, but nothing will cure her of this tendency! Please, take a seat."

"Thank you." Charity sat, feeling it was safer so. "It was good of you to invite me to visit again. I had not intended to intrude any more than I already have done."

"It is not an intrusion but a pleasure," Miss Greenaway said. "Now, tell me everything. How can your mother possibly refuse to house you? Did you explain the situation?" She stopped.

"Forgive me, I am impertinent. You are quite within your rights to tell me that it is none of my business."

"When you have been so kind," Charity said gratefully. "I think you have earned the right to call it your business, if you are sure you are interested."

Miss Greenaway laughed. "Unkind people might call it nosiness. I am glad you do not. Forgive me asking, but is your mother so very ill? I recall that you said she was taking the waters in Bath."

Charity felt as if she had lost a layer of skin: somehow, all the worst, most painful parts of her life were on show to Miss Greenaway. The lady had every right to ask, but oh! It hurt to speak of it. She hated to confess to her heroine that her mother cared so little for her that she had refused to help in Charity's deepest hour of need. How could she expect Miss Greenaway to like her when even her own mother could not love her?

"She is not ill…that is…" She stumbled to a halt and tried again. "I do not think my mother ever wanted children," she said baldly. "Certainly not one such as I. I am afraid I am a very bad daughter."

"That I am sure you are not," interrupted Miss Greenaway warmly.

"I am, though. I am not quiet, gentle or biddable. My mother and I never got on, and I can only presume that she has discovered in my absence that her life could be so much better. I do not…I *should* not blame her," she corrected herself. She looked up at Miss Greenaway. "I do blame her. I am angry and hurt."

"I am angry on your behalf," Miss Greenaway assured her. "If it were not for the fact that I will now be able to continue my friendship with you, I would be furious. Forgive me if I admit that I feel a little pleasure that you will be staying in London however!"

Charity's heart thumped irregularly. Was Miss Greenaway really so very keen to keep her friendship? It seemed impossible. Who was Charity really, after all? An ordinary girl, whose mother didn't even love her. Why should a rich, beautiful, gifted lady like Miss Greenaway show such an interest? She stammered something of this nature aloud, but Miss Greenaway just smiled and shook her head.

"I will not allow you to talk like that, Miss Bellingham. Now, should we continue to abuse your mother's behaviour, or should we get onto a new topic? Since we are going, I hope, to be such good friends, mightn't we drop some of the dreadful formalities and speak to each other on first name terms? As you know, my name is Isobelle. I know you mentioned yours at one point, but I am going to be brave and confess that I have forgotten it."

"Charity."

"Oh yes!" Miss Greenaway gave a little smile of reminiscence. "Not 'Sorry' but 'Charity.' Of course! But really, dear, are you always called by all three syllables? Isn't there some way of shortening it?"

"I don't know. No one has called me anything else." Charity thought, but did not say, that no one had cared enough to give her a nickname. Rebecca was Becca as often as not, but since their parents had tried to speak to Charity as little as possible, what need had there been to shorten her name? Especially when it reflected so well on her place in life: only kept by her parents out of charity, not because they wanted her.

"Well, take pity on me now." Isobelle pressed gloved hands to her bosom, a gesture which somehow set Charity's heart thumping more quickly than she could quite explain. "'Miss Bellingham' was long enough. 'Miss Charity Bellingham'…No, a thousand times no!"

"Just 'Charity' will suffice, if you truly do not mind?"

"But I have already asked you to be on first name terms. Nevertheless, I think we could do better than 'Just Charity'. An awful thought! Mayn't I call you something shorter, something more like you? 'Charity'…I couldn't. I honestly couldn't!"

"Call me anything." Charity could hardly believe that someone as kind and lively as Miss Greenaway should even want to be on first-name terms with her.

"But it must suit you," Miss Greenaway insisted. "Now," she said, reaching out a hand to draw Charity closer, "stand there. Let me look at you."

Charity stood motionless in front of her. Miss Greenaway examined her as if she were a piece of art. She cocked her head to one side to look at her, and then to the other. She walked around her. She looked her up and down. Charity flushed a little; she wasn't used to such close attention, and to have it from Miss Greenaway was exciting, perhaps, but terrifying too. The lady must have seen some sign of her discomfort.

"Am I distressing you?" she asked, stroking Charity's arm. "You mustn't mind me! No one ever minds me."

"No, no," Charity protested. "I don't...You mustn't...I don't mind in the slightest."

She smiled brilliantly. "Of course you don't. Now, about your name. Charry—no, that's so ugly. Carrie? Oh no, you could never be a Carrie. It doesn't suit your particular style of beauty." She looked up into Charity's face, so many inches above her own. "I have it," she announced. "Harry. Of course. You were born to the name. I shall call you Harry."

"But that's..." Charity stopped. *A boy's name*, she had wanted to say. But hadn't she always felt like a boy, somehow, in some ways? Hadn't that always been part of her problem? "That's perfect," she said.

Miss Greenaway looked up at her through lowered lashes. "Yes," she said. "Yes, I rather think it is."

* * *

Much to Charity's surprise and delight, Isobelle and she began a strong friendship. Difficult though she might find it to believe, it seemed that she was liked and valued by the one person above all others whom she would have most wished to care for her, and whom she would never had believed could possibly do so.

There were flies in the ointment, that was undeniable, but such was to be expected. It had usually to be Charity who went to Isobelle's house rather than the other way around, for reasons that hurt a little. Charity could not fault her heroine for anything, but she wished sometimes that there wasn't quite such a large gap between their social standings. Isobelle visited the Fotheringays' house a couple of times, but Charity was aware that it cost Isobelle something when she visited and was torn between shame and distress, even though she knew Isobelle's reasons and they had nothing to do with Charity herself. The truth was simply that Isobelle did not wish to give Mr Fotheringay any social advantage by her attendance at his residence. Her prejudice against Fotheringay was on two fronts: first because of the manner in which he had treated Charity, which of course Charity could understand, but second (and almost as strongly), because she and Fotheringay simply did not belong to the same social circle. When it came down to it, Charity thought sadly, the same could well be said for herself and Isobelle.

"Perhaps I am a snob," Isobelle admitted on one occasion, "but I would not like the information to be popularly known that I visited this part of London."

Charity tried hard not to be offended. It was not as if they lived in the slums. On the contrary, it was an elegant and extremely expensive part of town but, and this was the rub, utterly associated with trade.

"I imagine everyone knows that I live here," she said in response. As she came towards her second Season, she had taken to heart the principle that everyone knew everything, or nearly everything, about each other.

"Oh yes," said Isobelle, "but that is a little bit different. You are not involved in business, after all. And everyone has certain relatives who are…less than reputable, shall we say?"

Charity could not answer that. If Isobelle felt that way, then she must have some reason for it. All the same, she hoped and trusted that Isobelle was referring only to Fotheringay, and not also to Rebecca. It was true that Rebecca and Isobelle had not found much spark of friendship between them, much to Charity's disappointment. Rebecca, she knew, was intimidated by Isobelle's aristocratic background and, scared of doing or saying something wrong, had hardly been able to speak or move at all in her presence. Isobelle had quite evidently attempted to put young Mrs Fotheringay at her ease, but the blatancy of the attempt had only served to make Rebecca even less at ease. She stammered, and blushed, and spoke in tones so quiet that even Charity, used to her sister's voice, struggled to hear her.

"Of course, she's a lovely girl," Isobelle said politely afterwards. "Nothing like you, mind."

Charity had heard the latter statement many times over the course of her life, but this was the first time it had been said in her favour rather than to her detriment. She could not help a little guilty wave of pleasure wash over her.

"Much, much nicer than I am, I'm afraid."

"Oh, now, how could that be?" Isobelle asked teasingly. "Nobody can possibly be nicer than my Harry. But seriously, dear one, a lovely girl. Just a little…well, *staid*."

"She was shy," said Charity, half-defensively.

"Quite understandable. But come, let us speak of other things. What dress do you think I should wear to the Galloways' ball this evening?"

The more Charity met Isobelle at events, however, the more surprised she became that Isobelle had wanted her as a friend. Looking around, she could see so many people approach Isobelle for a chat or, if male, for a dance. On one occasion, when Isobelle had invited her to meet to walk with her at the park—a brave adventure in the chilly days of early December—Charity said something of this. She was in Isobelle's sitting room, waiting for her friend to decide which of a number of fetching hats she desired to show off this morning.

"You have so many friends. It is good of you to give so much of your time to me."

"Good of me?" Isobelle placed the fifth hat on her head at a jaunty angle and looked appraisingly at herself in the mirror. "No, not this hat. I like your company."

"I do not see why," Charity said honestly.

Isobelle flicked a mischievous glance at her over her shoulder and then replaced the fifth hat with the third one. "You do not need to, dear Harry. You have only to be who you are. After all, you are quite unique! But come. You promised to walk with me in the park, and I insist that you keep your promise, even though it be so cold. A lady must never go back on her given word, you know."

Charity followed her. "This lady," she retorted, "has no wish to do so, certainly not on this occasion. I would love to come with you."

It was a different experience walking in the park with Isobelle than it was walking with Rebecca, or with Charity's mother. Mrs Bellingham had always been on the lookout for acquaintances, especially those in the higher echelons of society, with whom to pass the time of day, or more importantly, to be seen passing the time of day. Rebecca, meanwhile, would walk soberly, gazing more at the trees or flowers than at the company. Isobelle, however, could hardly go a few steps without someone wishing to speak to *her*. It was a little frustrating for Charity: she would have preferred to have Isobelle to herself; but nonetheless it was much more enjoyable than any of those other walks she had taken in the past. The gentlemen tended to be much less polite than the ladies, directing the vast majority of their conversation to Isobelle alone. The time had been when Charity would have been distressed by this, but Isobelle made it more than clear that she preferred Charity's company to that of any gentleman, so Charity could bear the interruptions with equanimity. It also worked as a marker, as Isobelle pointed out to her as they watched a couple of children play, their governess hovering nearby, ready to intervene should any squabble break out.

"Any gentleman who is so rude as to ignore you is quite clearly not worth notice himself," she said, tucking her hand through Charity's arm. "And really, I had no idea that so many of the aristocracy were so badly behaved before I met you."

"I don't think they mean to be," Charity said, surprising herself with her defence. "It is just that they look upon me as being part of a different class. After all, none have spoken to the governess over there, have they?"

"Harry, you surely don't rank yourself alongside a governess!" Isobelle protested.

"Maybe not," acknowledged Charity. "But it is all of the same ilk. They just do not see me as worthy of their attention." "It is as I said." Isobelle nodded. "They are badly behaved." They walked a little further, and Charity looked wistfully at a couple of ladies riding by. She missed riding; it had been one of the only times at home in Forsbury where she had had a sense of freedom. Accompanied only by an uninterested middle-aged groom, she had been able to explore almost alone, released from the criticisms and disapproval of her parents. Rebecca had a horse in London, and Charity had borrowed it a couple of times; but Fotheringay had bought it with his wife's skills and likes in mind, and the frustrating sluggishness of the animal had driven Charity to the edge of distraction.

"Do you ride?" she asked, thinking to herself that Isobelle would look marvellous on horseback.

"No." Isobelle pulled a face. "I can, of course, but I don't enjoy it. Whatever one does, one ends up covered in horsehair and smelling so strongly of animals that it is quite distressing. The maids seem to be incapable of removing all the hairs, so that I am forever finding them for the week afterwards." She brightened. "I drive, though. I have the most delightful little phaeton, drawn by a matched pair of greys. I do think grey horses are the most beautiful, would you not agree?"

Charity had frankly not ever considered this. It was the temperament and the bond that one built up with one's horse which was most important to her, not their colour.

"Ye-es," she agreed doubtfully. "I suppose they are."

Isobelle laughed, correctly guessing her train of thought. "Confess it: you have never even considered the colour, now have you?"

Charity shook her head with a wry smile. "To be honest, no. Do you truly drive your own carriage?"

"I will take you out with me," Isobelle promised. "Then you will see the difference from mere riding." She smiled, and lowered her voice. "And I have other things to share with you, even better things, if you care for them."

Charity felt her heart thumping inside her. She was not sure what Isobelle meant, but she was very certain that she was willing to learn any lessons Isobelle wished to teach her. She did not have words to answer, but she suspected that Isobelle saw it written all over her face. Isobelle was...was everything, and Charity would follow her anywhere she wished to lead.

CHAPTER THIRTEEN

By the following morning, Charity had convinced herself that she was being foolish, reading far too much into Isobelle's comment. Her friend had made a vague reference to 'new things'; certainly she had done so in a meaningful tone, but the meaning might have been anything. It was ridiculous of Charity to feel such emotional turmoil over such a simple comment. Isobelle might have meant anything or nothing at all.

It was clear when she and Isobelle next met two days later that Isobelle really did have something she wanted to talk to Charity about. Ostensibly, it had been agreed that the two ladies would take a trip to the milliner's, for Isobelle wanted to buy a new hat (her particular obsession), and Charity had been putting off retrimming one of her own for long enough and must bite the bullet and at least buy some supplies. However, unusually, Isobelle was not so keen to go shopping when Charity arrived. She suggested tea and then decided against it; asked Charity if she did not think that it looked like rain and then dismissed the idea herself; spoke vaguely about staying in to make sure her mother was all right and then, seeing that Charity looked anxious, corrected herself and admitted that Lady Greenaway was no more ill than usual. Finally, flicking a glance up at Charity from below lowered lashes, she said: "The truth is, of course, that I want to speak to you about something, and am wondering how to find the words."

Charity had never known Isobelle short of words. "That sounds interesting," she said politely.

"I am wondering whether I dare tell you about something," Isobelle explained, a slightly mischievous expression on her face, for she must know perfectly well that Charity would allow her to ask anything she wanted.

"But of course," Charity said.

"I have a group of friends," Isobelle said. "Special friends. Particularly special friends."

"Oh." Charity tried not to feel downhearted by hearing about Isobelle's 'special' friends. What was she, then? A passing interest? Had it been arrogant of her to hope she was more than that?

"We call ourselves the Sisterhood," Isobelle continued, her eyes fixed on Charity as if making sure she did not miss a single fleeting emotion which crossed her friend's face, "and we are a particularly exclusive group."

"I see," Charity said, not seeing at all.

A smile flickered into life. "No, you don't. Anyway, we hold private meetings quite regularly. One of them is happening soon, in fact, to celebrate the beginning of the Season. Oh, I know it's a little early, when it's usually only considered to start in January, but most people are back in town by now."

Many of the *ton*, Charity knew, liked to be in town over Christmas, to take part in any festivities that were taking place. For herself, Christmas was a time to be survived rather than enjoyed: her childhood experience had been that enforced bonhomie brought out the worst in her mother, and she could not anticipate enjoying the time of year, even in her mother's absence, welcome though that would be. She turned her mind back to Isobelle's description of the Sisterhood.

"Is it a bit like…like Almack's?" Charity suggested tentatively. Almack's was a social club with strict rules and regulations. No one might attend without a ticket and invitation from one of the club's Patronesses, who ruled over it with a rod of iron. Charity, of course, had not been within any distance of attending, but she knew that Isobelle went regularly to their balls.

Isobelle gurgled with laughter. "No! Sorry, Harry, you were not to know. But oh goodness, the Sisterhood compared to Almack's! I must tell the other ladies! Cara—Lady Carolina Farrell, you know—will be so entertained." She paused. "And yes, by the way, we are all ladies. A very special sort of ladies." Charity nodded, and Isobelle moved nearer. "Aren't you going to ask what sort of ladies we are?" she murmured.

"W-what sort of ladies are you?" Charity asked, obedient but bewildered.

"Oh, now, I'm glad you asked that. You see, we are ladies who love ladies," Isobelle said. Charity had never heard of such a thing, and for a second she was open-mouthed with surprise. Yet suddenly, everything slipped into place. At last it all made sense: Charity's feelings for, Isobelle. How long had she been attracted to Isobelle? Perhaps since the very first moment she had seen her. "You are one of us, are you not?" Isobelle pressed. Her blue eyes glinted as if daring Charity to deny it.

Charity was too shocked to deny anything. Her whole world had changed in an instant, and it could never be the same. "How did you know?" she blurted out. "I…I mean—"

"I know exactly what you mean," Isobelle assured her, smiling.

"But you cannot be suggesting that…"

"That what? That I want to do this?"

Isobelle got up on tiptoes and placed a gentle kiss on Charity's lips. It should have been wrong, but it was so right. Charity trembled, her whole body tingling in response to those soft lips against her own. She wanted Isobelle to do it again, and then again. Unwanted, a comparison came into her mind: when Fotheringay had tried to do something like this, she had been repulsed. With Isobelle, she was anything but.

"I never…I didn't…I think…" But Charity could finish none of the sentences. She had no words to describe her feelings.

"Would you object if I kissed you again?" Isobelle asked, still looking up into Charity's eyes. "You did not pull away last time."

"I don't know." Charity was scared by the depths of her feeling, scared by how *much* she wanted Isobelle to kiss her again. But she could not say it aloud.

"Oh, Harry!" Isobelle laughed. "So unsure, so worried always. Why don't you trust yourself, trust me?"

It hurt, just a little bit, to be laughed at by Isobelle. Isobelle was beautiful, confident—everything that Charity would like to be. She was delicate, as a lady should be, not a mess of gawky long limbs and tiresome flyaway hair.

"I'm sorry," she said bravely, taking a breath. "Of course I trust you."

"Of course you do, silly," Isobelle said. "And you will attend the meeting?"

"A meeting of other ladies? Like me, like—" She took in a sudden, disbelieving gasp of air. "Like *us*?"

"Yes, dear Harry. Did you really think you were the only one?" teased Isobelle.

Charity had not recognised her own desires, let alone considered that another might share it. She blushed hotly. "I… don't know. I must speak to my sister, of course. She may have plans that can't be changed."

"I'm sure your sister will agree to let you come to me, even if she is busy." Isobelle brushed over Charity's anxiety. "She knows you will be safe with me."

Rebecca might know it, Charity thought, but she wasn't sure that she did. The feelings she had for Isobelle were anything but innocent: confused, tangled skeins of anxiety and desire, of worshipfulness and uncertainty. For Charity, Isobelle was anything but safe.

But it seemed that Isobelle was correct about Rebecca's response. Charity caught her sister that evening, as she was preparing to go out. Whilst the maid prinked and prepared

Rebecca, Charity explained in the simplest, most innocent of ways about the Sisterhood.

"It is a group of ladies. Lady Carolina Farrell is a member, I know, as well as Isobelle. To be honest," she added, apologetically, "I am not certain of many of the other ladies, but I will be able to tell you about them after the event, if you are not going to forbid me to go?"

Rebecca caught her sister's gaze in the mirror. "Charity...I, forbid you to go anywhere?" she asked. "Is it really likely?"

Charity gave a reluctant laugh. She had known that Rebecca would not object. Perhaps part of her had wanted her sister to do so however. It had all happened so fast—that kiss from Isobelle; the information that there was a secret group of ladies who met with the same unusual desires; a suggestion that Charity join them, that the kiss was not just 'a kiss' but an entry to a whole new world. Charity had found it hard enough getting used to the London that she knew. To change it all now and begin again, in a way, seemed terrifying. But Isobelle had asked her, and above all things Charity wanted to please Isobelle.

"I suppose not," she admitted. "But I had to ask you about it."

"Of course." Rebecca began to nod, but the movement drew a squawk of protest from her maid, who had just begun to arrange her hair. "Sorry Molly," she said to the maid. "When is the meeting?"

"Tomorrow afternoon." Charity tried to dampen down the anxiety inside her. "At Isobelle's house."

"Then you must go, of course, and tell me all about it afterwards."

But that, Charity thought grimly, was something she certainly would not do.

The night passed fast, and the morning faster, so that the time for Charity to attend the meeting of the Sisterhood seemed to rush upon her, like a torrent of water she could not hold back. She dressed carefully, as perhaps for the first time in her life her choice of dress seemed imperative. What impression would she give? What would these other ladies think of her? Indeed, who *were* these mysterious ladies who loved other ladies? Charity fretted and changed from one dress to another several times before making her choice. In the end, she chose a light-grey muslin: plain, almost Quakeress-like. She realised that she hoped not to be noticed, as if she could attend the Sisterhood almost as a ghostlike figure—someone who wasn't really there, who did not need to draw attention. But the dress was nonetheless one of her more expensive ones, and one both Rebecca and Isobelle had complimented in the past. Its simplicity suited her, and somehow the quiet colour seemed to minimise her height.

She was ten minutes later than she had intended by the time the rest of her toilette had been completed. The carriage was already at the door, and she had a moment only for a quick farewell to her sister before she climbed in and was borne away to her fate. As they drove up the street, Charity had her first glimpse of a member of the Sisterhood: the door was quickly closing behind an elegant lady in a pink, sprigged dress. It was no one she recognised, and Charity was not sure whether to be relieved or regretful on that level. Would it be worse to come face to face with someone she had met regularly on a different level, at picnics or concerts, or to walk into a room full of complete strangers? Neither option sounded comfortable and she had not come to any conclusion before the coachman was opening the door and assisting her out of the carriage. Perhaps that was as well, she thought to herself: if she had picked one, then the chances were high that the other option would be what she discovered. The front door opened to allow her in, and she saw Isobelle waiting in the hall for her.

"Harry, darling, it is so good to see you!"

"It was kind of you to invite me."

Though in truth, Charity wished that Isobelle had done no such thing. She had no time to dwell on this matter, however, for Isobelle was leading her towards the large downstairs drawing room.

"We usually meet down here. My sitting room would hardly be large enough to hold us all," Isobelle explained, driving more terror into Charity's heart with every word. "Come, in here."

Charity's heart beat fast, and she felt almost as if she was walking to her doom. "Welcome," Isobelle added, in her low, clear voice, "to the Sisterhood."

Although this was not the first time Charity had visited Isobelle's drawing room, she had never seen it so densely populated before. To her startled eyes, it looked as if there were tens—dozens!—of ladies in the room. Then, as her shock lessened, she saw there were really only five other ladies present, save her and Isobelle. Three of them she even recognised. That was Lady Caroline, wasn't it, that angular figure on the left of the fire? She was well known for her erudition, holding literary and other soirees for a specially chosen few. Charity had never attended one, but another debutante had pointed Lady Caroline out to her in hushed tones at a less impressive party. The second was Miss Musgrove, and Charity found herself bristling at the very sight of her in a pretty pink dress with her soft brown hair curling around her head in an elegantly styled coiffure. This was someone who had pretended to be friendly only so that she could laugh about it later. Realising that she was a friend of Isobelle's made Charity suddenly wary. Was Isobelle really as lovely as Charity had first thought? Charity shook herself. Just because one of Isobelle's lady acquaintances had once done something unkind, it didn't therefore mean that Isobelle would do so also. The last lady she recognised was Mrs Seacombe, a married lady a few years older than Charity. Seeing her, Charity wondered whether she had mistaken the nature of Isobelle's invitation. Surely a married lady could not…

She bobbed a curtsey, feeling dowdy and out of place in the company. Everyone else looked so comfortable, as if they were born to attend half-secretive meetings. Charity felt as if she had stumbled into a party to which she was not invited; every set of eyes was on her, watching, judging.

"Miss Charity Bellingham," Isobelle announced to the room. "But I call her Harry. It suits her so much better, does it not?" She smiled at Charity's look of amazement. "We stand on no ceremony here. And men, even servants, are forbidden the room. Are you terribly shocked?"

"N-no." Charity stumbled over her denial, and Miss Musgrove spoke up.

"Don't tease the child, Isobelle. Everything is new." She rose to her feet and walked over to Charity. "Nan Musgrove," she introduced herself. "It's a pleasure to meet you again." There was a certain hesitancy in her voice, but her hazel eyes were friendly enough. Then again, thought Charity, she had seemed so friendly on their first meeting. Appearances could be deceptive.

"And you." Charity heard her voice squeaking in an unaccustomed manner, and she coughed in an attempt to cover her embarrassment.

"And these others...Lady Caroline Farrell, I imagine you know. She is quite the most famous of our little group. Then Miss Garland, Mrs Seacombe, Miss Louisa Walters." Nan indicated each lady in turn.

Lady Caroline looked up from her position by the fire. "But it's all first names here, of course," she said, her no-nonsense tones contrasting strongly with Nan's quiet voice and Isobelle's sweet one. "Call me Cara. Everyone does. Mother was foolish enough to wish upon me the name Carolina, but I refused to be called any such thing. Even as a child, I believe, I was stubborn on the point. Never was a girlish Carolina type. Nothing like Caro Lamb, thank heavens! Cara, now. That's a sensible name for a sensible woman."

"I'm very glad to meet you," Charity said.

"No, you're not, not yet," Lady Caroline said gruffly. "You're feeling shy and awkward. Nothing unusual in that; first meeting and so on. But you will be in time. I'm told I am a useful person to know by my sisters here...Any meeting involving me will be safe from the slightest breath of scandal. Everyone knows my business, or they think they do."

Charity nodded, unsure how she was supposed to respond to this diatribe. She glanced at Isobelle for reassurance, but Isobelle had gone, butterflying across the room in her appealing way to swap confidences with Mrs Seacombe. Miss Musgrove saw her dilemma however.

"Have you been deserted by Isobelle already?" she said. "Oh, she's talking to Lydia. Rather ruthless of you," she called across the room to Isobelle, "to leave your new guest so quickly. The other two are Louisa and Mary."

"I know you would look after her, Nan of my heart," Isobelle retorted lightly. "And I simply had to tell Lydia the latest gossip about Lord Wendham and his servant. Too, too delicious not to share."

"Gossip," Cara said in a tone of disgust. "Why they describe gossip as the province of elderly ladies, I do not know. It seems to me that it is the younger generation who are the purveyors of such."

"Alas, too true," Isobelle acknowledged. "But you forgive us this one little sin, do you not, Cara?"

"Hmph." Cara looked back to Charity. "You come here and we can have a sensible conversation for once. If anyone here is capable of such."

"It's all right. She's not nearly as ferocious as she sounds, dear Cara," Miss Musgrove murmured into Charity's ear as she assisted her in moving a kneeler close to Lady Caroline's chair. "One of the old guard."

There was clearly nothing wrong with Cara's hearing however. "One of the old guard, indeed?" she demanded. "How dare you, Nan Musgrove?" Charity shrunk back a pace at Lady Caroline's severe tone, but it seemed that Miss Musgrove had been correct in her description of Cara. "I am not," the elder woman said, "'one' of the old guard. I *am* the old guard. One of them, indeed. I have never been merely a part of anything, ever."

Charity laughed, and Cara looked across to her. "That's better. A smile suits your face better than a frown, you know. Couldn't have you continuing to glare down at us all with beetling brows. Now, tell me about yourself."

Charity went home from the gathering full of whirling thoughts and emotions. The ladies had all been very nice to her: kind, polite, not treating her as if she were only one step up from a servant. She had been shocked by the very egalitarian nature of the meeting. First names for people she had only just met that very day! Everyone knowing everyone else's business. Indeed, everyone knowing the most private information about the others. If someone joined the group deliberately to spread gossip, how much more might they get than they had anticipated. Deep friendship between ladies, with flowery, loving language, was expected. But this group was so much more than that. She had seen Mrs Seacombe—Lydia—kissing, actually *kissing*, Miss Garland, in a fashion that Charity did not even remember seeing her parents kiss. Though given the cool state of their relationship, that was perhaps not so surprising. But to kiss in public!

Discovering that the famed Lady Caroline Farrell was a lady-lover had also taken Charity aback. Somehow, despite Isobelle's position in society, Charity had imagined the others of the group being less prominent. The realisation that such a respected lady was a member of the Sisterhood would take Charity some time to get used to. It had seemed curious to be ordered to speak of her own experiences to Lady Caroline (despite the encouragement, Charity could not yet think of her as Cara, not even in the privacy of her own thoughts), as if Charity herself was as important and interesting as any other member of the group. Charity had been cautious with her information, albeit taking punctilious care to make sure that Lady Caroline knew her social background. The other ladies might feel comfortable being totally open about their lives (and from what she had overheard, they certainly were open!), but Charity had been used her life long to keeping the majority of her thoughts and opinions to herself. It would take some time for her to change, if indeed she ever did.

Rebecca met her when she came in.

"Hello, Charity. Did you have a nice visit?" she asked. "Did you meet Miss Greenaway's friends? Pray, come and tell me all about it. I have been dull today in your absence. Won't you come and cheer me up?"

"Of course." Charity went rapidly through her thoughts, trying to find anything appropriate to share with Rebecca. She could find nothing, so she temporised: "Let me just take my cloak off and wash myself, and I'll be with you."

"Should I call for tea?"

Charity smiled at her. "Not on my account. I dare swear I have consumed more tea than the rest of this household put together!"

"Very well. I will be in the drawing room when you're ready. Mr Fotheringay is still out. I believe he is due home for supper, but I do not expect him any earlier."

Charity, aware of the listening ears of the servants—so cautiously kept out at the Sisterhood's meeting—merely nodded. "I will be with you soon."

Washing the grime of the city off her face and hands took only a minute, but Charity was still struggling with considerations of what she might and might not say to Rebecca as she allowed her maid to brush and restyle her hair. There seemed to be so much that she could not touch upon. However, when she rejoined Rebecca, she realised that it would be an easier conversation than she feared. Rebecca's mind ran on the 'who' rather than on the 'what' of the group meeting. She requested details of the ladies—their dresses, their manners, their place in society. She was overawed to hear that Charity had met Lady Caroline Farrell, and asked so many questions about the lady that Charity had to protest.

"Becca, I have no idea of the stones in her jewellery! You know how I am about noticing clothes. The fact that I can even describe the basics of Lady Caroline's dress is a miracle. Asking for more detail is impossible. You will have to meet her yourself and ask her."

"Oh, I could never do that," Rebecca protested quickly. "I would be too terrified to look at anything but the floor."

"I'm sure you would later be able to give a very good description of her footwear in that case," retorted Charity, smiling, and the girls laughed.

"And the others?" Rebecca asked. "Miss Greenaway? With a name like that, she ought to have a green dress."

"Oh no," said Charity seriously. "She usually wears blue. It matches her eyes so well, you see."

"Goodness!" Rebecca's surprise was evident, and Charity frowned, confused as to why Rebecca could find such a small detail so interesting.

"What?"

Rebecca reached out a hand towards her. "Do not be cross with me, dearest," she said. "I merely could not help being amazed that you had noticed the colour of her eyes, and that it matched her dress! It seems so unnatural in you, when you care so little for fashion."

Charity blushed. She noticed everything about Isobelle, if truth be known. She had not realised that she was doing so until now, but Rebecca's comment had brought it home to her that if it had been *Isobelle's* jewellery under discussion, she could have told Rebecca every piece her friend had been wearing. The necklace with the pretty blue stone in the middle—perhaps a sapphire. The way Isobelle's hair had been caught up and how the sparkling crystals on the ribbon had made it seem to shine in the light. The simple silver bracelet she wore, which seemed in so much contrast to the rest of her attire.

"You know I've always described her as the lady in blue," she said.

"That's true," her sister agreed. "Now, about the others. You mentioned a Miss Musgrove?"

"Yes." Charity felt as if a cloud had been cast over her afternoon's pleasure. "I'd met her before," she said at last. "She was...I don't know if you remember, Becca, but she was the one who teased me about my height. At least," she corrected herself, "she did not tease, but she laughed with the other girls behind my back. I wish...oh, I wish she hadn't been there."

"Oh, dearest, how awkward for you," Rebecca cried, her sympathy at once aroused.

Charity thought for the first time how glad she was that it was herself who had been teased and not Rebecca. It had hurt a lot to feel herself a figure of fun, but it would have hurt Rebecca that much more.

"It doesn't matter," she lied. "There are plenty of others. I'm sure I need not see much of Miss Musgrove if I choose not to."

"So you will meet them again?" Rebecca asked.

Charity nodded, realising for the first time how much she wanted to return. All of that worrying and fretting over meeting a group of ladies so friendly! Isobelle had been right—of course she would have been. It suddenly hit Charity: she felt like she had been with friends. And then the fear struck. Was this all to be snatched away from her? Had the Sisterhood truly liked her, or might they be speaking to each other in private, now that she'd gone? Criticising her, laughing at her...Miss Musgrove had done it once. She might well do it again. And this time it would destroy her, she believed.

"I think so. I believe Iso—Miss Greenaway has meetings quite often. I...I don't think I did anything to shame her," she said, suddenly doubtful.

"You didn't. You couldn't," her older sister said, always loyal. "Of course she will want you to attend again. Miss Greenaway has been so very kind to you already. It was silly of me to ask."

"I hope you're right." Charity's thoughts were troubled. "I hope you're right."

CHAPTER FOURTEEN

Charity did not have to live with her concerns for too long. Visiting Isobelle the next day, she was greeted with a sparkling smile and the warmest of welcomes.

"Well! That went beautifully yesterday, did you not think?" Isobelle asked.

"I…I hope so. I did not let you down?"

"Let me down? How could you possibly have done that? Anyway," Isobelle said gaily, "I hope you felt welcome?"

"Very much so. Your friends are delightful."

Isobelle shook her head reprovingly. "Don't say 'your' friends, say 'our friends'. You must not be unfriendly, you know! You are one of us now. As long as you want to be?" she added inquiringly. "I know I pulled you into this half-unwilling. Do you forgive me now that you have met the Sisterhood?"

"I was honoured to be invited. But yes," admitted Charity, "I was scared in advance. Can you blame me?"

"Of course I can! What sort of person do you think I am, who would force you into a situation in which I knew you would be uncomfortable?" Isobelle rearranged some flowers in a vase as she spoke. "There, that is much better. I knew you would be scared at first. But you were not uncomfortable for too long, I hope."

"No, indeed." Charity pushed the thought of Miss Musgrove firmly to the back of her mind. "How could I be? Everyone was so friendly!"

"I hoped you would say that." Isobelle grasped Charity's hand and laid a kiss upon it. She seemed to find it so easy to perform such gestures; Charity herself would never dare even to take Isobelle's hand in hers unless it was clearly offered, let alone to kiss her. Would she ever learn to be so free and confident in her desires? "Because," added Isobelle, "for once we have another meeting following close upon the heels of the first. It is unusual for us. We usually have so many other commitments, and we try not to make the Sisterhood too visible by meeting too often in private. But yesterday's meeting…Shall I shock you now? Yesterday's meeting was really called to welcome you to our midst. Our intended meeting was to be in three days' time, on the last Saturday afternoon before Christmas. A celebration, if you will. Can you…would you possibly agree to join us once more?"

"I…" Charity's mind was racing. The Sisterhood had welcomed her; that was wonderful to know. But to discover that the meeting she had attended was solely for the purpose of introducing her to the group was shocking. She was glad she had not known in advance: her nerves would have been unbearable to cope with. And now, she was invited to a second meeting, not a week later than the first!

"Have I shocked you terribly, dearest?" Isobelle asked, with amused sympathy. "They told me not to overpower you too much, and I fear I have done just that. Have I overpowered you?"

"I'm…well, I'm not certain what to say," Charity stammered, reaching out a hand that she might lean upon a chair back for support. "They gathered to meet me?"

"Well, yes. Sit down, dear Harry, before you fall down." Isobelle suited her movement to her words, sitting herself comfortably down on the chair to one side of the window. Charity, too stunned to do anything but what she was told, followed suit. "And they liked you a lot."

"All of them?" Miss Musgrove would intrude herself on Charity's mind. How could someone who had previously been so unkind to her claim to like her?

Isobelle reached over and patted her knee. "All of them who were present. Of course they did! Why, which of them were you unsure about? Cara? I know she can be an imposing character. Lydia? Were you scared by her self-confidence? You surely can't have been worried about me!"

"I...I..." Charity pulled herself together firmly. There were enough ladies in the Sisterhood to mean that she was not obliged to speak more than occasionally to Miss Musgrove. And if Isobelle wanted her and the others were happy to welcome her... That was all that mattered. "I'm overwhelmed," she said, avoiding Isobelle's question. "Wh-when is the next meeting, did you say?"

"Saturday. Of course, you have not met everyone in the Sisterhood yet, you know," Isobelle said seriously. "It was not possible for us all to attend at such short notice. But you must not mind that. You know enough of us now that Saturday will not be too much of a trauma to you." She clapped her hands suddenly, in a burst of pleasure. "Saturday! I can hardly wait!"

Charity was not sure whether she could hardly wait for Saturday or hardly wait for Saturday to be over. Rebecca had shown no concern about Charity attending another meeting so soon after the first. Six months into her marriage, Rebecca seemed to have settled down a little more. Fotheringay was often out, and Rebecca seemed happier for it.

"In truth, Charity," she said, "it will be quite useful. I have a few friends coming around myself—Mrs Hollings, Mrs Davison and Miss Clay—and it is just the sort of event that you would hate, you know. Gossip and embroidery, I'm afraid! But if you're safely somewhere else, none of the ladies can take offence at you not appearing."

"Do they take offence?" Charity asked guiltily, aware of several previous meetings which she had avoided with much less excuse.

Rebecca put her hand to her mouth in dismay. "Oh dear! I ought not to have said that. Well, you know what they are for talking about everything, and I'll admit that I found it hard to keep my countenance when they were asking whether you were deliberately avoiding them!"

"Because I was." Charity sighed. "Becca, I'm sorry. I will try and come to another one, but if you really think that it is all right for me to go with Isobelle instead, I'll be very grateful to you!"

Rebecca smiled. "Dearest, you are mixing with the elite. Mrs Hollings would never dare object, and Miss Clay will be quite overcome by her close brush with the top echelons of society! You know that she is the daughter of one of Mr Fotheringay's friends, do you not? A nice girl, but not used to the *ton*. It will take the rest of us to keep her feet on the floor when she discovers whom you are with!"

The sisters laughed, and Charity went up to her room, with one more reason to be grateful to Isobelle and the Sisterhood before the meeting ever had started.

The time for the meeting came soon enough, though, and Charity realised with relief that it really and truly *wasn't* as frightening this time. She had met several of the Sisterhood; had talked to them and had had confirmation from Isobelle that they liked her and wanted her as one of themselves. And, as an added advantage, she had every excuse for avoiding Rebecca's dreary social gathering. All in all, she thought, looking out of the window and seeing the sun pouring down its rays onto the world, life was fairly wonderful.

As she was driven over to Isobelle's house for this second meeting, hot on the heels of the first, she wondered who would be there. Would it be all the same people? Or, as Isobelle had suggested, might there be more new people to meet? But at least this time she would know some of the others apart from Isobelle;

and the meeting itself would not be so strange. She wondered if Mrs Seacombe would be there again and if there would be more kissing. She had felt embarrassed and uncomfortable about the public display of such deep affection, but it had also been exciting, in its way. She was not sure whether she hoped that it would or would not happen again; it made her feel funny all over, and gave rise to a strange throbbing between her legs when she remembered it.

Isobelle met her in the hall once more, and escorted her through into the drawing room, which had sprigs of holly and mistletoe around it in festive fashion. Charity saw on a quick sweep of the room with her eyes that many of the same ladies as last time were indeed there. Miss Garland—Louisa; Mrs Seacombe—Lydia; Lady Caroline; Nan Musgrove. But there were a couple of new ladies also, sitting quietly together by the back window. Isobelle caught the direction of Charity's gaze and then took her over to the pair.

"These are our lovebirds, Emily and Jane," she said, by way of introduction. "I don't think they were there at our last meeting. They scorn my little events, you understand! They are the Sisterhood's first married couple, you know."

"I beg your pardon?" Charity said, very much disconcerted.

Isobelle pealed with laughter. "Oh, Harry, your expression! Ask them yourself. I'm sure they will be happy to explain."

Charity looked expectantly at the two ladies. Emily was fair-haired: not golden like Isobelle, but with a riot of almost-white curls surrounding her face. It was clear that her hair had once been pulled back in an elegant style, but little strands had escaped, giving an almost halo-like effect to her appearance. But she was clearly shy—shyer, even, than Rebecca at her most uncertain. She looked terribly young and in need of protection, grasping Jane's hand tightly, and staring down at the floor. Jane was very different: her straight brown hair was parted at the middle and pulled back in a very severe fashion, which reminded Charity of the governess she and Rebecca had had for a couple of years, before their father had declared that educating girls was a shocking waste of time and money and sent her away. It was Jane who explained.

"Emmy and I have been friends for some years now. Closer than sisters, closer than most gentlemen and their wives," Jane said. "We thought for a long time that we were the only ones. I suppose most people do, so finding the Sisterhood was a great joy to us."

Charity wondered how they had discovered the Sisterhood, but did not quite like to ask. "But you had each other," she said instead.

Jane smiled, and there was a sudden warm glow in her looks. Charity had been wondering how someone as young and shy as Emily seemed could have dared even to speak to Jane, let alone to become so close to her. However, looking at Jane's face as she smiled, it made more sense.

"We did. We are the lucky ones. Of course, Isobelle was teasing to call us married, but a few months back we plighted our troth in front of the rest of the Sisterhood." Jane laid her other hand protectively over her own and Emily's clasped ones, and Emily almost unconsciously moved an inch or two closer to her 'wife's' side. "We can't have rings, as you can understand, but we have these keepsake necklaces to remind us."

Charity saw the matching chains around the two ladies' necks. It was a beautiful idea, and the necklaces were equally beautiful. Perhaps one day... But she refused to follow that train of thought. It was much too early, and anyway, Isobelle was much too beautiful and important to... She smiled back at Jane.

"That's lovely," she said sincerely. "Congratulations to you both."

Emily just dared to raise her gaze and gave Charity a happy glance. Jane looked embarrassed.

"Of course, we can't tell anyone, nor live together officially like man and wife. But we're lucky to have the Sisterhood, where we can be ourselves, and luckier still to have each other."

Charity would never have considered herself a romantic. Rebecca had always been much more inclined in that direction, devouring the few three-volume novels which had come her way, and reading them over and over again, but Jane's simple love story touched Charity deeply.

"I hope you will be very happy."

"They will!" called Isobelle, whose flitterings from lady to lady in the room had brought her back close enough to overhear Charity's remark. "If they are not, the rest of the Sisterhood will join together to demand the reason why!"

Unexpectedly, Emily giggled at this. Charity had begun to wonder if the girl *could* make a sound, so silent had she been. Jane caught Charity's surprise and responded to it.

"Emmy does talk, don't you, my dear?"

"Sometimes," the girl said shyly.

"I'm sorry. I didn't mean to be rude," Charity apologised.

"I don't mean to be shy. It just happens."

Jane ruffled her hair affectionately. "She didn't have the best of times in society when she first came out, and—"

"Too many people?" Charity asked sympathetically.

"No, it wasn't that. It…" Emily looked appealingly at Jane.

"They didn't understand her," Jane said. "She's very intelligent, you see"—Emily blushed, but did not deny the statement—"and her conversation about Sophocles and others of the Ancient Greeks somewhat baffled the *ton*. It was not quite what they expected from her!"

Charity tried to suppress a smile. She could imagine only too well the reaction of the society belles, and the vast majority of the gentlemen, to a pretty young girl attempting to draw them into a serious discussion about Greek philosophy. Jane and Emily both laughed, easily able to read her mind.

"You see?" Jane asked.

"I certainly do!"

"Fortunately," Emily said, encouraged into speaking, "I met Lady Caroline. She understood about philosophy. And then," she looked adoringly at Jane, "we learned of the Sisterhood. It had never seemed so wrong to me, our relationship—Sappho, you know—but I never thought we would find other people who understood."

"I didn't understand myself until lately," Charity admitted, amazed by the transformation in Emily now she felt comfortable enough to speak.

"Have you been to any of Cara's Greek evenings?" Jane asked.

"Goodness, no!"

"Would you be bored?" Emily's tone was wistful, as if Charity had let her down.

"No, not bored." Charity flushed. "I am not," she began with difficulty, unsure how to explain, "of the same…well, circles as Isobelle or Lady Caroline. Isobelle has been kind enough to take pity on me, but I don't think…"

"Oh, if that is all!"

Isobelle had stayed to listen to the conversation. "Emily is unimpressed with titles and great names," she said gaily. "I fear I am far too ill-educated for her."

"You know that is not true," Jane retorted, in her 'wife's' defence. "Don't tease her so."

"All the same," Isobelle said, "Emily is correct about one thing. If you care about such things, Cara will be delighted to invite you. It is one of her pet projects, you know. That and slavery. Both Nan and Cara are keen on slavery."

"I don't understand." Charity felt totally confused by this statement. The conversation had veered off in an incomprehensible direction. Philosophy and slavery? What was the link? And why on earth were Lady Caroline and that awful Miss Musgrove so enthused about the latter?

Fortunately, Lady Caroline had caught her own name. "Neither would you with an explanation like that!" she exclaimed in her usual forthright fashion. "Honestly, Isobelle, sometimes I think you don't have the sense you were born with. Nan and I are 'keen on slavery', for goodness sake. Come here, child," she said to Charity, "and I will tell you about the Abolitionist movement."

Rather as she had in their first meeting, Charity found herself sitting by Lady Caroline. Unlike last time, however, it was Cara who did the speaking, a change for which Charity was most grateful. Miss Musgrove—whom Charity still felt too uncomfortable to think of as 'Nan'—was sitting there too, however, and Charity regretted it somewhat. She still felt awkward around her, remembering the feeling of betrayal she had experienced when she discovered that Miss Musgrove had been gossiping about her behind her back. At the last meeting, they had done little more than exchange polite greetings; to sit and talk with her, even in Lady Caroline's company, was an uncomfortable thought. It was evident that Lady Caroline valued Nan highly. Whilst Charity could not in her wildest imaginings think that Cara would take part in malicious gossip, Nan's presence made Charity feel on edge, as if she were a cat whose fur had been stroked in the wrong direction.

"Please do tell me," Charity said, attempting a lightness of tone she did not feel. "I know a little, a very little, about Ancient Greece, but I fear I am ignorant indeed about slavery. It feels so very detached from my own experiences."

"Hmph," said Lady Caroline. "Well, that is precisely what it is not. Granted, since Somersett's case in 1772, slavery in England itself has been unknown, but out in the colonies—Jamaica, for example—it is rife. Shocking conditions, some of them too."

"The traders are the worst," Miss Musgrove put in. "They haunt the shores of Africa, I believe, taking the natives and shipping them across the Atlantic in the most awful conditions. If one of the slaves dies, or even just gets badly sick, they throw him overboard. There are plenty more to replace them, you see."

"It is a terrible thought." Charity knew that her words sounded stilted, but for the life of her she could not feign naturalness when speaking directly to Miss Musgrove. She looked at the other lady with bewilderment. Here she was talking with such sympathy about slaves on the other side of the world, yet she could deliberately hurt someone she had actually met. It didn't make sense.

"Most people in England don't want to know," Cara said. "Too much money involved, and most of the cruelty taking place too far away. But even if it is not on our homeland soil, there are English slavers sailing the seas, and plenty of English gentlemen have fortunes which have been built through slavery.

You may have noticed I don't take sugar in my tea?" She looked enquiringly at Charity.

"Um, no, no, I didn't," Charity stammered, yet again taken aback by the sudden change of conversation. Her head, she was sure, would hurt from all the subjects which had been thrown at her this afternoon.

"Perfectly reasonable. No reason why you should," Lady Caroline said. "But all the sugar in this country comes from slavery. Sugar-beet plantations, you know." Charity nodded. It all sounded vaguely familiar, and Cara clearly knew precisely what she was talking about. "There's a movement," Cara continued, "a very small movement, a shamefully small movement," she added severely, "to boycott sugar to demonstrate one's opposition to the use of slaves. That's why."

"Cara was one of the first female subscribers to the Committee for the Abolition of the Slave Trade," Miss Musgrove said. "Being a lady, she could not, of course, take part in public meetings, but she has set up her own female-only meetings here in London."

"With a lot of help from Nan," Cara added. "Incidentally, I couldn't help hearing a bit of what Isobelle was saying to you. Think you should know that the Sisterhood is just that. We're close as sisters, and some of us," she added with a nod at Emily and Jane, "closer than that. But any Sister is welcome at any gathering organised by another. Some don't want to, of course. Try inviting Isobelle to talk about Ancient Greece and see how keen she looks, while Emily and Jane don't come to a great many of Isobelle's tea parties. Not really a great talker, Emily, until you get her on her own subjects."

"I thought she was shy."

"So she is. Doesn't know how to talk to many people, poor lamb. Her father believes in educating girls as much as boys, which is just as it should be, of course. But if you're going to let a girl loose in society, she needs some other knowledge too. I take it you had a governess?"

"For a couple of years. My father baulked at the cost at that point. He did not share Emily's father's opinion. What is her surname, incidentally? I know my sister will ask."

"Summercourt. Jane's a Blackthorne. The Norfolk branch originally."

"Well, my father decided that it was more sensible to save the money rather than spend it on teaching us, given that the house would be entailed away. And I'm not sure he was wrong," she admitted fairly.

"See your point. Anyhow, the thing is, whatever your status of birth or education, a Sister is a Sister. Got my eye on another young thing, incidentally. Miss Kate Smyth. Gossip has it she's on the catch for a husband, but I'm not so sure. Mind, the *ton* also seem to think she's a commoner, but I have a feeling that her grandfather…But never mind that. Give me your address, and if you're interested, I'll ensure you get cards for the next Abolitionist meeting. We're always looking for new members and would be very glad to put you down as another. None of this 'not good enough' nonsense."

"Thank you. I'd like that," Charity said. She was wise enough to see the kindness behind Lady Caroline's gruff comments. "I know very little, but I'm anxious to learn more, if you would not mind my attendance."

Cara gave a quick nod. "And I'll let you know about the Greek group. We will be discussing Lord Elgin's marbles. There are mixed views within our members as to whether they should be on display in London, or even whether they should be in London at all. Hope you don't mind heated discussions. Strange that something related to a time so long ago can cause more controversy than modern events of our time, but so it is."

CHAPTER FIFTEEN

Christmas had come and gone before Charity heard anything further from Lady Caroline Farrell about her various meetings. But in the first week of January, Charity received an invitation to an Abolitionist meeting taking place a few days later. Half-excited, but with no idea of what to expect, Charity was keen to attend. Rebecca had expressed concerns about her attending alone, so Isobelle had arranged that she and Charity would be chaperoned by Mrs Seacombe for this occasion. Isobelle's mother, Lady Greenaway, rarely left the house thanks to her ill health, so it was not unusual for Isobelle to be accompanied by one member or another of the Sisterhood. Lydia Seacombe, as a married lady, had the privilege of attending places alone, though she freely admitted that she was rarely to be seen at Lady Caroline's more serious events.

"But for you and your little protégé," she had told Isobelle in front of Charity, "I will do so this once. Though honestly, Cara would be perfectly happy to do the honours herself, you know."

Charity had blushed, both because of the description of the relationship between herself and Isobelle, which implied that Isobelle saw her as more than just another member of the Sisterhood, and because of the reference to Lady Caroline, which was identical in nature to something Isobelle herself had said. Despite Cara's own comments to her, Charity did not feel quite confident enough to throw herself entirely under Cara's protection. It still seemed too much of an imposition. She had been grateful when Isobelle had shrugged and said that she would ask Lydia instead.

"Little protégé," however, had been Isobelle's response to Lydia. "Harry, little?"

The ladies had both laughed then, but Charity had not minded.

Now, however, she wished herself smaller, that she might more easily slip into the background. In a meeting attended solely by women, her height made her even more conspicuous than usual. And now they had arrived, both Isobelle and Mrs Seacombe had vanished on errands of their own. Lydia Seacombe had been quite frank about the fact that in her eyes this was likely to be the most interesting part of the whole evening. Charity sat quietly on a chair near the back and waited for the meeting to begin.

When it did, she found herself transfixed from the very first moment. The first speaker was a plump lady whom Charity had never seen before. Her dress was peculiar, in puce with light pink ribbons; she seemed a figure of fun, and yet Charity was certain that Lady Caroline would not invite someone to speak merely to laugh at them. She looked enquiringly at Isobelle, who smiled.

"Wait. Even Lydia occasionally enjoys these moments."

Lady Caroline introduced her speaker, and without further ado, the lady began.

"Little child, little child, why do you cry?
Your clothes are all tattered; there's mud in your eye.
The marks of the slave whip show the reason why
A tiny young child begins now to cry."

There were four more verses, and the audience listened quietly. It was the merest doggerel, almost humorously bad, and yet—and yet the sincerity of the speaker and the simplicity of her words brought it home. Children were beaten and forced to labour with no payment and no hope of anything better, ever in their lives. No payment, no freedom. To labour without hope. The children might look different to the pampered sons and daughters of the elite, but they were still human. The lady was applauded when she finished for her evident passion more than her attempt at poetry, for the kindness and humanity which led the ideas, rather than the words themselves.

"They often start with some sort of story or poem," Isobelle explained under cover of the applause. "It breaks the audience in gently. Once Cara managed to get Amelia Opie to start us off with her poem *The Negro Boy's Tale: a poem addressed to children.* Although it was originally written for children, a few ladies actually cried."

"I've never heard of her," Charity admitted guiltily.

"Not? But she's famous! A novelist, you know. And Josiah Wedgworth himself praised her. I suppose you know who he is?"

"Ye-es," Charity said. She knew he was a jeweller, certainly, though his association with a lady poetess seemed tenuous.

"The Quaker. They've been against slavery for centuries, you know," Isobelle informed her.

For someone who claimed to have little interest in the abolition of slavery, Isobelle appeared to Charity to know a great deal. Fortunately for her, before she could continue to demonstrate her own ignorance, the evening continued and the audience fell quiet once more. Lady Caroline herself gave a speech dealing with certain issues which were currently forming in terms of changing legislation: "Although we, as women, have no part in the legal process, we can perhaps encourage our menfolk to work through such channels," she had said at one point.

It seemed odd that someone who not only had no gentlemen in her life and was committed to a society of ladies that in and of itself precluded gentlemen should speak in this way, but Charity learned that Cara was a pragmatist. Many of the ladies attending had husbands. By speaking to them in this way, she hoped to garner more support for the cause. It was well known, it seemed, that some of the most vehemently anti-slavery gentlemen in Parliament resented what they saw as the interference of ladies, and therefore asking men to voice the concerns might have more influence.

All in all, Charity was fascinated. She was humbled by her lack of knowledge and the strength of feeling apparent in the room and torn with the desire to learn more and do more. When the meeting drew to a close, she sat still in complete silence for several minutes until her attention was drawn back to herself by Mrs Seacombe. Isobelle had disappeared, she noticed for the first time; it was Lydia only who stood by her.

"You enjoyed yourself, then?" Mrs Seacombe asked gaily.

Charity was not sure that 'enjoyed' was quite the right word, but she nodded.

"There's so much to understand," she said.

"Yes, and all of it so dull!" mourned Lydia

Isobelle joined them at this point, arrayed in a grey evening cloak that shimmered in the candlelight.

"Lydia, darling, are you never serious?" she scolded gently. "You know it is important work Cara does."

"And you, of course, find it fascinating," Lydia tossed back.

"No," said Isobelle slowly, "but I think perhaps I ought to. Listening to Cara and her guests speak, I can't help feeling that I should be doing more."

"Yes," cried Charity eagerly, "that is what I felt!"

Lydia Seacombe shrugged. "My advice is to drink a cup of tea and wait for the feeling to wear off."

"You're hopeless." But Isobelle smiled at her friend. "Harry, I saw Cara speak to you at the end. Do you feel now that you are welcome to attend? Even without this hopeless creature here," she added, shaking her head at her friend.

"She was very kind. I'm not sure whether my sister, Mrs Fotheringay, would feel comfortable about that, though."

"That's easy," Isobelle said. "Ask Cara to invite her too. The more the merrier, you know…or perhaps not quite that!"

"If you call that merrymaking," put in the irrepressible Lydia, "you need more than a cup of tea. Allow me to correct my prescription to two glasses of champagne! And allow me also to carry you off to your respective dwellings. To think I missed Miss Jameson's party for this!"

"I'm very grateful," Charity said. Whilst she could not condone Mrs Seacombe's comments, she appreciated even more the generosity that had made Lydia agree to chaperone her. "It was especially kind in the circumstances."

"The things I do for a Sister," Lydia said, and would brook no more gratitude.

"All the same," Charity said to Isobelle the next day, as they met to discuss the evening before, "it was generous indeed of Mrs…of Lydia," she corrected herself, seeing the correction on Isobelle's lips, "to agree to go. I could see she felt little interest in the subject."

"Oh, Lydia is a kind-hearted soul, if she is such a flibbertigibbet," Isobelle agreed. She looked up at Charity with a quick glance, her eyes alive with mischief. "Will you think me just as bad if I admit that it is not my preferred method of entertainment either?" she asked.

"How could it be?" Charity said sadly. "It was all so…so—"

"Serious?" suggested Isobelle.

"Shocking. I had not realised…I suppose I never thought about it. Well," Charity said with determination, "there is one thing I can do right now. I will take sugar in my tea no longer until I can be certain that I am not supporting such a dreadful trade."

"Oh, Harry," Isobelle said, laughing. "What a disappointing end to that sentence! For a moment I quite thought that you were intending to…I don't know, perhaps go and work as a missionary for those poor benighted savages, or something of the kind."

"I know it is only a small thing," Charity acknowledged, "but I want to do something, and in truth it is the only think I can think of as yet. I will ask Lady Caroline—"

"Cara," Isobelle corrected her.

"Cara, then, if she will be good enough to point me towards some literature on the subject. I feel I have barely begun to understand what is happening, beyond our sight but in our names."

"Cara will be delighted to have made such a conquest of you." Isobelle sipped her (sugared) tea. "I quite see that something must be done, Harry, but—and I know this is sacrilege to the Sisterhood, but I must say it—can we not leave it for the gentlemen to sort out? They have made this mess, after all. Let them solve it."

"I see your point, but…" Charity was just beginning before she was interrupted by the entrance of a footman.

"Miss Musgrove to see you, Miss Greenaway."

Charity got to her feet again, still fighting shy of Miss Musgrove. She couldn't understand how the lady could seem so genuinely considerate and thoughtful and yet have treated her so badly. She had kept a watchful eye on Nan Musgrove since the first Sisterhood meeting she had attended and had become more, not less, confused. She was *nice*—or at least, she came across so. She had a gentle sense of humour that would have attracted Charity under any other circumstances, and she was always ready to help others.

"I must be going," she said abruptly, wondering whether there was something she might have done to spur Miss Musgrove to such unkindness. "My sister will be wondering what has become of me. Pray excuse me, Miss Musgrove. Goodbye for now, Isobelle. And thank you."

In fact, as Charity had known, Rebecca showed no concern over the length of time her sister had been absent. She did, however, have another subject that she wanted to raise with Charity. The conversation came up as they were sitting together, Rebecca with her sewing and Charity reading a book in the window seat. It was companionable being in the same room, even when the girls were not chatting to each other. But as Charity finished her chapter and put the book down with a sigh, Rebecca looked up at her suddenly.

"Charity…" She sounded shy, and Charity looked at her with surprise.

"Yes?"

"Miss Greenaway…she calls you Harry."

"I'd noticed."

"But don't you mind?"

"Mind what?" Charity leaned back against the deep window seat and eyed her sister quizzically.

"Well, it's a boy's name."

"And hasn't everyone always said I'm half a boy?" Charity asked. "The wrong half," she added, and a note of bitterness would creep into her voice, no matter how much she tried to conceal it.

"I've never said that." Rebecca walked over to her and put a hand on her arm. "My big little sister," she said, smiling. Her conversation turned back to Isobelle. "You like her a lot, don't you?"

"Yes. Yes, I do." Charity put her own hand over Rebecca's. "So no, I don't mind if she calls me Harry. Are your fears quenched, my dear?"

Rebecca nodded. "You didn't mind my asking?"

"Not at all."

But Charity's mind went back to this conversation later, when she was alone. Rebecca, of course, did not know about the relationship between Charity and Isobelle; it would certainly never have occurred to her. And although Charity did not consider herself a man, she always had had boyish tastes in so many ways. 'Harry' suited her far more than 'Charity' ever had, she thought. And the other ladies in the Sisterhood had followed Isobelle's lead: Charity was probably, she thought with amusement, called Harry more often than Charity these days.

She had never thought to find a home in London. She had not even realised who and what she was. But she was happy— happier than she had been in her life. Happy to be Harry, to be accepted for who and what she was. It had seemed, growing up, as if Rebecca had it all: the love of her parents (in as much as they were capable of such an emotion); a delight in the feminine pursuits which society considered suitable for a girl of the Bellinghams' class. But where had it got her, in the end? A circumscribed life, married to a man who was no gentleman—not because of his birth but his behaviour—and forced to pander to his every whim. No, Rebecca was not so lucky after all.

But I am, Charity thought, her happiness flowing through her veins, more intoxicating than champagne. *I have Isobelle, I have the Sisterhood. However did it come to this?*

However had it come to this?

CHAPTER SIXTEEN

To Charity's surprise, and not a little amusement, Lady Caroline had been speaking nothing but the truth when she said that the Ancient Greece discussion would be more heated and angry than the Abolitionist meeting. When Charity thought about it later, it seemed more obvious: of course, it was likely that only Abolitionists would attend the anti-slavery group, whereas it was quite possible to have a deep and abiding interest in antiquity and yet disagree profoundly with a fellow enthusiast. Charity had not been able to persuade Isobelle to come with her—"No, Harry, not even for you!"—but Emily and Jane had picked her up in Emily's carriage.

Emily herself made a strong, stirring speech at the event, criticising Lord Elgin for the removal of marbles from Greece as vehemently as if he had stolen the crown jewels of England. Charity thought of the quiet, timid girl she had seen, first at Isobelle's party, and then at a couple of balls, and was privately amused by the difference. Here, at last, Emily was in her true element. Her opinions, to be sure, were shouted down by a number of other people, but Emily seemed little concerned by this. On the journey home, she explained calmly that her father had always made it quite clear that opinions might vary, and that the important thing was to state one's own point of view as specifically and with as little unnecessary emotion as possible. Charity had originally considered that Emily's speech had been extremely emotive, but when she thought it over later, she realised that Emily had backed up each of her arguments with clear, precise facts. The emotion was in the power she gave to the words, not in the words themselves.

Charity herself was beginning to feel more at home in London than she had done throughout the whole of her first Season. Partly, she knew, this was because she was more used to the city life. It was partly, too, the absence of her mother, who had always been capable of throwing a dampener onto anything that Charity did, but mostly it was because of the Sisterhood's wholehearted adoption of her. For the first time in her life, she had friends who cared for and supported her. With Rebecca at home, and her friends around her, Charity was happy.

Fotheringay and she had held an uneasy truce since the day he had assaulted her. He was clearly uncomfortable in Charity's company, and she made no effort to change this. She knew perfectly well that if it hadn't been for her well-to-do circle of friendships, he would not have thought twice about forcing her to do whatever he wished. She was concerned for her sister's well-being, but Rebecca was beginning to regain the bloom she had lost in the early days of her marriage. Her gentle, agreeable nature almost disarmed Fotheringay, Charity suspected. Whilst he had presumably married her in the idea of having an obedient young woman to fill his needs, Rebecca's willingness and lack of complaint about anything he said or did was quite probably beyond anything he had hoped for. Charity had forced herself to check with Rebecca that all was well, but her older sister had reassured her that she was content with her lot. She offered little information to her husband about her doings, and it seemed that he was prepared to allow her a surprisingly high degree of freedom provided that it did not inconvenience him in any way. It was not the lifestyle that Charity would have wished for herself, and she suspected it could hardly be what Rebecca had wanted, but they all—as Fotheringay himself might have described it—"rubbed along together rightly enough".

The meetings of the Sisterhood did not all take place in Isobelle's drawing room, either, to Charity's great delight. Though she loved Isobelle's beautiful home, it was a thrill to see new places and discover new things. Therefore, in mid-February, she received an invitation to visit a large house on the outskirts of London with her Sisters. The owner was a friend of Lady Caroline Farrell's. He was currently away, travelling abroad, but he had given Cara explicit permission to show guests around whenever she so pleased. The weather, which had been rainy for some days, had obligingly cleared up just in time for the picnic, and Isobelle had arranged to pick Charity up in the morning.

Charity discovered, to her surprise, that when Isobelle had promised to pick up her, she literally meant that she would do so. Awaiting the carriage, she was disconcerted when she went outside to see a small vehicle approaching. Waiting for it to go past, she realised as it stopped that the driver was Isobelle herself, in the phaeton she had once told Charity about. There was a groom up behind, who leapt down and held the horses as Isobelle went to greet Charity.

After the hellos, Isobelle said proudly,

"There, Harry! Isn't she a beauty? I know it isn't really the right time of year for this, but I could not resist a moment longer."

"She's amazing," Charity agreed, awestruck. The phaeton was picked out in light blue designs, the colour of the sky on the morning of a warm day. It hung beautifully and seemed to be perfectly weighted. The horses drawing it were as close to identical as two animals might possibly be, and Charity acknowledged to herself that their markings did indeed work exceptionally well with the colour of the phaeton. "Isobelle, you can truly drive this?"

"Oh ye of little faith," Isobelle mocked, leaping lightly back in and scorning the hand of her groom. "Of course I can, can't I, Jem?"

"When you concentrate, Miss," the groom said cautiously.

"Which I always do," she tossed back at him.

"Which you usually does, Miss," he replied. "Can I let 'em go now?"

"Just let Miss Bellingham in." Isobelle reached down to Charity. "Jump up, Harry." Obediently, Charity settled herself beside Isobelle, who took up the reins in confident fashion. "I wasn't sure until this morning whether the weather would be fine enough to allow me to bring the phaeton," Isobelle confided. "We will be in dreadful trouble should it start to rain, because I fear there is no cover at all."

"Never mind. We won't die from a little wet," Charity said practically.

"No, but it would be rather uncomfortable. However, Victor—the coachman, you know—says that he believes it's set to stay fair all day, and he is usually right about such things. And I wanted to show you my phaeton, so I simply leapt at the opportunity! Plus," she added happily, "it is so very much quicker and lighter than trundling in the big carriage, as well as being ten times more elegant."

"It's certainly beautiful. Oh Isobelle!" Charity cried in alarm as Isobelle narrowly missed running over a stray dog that had darted out into the road.

"You concentrate, Miss," came the voice of Jem from behind them.

"Yes sir," Isobelle said. "Now really, how can I be expected to predict the every movement of a horrid little mongrel? Don't worry, Harry. I won't spill you."

Isobelle was true to her word, but in truth Charity found it a somewhat alarming journey. Isobelle's hands were light on the reins and the horses were obedient; everything was perfect so long as Isobelle didn't spot something she was interested in, or turn her head to speak to Charity, forgetting to check the road ahead. However, they reached the house with no mishaps, and Isobelle left the vehicle in the capable hands of Jem as they went to greet Lady Caroline, who with Nan Musgrove and the 'lovebirds' Emily and Jane, had already arrived and were standing on the terrace.

"Drove, did you?" Cara asked, looking at Isobelle's driving dress with interest. "You're lucky you had a nice day for it."

"Of course it is a good day! It wouldn't dare do anything so cruel as to rain when I wanted to drive," Isobelle said.

During the next hour, various others of the Sisterhood arrived, until there was a merry group of revellers. Emily and Jane, as usual, tended to go off together by themselves to explore certain rooms (the library, for instance) in more depth, but the rest of the Sisterhood mixed merrily—with the exception of Charity and Nan Musgrove. Charity avoided Miss Musgrove whenever possible, though she found herself watching the lady from afar, trying to make sense of her character. But she had thought her dislike of Nan was subtle enough not to cause comment until now.

Isobelle, touching her arm lightly, said seriously,

"Now Harry…" Her face was as stern as her voice.

"Yes?" Charity tried to think of anything she might have done wrong. She could think of nothing, but that only made her more anxious. What on earth had she managed to do accidentally?

"I need to talk to you about something."

"Very well."

"Stop looking at me like that," Isobelle chided. "I'm not going to eat you, silly child. I just want to know what it is that you have against Nan. Of all the inoffensive people I know, Nan must top the list!"

"Really?" Charity was uncommunicative. To explain her reason for disliking Nan Musgrove felt like telling tales, but she hated to think that Isobelle thought badly of her.

"Really." Isobelle put her hand over Charity's. "You might as well tell me now, you know," she said gently. "I'm determined to find out."

"It's nothing. Nothing much."

"Even better," Isobelle said briskly. "If it isn't anything much, it is easily dealt with. What did she do, stand on your best dress at a dance and rip it? A sin indeed, but like the dress, easily mended."

"Of course not." Charity hesitated. Isobelle looked determined, and it was hard to resist explaining. Yet at the same time, she felt a sort of shame: she was embarrassed about having trusted the wrong person, and she couldn't help wondering whether it was something about herself which had caused the problem. If everyone else thought Miss Musgrove was so wonderful and yet Nan had been so unkind to Charity, perhaps Charity was the problem and not Nan Musgrove. She sighed. "It's silly. I told her something, something a little bit private, and I thought she'd keep it to herself—"

"You're not telling me she told someone else your secret?" Isobelle interrupted.

"It wasn't a secret. It's just…I hadn't expected her to laugh about it behind my back. Like I said," Charity added hastily, "I know it's silly. It's nothing important. I didn't ask her never to tell, after all. But…" She trailed off.

"Nan did that?" Isobelle opened her eyes to their widest extent. "You're sure?"

Charity bit her lip. She was sick of hearing what a paragon of virtue Miss Musgrove was. She remembered the way she'd felt, hearing the other girls giggle about her. She couldn't blame everyone else for trusting Nan—Charity had done so herself, after all. She had been honest about herself, for the first time since coming to London, and this was how Miss Musgrove had repaid that trust.

"I'm sure," she said curtly. "I heard the girls laughing about what Miss Musgrove had said, how I'd answered. I just…oh, I don't know, maybe she's different with you. I've seen how kind she is to people usually. But not with me. Perhaps it was something I did, I don't know. But I'm certain enough of the truth."

"It does sound very unlike Nan," Isobelle said. "I'll ask her, see what she says."

"You can't!" Charity put out her hand, as if physically to stop Isobelle, but her friend was taking no notice.

"Nan!" she called across the room, to where Nan Musgrove and Louisa Garland were chatting animatedly about the family portraits hanging on the wall in front of them.

Miss Musgrove turned and smiled at her. She was wearing a green dress, an elegant shawl flung over her shoulders. She looked, Charity thought with vague annoyance, rather pretty. Charity had never considered her in that fashion before, but then of course even the greatest beauties faded to nothing beside Isobelle in Charity's mind. Nan Musgrove, though, was always so…so interested, so involved in what she was doing. She treated everything and everyone with an eager fascination that lit up her features. Bother her!

"How can I help you, Isobelle?"

"Oh, it isn't I who needs you. Can you come here a second?"

"Isobelle please," whispered Charity. "Don't. I trusted you. Please, not again."

Isobelle patted her hand gently. "But I am showing why I am worthy of that trust. I will not laugh at you, and I won't allow Nan to do so. Have faith, my dear." Nan had reached them now, her blue eyes inquiring. Isobelle kept hold of Charity's hand, preventing her from sliding away without making a scene. "Nan, I gather you met Harry before she came here?"

"I did indeed." Nan looked straight at Charity. "At the Carrington's ball, wasn't it? You weren't dancing."

"No," Charity said, in a small tight voice. "I wasn't."

"I've often thought about that conversation. It had never occurred to me that height could be such an impediment until you mentioned it." Miss Musgrove smiled. "Well, it was never a problem I would suffer from."

Charity didn't—couldn't—answer. Hearing Nan Musgrove speak so lightly of something that had hurt her so much made her insides turn over.

"But Nan," Isobelle said guilelessly, "why did you mention it to anyone else? You must have known what some of the debutantes are like. Gossip is their middle name."

Her friend frowned. Charity noticed that Lady Caroline had shushed Lydia Seacombe and was listening unashamedly. "I didn't. It was none of their business." She put her hands on her hips and glared at Isobelle. "You're forever scolding me for my lack of interest in gossip, Isobelle. As you know well, if I'd intended to mention the conversation to anyone, it would have been the Sisterhood. But I'm not one for talking over this or that event. It's no one else's business."

"But…" Charity began.

Miss Musgrove turned to face her. "But what?" she asked. "I saw you again, of course, at the picnic, but you were…busy, as I recall."

Charity blushed. She knew she had been rude that day. It had seemed reasonable at the time, knowing what she'd thought she knew about Nan's behaviour. But if Miss Musgrove hadn't talked… Oh, Charity thought, helplessly, what had she done? What had she said? But it must have been Nan. It must have been.

"The other girls knew," she said.

Nan's gaze was steady. She looked almost hurt. "Not from me."

"She wouldn't, you know," Isobelle said.

"How did they know, then?" demanded Charity. Miss Musgrove's sincerity seemed so genuine and her expression so hurt that it was difficult to doubt her. But *someone* had told.

Nan smiled wryly. "You are rarely more than a few inches from another person at such crushes. It was perhaps foolish of me to speak so openly to you, leading you into saying more than was safe. I'm sorry for that. But I told no one, and I would not laugh at you for worlds."

"I see." Charity felt confused by the mix of emotions. "I'm sorry. I'm so very sorry."

"It was an understandable mistake," said Nan, though Charity thought she still sounded upset, however much she tried to hide it. They both glanced at Isobelle, who was about to speak. Miss Musgrove got in first however. "No, Isobelle, don't say it."

"What mustn't she say?" Charity asked, her guilty mind suggesting that Isobelle might turn on her, unforgiving, for misjudging Miss Musgrove so badly. Had she not only hurt Nan's feelings, for it was clear that this was so, by misinterpreting her actions, but also lost Isobelle's esteem as well? She did not think she could bear that burden.

"I have," Nan Musgrove said, "a great suspicion that she wishes to say 'I told you so'. Am I right?"

Isobelle blushed prettily. "Would I say a thing like that?"

"Quite definitely," said Nan drily. She turned back to Charity, who felt almost faint with shame. "I'm sorry," she said, looking at the other girl with frank, sympathetic eyes. "They teased you, did they not? I know how the debutantes can be when they sense a weakness. Like a pack of wild hyenas."

Isobelle laughed, and even Charity managed a smile at this improbable simile.

"Oh Nan!" Isobelle exclaimed. "Hyenas? Really? In *those* dresses?"

Nan gurgled with laughter herself. "Well, perhaps not. But you know what I mean. They can be cruel, and they hunt in groups. If I had not been out of town that while, I might have been able to prevent it, but I honestly had no idea of what had occurred."

"So," Isobelle began briskly, "is that settled? No more awkwardness between you two?"

"Not from my side," said Nan.

Charity felt guilty. She felt that she should apologise again, but her throat seemed all stuck up as if she had swallowed glue. She nodded and cleared her throat. "Nor mine," she said.

"But I must speak to Emily," Nan said. "Excuse me."

Charity knew it was an excuse, but she was grateful for Nan's tact. She could not have said another word to the lady if she'd tried. Isobelle, far from saying 'I told you so', touched Charity's arm lightly.

"All right?" she asked gently.

Charity nodded. "I feel silly. And guilty."

"Don't." Isobelle's hand stroked her arm, soothingly. "Nan won't mind. She understands."

"She might not mind, but I do." Charity once more looked across to where Nan was determinedly engaging Emily Summercourt in conversation, loudly enough to make it quite certain that she could not hear the conversation between Charity and Isobelle. "I should at least have asked her."

"You should indeed," Isobelle said with false severity. "And next time, dear Harry, trust your Isobelle when she tells you something. Do you promise?"

"I promise."

"I am very wise, you know," Isobelle said laughingly. "And pretty. Do you not think I'm also pretty?"

"I think you are the most beautiful person I've ever met," Charity said.

She knew by now that Isobelle lived for praise, soaking it up like a cat soaked up the sun. But Charity didn't speak the words because of that: to Charity, flowery compliments did not come easily. It was simply that Isobelle truly was the most beautiful lady she had ever seen. She saw Isobelle's face flush with pink at her words. Her cheeks gained a blush the same colour as the roses pinned to the dress she was wearing. Charity's heart caught a little. Isobelle was irresistible at moments like this.

"You mustn't flatter me," Isobelle scolded, meaning, as Charity well knew, nothing of the sort. She caught up Charity's hand and pressed a kiss to the inside of her wrist. Her dress rustled as she moved, as if it were whispering to Charity.

"I don't." Charity looked straight at Isobelle, a startling realisation rushing over her. How long had she been in love with the other lady? Now the thought had crossed her mind, she knew that this was no new feeling. But then, how could anyone do anything but love Isobelle? "You know I don't flatter. I would not know how."

Isobelle laughed at this. "Oh, Harry, you are so sweet, and so funny. I never met a girl like you before."

"Nor I one like you." Charity drew her hand back gently. "But most people use the word 'strange' when speaking of me."

"It is easy to hate what one doesn't understand."

Sometimes Isobelle's statements shocked Charity with their clarity. It was all too easy to think of Isobelle as a frivolous young lady, caring only for clothes and attention. But there was more to her than that, Charity thought, the warmth of her love spreading through her. She was so much more than merely a pretty face. Perhaps knowing that her interest was in other ladies, rather than gentlemen, had led Isobelle to think more seriously than otherwise might have been the case. Certainly that sentence might apply in more than one way—both to Charity herself, and to Isobelle.

"Is it? I tend just to feel ignorant."

Isobelle giggled again, tucking her arm through Charity's. "Well, never mind all this nonsense! We have grounds and gardens to explore. Let us do so right this very moment!"

CHAPTER SEVENTEEN

A week after the visit to the large house, Charity—misgivings notwithstanding—went to call on Miss Musgrove. Isobelle had willingly given her the address, but as Charity stood nervously on the doorstep, waiting as her name was sent up, she was not at all sure that she would not be turned away. And she could not blame Nan if such was the outcome. But it was not, she was glad to discover. Indeed, anything but. Miss Musgrove herself came down with the footman to the door, smiling a welcome.

"Harry!" she exclaimed and then hesitated. "I may call you that, now, may I not?"

"Of course," Charity said quickly.

Nan smiled. "I'm glad. It suits you. Come in. My parents are otherwise engaged at the moment, so I was feeling very dull until you appeared."

Charity stepped into the house. It was smaller than Isobelle's, though not by a great deal, and was very different in style. The Greenaways' house was light and airy, full of white and open spaces. The Musgroves' house, in comparison, was cluttered. An old oak table, polished to a fine sheen, stood in the hallway, with a number of curios atop it. There was a grandfather clock in the corner, ticking steadily; and the walls were covered in hangings. Charity did not need to be an expert to know that many of them were precious, perhaps centuries old, and well looked after. Nan Musgrove took her down a little corridor to a room that opened onto a small courtyard garden.

"I know this isn't a very big space," she said apologetically, "but I do like the view. We get sparrows and other birds down here. See the bushes around the sides and the little bird bath at the back? It's such a comforting room. It used to be my brother's and my play room when we were children."

"You have a brother?" Charity realised that she did not know even the simplest details about Nan.

"Yes." Miss Musgrove smiled suddenly, as if the thought of him made her happy. "He is a couple of years older than I, but we have always been the best of friends. He is a sailor, you know. I saw you looking at some of the ornaments in the hall. He brings us home the oddest objects from his voyages."

"It sounds fascinating."

"He is in the navy," Nan explained.

"Oh." Charity paused. "Then…he was involved at Trafalgar?"

"He was," Miss Musgrove said, absent-mindedly twitching the curtains to their furthest extent, so that the view out of the large picture windows was at its clearest. "But not in the main action. He had been injured a few months beforehand. It was the reason that I was out of town, in fact, last Season," she added. "We all went to the country, when my brother was well enough to be moved, to help with his recuperation. He was sorry to take me away from London during the Season, but I much preferred to be with him. He is so often away, you know."

"Yes. I never had a brother," Charity said thoughtfully. "It must be strange."

"Oh, everything is strange if one has not experienced it oneself, I think. I myself have not a sister. At least, not in the usual sense! Isobelle, of course, has no siblings at all, though there was a boy once, who died before she was born."

"You seem to know about everything." It felt odd to Charity to have a comparative stranger tell her things about Isobelle she did not already know. Of course, Nan must have known her for far longer than Charity had, but somehow, Charity was in the way of thinking of Isobelle as somehow hers. It jarred that she had not known about her dead brother. "You know so much about slavery, as well."

"Oh, well, that is through my brother too, you know," Nan said. "In his time in the Atlantic, he and his crew boarded many a slave ship, and what he saw doesn't bear thinking about. It seems too terrible that such things should happen in our world. I want so much to make things better, but it is difficult."

"Yes, I see you do. Nan, I'm sorry." Somehow, it was easy to refer to the lady in front of her as Nan now, when previously it had seemed so hard.

"I beg your pardon?" Nan looked up, as if checking that Charity had not suddenly lost her mind.

"For misjudging you. I've felt terrible about it since I discovered, but didn't know how to say it."

"Oh." Nan was silent for a moment. "Oh dear," she said at last, smiling but blushing. "Must I confess?"

"Confess what?" Whatever path Charity had anticipated this conversation taking, this was not it. "I don't understand."

"If you must know, you were perhaps not the only person to misjudge another." Charity raised her eyebrows. "When you snubbed me...I was hurt, of course. But shortly afterwards, I thought I had found out the reason why. The news of your sister's betrothal was the talk of the *ton*, you know."

"I still don't...Oh."

"'My sister requires my attention'," Miss Musgrove said reminiscently. "And shortly afterwards, that same sister's betrothal was announced...to a rich man."

"And you thought I only cared about money. Oh, Nan!"

"Whereas you thought I was cruelly laughing at you behind your back," Nan threw at her teasingly. "Shall we acknowledge that we were both unfairly prejudiced and move on?"

"I..." Charity stopped and shook her head, amused. "Well, they say that confession is good for the soul," she said. "We must both have spotless spirits after this moment."

Miss Musgrove laughed. "Trust you to come to that conclusion, Harry. Spotless spirits or none, I'm glad we've talked about it and got everything out in the open. It's so much more comfortable that way, do you not think?"

"I hadn't thought of it that way, but yes, of course it will be. I like your way of looking at things."

"I think we in the Sisterhood," Nan began thoughtfully, "tend to be a bit inclined that way. Having hidden a part of ourselves, sometimes for years, now that we have the freedom to be who we truly are in one sense, there's an inclination towards honesty in all things, at least to our Sisters. Or that's how I feel, anyway."

"That does make sense. Goodness, if you knew how scared I was of you to begin with. Lady Caroline in particular."

"Cara?" Nan said. "Oh, she's just a pussycat. You surely know that by now. Gruff on the outside, but soft inside."

"I know someone else a little like that." Charity propped her head on her hands and looked thoughtfully at Nan.

"Me?" Nan asked in some surprise. She laughed. "No, I'm more of a dog. Running eagerly around, wanting to help and only succeeding in bringing back the stick that her owner had wanted to throw away!"

Charity giggled. "What an image! So what animal would you compare me to?"

"Hmm." Nan looked at her consideringly. "Are you sure you really want me to answer that? After all the misunderstandings we've had in the past, I'm loath to risk another."

"Why? Is the creature which came to mind so terribly fearsome?" Charity asked. "It's no use, Nan. Having gone so far, you will have to continue, or I'll believe forever that you wished to compare me to a cockroach!"

"That was not the animal I had in mind," Nan assured her seriously. "No, really, I just don't want to say the wrong thing, and it is so easy to get offended, even if a statement is not meant that way."

"Stop, stop!" cried Charity. "An easily offended cockroach!"

"Well, I shall stop digging myself into an ever deeper hole. You were, perhaps, prickly to start with, but I don't see you as a hedgehog either! No. I wonder if I can explain…" She was looking Charity up and down, as if sizing her up—not just considering her length, but the quality of what was inside her as well. "There is something…When I first saw you, last season, you seemed…how can I say it? As if you were in a cage. A polite, velvet, smart cage, but one you hated. Somewhere you could not feel at home. Now, seeing you with the Sisterhood, it is as if you have been freed. A wild bird, caught and kept in a cage for others' amusement, now flying again. Or perhaps learning to fly for the first time."

"Oh." Charity looked at Nan with startled eyes. "That's beautiful. Poetic."

"Poetic nonsense." Nan blushed a little.

"Of course, you probably mean a goose," Charity added, trying to lighten the atmosphere, and succeeding as she saw Nan grin. "But still, you have something there. I think of late, this is the first time I have felt I have belonged anywhere. And whilst we were still at odds—all right, I will not speak of that any more," she promised hastily, seeing Nan open her mouth to protest. "But it made it harder to feel at home. Now…Well, now it is all different. I feel as if I have found a friend. At least, I hope so?" she finished, an inquiring note in her voice.

"A friend in me? Of course," Nan said, too heartily to be doubted.

And so the friendship was cemented.

CHAPTER EIGHTEEN

Even though she had said that she felt like she belonged, it took time for Charity really to get used to being part of the Sisterhood, with all the benefits and challenges it involved. After making up the quarrel with Nan Musgrove, she was now spending time with the lady and liking her even more than she had on that first occasion. She was as familiar to Nan's parents as she was to Lady Greenaway, having visited so often. Sometimes Charity mourned for all time she had lost with her mistrust of Nan, but she was so happy in other ways that she could not be too regretful.

The moment she realised that she was completely comfortable with the Sisterhood was when she noticed that she could start a conversation with Lady Caroline without thinking twice about the differences in their age and status. It seemed a peculiar way to discover you were at home, but then, Charity thought idly, they were a peculiar bunch of ladies, all in all. She mentioned this to Cara, tentatively.

"I was just thinking," she said, "about how different we all are, in our situations and selves and…well, everything."

"Most people are," Cara said.

"Yes, of course. It was silly of me to be so surprised, but…So many different ladies, so many backgrounds, and yet we are all invisible, secret, unable to be whom we truly are."

"I think you'll find many ladies, even within the normal ones, who feel the same way. But I know what you mean. It is not a total secret, our type of deviancy. There have always been ladies who have either been public about their love for one another, or who have been found out. Common understanding is that such ladies attract each other because they are incapable of attracting a man. But that's clearly not so. You see Lydia and Charlotte Wentworth with their husbands. Then there is Isobelle, who has had more offers of marriage than the rest of us added together, no doubt. And even I…"

"Yes?"

"Well, I was engaged once," Lady Caroline said. "Nice feller. Loved him like a brother."

"But you never married?" Charity asked, with interest.

"He died. Horse-riding accident. A few too many brandies, and"—Lady Caroline made a wide gesture with one arm—"*whoomph*. They said it was immediate. Not sure how true that was. I cried for days. Often wonder how life might have been."

"I'm sorry." Charity leaned towards her. "That must have been…I don't have the words."

Lady Caroline lifted one of Charity's hands to her lips and kissed it. The gesture was quite matter-of-fact—unemotional, even. "Bless you, child. No need to fret on my behalf. It didn't turn me to women, y'know." She smiled. "Knew at the time it wasn't love, but then marriage ain't supposed to be. I liked him well enough. Sad to see him die. But I don't know whether to be amused or sad when people presume—for they do, you know— that I never married for the sake of Duncan. As I say, nice man. But he never interested me *that* way."

Charity could feel herself blushing and was irritated by her own body's betrayal. "I didn't…"

Lady Caroline looked at her thoughtfully. "You knew about yourself, didn't you?"

"I…"

Lady Caroline gave her characteristic nod. "That it ain't men. Fact. You know it."

Charity thought of all the gentlemen she had met. There had been not one tenth of the emotion, the attraction, she felt for Isobelle.

"I suppose that's true," she acknowledged. "I didn't always, though. I suppose I just thought…that I wasn't old enough to feel the emotion, or hadn't met the right gentleman. That there was a reason which I hadn't quite discovered yet."

"Nothing to be ashamed of," Lady Caroline said briskly. "Not here, at any rate. Neither in loving ladies nor in taking your time to realise it is so." She smiled at Charity. "Still, young Harry, I believe you are beginning to feel at home in our company, are you not? Not just when we are discussing matters you know about, or wish to know about. But in general. Perhaps you wondered why we felt the need to have these meetings. Like Emily, who finds it hard to grasp the concept of a meeting without a point at stake, without a purpose. Bless her," she added tolerantly. "But you're beginning to understand, I think."

"I think so too. Just to be somewhere…" Charity grasped for words, "where we can be all of ourselves. No one expects Emily to partake in gossip, nor Mrs S—Lydia—to care about the Ancient Greeks. They do not have to pretend."

"Not on any level. Quite right." Cara nodded. "If Jane wants to hold Emmy's hand as they talk about Plato; if Lydia wants to give out kisses to any lady who welcomes them; if I want to look appreciatively at you young, attractive girls…why, we may do so. We ain't together to talk about the love of women for women, not unless we want to. We come that we might be whoever we please, and say whatever we please, with neither fear nor favour."

Charity smiled. "Yes, that."

"So you'll forgive me if I say what I think, I take it?"

"Of course," Charity said, much surprised that Lady Caroline might even consider her feelings before speaking.

"Can't help noticing, you see," Cara said. "The way you look at her, it's clear."

"At whom?" Charity said, but the words were hollow. She knew what Cara meant, even if she pretended for the moment that she didn't.

Lady Caroline looked across the room, to where Isobelle was sipping her tea and chatting eagerly to a group of other ladies.

"You're in love with Isobelle." Lady Caroline gave a sharp, decisive nod. "Not a surprise, really. Wouldn't usually mention it. After all, think all of us are, to some extent. Not counting Emmy and Jane, of course, but they're a class apart. But the rest of us, just like all the gentlemen who ask for her hand in marriage. We're no better. We all look at her a little like that. Apart from Nan, perhaps. Good girl, Nan."

Charity looked up, and her eyes met Nan's across the room. She could tell from Nan's ironically amused expression that Lady Caroline's words had carried. Charity bit back a grin as she turned back to Lady Caroline.

"Yes, I suppose I am." She was still unused to being able to speak about these things. She thought of her childhood pining over a pretty dark-haired girl she had passed occasionally in the village street. If anyone had asked her, Charity would have said that she wanted to *be* that girl—Emma, her name had been, she recalled. Emma Ponsonby. But in fact, she had wanted more desperately to be the boy her parents never ceased to remind her she was not. She felt like a boy. She had thought that maybe, had she been like Emma—like Rebecca—her parents would have forgiven her the sin of being born female. Instead, she was born a boy in a girl's body, and the body was the only part that mattered. Her feelings towards Emma, however unwittingly, had been of a very different ilk.

Lady Caroline threw a faggot on the fire. "Never get a chance to do this at home. The servants do it before I get a moment to myself. Always liked tending a fire. M'father and I used to light the big bonfire in November, outside. The smell of wood smoke, and the feeling of dead wood against my palm takes me back there, even now." She picked up the poker and prodded it experimentally into the flames several times. "There. That's better. But yes, about Isobelle. Wonderful lady, but be cautious, Harry. No one will ever pin her down, not even you."

"I don't want…" Charity caught herself up. Why not admit it? She wanted Isobelle to herself; wanted Isobelle to lie in her arms and think of no one else. Wanted to touch Isobelle's beautiful, creamy skin.

Lady Caroline glanced at her. "No, you couldn't finish that sentence, could you?" she asked gruffly. "Never mind. We won't speak of it any more. Go and chat to Nan. Now *there's* a forever girl, if you want one."

But Charity didn't want a forever girl just for the sake of having one. She wanted Isobelle. Still, there was no point in saying that to Lady Caroline, so instead she got up obediently and walked over to Nan, hoping that the other lady hadn't heard Lady Caroline's final words. Nan looked busy over her crochet, but then Nan never did give very much away. She glanced up as Charity came near.

"Oh, good. Now, do you think I should complete the next square in red, or choose a darker colour?"

It was the sort of question that Charity had never been able to answer sensibly. Crochet, like most handicrafts, was a sealed book to her. But she suspected Nan didn't really want a response, at least not about that. It was a kindness, a chance for Charity to recover her senses. It was one thing to adore Isobelle—another to have it noticed and commented on, even in the calm, practical tones of Lady Caroline. Cara was right, of course: it was foolish—more than foolish, it was arrogant—to hope to keep Isobelle to herself. She was no Emily, and Isobelle was certainly no Jane. Keepsake necklaces and commitments of love were not Charity's lot. She looked once more, wistfully, at Isobelle, and reminded herself to be grateful for what she did have: Isobelle's friendship, entry into this wonderful world of the Sisterhood, with the privileges in terms of invitations and status allotted to those who counted themselves in its number. She had never anticipated even feeling at home in London, let alone a welcomed visitor at some of the best known events and occasions. She would be, if it killed her, grateful.

"Oh, red," she said randomly, hardly knowing what she replied.

It was funny, then, that soon after this conversation Lady Caroline was proved wrong. Charity and Isobelle were sitting together on the sofa in Isobelle's little white sitting room, and Isobelle had her head on Charity's shoulder when she spoke.

"Have you ever been with a woman?" she asked delicately.

Charity shook her head, knowing what Isobelle meant. "No."

She felt suddenly shy—uncomfortable, almost, as if the sofa had lost its cushion. Isobelle seemed to divine this.

"It is all right, Harry. It's easy. There's nothing difficult about it."

Nothing difficult, except that Charity was sitting next to her idol. Nothing difficult, except the fact that even breathing seemed to be difficult with Isobelle's hand on Charity's leg, Isobelle's mouth just centimetres from her own. Charity reached out a tentative hand and stroked Isobelle's hair. Her fingers felt clumsy and sausage-like, her movements jerky and uncoordinated. It was silly: she had touched Isobelle like this many times, yet somehow the promise of intimacy Isobelle had made turned the same gesture laden with importance. Isobelle leant in and kissed her lightly on the lips.

"Don't be afraid, Harry."

"I'm afraid I'll disappoint you." Charity looked away, too embarrassed to meet Isobelle's eyes.

"You won't," Isobelle promised. "Come into my bedchamber. We can be private there. No servants enter unless I give explicit permission. It is understood."

Obediently, Charity stood up, reaching out a hand to assist her more feminine friend to her feet. Isobelle's hand lingered in hers for a few seconds before she withdrew it.

"After you, Harry," she said.

"No, after you," Charity said firmly. It was Isobelle's right to go first and Charity's job to hold the door open for her, as a gentleman might do.

"Very well," said Isobelle, looking up at Charity knowingly. She led Charity through the door into the beautiful bedroom beyond, and when they were, indeed, private—and Isobelle had locked both doors—Isobelle looked over at Charity and smiled.

"Now, it is not too bad here, is it?"

"No." Charity's words were as awkward as her movements had been. She could not think of anything to say.

The feeling continued as Isobelle slowly but deliberately began to undress, each motion drawn out. There was a half-smile on her face as she did so; she was watching Charity closely, noting every emotion that played out across the other girl's face. Charity knew it, and was made embarrassed by it, but she could not remove her eyes from Isobelle.

"Won't you help me with the fastenings?" Isobelle asked demurely, smiling up at Charity.

"I...yes." Charity cursed her clumsy fingers as she fought the buttons and laces, but Isobelle seemed to notice nothing wrong.

"Thank you, Harry." Isobelle slid out of the dress, her gaze locked with Charity's. Charity's heart beat faster as she looked at Isobelle with awe. "Sit on the bed next to me, dear one," Isobelle invited, sitting down and casting a look up at Charity through lowered lashes.

She was beautiful—beautiful! With the dress discarded (neatly, for Isobelle was always neat; she made Charity ashamed of her own haphazard ways), sitting on the bed in her flowing petticoat, she took Charity's breath away. It was difficult, too, to believe that a goddess like Isobelle could possibly condescend to speak to Charity, let alone go further. Charity felt that far from being asked to sit beside her, Isobelle should have ordered Charity to kneel at her feet and worship.

She sat down at Isobelle's side, and Isobelle touched her hand to Charity's face, gently drawing her in for a kiss. Whereas before Isobelle's kisses had been gentle, almost platonic, this time the moment was lengthened, deepened, until Charity's head was spinning and her body was throbbing for more.

"You see?" Isobelle said. "Like so."

"Yes." Charity could say no more. She ached with desire, actually ached.

Isobelle's fingers lay on the fastenings of Charity's dress.

"May I?"

Charity nodded dumbly, and Isobelle undid fastening after fastening with the same deliberate slowness she had used on her own.

"Please," Charity begged.

In response, Isobelle leaned over and kissed the top of Charity's breast.

"There is no hurry."

But there was! Charity wanted… She did not quite know what she wanted, but she knew she needed it now. Finally, Isobelle slipped the dress down. They were just two girls sitting in their petticoats, Charity told herself fiercely. She had done this before, so many times, but it had not felt like this. She had not felt as if her bones were melting; had not had this curious desire to push a friend back so that they lay together, limbs entwined, across the bed's perfect white sheets. Gently, Isobelle helped her to her feet and divested her of her dress and petticoat almost together, tugging on the strings of Charity's corset so that she was left wearing the light shift alone.

"Oh, Harry. So tall. So handsome," Isobelle murmured.

Charity blushed. Could Isobelle really be using such words to describe her? Isobelle, so perfect in her beauty: curved, and soft, and white and inviting, where Charity herself was so angular and awkward.

"Don't tease me."

"I am not," Isobelle said, standing up and onto tiptoe to kiss Charity. "Do I seem as if I am teasing?"

"I don't…I'm not…You're so…" Charity stumbled through the beginning of sentences she could not finish.

Isobelle slid out of her petticoats and turned to allow Charity access to the stay laces.

"I'm so what?" she asked lightly. Then, gently, she said, "No, I promise I will not tease you, Harry."

If Charity's fingers had fumbled before, this time her hands shook too much to untie the knot. Isobelle laughed a little.

"I can't," Charity said in an agony of humiliation.

"Yes, you can. Just a little bit more, dearest," Isobelle encouraged.

Finally, she managed and saw Isobelle for the first time unfettered, dressed only in the light shift.

"Oh!" Charity was drawn by the need to touch, to hold, to taste. "May I?"

"I rather hoped you would," Isobelle murmured.

Charity, breath catching in her chest at her own daring, put her hands underneath Isobelle's large, full breasts, as if weighing them. They were heavy and firm and *wonderful*. If Isobelle had been beautiful while dressed, now she was exquisite. And somehow there was something just right about what was happening. Charity still shook a little with nerves, but touching Isobelle...it was as if she had been born to do so. Isobelle's smooth, warm skin felt perfect to her touch, and the look of blissful encouragement on Isobelle's face as Charity laid hands upon her took away the worst of Charity's fears.

"Let me take this ridiculous shift off." Isobelle shrugged her way out of the garment, and Charity could hardly bear to look. That she should see Isobelle, like that. "Now, dearest," Isobelle said, "where were we? I believe your hands were..." She took Charity's hands and placed them on her breasts, humming with pleasure at the touch.

"I want...I don't know."

"I will teach you, Harry. That's right, touch me there. Hold me close to you."

Isobelle guided Charity through each movement in turn, murmuring encouragement and sweet words. She reached behind herself to pull the pins from her hair, so that golden curls fell down around her shoulders.

"Now," she said at last, "let me touch you."

Isobelle slid Charity's shift up around her waist, slipping her hands underneath it and running her fingertips across Charity's belly. The fingers tickled and heated where they touched. There was warmth and wetness and throbbing between Charity's legs. She found it hard to lie still as Isobelle, having removed Charity's shift also, moved her hands from place to place, caressing the sharp shoulder bones, the small, high breasts, running down over the flat plains of Charity's stomach to the dark curls at the apex of her thighs. Then lower still, sliding between Charity's legs with a rubbing, repetitive motion that made Charity cry out.

"You like that?" Isobelle asked softly.

"Oh...oh, yes." Charity's arms, somehow, had found their way around Isobelle. She wanted to close her legs, too, trapping Isobelle's hand in that magical place. "Please," she begged, not knowing for what she asked.

"I will," Isobelle promised.

Her hands grew firmer, her movements stronger. Unexpectedly, Charity felt a finger dive inside her. She could not stop her hips from bucking up against Isobelle, who had somehow, with her other hand, found a magical place a little further forward that ached in a way almost too wonderful to bear. Charity's breath came out in little gasps, which grew faster and faster as Isobelle rubbed, until the whole world exploded around her. For several moments, she did not understand what had happened—then she was breathing more normally again, tears in her eyes, Isobelle smiling down at her.

"Didn't that feel good?" Charity's lover asked her.

Charity nodded dumbly, pulling Isobelle close down on top of her, tangling arms and legs around her as if she would never let go. She had no words; all she could do was try to show Isobelle how much she meant to her by gestures alone. She had known she wanted something from Isobelle. She had not realised it was this.

"Thank you," she whispered at last.

"My pleasure," Isobelle assured her, tossing dishevelled curls behind her shoulders.

It would not be the only time they spent making love. Charity learned ways to pleasure Isobelle, in turn. Indeed, they found new ways of pleasing each other, and Charity looked forward with almost painful desire to the moments they found to spend in bed. It could not be very often: Isobelle had so many engagements to attend, and even when she was at home, there were regular visitors—not to mention the fact that she spent a great deal of time with her mother.

There, too, Charity found something to cherish. The love between mother and daughter in the Greenaway household was like nothing she had ever experienced before. Lady Greenaway clearly thought her daughter the most wonderful being in the world—Charity wholeheartedly agreed—and Isobelle returned her affection with interest, always ready to give up plans at a minute's notice if her mother wanted her. Charity loved to watch the two of them together: their playful teasing, the physical displays of affection (gently given, for Lady Greenaway's rheumatism meant that she was often in a great deal of pain, though she rarely seemed to complain) and the whole feeling of joy that ran throughout the house. Visiting Isobelle, whether they made love or not, was always a wonderful experience.

This did not mean that Charity did nothing save spend time with Isobelle. There were various events to attend, both with the Sisterhood and with Rebecca. Isobelle's love of concerts meant that Charity had a chance to see good musicians perform without the guilt of having dragged her sister along to something that she was not very interested in. There were also the soirees and events run by friends of Fotheringay's, to which Rebecca must always go, and Charity must on occasion. She felt rather as if she had been invited by default, as it were, for her attendance often threw the numbers in a gathering right out. However, whether it was in politeness to Fotheringay or because they knew of Charity's links with the cream of the *ton* and hoped to gain favour themselves through her, she had at least one occasion in every week where she must dress up and do her best to make polite conversation with a group of people with whom she had precious little in common.

These events always made her think of Emily Summercourt: this, presumably, was how she felt most of the time in polite society, where people gossiped and flirted and spent so little time talking about the things which were important in Emily's world. The idea of comparing herself to Emily amused Charity enough that she got through the occasions with a good grace. She even heard Fotheringay say on one occasion to Rebecca (when he thought Charity was out of ear shot) that: "That sister of yours has improved in society of late. Noticed it meself, and Bulstead mentioned it the other day".

When it came to the time for the next Abolitionist meeting, Charity was appreciative to note that Cara had sent the invitation to Rebecca as well as Charity. It was good of her, Charity thought, to have remembered after all this time. Rebecca and she were sat in the drawing room, sorting through their invitations. Fotheringay had disclaimed all interest in any of them, and, aside from telling Rebecca of the engagements he expected her to fulfil with him or on his behalf, had left them to get on with it. Fotheringay had a deep lack of interest in feminine matters. It was perhaps why it had taken him so long to marry. Ladies, and the concerns of ladies, seemed so entirely irrelevant to a gentleman whose business interests, even now when he could easily afford to have little input, were his first concern. When not working, he preferred the company of other men—probably drinking, smoking and gambling, Charity thought disparagingly. Possibly he had a mistress or two to his name; however, he did not intrude them upon his wife's life, and Charity could only think that Rebecca would be grateful for the respite. With the knowledge which had come to her through her joy in her own physical relationship with Isobelle, she could see that although Rebecca (she was sure) performed all wifely duties without complaint, she had little interest in them. Charity shuddered. She could hardly blame her sister for that.

Rebecca was surprised by and not a little apprehensive about Lady Caroline's invitation. She was fearful both that she would be out of place and that she knew so little that she would be despised for it. Charity reassured her on both points, telling her that all sorts of people attended the meetings and that there was no need for her to say anything, so she could just sit and listen. Rebecca relaxed a little bit.

"You are sure?" she asked. "I confess, I would like to come."

"Would you?" Charity was much surprised. She had known that Rebecca would be willing to come as a chaperone, but had hardly anticipated her sister taking any pleasure in the occasion.

"I know so little about the matter," Rebecca explained, "and don't know where to start to learn more. So if you are certain Lady Caroline would not object..."

"Why, that is exactly how I felt myself!" exclaimed Charity. She gave a mocking grin. "Anyone would think we were related, Becca. But as far as attending, of course you must. Lady Caroline has explicitly asked you."

"Then I shall," Rebecca said with relief.

CHAPTER NINETEEN

By the time of the meeting itself, however, Rebecca's nerves had returned. Charity had watched her get visibly more nervous as the evening wore on, and by the time they entered Lady Caroline's house, she was literally shaking with fear.

"Are you sure I should be here?" she whispered anxiously to Charity.

"Certainly sure," Charity said, all the more robustly to cover her own agitation. She had only attended that one meeting herself, and in truth was also feeling a sense of alarm. She was determined not to let Rebecca see that, though, but her eyes were searching busily for Cara or at least *someone* she knew from the Sisterhood. "Oh, Nan!" she said thankfully, seeing a familiar plump figure.

There was no possibility that Nan could have heard her, but somehow she looked up at that moment, catching Charity's glance. She hurried over to the two girls.

"Oh, Harry, nice to see you. Is this your sister?" She turned interested eyes on Rebecca and gave her an encouraging smile.

"Yes. Rebecca, this is Miss Musgrove. Nan, my sister, Mrs Fotheringay."

Nan curtsied to Rebecca, who blushed a little as she returned the courtesy.

"I'm so pleased to meet you," Nan said cheerfully. "Harry has talked about you a lot."

"Thank you." Rebecca barely spoke above a whisper.

Nan, a practical person, saw her anxiety. "Can I find you a seat?" She looked around, assessing the room, and then moved purposefully towards a row of chairs set to one side of the room. "Here. You're a bit out of the way here, but you looked as if you might prefer that. Everyone attending is very nice, but in bulk perhaps a little alarming."

"Thanks Nan. It's good of you." Charity remembered how she had misjudged the other lady and felt guilty all over again. Nan was one of those rare people who really was as nice as she first seemed.

"Everyone is new sometimes," Nan said. "Goodness, I must go over and speak to Lady Caroline. It has been lovely to meet you, Mrs Fotheringay. You're very like your sister."

"Hardly," protested Charity with a laugh. "Nan, you're terrible. You've only just met her and already you are insulting her."

"Charity!" exclaimed Rebecca, mortified. "You mustn't say things like that!"

"Don't worry, Mrs Fotheringay, I know just how seriously to take her," Nan responded. "Pray excuse me." She bustled off.

"Charity, she's *nice*." There was a wondering tone in Rebecca's voice.

"Why, did you expect me to have dreadful friends?" Charity teased. "Is Isobelle so terrible?"

"No, of course not! But they're all so very much above us in society. I don't know why they should be so kind to us."

"I've noticed, of course," said Charity, still in a teasing mood, "how rude you are to those below you on the social scale, Becca."

But her mood sobered as the meeting drew close to opening. She remembered how she had felt after the last one—the mixed feelings of guilt, shock and thankfulness for her own lot in life.

"Will I like it?" Rebecca asked suddenly.

"No." Charity could not honestly say anything else. "No one could like hearing what we're going to hear, Becca. I believe many people do not come because they do not want to know, because it would hurt too much, because they would feel as if they ought to do something, and that would be uncomfortable."

"I see. I think. Sometimes it is better not to ask." Rebecca's face was clouded with her own thoughts.

"Better for oneself, anyway," Charity retorted.

"Indeed." Rebecca turned to her. "Charity, I—"

But whatever it was she had been about to say was cut off as the first speaker stood. It was not a poem on this occasion, but a short tale, written for children. Charity, glancing at her sister, saw that Rebecca was concentrating hard. But it was the second lady who drew a comment from Rebecca when she went to the front of the room.

"But she's…"

"Black," Charity finished for her sister, almost as surprised as Rebecca was. Although it was not uncommon to see Black or Mulatto people around the town, they were usually servants. But to have one standing up and talking… Charity looked around the room. All the ladies gathered there seemed to be of good birth and standing. Would they really listen to a servant? But then her eyes went back to the woman standing at the front, who was hardly dressed as a servant. Confused but fascinated, she waited.

"I am a woman," the lady announced. "I am one of you. Some of you may have met me in drawing rooms or at picnics, but many of you will not have done. Because, of course, I am not one of you. I am Black."

She paused. Charity, looking around the assembly, saw a number of different expressions on the faces of the listeners. The lady speaking was clearly well educated and spoke well, albeit with an accent which had marked differences to the one commonly heard in ballrooms and parlours. But her presence lent an air of discomfort to the room. It was all right, Charity could almost hear some of the ladies thinking, to support the end of slavery in some far-off place—but it was another thing entirely to speak on terms with a Black lady. What was Lady Caroline thinking of to invite her? But then, Charity thought, there were others like herself coming face-to-face with prejudices they had barely known they had. Her first thought on seeing this woman, whoever she was, had been to presume her a servant. Any lady whose skin was not that unusual colour would not have drawn that response from her, and certainly not one dressed in the warm, deep-red silks this lady was wearing.

"My name is Miss Leigh," the lady continued, having allowed them a moment to get over their shock. "I was no more born to slavery than any of you, but because of the colour of my skin I have a sense of kinship with those who were. London is my home, and my people are your people. Among you, I see friends of mine. But across the seas, I see people who might have been family of mine enslaved and treated as less than human. And I stand here today to say that *this is not right*."

She paused again, as applause broke out. Charity, starting to clap, realised that her sister had beaten her to it. As she looked around the meeting, however, she was entertained and a little ashamed to note how patchy the applause was. By no means was everyone reacting quite so positively to Miss Leigh. Glancing back at the speaker, she could see that the lady was aware of this herself; there was a glint, perhaps of amusement, in her eyes. She had in two short minutes taken out the hypocrisy of the gathered ladies and waved it in front of them. Not everyone, no matter their principles and feelings towards slavery, was quite ready to accept a Black lady as one of themselves. The rest of the speech passed in a bit of a blur, and Charity barely heard a word the third and final speaker said. A minute later, it seemed, Lady Caroline was bringing the meeting to a close.

Charity looked around, a thought which had been growing within her all through the comments of the final speaker crystallising in her mind. "I wonder if I might speak with Miss Leigh," she said. Part of her wondered whether she was foolish and, in fact, whether her suddenly felt desire would be welcomed by the lady in question. But having seen and heard not only Miss Leigh's comments, but the reaction of the meeting, Charity could not help but wish to say something to her.

Shy Rebecca recoiled at the thought of accosting a stranger. "Oh, goodness, Charity! Will she not be terribly busy with other people?"

"I'm not sure," Charity said slowly. "I fear she may not be, which is why I would like to speak to her. You must have noticed that not all those present welcomed her."

"No." Rebecca looked concerned. "That surprised me. I thought—the meeting being what it was—that the lady would be an honoured guest. I don't quite understand…"

"The difference between the theoretical and the actual," Charity said absently, still looking about the room. "There's Nan. She may be able to introduce me. Are you sure you will not come?"

"Quite sure, thank you," Rebecca said firmly. "I will wait here for you."

Charity nodded, and moved briskly across the room to speak to her friend. "Nan!"

Nan turned. "Charity. What did you think of the meeting?"

"I liked your second speaker greatly," Charity said. "I was wondering whether I might be introduced. Do you know her?"

"Miss Leigh?" Nan smiled. "I certainly do. She is a friend of my parents. Or a friendly acquaintance, at any rate. Come with me." She led Charity over to the other lady. "Miss Leigh, may I introduce my friend, Miss Charity Bellingham?"

"A pleasure to make your acquaintance," Miss Leigh said.

Charity felt suddenly shy, unsure what to say.

"Thank you for your speech," she said tentatively.

Logically, she knew that talking to Miss Leigh should be just like talking to anyone else, yet somehow the colour of Miss Leigh's skin *did* matter, making Charity feel self-conscious in a way she would not have done if she had been talking to a white-skinned lady. She could see in Miss Leigh's face that her new acquaintance was reading her thoughts accurately, which embarrassed her further. Nan had moved away, to speak to someone else, leaving Charity and Miss Leigh alone.

"It is good of you to speak to me," Miss Leigh said.

Charity frowned. "No, that it is not," she said, suddenly vehement. "Are we not both ladies, both people?"

Miss Leigh's eyes twinkled. "Now, that," she said, "is indeed the question. Many of the people in this room are not quite sure about the answer to that. Am I, indeed, a person such as yourself? Or does the colour of my skin bar me from being quite the same?"

"I feel as if I should apologise for them," Charity admitted. "Yet I cannot help but be aware—forgive me—of...of..."

"The fact that I am Black?" Miss Leigh smiled. "I would not trust someone who claimed not to notice. But when ladies such as yourself make the effort to speak to me, perhaps to get to know me and realise that I am not so very different after all, why, sometimes I begin to have hopes for this world after all. It has been a pleasure speaking with you, Miss Bellingham. I hope we meet again."

"I too," said Charity. She curtsied and left.

"What was she like?" Rebecca asked, when Charity returned to her.

"She was very pleasant," Charity said, thoughtfully. "I never thought before to be grateful for the colour of my skin."

And as Rebecca and Charity waited for the carriage to take them home, they were both silent.

Charity wondered later what it had been that Rebecca had been about to say to her when Miss Leigh began speaking. She had not long to wait to find out. The two ladies had gathered in the drawing room the next day to perform their various pursuits in mutual silence. Charity knew she had been neglecting her piano of late and was determined to put in a good hour's practice, whilst Rebecca was knitting something small and white and fluffy. Scales and exercises took half an hour, and then Charity turned to some pieces, revelling in the magic of Haydn and Beethoven before turning to lighter dance tunes—Scotch and Irish airs, a folk song or two. An hour and a half later, she finished the final piece with a flourish, then carefully lowered the lid on the piano.

"There. That will do for today."

"I wish I could play like you," Rebecca said, finishing her row of knitting and holding the piece up to the light to examine it.

"It's just practice." Charity was always embarrassed by compliments, no matter the giver.

She stood up and walked over to look out of the window over the busy street. London was always busy, always full of life. Some parts—such as the area where Isobelle lived—were quieter. But even there, it was only as if the city was holding its breath, ready to exhale with a long sigh of noise and action elsewhere.

"Perhaps I wish I had the patience to practice, then," Rebecca said. Changing the subject, she added, "Do you see Miss Greenaway today?"

Charity started, wondering whether Rebecca had been reading her mind in order to mention Isobelle right now. Then common sense kicked in, and she realised that she almost always *was* thinking about Isobelle.

"Yes. We're going to the concert at St Bartholemew's Church Hall." St Bartholemew's was a medium-sized church, not anything large and important, but it happened to be the nearest church to Lady Caroline's home. She had thus taken it under her wing as a "project", persuading far more talented musicians to play there than might otherwise have been the case. Charity smiled at her sister. "Isobelle asked if you would like to come, but I thought you probably would not."

"I do like music," Rebecca defended herself, "but I always feel a little out of place at concerts. Everyone says such clever things, and I don't know what they mean."

Charity laughed. "Nor do half of them, in my experience. Thankfully, Isobelle isn't like that. She knows what she's talking about."

"You like her a lot," Rebecca said again.

Charity swung round to look at her sister, a funny feeling in her throat. She had been wanting to speak to Rebecca about Isobelle for some time now, yet fearing to do so. How would

Rebecca take the news that Charity wanted to impart? But Rebecca's words seemed almost set up to encourage Charity to speak. Taking a deep breath, she did so.

"You said that before. But it's worse than that, Becca. I'm in love with her."

She waited on tenterhooks for her sister to reply. Was she to be condemned, rejected? Charity could not believe that Rebecca would forbid her the house, but might not Charity's confession drive a wedge between the two sisters that time could not heal? And yet...was it not true that living with this secret between them formed a wedge of its own, even if Rebecca was unaware of it?

A little crease appeared between Rebecca's eyes, and she ceased her sewing. "But she's a lady," she said, looking up at Charity.

"I'd noticed," Charity said dryly.

"Does she know how you feel?"

"I hope so! I should perhaps have said that *we're* in love."

"But two ladies. It's unnatural."

"And being sold into marriage with a drunken sot more than twice your age isn't?" Charity snapped, her nerves getting the better of her. She had always a tendency to hit out when upset, and when Isobelle was so precious to her, it was hard to hear their love described as 'unnatural'.

Rebecca winced, looking back down at her embroidery as if it were the most interesting thing she had ever seen. But Charity knew there were tears in her eyes. Impulsively, she ran over to her sister and sank onto her knees on the floor beside her. "I'm sorry. That was unkind." She reached up to wipe away Rebecca's tears with her thumbs.

Rebecca rubbed her eyes a little and sniffed, trying to compose herself. Then, bravely, she tried again. "But can it really be true? You...and Miss Greenaway? It does seem—" She caught herself up short and reached out to take Charity's hands in her own. "I don't mean to hurt you, Charity."

"Whereas I aimed to hurt," Charity said ruefully. "I'm sorry, Becca." She hesitated and then braved going on, turning away from her sister, fearing what Rebecca's response might be. "If you have to know, Isobelle saved my life." She gave a little laugh. "That sounds melodramatic, doesn't it? But that's what it felt like."

She had not heard her sister get up, but felt Rebecca's light touch on her arm. "Forgive me. I did not mean to be unkind," Rebecca repeated. "But...she saved your life?"

Charity turned to face her sister. "You never asked me why I wrote to Mother, why I wanted to move to Bath." She had been shocked at the time by Rebecca's lack of response to that explosive letter. It made no sense, even now.

Rebecca brushed the front of her dress with her fingers, as if trying to remove invisible specks of dust. "No," she said, her eyes meeting Charity's. "I never did." Her hand had stopped, resting gently on her stomach. It was a gesture Charity had seen before, in other ladies, but never in her sister.

"Becca!" Rebecca's gaze dipped for a second before she glanced back at Charity. "You are, aren't you?" Charity said slowly. "Expecting."

"In about fourteen weeks, I think."

"And Fotheringay. Does he know?"

"Of course." Rebecca smiled ruefully. "'For better, for worse'. He is my husband."

"And will be the father of your child," Charity said softly.

"That too. So no, Charity I did not ask. Perhaps I was cowardly, but I did not wish to know the answer."

"You knew about this even then?"

"Yes. Not for sure, but I knew."

Rebecca turned away, bending to pull the cushion covers straight on the seat where she had earlier been sitting, and then to smooth a humped corner of the Oriental rug.

"Should you do that in your state of health?"

"Darling, I'm expecting a child, not dying!" Rebecca retorted. "At least, I hope."

Charity said nothing. It had been only six weeks since shockwaves had gone round the polite world after the unexpected death of Lady McFadden. It had been the lady's third baby, and—as far as anyone knew—she had had no problems with her earlier lying-ins. Nor had she been particularly old, still in her early twenties. Of course, it was not unusual for women to die in childbirth, but nonetheless the news had caught the *ton* by surprise.

"I'll be fine," Rebecca asserted, and Charity mentally shook herself. It was Rebecca who was pregnant, and yet Charity's sister was still trying to reassure *her*.

"Of course you will!"

Rebecca laughed suddenly. "Goodness, we seem to have strayed far from the original subject. 'Grasshopper minds', father would have called us."

Charity had never experienced her father calling her anything but her given name. There had been, too, something in the way that he pronounced it that had always make the original meaning of the word spring to mind. She tried to compose her face into an appropriate expression, but Rebecca must have seen the struggle, for her laughter faded. Serious now, she said: "Anyway, Charity, if you are happy, then I am happy." She paused for a second before continuing. "I think perhaps you have not had all that much happiness in your life, dear."

"And you?" Charity asked.

Rebecca gave a little sigh. "I am content."

"Really?"

"Really." She smoothed her hand across her belly once more. "The little one will be here soon enough. I have always wanted children, you know. Perhaps this is not…what I dreamed of. But not many people get that. Really and honestly, I am content."

"And I am happier than I ever thought I could be." Despite her worries about her sister, Charity could not keep the joy from her voice. Isobelle. Isobelle. Even thinking her name filled Charity with happiness.

"Then I am glad."

Charity remembered this conversation that night, as she was lying in bed. Her thoughts, as always, had started with Isobelle, but she had quickly passed on to thinking about Rebecca and what her sister had said. Rebecca had known, then—or guessed—what had caused Charity such distress. Known something of what her husband had done. Charity remembered the time when Rebecca had been unwell. Her whispered admission that she did not want to get better, and the implication that some of her womanly duties were unwelcome—or worse. Charity thought of the way that, after their mother's letter, Rebecca had made more excuses to spend time with her sister: Charity had thought that she was just trying to make Charity feel wanted, but perhaps it had been more about protecting Charity. Fotheringay could hardly accost his wife's sister in front of his wife.

Should Rebecca have spoken? It was pointless to wonder how things might have changed. But Rebecca, so retiring, so quiet, so newly pregnant... It would have been impossible for her to speak out. Instead, her sister had given wordless support: delicate, tactful and kind. All the things her sister was, Charity thought ruefully, and she was not. Perhaps she should even be grateful to Fotheringay, improbable though that might seem. For it was due to him, to his attack, that she had met Isobelle.

CHAPTER TWENTY

"God be damned!" Fotheringay had slit open a letter as they sat at the breakfast table six weeks later and was looking at it with an expression of deep disgust.

"Thomas!" Rebecca exclaimed, genuinely shocked.

Charity continued eating placidly. Since "The Day", she and Fotheringay had preserved a hostile truce, neither of them acknowledging the other's existence save when absolutely necessary.

"This damned—dashed letter. It's from Monroe. Trouble on the plantation, he says. I pay him for there not to be trouble. And I pay him enough lucre as it is. Trouble indeed!"

"Oh dear," said his wife, a comment so mild that Fotheringay smacked the letter down in indignation.

"Oh dear? It's more than that. Do you think your precious mother would have been so keen for me to wed you if my plantation hadn't been doing so well?"

Charity lifted her eyes to give him a steely glare, but for her sister's sake kept her silence. Rebecca, too, was quiet.

Fotheringay gave a grunt and forked the last piece of ham into his mouth, masticating thoroughly before swallowing it. Less brusquely, he said, "You don't want the carriage today, do you? With the curricle with the wheelsmith, I'll have to take it to see Sanders, m'financial advisor, you know."

"I was thinking of—"

Fotheringay cut her off. "Well, don't." He stood up. "I'll be gone, don't know when I'll return. You can have a quiet day. It will do you good."

"Yes Thomas."

Charity knew, and she knew that Rebecca knew, that this apparent concern for his wife's well-being was merely a sop thrown to back up his argument. As he left the room, Charity said in an undertone, "Or you could just leave and not return. *That* would do her good."

Rebecca smiled across the table at her sister. "He'll hear you one day," she said chidingly, but she did not either look or sound cross.

"If it were not for you, I would hope he did!"

"I know. And I am grateful. I must live with him, and I would prefer to do so as peacefully as I can. As peaceful as life can be, in the circumstances."

"Should I have tried harder to dissuade you from marrying him?"

Rebecca sighed. "No. I would not have had the courage, and would have felt worse about it. Besides"—she stroked her protruding belly, and Charity wondered how she could possibly not have realised earlier that her sister was pregnant—"I believe I was made for marriage and children. Few people, I think, get precisely what we want. We are all required to make do."

"That's very philosophical. A lot easier to say than to feel, I imagine."

"Oh, for a certainty! Do you think I do not resent my fate sometimes? But what good would it do to fixate on that? Fotheringay is my husband, and I must make the best of him. But I confess," Rebecca added ruefully, "that I prefer it when he is absent!"

"Then here is to his absence!" Charity said, raising a tea cup in mock salute.

When Fotheringay returned, late that afternoon, his mood was worse. The two ladies looked at each other and asked no questions. Over the evening meal, Fotheringay brought the subject up himself. "Sanders hasn't been happy with Monroe for a while. Won't go into the details—don't want to confuse your pretty head with things, m'darling—but long story short, looks like I'm going to have to take a trip out there to the plantation and see what's going on."

"A trip?" Rebecca faltered. "Isn't it a very long way?"

"The Indies, yes. No help for it, though, it seems. Of course, I'm not going till I've seen my son born. First things first, and all that."

Charity felt herself bristling at that "my son". Presumably if there was a way of telling that the baby would be a girl, he'd be straight off before the birth. Or maybe not, she reconsidered. After all, that would leave them still in need, as gentlemen seemed to think it, of a son. A remedy for which could not be implemented until after the first child was born.

"I see. H-how long would you be away for?"

Fotheringay shrugged. "A year. Perhaps more."

"A year?"

Charity looked over at her sister, having heard clearly the panic in her voice. She might not enjoy Fotheringay's presence, but the thought of having him on the far side of the world was a frightening one. Rebecca had always had someone to lean on: first her mother, now Fotheringay. Charity had no doubt that her sister could cope without them, but it was understandable that she should be concerned, especially as she was shortly to become a mother as well.

"Can't just nip over there on a day trip, Rebecca," Fotheringay said sternly. "It's a damnable business all round."

"I know. It's just…a year? It seems such a long time."

Longer than Rebecca and Fotheringay had been married, Charity realised. No wonder that it had shaken her sister. For herself, it seemed marvellous—far too good to be true. Could they really get rid of Fotheringay for an entire year? Fotheringay and Rebecca were still talking, discussing the proposed venture in detail. Charity rose.

"Would you mind if I left the table, Rebecca?" she asked, following her usual pattern of ignoring Fotheringay entirely.

"Oh! Yes, that's fine. I'll talk with you later, Charity?" her sister asked.

"Yes, of course."

Charity left the room, her mind still running over the news that Fotheringay had dropped on them and trying to think of all of the ramifications. A year! A whole year without him. She hoped that in her concern about the future, Rebecca would not attempt to persuade Fotheringay against the trip, for Rebecca's sake as much as Charity's own. Rebecca was forever frightened of new experiences and had been encouraged in her tendency to be guided by older minds, first by her parents and then by Fotheringay himself. Rebecca would feel anchorless, Charity knew, at least initially. But surely it was worth it, when the prize was Fotheringay's absence?

It was not until Charity was being readied for bed by her maid that Rebecca sought her out. With a quick word of thanks and dismissal, the maid was let go to her own room, and Rebecca carried on with the task of brushing out Charity's long, dark mane of hair.

"Well?" Charity asked, catching her sister's eye in the mirror.

"He insists on going," Rebecca said, separating out a chunk of hair to brush more thoroughly.

"Good!" said Charity robustly. "We don't need him here, and we certainly don't want him here."

"Charity, how can you?"

"I'm only saying what you're thinking, certainly about the 'want'," Charity retorted. "You are just worried about coping alone, but you will still have me. And other families seem to manage quite convincingly without a gentleman in the house. The Greenaways, for example."

Rebecca laughed softly, taking up a new section of hair. "I hardly think we can really compare ourselves with the Greenaways, dearest. The situation is very different."

"Yes. Lady Greenaway is crippled," Charity said. "And they still manage. Becca, it will be fine. No, it won't be fine, it will be delightful! Can't you hurry up and bring your baby into the world so that we can get rid of him the quicker?"

"The baby will come when he, or she, chooses. And hasn't anyone told you that it's impolite to speak about such matters?" But Rebecca was not cross.

"You know I would not do so to anyone but you," Charity said. "Come, dear, smile. Think of our freedom! I'm having tea with Nan tomorrow, and can hardly wait to tell her!"

"Just be careful what you say, Charity, please? For my sake if not for your own, or Fotheringay's. You can be very outspoken, and sometimes it is better that things are kept private." Rebecca put the hairbrush down on the dressing table. "There. Your hair is beautifully brushed. Do you want to plait it before bed?"

"Not tonight. And I will be careful, Becca, I promise. Sleep well. Dream of a future with no Fotheringay."

Rebecca laughed, kissed her and left.

CHAPTER TWENTY-ONE

Charity visited Nan full of news and excitement the next morning. She would have preferred to go straight to Isobelle and tell her everything, but the arrangement with Nan was long standing and she could not let her down. She had written a brief note to Isobelle, telling her that there was exciting news. Charity knew she must content her heart with that until the evening, when both ladies were to attend the same ball. Nonetheless, if Nan was second best, she was a very good second best, and Charity could hardly wait to talk over everything with her friend.

But the conversation was not to go as planned. Charity spilled the news about Fotheringay: his manager, his business and his desire to see the plantation for himself and discover what was happening there. She looked up to find Nan staring into the distance, a crease between her eyebrows.

"What is it?" she asked. "Surely you, like Rebecca, do not think that we are incapable of coping alone?"

"No, of course not. But...you said plantation?"

Charity looked at her friend in perplexity. "Why, yes. I confess I thought he merely transported things, but it seems not. Nan, I thought you'd be pleased. Can't you understand that I'm thrilled to have Fotheringay out of the country, especially after—"

"I am. Of course I am. It's just…" Nan put a hand to her forehead, pressing her fingers hard against the creases of her frown. "Harry, you said India. Fotheringay's money is from tea, is it not? He trades with China, or that is what I always believed you meant."

"As far as I know, that is true," Charity said. "He has links with an island out there. Is it important?"

"India, not…not Jamaica?"

"No, India. Western India, I believe he said, which makes sense. It would be the closest side of the country to England, after all."

Nan turned away, striding across the room as if trying to move as far away from Charity as possible.

"You don't understand." There was still the sharp note in Nan's voice. "Not Western India. At least, I do not believe so. The West Indies. Harry, have you not realised that your brother-in-law's money comes from sugar, the plantations? From slavery?"

For a moment, Charity thought that she must have misheard. Either that or have misunderstood. Those two Abolitionist meetings… She had heard ladies talk about islands such as Jamaica, and a place called the Caribbean, which appeared to have the largest amount of African slaves. India itself was not entirely free of slavery, but the problem there was less vicious. She could half-believe that Fotheringay had servants out there whom he barely paid, but nothing more sinister than that. But now—Nan surely could not mean what Charity had thought she did? Fotheringay's fortune… Could it really be built on the back of slave labour?

"No." Her lips framed the word, but no sound came out, and Nan's back was turned. Charity took a few deep breaths and tried again. "You cannot mean that," she said, attempting to keep her voice steady.

"You must have heard us speak of Tobago, Jamaica, Trinidad." Nan turned to face her.

"Yes, of course."

"They're known as the West Indies. Not Western India, Harry. The West Indies."

"But it's none of those. It's a little place, I believe. Tortola. And Mother said..." Charity had never expected to quote her mother's words in her own defence. But what precisely had her mother said?

It is to be hoped that this modern desire for hot beverages continues. Why, Rebecca, in a few years he may be worth even more money!

Was that truly what Mrs Bellingham had said? Surely she had mentioned tea?

"What did she say?"

Charity winced. She felt as if she were on trial. Nan's voice was so harsh, almost accusing.

"I...I hardly know," she stammered. Then, suddenly angry, she said, "Of what are you accusing me? Do you call me a liar?"

Nan softened, almost visibly. "I'm sorry. It is quite a shock."

You think it's a shock to you? But Charity did not say the words aloud. She felt shaky, fighting to stop herself from trembling. Something must have shown on her face, for Nan came to her side quickly.

"Come, sit down." Nan guided her to a chair. "I did not mean to hurt you, Harry. But...West India, plantations. It must be so, yet you seemed so sure when you said tea."

"I feel so stupid," Charity said, clinging to Nan's hand. "I did not lie, Nan."

"I know," Nan replied quickly. "I should not have said what I did."

"Mother...she spoke about hot drinks, and our modern society's desire for them. I thought she said tea, but now I am not so sure. My mind would have leapt to tea, that being my mother's drink of choice. I thought...I assumed..." She dragged her hand away from Nan and clasped her hands together in front of her. "Why would she say that about sugar? Sugar is not a drink."

"No." Nan sighed. "But everyone takes sugar in their tea. You did, until recently. Also, there is the new beverage, chocolate. Warm chocolate is taking the *ton* almost by storm. When I was a young girl, no one ever considered drinking sweetened chocolate. Of late, though, it seems that if you do not start or end your day with a warming cup of chocolate, you are almost beyond the pale. And one of the main components is sugar. The only people who do not drink it are people like the Sisterhood—we who oppose slavery and choose to make it known by boycotting sugar."

"I never thought of it that way. And Isobelle drinks chocolate, still."

"And takes sugar in her tea. I know." Nan did not say more, but Charity could sense the unspoken criticism.

"I'm sure she has her reasons," she said, defending her love. Nan turned away from her again. "I'm sure she does."

But Charity had bigger concerns than Isobelle's choice of beverage. "What can I tell Rebecca?" she asked. "She has been so moved by what I've told her about slavery, so keen to promote the abolition."

"Can she really not know from what her husband's money comes?"

"If I did not know…" Charity hesitated, not knowing how to explain Rebecca to Nan, such a different character to Charity's gentle, innocent sister. "Nan, Rebecca…I do not think that it would occur to her to ask. Fotheringay's business is his own. Rebecca contents herself with house and home. She…" Charity felt her face flushing as she stumbled on. "She is expecting, you know. I do not think she concerns herself with his financial status, only with getting the house ready for the child." She felt suddenly defensive of her sister. "It is not that she does not care. It is just that her priorities are not the same as ours. And why should they be?"

"I did not criticise her," Nan said softly. "Perhaps it was unfair or unkind of me to ask the question, though. I am sorry, if so."

Charity sighed. "I can't forgive my own idiocy, in truth. It would not occur to Rebecca to consider the source of Fotheringay's wealth. Enough for our mother that he had it. And Rebecca just did as she was told, as she always does. And you are not to criticise her for that," she added defiantly. "She is a wonderful person. Kind, loving. A million times better than I."

"Do not accuse me of sins I have not committed," Nan said. "I am no one to judge her. And she is with child, you say?"

"Yes. We are expecting the baby in a few scant weeks' time."

"Then you must not tell her any of this now," Nan said firmly. "You cannot upset her when her life must be so upturned anyway. A baby on the way, a husband about to leave her...No, Harry, it would be unkind indeed to tell her any of this now."

"That's what I thought," admitted Charity. "But I wasn't sure whether I was just trying to deny myself a difficult task. Besides," she added honestly, "I do not think that Fotheringay's departure will distress her much more than it distresses me."

"But with the child...no."

"*He* won't leave until the baby is born, anyway," Charity said. "He wants to make sure of an heir, of course. Don't they always?"

Nan smiled. "By the time I was born, my parents already had a son. I did not have to live with that particular concern, and I did not ever feel that I was resented or judged for being a mere female."

"Then you were lucky." But Charity said no more on the subject. It was a matter on which she was too sensitive to discuss right now. "I hope for a girl," she said instead. "I like to think that it is not just to spite Fotheringay, though I fear that may be part of it."

Nan laughed reluctantly. "Unkind but irresistible. Though it is like you to own up to it, Harry."

"If I had known about—" Charity started, but Nan interrupted.

"I know. I do know, I promise. Please do not hold me forever in anger for my immediate reaction."

"As if I could," Charity said. Then, "Oh, Nan, what should I do? I just never thought anything like this could happen."

"I don't think there is anything you can do," Nan said, with her usual practicality. "Fotheringay is breaking no law. Although we have no slaves on English soil by law, most people in England would say he is well within his rights to own them abroad. It is we who are unreasonable."

"But..."

"I know," Nan said grimly. "The thought appals. All we can do, though, is to campaign, to support, to hope that things will change. Will we have slavery in fifty years' time? In a hundred? Perhaps we will. We cannot affect what has already happened. We can only fight for things to change in the future. In the hope that one day, all people will be free."

If Charity had wanted to see Isobelle before, that was nothing to her need now. A ball was hardly the best place to have any sort of private conversation, but Charity's desire to speak to Isobelle was too strong to be denied. She could think of nothing else. The ballroom was crowded with ladies in bright dresses and suave gentlemen with costumes varying from the gaudy to an almost sternly sober black. At first, Charity had thought she preferred the colourfully dressed men, but after such a riot of colours, the quiet black began to have a distinct appeal.

However, this evening's clothes were the least of her concerns. She was hunting for Isobelle, looking out for her lover's trademark blue. It was not that Isobelle wore nothing but blue, but it was certainly her first colour of choice. Seeing the way it matched and drew attention to Isobelle's glorious eyes, Charity could not criticise her choice. But in an overcrowded ballroom, searching for one specific lady was no easy task. Mentally, Charity blessed her height: she could at least see over the heads of most of the ladies present. She glanced across at where her sister sat quietly in a corner. Charity had not been certain whether it was appropriate for Rebecca to come out in her state of health, but she would not have been able to come without her, and Rebecca had said in her quiet way that an hour or two's jollity would not hurt.

A flash of blue caught Charity's eye—no, that was not Isobelle. The combination of blond hair and a blue dress had fooled Charity for a second, but this lady was much older and more… Charity struggled for the right word. She was more angular than Isobelle. Isobelle was all soft feminine curves and delicate, pink-tinged skin. Charity sighed. She had not really wished to come out tonight, her mind taken up as it was by the shock of discovering that Fotheringay's wealth came not from tea but from sugar. But it was too hard sitting home with Rebecca and saying nothing of her new knowledge, especially when she longed to unburden herself on Isobelle, seeking the comfort and reassurance she could only get from her.

"Good evening."

Charity started at the voice. She had been too taken up in her own concerns to have seen the lady approach.

"Oh, Lydia!" She forced a smile. It was rare that she was displeased to see one of the Sisterhood, but right now was one of those few occasions. "What a lovely dress. That green suits you."

Lydia Seacombe pealed with laughter. "This old thing? Harry, you have seen me wear it a hundred times!"

"Oh." Charity blinked and looked at her friend more closely. "Sorry. I was thinking of something else."

"Something, or someone?" Lydia asked archly. "Oh, I see your blush. I take it Isobelle is expected to attend this evening?"

"Have you seen her?" Charity did not bother to deny it.

"Not yet. But the evening is still young. Come, are you not going to dance?"

"No one has asked me. But no, I'm not in the mood just now."

"You and your moods!" Lydia exclaimed. "Don't you realise that a lady should always be in the mood to dance?" Charity mumbled something—even she did not know what—and Lydia shrugged elegant shoulders. "Well, you stand here and pine after Isobelle if you so wish. *I* am going to dance."

Charity saw her walk away with a good deal of relief. Lydia rarely took anything seriously—like Isobelle, perhaps, but Isobelle had more to her, somehow. Lydia cared for nothing above her own amusement, which made her excellent company but not someone Charity would choose to confide in. Isobelle, though... Where was she? Charity returned to her self-appointed task, scanning the crowd once more. And this time her efforts were crowned with greater success. Isobelle, as if intentionally to confuse Charity, was wearing a rose-pink frock this evening. As always, she looked ravishing, but that was almost an irrelevance to Charity right now.

"Excuse me." She wriggled and pushed her way through the throng until she reached Isobelle's side. When she got there, she caught up Isobelle's hand and pulled her away from the dancing she had been about to join. "Isobelle!" she said urgently.

"Harry! Such unanticipated joy to see me!" Isobelle said laughingly. Then, apologetically to her would-be partner, she said, "Pray excuse me. It seems I am needed elsewhere. But Mrs Seacombe is in need of a gentleman with which to dance. I would be forever in your debt if you would but ask her."

The gentleman bowed stiffly, casting an unfriendly look at Charity. However, his society manners would not allow him to do anything further to express his displeasure.

"Your word, Miss Greenaway," he said, "is my command."

"And now," said Isobelle, watching him stalk off before turning to Charity. "What can I do for you, my dear one?"

"I need to speak to you," she said urgently.

"I can see that much!" Isobelle smiled gaily at her lover. "Well. You want me, and here I am. Pray tell me what the matter is!"

"We should find somewhere private." Charity looked round the crowded room in something nearing despair. "Where can we go?"

"Follow me," Isobelle ordered, setting briskly off towards a curtain. "Behind here. It looks as if it is just a window, does it not? But in fact it is a small, private room. You can always trust me," she said, her lips turning up into a mischievous smile, "to know where the private rooms are." She threaded her fingers through Charity's and led her into the space. It was more of an alcove than a room, but it was large enough, and private enough, to suit Charity's needs. "Now," said Isobelle, turning to face Charity. "Do you mean to ravish me, or is that too much to hope?"

"It's Fotheringay."

"Indeed?" Isobelle sobered. "What has he done?"

"I talked to Nan." Gently, Charity disentangled her hand from Isobelle's.

"Not me? Harry, I am hurt!"

"Isobelle, it's more serious than that. I wanted to speak to you so desperately, but I did not realise until I talked to Nan that...oh!" Charity dashed a hand across her face. "I shall not cry, I shall not!"

"Tell me, dear one."

"Fotheringay's fortune. It comes—"

"Goodness, is he thoroughly undone? Gambling? Are you to be impoverished?" Isobelle's questions burst out excitedly.

"No. Nothing like that. Oh heavens, it's worse. His money comes...from sugar."

Isobelle frowned. "That is a great comedown. I thought something was dreadfully wrong!"

"Isobelle, from the plantations, from the West Indies! From *slavery!*"

"Many people's do." Isobelle looked quizzically at her.

"But not us. To think that I have wanted so much to have slavery abolished—those meetings, that reading—and all the time I was living off slave money, blood money."

"Embarrassing, certainly," Isobelle agreed.

"Worse than that. Every part of me rebels! And yet, what can I do?"

The room was small. Charity wanted to pace back and forth but could only take a couple of steps in any direction before having to turn back. And Isobelle... Isobelle was standing in the middle of the room, as calm as anything, apparently unable to realise what a real crisis this was.

"Harry," Isobelle said gently. "Look out there, at all the ladies and gentlemen dancing. Do you not think that at least a quarter of them are slave owners? It is part of life. An unpleasant part, certainly, but not uncommon. In a perfect world, of course there would not be slaves, but we do not live in a perfect world."

"I thought you understood. I thought you cared!" Charity flung at her.

"Oh, Harry dear! You do take everything so seriously," Isobelle complained, half-amused still. "It is business. Heaven knows what gentlemen get up to in the name of business. Can't you just put it aside for the moment and come and dance?" She reached for Charity's hand and then placed a kiss on the palm. "Forget it. Forget him. Why, you are barely related to Fotheringay. Just pretend you don't know, and we can go on as before. It is not as if you will want to take him to task about it!"

"No. And he is going over there, to the Indies, soon," said Charity dully. "I will not have even to see him, let alone speak to him."

"Well, then. All the more reason to celebrate. And," she added laughingly, "to be grateful to slavery. It cannot be all bad if it is taking Fotheringay away. Come, let us go and dance."

Charity watched numbly as Isobelle left the room. How could she take it so lightly? How *could* she? Surely that could not have been Isobelle speaking those words! Surely the lady who had accompanied her to the first Abolitionist meeting she attended could not be as unconcerned with slavery as she seemed. Charity remembered Nan's shocked reaction, unwillingly comparing it with Isobelle's. Nan understood about slavery. But surely Isobelle was no less humane than Nan? How could she be so unaffected by Charity's crushing revelation? She had hoped—no, she had been sure—that Isobelle would understand. Charity had needed her to sympathise. Neither had happened. She had come to Isobelle to help mend the tear in her heart; instead, it had been torn still further. As she walked slowly back into the ballroom, the candles in the room seemed to burn too brightly. The heat made her feel almost faint, and the noise assaulted her ears.

"Rebecca," she said quietly to her sister, "can we not go home? I am not feeling well."

For the sisters, the ball was over, and for Charity, so was her peace of mind. It was with a heavy heart that she readied herself for bed.

CHAPTER TWENTY-TWO

By the next morning, Charity had recovered her spirits a little. It was not fair to judge Isobelle too harshly for her lack of understanding. As she had so rightly said, many of her friends and acquaintances must be slave owners too. She had had to learn to live with it, to understand it was possible, as the *Bible* said, to hate the sin but love the sinner. Charity's background was so very different. Her father's money had come from land owned in England—a land free of slavery for many years now. To her, the idea of slavery had been a vague one, something other people did in other countries. To Isobelle, it was a fact of life. Nan saw it in a different light, certainly, but she had the descriptions her sailor brother had given her of slave ships to consider. She was a little closer to having seen the true horrors of slavery. No, Charity told herself as she washed her face and hands that morning, it was unfair to judge Isobelle.

They had arranged to meet to walk together in the park, and when Charity saw Isobelle again, she felt her heart leap inside her. Isobelle was so beautiful and so much fun. Nothing she could say or do could be that wrong.

"Harry!" Isobelle greeted her warmly. "Now, why did you run away so quickly from the ball last night? Was your sister unwell? I have seen, of course, that she is in an 'interesting condition'."

"No, Rebecca is quite well, in the circumstances." Charity found it a little bit of a struggle to sound natural, but she hoped that she was making a fair impression of it. "We just...preferred to go home."

"Well, I do hope that Lady Kingston didn't notice. To come to her ball and stay less than an hour! Criticism indeed!"

"I was not feeling altogether the thing," Charity said truthfully. "I will of course explain that to Lady Kingston if need be."

"Oh, I was only teasing you." Isobelle tucked a hand through Charity's arm companionably. "Did you see the crush? I don't imagine she had time to notice anything."

"That's good."

They walked a little way. The flowers were not at their best at this time of year, but the park was full enough of ladies and gentlemen taking a morning promenade to make up for it. Of the light muslin dresses of the ladies, many had sprigs of flowers patterned across them. They were almost, Charity thought absently, more floral than the gardens themselves. She spotted Emily and Jane chatting seriously a little way distant. Isobelle had clearly seen the same thing.

"Shall we go and speak to them?" she asked. "Or would it be unkind? I would hate to interrupt a conversation about the relative merits of a few bits of mouldy old stone, or whatever it may be that they are discussing in such depth!"

"Isobelle, you are awful!" Charity remonstrated. "Do you care nothing for the works of the ancients?"

"Very little, I'm afraid," Isobelle said unapologetically. "A few bits of stone here, a beheaded statue there. Give me modernity. Colour, life, music! Give me fun!"

"You do have a point," Charity admitted. "So often the statues are incomplete. It is sad."

"It is sad, and I do not like sadness. So come, Harry, let us talk about something else. Did you really say last night that Fotheringay was going away?"

"Yes. After the baby is born. He thinks he may be gone for a year or more." There was a certain reserve in Charity about speaking of it, bound up as it was by with the issue of slavery. She tried to put it to the back of her mind.

"How splendid! And he might die out there, you know," Isobelle said in a hopeful tone. "They say the climate does not suit everyone."

"I don't want him to die," Charity objected. "But I confess," she added, smiling, "that I do not regret his proposed absence. The sooner the better, as far as I am concerned!"

But she would have done anything to take back that last line a few days later. Fotheringay's departure was dependent on the birth of his child, and it had been believed that Rebecca had another month at least before her lying in. When her pains had started unexpectedly, Rebecca had first declared that it was nothing. Then, as they had progressed, getting worse and not better, she had grown suddenly silent on the matter. Fotheringay, for once showing some concern, had sent for the midwife, and Rebecca had retired to her room with the woman. But a couple of hours later, the midwife herself had spoken privately with Mr Fotheringay. Shortly after that, a doctor was called.

No one had time to explain anything, and Charity was left hanging, uncertain of what was going on, afraid for what it might be. Death in childbirth was no rare thing; the death of the baby would be preferable but still devastating to her sister. But if only—if only Rebecca lived, anything would be acceptable, Charity told herself.

She paced the drawing room, heart pounding. It was now several hours since the doctor had been sent for. Rebecca, she knew, had had no intention to have a medical man present at her lying-in. Yet the doctor was here. What was happening? Charity had even steeled herself to ask Fotheringay (the frigid silence between the two of them remained otherwise as strong as ever). He had muttered a testy "I don't know" before barricading himself in his study. Charity would not have been surprised if he had answered that way deliberately to provoke her, but something about the fearful expression on his face suggested that he had spoken nothing but the truth. *Gentlemen have little place at a birth*, Rebecca had once told Charity, apparently assimilating maternal knowledge through the sheer fact of being pregnant. Fotheringay was as ignorant as Charity herself. Indeed, Charity thought, this might perhaps be the one and only time she and he were in sympathy, though his concern was for the unborn child and Charity's for Rebecca.

Charity was sure—fairly sure, at least—that she would take an interest in Rebecca's baby once it was born. At the moment, however, she found it difficult to care much for someone she had never met. Not when the doctor had been closeted upstairs with her sister for so long.

Charity stood in the centre of the cluttered room and looked ruefully at the piano. If she could only sit down in front of its keys and distract herself with music, it would at least apply a little balm to her worries. But the room lay directly beneath Rebecca's, and she was not certain whether this might disturb her sister. On no account would she do anything that might negatively affect Rebecca's health. Instead, with a deep sigh, she returned to her pacing, leaving a track mark across the luxurious shag carpet.

Finally, she heard footsteps on the stairs that did not belong to a maid. She hurried to the door and looked anxiously up and the descending doctor. Fotheringay was doing the same a little further on. They must look like puppets, Charity thought, to the gentleman observing their behaviour.

"Well?" snapped Fotheringay.

"I am glad to tell you, sir, that the birthing was successful. Your wife is currently resting, and is very tired. She must be cared for very carefully over the next few—"

"Never mind that," Fotheringay interrupted. "The child. The child, man!"

"You have a healthy daughter—" The doctor stopped for a second as Fotheringay gave a disgusted grunt. "And," he continued, "a healthy son."

Both Charity and Fotheringay stared at him.

"Good gad, twins?" Fotheringay asked disbelievingly.

The doctor nodded solemnly. "Twins. They are small babies, twins always are, but healthy, both of them."

Fotheringay strode to the staircase. "Well, let me past, man. Let me past. I have to go and see my son."

The doctor looked as if he was keeping quiet only by force of will. He must, Charity thought, be used to gentlemen's obsession with boy children. She wondered whether he had mentioned the mother and daughter first deliberately. If so, she thought she might have found the first man she actively liked. She gave him a swift smile.

"And his wife, and his daughter," she said. "I will be happy to see them. My sister, Mrs Fotheringay, particularly."

He returned her smile. "I am glad to hear it. Mrs Fotheringay will need to be kept very quiet for some time to come. I was pleased to hear that the nursemaid was already engaged and on the premises. First births are often the most difficult, and twins more difficult still. Mrs Fotheringay was very brave, caring little for her own pain and more for the babe. Or in fact, as it turned out, babes."

Charity nodded. "She would be. When may I see her?"

"Tomorrow, perhaps. The excitement of the children, and the visit of her husband..." He trailed off, and he and Charity exchanged a knowing glance. "At least, maybe for five minutes tonight," he amended.

A door upstairs closed with a bang, and tuneless humming preceded Fotheringay down the stairs.

"Off to wet the baby's head," he said cheerfully. "My son. Jolly good show. And I'll book tickets for the Indies tomorrow."

With that, he was gone. A meaningful silence remained in its place. The doctor, knowing his position, could make no comment, but Charity had no such professional qualms to prevent her.

"It's the best thing," she said briefly. "The sooner we get him out of the country, the better. Mrs Fotheringay might not admit it, but it's true nonetheless. Good riddance."

The doctor gave a discreet cough. "Well," he said. "I will leave now. My bill will be here tomorrow morning, and..."

"Address it to him. That way he can be of some practical use," Charity said. The relief of knowing that her sister was alive and as well as possible had made her more forthright than she otherwise might have been to a stranger.

"I feel sure that you will make certain that Mrs Fotheringay is looked after properly."

"Yes," Charity said soberly. She thought of her patient, brave sister, who was now a mother twice over. "That I can certainly do."

"It has been a pleasure meeting you, Miss...?"

"Bellingham."

"Miss Bellingham. Please excuse me."

Charity reached out a hand as he went to pass her. "Thank you," she said. "For caring about my sister as well as the birth of the baby...babies," she corrected herself.

The doctor broke out of his professional demeanour. "An extremely nice lady, your sister," he said unexpectedly. Then, slightly pink in the cheeks, he left.

For a moment or two, Charity gazed after him. She was not sure what she would have expected in a doctor—and certainly in a Fotheringay-approved doctor—but the man had not been it. And Rebecca was recovering, and the twins... Her thoughts broke down there, lost in a whirling mass of emotions. Turning to the stairs, she ran lightly up to spend her allotted five minutes with her now much-increased family.

Just outside the doorway, she paused. She was almost afraid to go in, which was ridiculous. It was Rebecca in there, her gentle older sister. Nothing to be afraid of. And yet...and yet... Something mysterious and magical had happened in that room in her absence. Something Charity would never experience herself: that moment when one person became two—or, in Rebecca's case, three. And so she paused, wondering whether she would see the same sister she had always known or something new, different, incomprehensible. Telling herself not to be stupid, she pushed open the door and looked across at the bed.

"Charity!"

Rebecca looked flushed and untidy, and very tired, but she was still Rebecca. No stranger faced Charity.

"Becca." Charity went over the bedside and gave her sister a gentle hug. "How are you? I've been so worried."

"I'm fine," her sister said, smiling, gesturing to the nurse to leave them alone together. "And oh, Charity, look!" She gestured to the Moses basket where two tiny babies lay, squashed a little together. They were wrinkled like old ladies, one with little tufts of blond hair, the other with a soft, fair down upon its head. "Aren't they beautiful?"

Charity went round to examine the babies more closely. Tentatively, she reached out a finger and stroked the cheek of the closer child.

"Which is which?"

"The tufty one is our boy. The downy one is my girl."

Charity noted the different possessive phrases: the boy was "ours", the girl "mine". She wondered how the girl would feel, growing up, knowing that she was so much less important— unwanted, almost. She was suddenly filled with a fierce protectiveness for the girl. Then she shook herself. The girl would have Rebecca. She would have no doubt that she was loved and important to her mother.

"Do they have names?"

"Mary does. She's the older, you know." It had never occurred to Charity that there were older or younger when it came to twins. "As for my baby boy, I like Patrick, but Thomas thinks it's too Irish, or not genteel enough."

Charity gave a snort. "As if he'd know about things like that." She stopped herself. "Sorry, was that catty?"

Rebecca's mouth twitched, and Charity knew she was holding back a smile. "A little."

"You're right. If I have to criticise Fotheringay, I have many more routes to go than that," Charity agreed.

There was a stifled noise as Rebecca tried to hold back a giggle. "That was not the message I was trying to get across, dearest!"

Charity laughed. "Well, I shall stop criticising your husband altogether and instead praise you."

"And the children."

"And them," she agreed. She bent down to kiss Rebecca lightly on the cheek. "I was only allowed five minutes, and they've more than passed. I don't want to tire you. But oh, Becca, twins. How clever of you!"

Rebecca grasped her hand. "I'm glad you came," she said. "So glad. I am tired. But I'm so thankful I have you with me here, there aren't words for it. I know we're not a family for talking much about emotions, dearest sister, but I love you very much."

Charity squeezed her sister's fingers for a few seconds before letting go. "And I you. Sweet dreams—all three of you!"

CHAPTER TWENTY-THREE

Within a week of the babies' birth, Mr Fotheringay had made arrangements to sail to the West Indies. Charity did her best to hide her pleasure, but she strongly suspected that beneath her concerns about coping alone, Rebecca felt similarly. Having admired his son on the day of his birth, he had had barely more than a few fleeting glimpses of him since. Rebecca told Charity that Mr Fotheringay had eventually agreed to Patrick's name, though, with the addition of his own Thomas as a middle name, so the children could be christened when they were old enough to leave the house. His daughter, it was clear, he had only seen by default: she shared a crib with Patrick, so he could hardly see one without the other. His mind at rest about his heir, however, he clearly felt no need to stay in the country with business calling his name from abroad.

To Charity's relief, it had not occurred to Rebecca any more than it had originally occurred to Charity herself that there might be any link between the place to which Fotheringay was travelling and the slave trade. Although she knew he was visiting an island, Rebecca continued in the fond belief that she and Charity had once shared that it was an island off India. Tortola was not mentioned by name in any of the slavery literature either Charity or Rebecca had seen, being small compared to islands such as Jamaica and Antigua, so it was easy to be ignorant of the link. Until the twins were very much bigger, and Rebecca herself recovered fully from the birthing of them, Charity hoped to keep her in ignorance.

By the time the children were three weeks old, Fotheringay had left—"And good riddance!" Charity had commented to Nan, a trace of bitterness in her tones. Rebecca was so bound up in her children that Charity suspected that she barely noticed her husband's absence. Charity did, however, and revelled in it. With the household just consisting of two babies, Rebecca, Charity and the servants, there was an air of contentment that was almost tangible. Charity herself, in love and happy beyond anything she had ever experienced before, was in a constant state of rejoicing. Although she knew that Rebecca did not approve of her relationship with Isobelle, she also knew that Rebecca would not criticise her, nor do anything to make her uncomfortable.

As for Isobelle, Charity marvelled every time she saw her that she could be so lucky. In Charity's eyes, there had never been someone more beautiful, more wonderful, in every conceivable fashion. When Isobelle kissed her, she felt as if the world was complete. The one trouble had been in finding times, of late, to make love. Isobelle was ever popular, and could have been out every minute of every day if she so wished. It was difficult to spare the time for the two girls to lie together alone, without any fear of interruptions. But then, Charity told herself firmly, it made the few occasions on which they did manage that much more special. No, she had nothing to complain about.

And neither did Rebecca. Charity could see her sister growing more and more confident in her role as mistress of the house, but also in that of mother. It was often said that a woman's true purpose in life was to nurture her babies; that was certainly not true for Charity, but in Rebecca's case it seemed undeniable. When she saw her sister with the two babes, it just looked so natural, so right.

Charity trotted up to Rebecca's room that evening. Her sister looked up at Charity, her face full of a joy and yes, serenity, that Charity had not seen in Rebecca before. One baby lay cradled in its mother's arms—Charity still could not tell which was Mary and which Pat—and the other was asleep in the double rocker.

"She's just dozing off," the mother said quietly, looking down at the baby she held. "Pat has been sleeping for some while now, but this little miss had a touch of wind, poor lamb. But you're better now," she crooned to the child. "Aren't you, lovely?"

"You're so good with them."

"Of course. I'm their mother. Wait." Rebecca stood up and gently laid Mary next to her brother. "She's sleepy enough now."

"Shouldn't nurse be looking after them?" Charity asked. Rebecca, after all, was only a month post her lying-in and the nurse was being paid a small fortune to look after the twins. Rebecca had refused a wet nurse—the first time Charity had ever known her to rebel—but she admitted that she had been grateful to have nurse's help.

Rebecca laughed. "She should, I know. She regularly tells me so. But I find I do not care to part with them. Oh, Charity, aren't they such angels?"

"They're lovely," Charity said awkwardly. "They're very small still." She hung over the cradle, looking at her nephew and niece.

"That's because there's two of them. But they're growing. I'm sure Patrick's put on a pound or more this last sennight."

"You seem to know just what to do."

"Yes." Rebecca looked at Charity. "It is strange, you know. Mother always told me that I would not be able to cope alone. That I needed someone, a gentleman, to look after me. I believed her too. That is partly why I agreed to marry Fotheringay, for I had not the confidence to refuse. Yet now, with my husband hundreds or thousands of miles away, and I with more responsibilities than ever. Better responsibilities," she added, smiling. "I feel happier and more confident than ever before. Isn't that strange?"

Charity regarded her sister thoughtfully. "I'm not so sure it is," she said. "It was always there, inside you. You just didn't believe it. Such mothering as I had came from you, you know."

"My big little sister," Rebecca said, looking at her.

"Precisely. And now you have your own children to mother. And Becca, you deserve your happiness more than anyone I know." And Charity gave her sister a clumsy hug.

The next morning, Charity had an arrangement to walk with Nan. She was just sitting with Rebecca, who was beginning to tire of keeping to the house, and was beginning to speak of inviting a few visitors round in the near future, when a note was delivered to her. Upon breaking it open, she scanned through it. Nan sent her apologies, but was unable to make it that morning; a family situation had come up. Charity remembered the way she'd felt when Rebecca was taken suddenly ill. She hoped Nan was not facing any similar circumstances, though certainly a birth was out of the question. Nan's parents were elderly and past the age of childbearing, and her only sibling was her brother, currently at sea.

"Bother," Charity exclaimed, reading the letter aloud to Rebecca. "I hope it's nothing serious, I must send Nan a quick response to check. But I can't imagine it is anything too disastrous. Nevertheless, that leaves me with no plans for today." She hesitated, looking at her sister. "Do you want me to stay in with you?"

Rebecca shook her head. "Not if, as seems likely by the look on your face, you have other ideas. What are you thinking: to devote yourself to the piano, or to go shopping? If it's the second, do you think you could buy me some more embroidery silks? I seem to be running short."

Charity blushed. "I wasn't intending to go to the shops," she said evasively.

In fact, the notion that had occurred to her was that she might take this opportunity of visiting Isobelle—perhaps, even, spending a happy hour or more in bed with her. They hadn't managed this of late, and Charity missed it desperately. The stolen kisses, the moments at the Sisterhood meetings where they could touch if they wanted to… These were nice, but they weren't enough. Charity ached to have her body pressed against Isobelle's, to rub her palm against Isobelle's private place and watch her lover convulse with ecstasy. Kisses were good—they were lovely—but they weren't enough. None of this, however, could she say to Rebecca.

"Then do not bother on my account," Rebecca said, cheerfully enough. "I think I must have done more than enough of it in the last month! I need a new hobby, I think. Perhaps I too shall learn the piano!"

"You hated it," Charity pointed out, remembering their childhood when the one time that Rebecca had not pleased her parents was in her quietly spoken but determined objection to learning music.

"Not as much as I hate being alone. No, dear," Rebecca added, "that was not a veiled request for you to stay. I think I will spend this morning organising my first few outings. If you could bring me paper and pen, that is all I need."

Charity obliged. "You're sure you don't mind my going out?" She hesitated in the doorway.

"Oh, go away!" Rebecca laughed. "I see more than enough of you. Go and enjoy yourself."

"Then I will."

The carriage was brought round, and before another half-hour had passed, Charity had arrived on the Greenaways' doorstep.

"There is no need to announce me," she said, smiling at the footman as he opened the door. "I know my way, and Iso—Miss Greenaway will not be shocked."

James gave a ponderous nod. "Very well, ma'am. I believe…"

But what the footman believed, Charity did not wait to find up. She was halfway up the stairs before he began his sentence, and fully up and out of earshot before he got any further. She knocked lightly on the door of Isobelle's pretty sitting room and then opened it. The sun was shining through the windowpanes, lighting a path across the room. Charity took a second to admire the décor: the beautiful mix of books and ornaments, and the neatly laid fire in the grate. But it was Isobelle herself she wanted, not her room. The door to Isobelle's bedroom was slightly ajar, and Charity went towards it.

"Isobelle?" She pushed the door further open. "Are you— oh!"

Charity grasped for the door frame, feeling dizzy. Isobelle was indeed in her bedchamber, but she was not alone. Lydia— Mrs Seacombe—was sat on the heavy-backed chair Isobelle loved so much, Isobelle on her lap. The white undergarments, which were all that the pair was wearing, showed brightly in the darkened room. Isobelle's stay laces hung down, her corset attached only because of Lydia's grasp around her. They were lips to lips, kissing and giggling. The scene was so familiar—so painfully familiar. Charity had been there, had been the lady that Isobelle was embracing with such unrestrained pleasure.

She stood, stricken, in the doorway, unable to look away, unable to move. Isobelle glanced up and saw her, and the dreamy expression in her eyes faded.

"Harry…" she faltered.

Lydia looked round also. "Oh," she said merrily, seeming unaware of the tension in the room, "have you come to join us?"

Charity looked at her for a second, then back at Isobelle. "No," she said quietly, trying not to embarrass herself, to fall to the floor in tears. "No, I am not. I…" She took a sudden breath, realising that she had forgotten to breathe since seeing the two ladies together. "I have…I have other plans. Pray excuse me."

She stumbled from the room, taking a second or two to compose herself in the sitting room. It seemed less beautiful now, as if what she had just witnessed had tainted the room itself. There was the painful prick of tears at the back of her eyes, but she would not shed them. Not here, not publicly. Alone, perhaps, when she got home. She needed to be home. She heard a rustling from the bedroom, footsteps on the floor.

"Harry, wait," Isobelle begged. "Please."

Charity ignored her, flitting to the door and then shutting it firmly behind her. She would not make a scene; she couldn't do anything to hurt Isobelle, no matter how much Isobelle might have hurt her. So she walked, outwardly calm, down the stairs, even managing to smile at James as she passed him in the hall.

"Thank you," she said quietly. "I just wanted to see Miss Greenaway for a second. Please excuse me." James opened the door, and Charity walked through it. Half-dazed, she clambered back into the carriage. "Home please."

The coachman clicked his tongue, and the carriage set off. Charity had made this journey so many times, but never had it seemed as long as on this occasion. Longing for home, for privacy, every second stretched out beyond its normal due. It hurt. It hurt so much. Isobelle and Lydia. She kept remembering the way they had looked, clinging to each other. Isobelle's face had been flushed a pretty pink; strands of her hair had whispered down around her shoulders. She looked beautiful and desirable, as always. Beautiful, desirable and in the arms of another lady.

The carriage pulled up, and Charity stepped out, almost falling over in her hurry to retreat to the safety of her own house. As she entered, Rebecca came out of the drawing room, a neatly inscribed list in one hand.

"Why, Charity!" she said. "I thought you were visiting Miss Greenaway."

"She was...otherwise engaged." Charity swallowed down a sob. "Becca, please, don't ask questions. I just need..."

"Charity!" Rebecca exclaimed again, going over to her sister and looking up into her face. "What is wrong, dear?"

"Please." It was all Charity said as she pulled away from her sister.

Rebecca was silent for a moment. Then, just before Charity moved out of sight, she called, "Charity." Charity turned to look down at her, and Rebecca said softly, "I love you. I'm here if you need me."

Charity produced a watery smile. "I know." Then she bolted for the safety of her room.

CHAPTER TWENTY-FOUR

The rest of the day and the night passed slowly. Charity sent her sister a little note, still unable to speak of what had gone on, begging that she should be left alone for a while, that she was unwell. It was true enough. Charity rarely cried, and the storm of tears which had burst from her when she reached the privacy of her bedchamber had left her shaken and worn out. Isobelle— how could Isobelle have done such a thing? How could she?

Then the pernicious thoughts started. How often had Isobelle been making love with other women? Charity had not thought that there was any particularly fond relationship between Isobelle and Lydia: they were friends, of course, but not close. Not close enough to be lovers. Surely not that. What had Charity missed? How could she have been quite so wrong? The tears came again, but slower. The exhaustion of despair had claimed her, and Charity could only sit on the floor, her head buried in the bedclothes and let the tears trickle down her face.

Isobelle. Oh, Isobelle.

There was a knock at her bedroom door, but Charity did not answer, and the knock was not repeated. Later, when she looked outside, she saw a tray with food on it, and a note from her sister. She brought it inside the room, but had not the stomach to touch the food, though she read the note. It was a simple enough letter, though Charity thought she might have handled criticism better than this generous sympathy.

Oh, Charity, dear, I hope you are all right. At least, I know you are not and I wish I could help. I'm here if you need me, dearest—you know that. All my love, Rebecca.

"All my love." That was what Charity had thought she had from Isobelle: all her love. When in fact, she was sharing it with who knew how many others? But then, thought Charity, turning to maudlin self-blame, why should she have been so arrogant as to assume that? Why had she ever thought that she, Charity Bellingham, could be enough for Isobelle Greenaway? How foolish. How naïve and yes, arrogant, she had been! She had got no more than her just desserts.

But Isobelle! Why had Isobelle not just said something? Why had she let Charity believe that they were equally in love? She must have known how Charity felt. It had hardly been a secret. Why not point out to Charity that she was fond of her, of course, but that it was nothing serious? Nothing exclusive. Perhaps she had not thought that Charity would think any such thing. Charity cried, occasionally slept for a while, woke up and cried again.

When the morning came, she felt as if she were recovering from a bad illness. Perhaps she was. A fever of the brain—a few months too happy to be real. It had all been a fantasy, a silly girl's dreams. Rebecca was right: no one got perfection in life. She had just had an earlier opportunity to discover it than Charity had. There was another knock on the door.

"Come in," Charity called, expecting the maid. But it was Rebecca, carrying the jug of warm water for the morning's ablutions. Charity woke up to reality again with a jolt. "Surely you shouldn't be carrying something like that?" she asked anxiously, taking it from her sister.

"If I were a servant, I would be expected to be back at work by now," Rebecca said. "Anyway, I preferred to come myself." Her face was troubled. "Oh, Charity, I wish I could help you, dear."

"You do." Charity splashed the water into a bowl and sluiced her hands. Looking in the vanity mirror, she could see that her face was blotchy and her eyes swollen with tears. "It's over. Between me and Isobelle, I mean. It's over."

"I'm so sorry," Rebecca said quietly.

Charity made a noise that was not quite a laugh or a sob. "So am I. It was stupid. Becca, I thought she loved me."

"And she did not? I do not want to pry, dearest, but I want to help."

"No. She has"—Charity attempted a wobbly smile—"someone else. Please, Becca, I can't talk about it, even to you."

"I know." Rebecca put her arms round her sister and held her tightly, almost as if she were one of the twins. "I love you, Charity."

"I love you too. It was just...oh," she sighed. "I will be down soon, Becca."

"There's no hurry," Rebecca said softly. "Let me call Sarah for some cold water as well, to splash on your face. It helps when your eyes feel so swollen."

"Thank you."

Rebecca went to the door and called the maid. Then, armed with a bowl of water and a napkin, she gently washed her sister's face, still treating Charity as if she were one of her precious babes.

"You are kind," Charity said gratefully.

She thought about what Rebecca had said. *It helps when your eyes feel so swollen.* The words had the ring of experience about them, and Charity wondered how many times she had left Rebecca to cry alone, never thinking to come and sit with her, or offer support. Charity's own bleak unhappiness at home with their parents had made her selfish. She hadn't considered that Rebecca might be miserable too. And had Charity ever asked Rebecca about her marriage, in all of the months they had been living in this house? She had a horrible feeling she had not. Yet it was clear that Rebecca felt no resentment of her sister.

"I wish I could help in other ways," Rebecca said. "It seems so little."

She was brushing Charity's hair now, with a soft-bristled brush that removed tangles without tugging. Charity knew that when Rebecca had finished, her hair would shine like silk. But that didn't matter. Nothing mattered, save Isobelle's betrayal.

"You can't. No one can." Charity felt the tears threaten her eyes again, and she blinked them back.

"I know," Rebecca said softly.

"I'm sorry. I am being unkind."

"No, dearest, you are upset. There, your hair is brushed out. Let me help you into a new dress."

The unexpectedly practical solutions Rebecca offered were surprisingly helpful. Nothing could mend a broken heart, but when, thirty minutes later, Charity looked once more at herself in the mirror, she could see the difference. Her face was still a little blotchy, but she no longer looked crumpled and broken. Physically, too, she felt better: not so sick and uncomfortable, and the worst of the headache had passed. She gave Rebecca a wobbly smile.

"If nothing else, I at least look a bit more human."

"Come and have breakfast," Rebecca urged.

Rebecca stayed almost by Charity's side for the whole morning. She did not press or worry her sister for details, but Charity could feel the wordless sympathy enveloping her, even as they sat together in the drawing room some hours later, involved in their different pursuits. The quiet mood was ended, however, by the entrance of the footman.

"Miss Greenaway," he announced. The sisters exchanged looks.

"I'll be upstairs," Rebecca said hastily, gathering up her embroidery. She hesitated. "Unless…?"

Charity knew what she meant. "No. It is kind of you, but no. I must face her myself."

Rebecca left, and a minute later Isobelle arrived, beautiful in palest blue, her gloves immaculate white.

"Harry, darling," she fluted, her hands held out to Charity in her usual appealing gesture. Strangely, the gesture meant so little—now. Charity flinched.

"Hello Isobelle," she said gravely. "Please, take a seat."

"You are so stern, Harry! Tell me you are not upset about yesterday? It was nothing, you know. Lydia was there, and one thing led to another..." She gave a helpless shrug.

"I see. I thought...but never mind what I thought."

Isobelle's words, her carelessness, hurt more than anything. It was not true love that had made her do it, impelled her to make love with Lydia, just a morning's entertainment. Charity knew, too, that Lydia would have treated it just the same. It was nothing important to either lady. They had flirted a little, both socialite butterflies who cared only for the moment, nothing deeper. Charity had thought that Isobelle was different, but she had been wrong. It was her own mistake, Charity thought. No one else's.

"Harry, darling, you're not angry with your Isobelle?" Isobelle's voice had a slight quaver; her eyes were big and appealing. "You know what I am. I can't help it."

Charity swallowed hard, trying to dislodge the metaphorical stone stuck in her gullet. Isobelle was right. It was just what she was like. If Charity had taken her own image of Isobelle and put her on a pedestal, that was hardly Isobelle's fault. And Charity had been warned—gently, lovingly warned—by some of the Sisterhood that Isobelle was...as Isobelle was. Charity hadn't wanted to believe it; she had wanted to keep her idealised lover perfect in every way. Even when she had discovered something of Isobelle's feet of clay, when she had gone to her in distress about Fotheringay's slaves, she had pushed the knowledge from her, still determined to keep Isobelle as a goddess who could not be wrong. How could she now feel betrayed when the betrayer was her own mind, not Isobelle?

"I know."

"You forgive me?"

Taking a deep breath, Charity looked straight into Isobelle's eyes. "Of course."

She watched the smile dawn slowly on Isobelle's lips. "Of course you do. I knew you would. You understand me."

I didn't, Charity wanted to say. *But I do now. All too well.* She knew it would never be the same for her now; could never be. The adoration had lost its shine. But Charity kept the words to herself, just as she kept the hurt tucked closely to her soul. Isobelle should never know how much she had hurt Charity.

"Yes," she said, amazed to hear how steady, how normal, her voice sounded. "Isobelle, you must go. I have to get ready for a picnic this afternoon. I'll see you soon."

She turned to go upstairs, but Isobelle grasped her sleeve. "Without a kiss? Harry, how can I believe you forgive me if you leave without a kiss?"

Charity looked down at Isobelle, and for a second she thought her grief would overwhelm her. Isobelle might never have been the wonderful, trustable character Charity had envisioned, and therefore Charity had not lost a real person. But she had lost her belief in that person, in the Isobelle she had thought she'd known. She leaned down and kissed Isobelle gently on the lips.

"Goodbye Isobelle."

CHAPTER TWENTY-FIVE

It was hard, at first, spending time with others of the Sisterhood. Charity knew that they all had some idea of what had happened. Even if Isobelle had not told, Lydia would have done, giving one of her expressive shrugs and asking, "How should I have known that Harry would take things so badly?" Charity had done her best not to add grist to the rumour mill, but she knew she did not seem quite as joyful as she had once done. Even when she acknowledged that she had no logical reason to be upset, it did little to stop the real emotional hurt. Isobelle was sweet to her, and Charity did not want to lose her friendship on top of everything else, so she responded, albeit with a touch of reserve. Their tête-à-têtes still occurred occasionally, when Charity could find no excuse to avoid them, but she shied away from Isobelle's kisses even then. To begin with, Isobelle had attempted to treat her just as she had done previously, but no matter how much Charity wanted to keep her former lover as a friend, she could not go back to those halcyon days of before.

Cara was gruff as always, but Charity could feel the understanding behind her matter-of-fact phrases. She had tried to tell Charity once how such a passion for Isobelle was liable to end. Charity wondered whether Cara had been in a similar situation once in her own life—perhaps not with Isobelle herself, but with another bright, vivacious, unreliable lover. Cara had no partner now, and seemed not to wish for one—as if she had been there herself and learned the hard way to stay safe. Or maybe that was just Charity projecting her own feelings onto the older lady. Would Charity end up like Cara one day, childless and loveless, but without the riches and title which must ease Cara's path, at least a little? She tried to stifle such morbid wonderings but could not altogether shift them.

Jane was friendly, in her way, but it was plain to see that her whole life was bound up in Emily. Since Emily had little interest in social gatherings, it followed that Jane too was rarely to be seen at them. Emily herself was—just Emily, Charity thought with a reluctant smile. She had never met anyone quite like the diminutive, pretty blonde, with her fascination with academic study. Emily was as friendly to Charity as she was to anyone bar Jane, but the normal ideas of friendship meant little to her.

Charity's one anchor in the Sisterhood was really Nan—an idea which would have been unthinkable when she first met the group. Nan was neither outstandingly beautiful nor fearsomely intelligent, though she was both pretty and clever in her own way. Nor did she have the immediate charisma that Isobelle undoubtedly held. She was no one to fall in love with, despite Cara's suggestion, but she was a good and loyal friend, and Charity valued her support above all. Most importantly of all, whilst Nan did not bring up the subject of Isobelle's past relationship with Charity, she did not make it obvious that she was avoiding the issue. If Charity spoke of it, Nan responded honestly but without embarrassment. Charity suspected it was a tactful lie but was grateful.

Sitting together with Nan one afternoon, Charity decided to bring up the subject of Isobelle. Sometimes she felt the need to speak of it, to explain to an understanding friend how she felt.

Rebecca had been sympathetic, but she could not understand, no matter how hard she tried.

"I'm not...in love with Isobelle," Charity said. "Not any more. But I love her, as a friend. As...well, as Isobelle. I know what she is like, and asking her to be different would take away part of what makes her who she is. But however fond I may be of her, she is not for me. Not as a love." She looked up at Nan, a wistful expression on her face. "I suppose I am just too boring. I can't live with extremes of emotion as Isobelle can. I want to come back to someone and know they'll be there for me, no matter what. Perhaps I want too much."

"No," said Nan. "That doesn't sound unreasonable." She smiled suddenly, and Charity thought unexpectedly how pretty Nan was when she smiled. "But nor does it sound like Isobelle."

Charity laughed. "Hardly." She sobered up. "I would not want to change her, but I cannot have her as she is. And that is a contradiction I will just have to work out for myself."

"You're very wise."

Charity stared at Nan, startled. "I? Of all the things I've ever had said of me, that is not one!"

"Often," Nan said slowly, "people think that they can change someone. Either the other person, or failing that, themselves. By the time they realise that this isn't possible, they've torn each other apart."

"You see, that's just what I don't want." Charity traced a little pattern on her dress with her finger. "I don't want to hate Isobelle. And she's done so much for me. But I can't, I just can't..." She broke off.

Nan, ever practical, refilled Charity's tea cup and passed it back to her.

"Of course you can't," she said calmly. "As I say, I think you're wise."

"Either that or a coward." Charity fought to keep her tone light. She took a sip of tea.

Nan smiled, understanding that the conversation was over. "Let's stick with wise, shall we? And now, are you and your sister attending the concert tomorrow evening? I've heard it's going to be the most terrible crush."

"Rebecca will be gladder than ever not to be attending, in that case!" Charity replied. "She doesn't care much for music at any time, though she does her best to pretend for my sake. No, we are going to a quiet soiree with Mrs Hollings."

"At which you," said Nan, "will do your best to pretend for her sake! Well, I wish you luck. I don't know when the Sisterhood are meeting again, but I feel sure we will find out in due course." She stood. "Bless you, my dear. Remember what I said. And thank you for the tea."

The next excitement to befall any of the Sisterhood, however, was not a meeting but the return on leave from his ship of Captain Musgrove, Nan's brother. Charity, knowing that Nan had become passionate about the abolition of slavery after hearing his stories of slave ships he had encountered, was interested to know he was returning but privately a little concerned about meeting him. She herself was in a difficult position as regarded meetings about slavery: her knowledge about Fotheringay had shaken her badly, and she still had not found the right moment to break the news to Rebecca. The twins were still very tiny, and any shock for her sister might rebound onto them. Charity's new-found knowledge about the origin of the wealth on which she lived made her uncomfortable; and she fought shy of Captain Musgrove, certain that he would see her guilty secret in her eyes, or have discovered it from Nan. Consequently, she found reasons to refuse Nan's invitations to tea whilst he was around, explaining that her sister needed her; she must visit the haberdashery; her library books needed changing. Charity knew, and Nan knew, and Charity knew that Nan knew, that these were excuses, but her friend was kind enough not to push her point.

In the end, the meeting with Captain Musgrove came entirely unexpectedly. Charity, under Cara's chaperonage, was attending the Carborys' ball. It was a large event arranged to celebrate Miss Carbory's newly announced betrothal to Lord

Worcester, a rotund and genial lord in his early thirties whom many saw as an excellent match for the beautiful young lady. Charity had ducked away for a moment, seeing Isobelle and Lydia talking together, something that even now retained the ability to hurt—and she had walked straight into Nan, who was accompanied by a gentleman. To Charity's surprise, he was on an eye level with her; she had no need to ask who he was, for the similarities between himself and his sister were marked. They had the same light-brown hair, the same bearing. Captain Musgrove did not have Nan's plumpness, but a physical, seafaring life might explain that. There was also one major difference, which drew the eye the moment Charity met him.

"Oh Harry." Nan smiled. "This is my brother, Captain Musgrove. Forgive me if I leave you to introduce yourselves. I am supposed to be dancing with Mr Foster, and I feel sure he will start pursuing me indignantly if I do not find my place."

Charity, who had occasionally danced with Mr Foster herself, smiled. He was a kind gentleman, in his way, but he liked everything to run in its proper order. Finding the orchestra starting their music and his dance partner nowhere to be seen, he would be quite upset.

"Of course." She and Nan exchanged an understanding glance as Nan hurried off. Then she turned her eyes to Captain Musgrove, curtseying. "Captain Musgrove, it is delightful to meet you. Nan speaks highly of you, which says more than I need to explain."

"She does of you, also," he said, bowing. "I believe it is usually the custom to shake hands at this point," he added seriously, "only…" He looked ruefully at the pinned right sleeve of his coat where an arm must once have been.

"If you think I'm taking that for an excuse," Charity retorted. She held out her left hand to him, and he grinned. He put his own left hand over hers, then lifted it to his mouth.

"Miss Bellingham, you are an unusual lady, just as my sister told me."

Charity's smile faded, and she pulled her hand away gently. "So I am told."

She tried to keep her tone light, but she could tell he knew better. His eyes met hers.

"That, Miss Bellingham, was a compliment," he said.

She met his gaze openly. "Usually, it is not."

She remembered all the gentlemen who had shied away from her honesty. All the ladies who had mocked her behind her back. The humiliation of being left at the edge of the room whilst gentlemen stood watching the dances in preference to leading her out. How could she blame them? She was different, in a world where convention was king. But he was truly Nan's brother, in personality as well as blood.

"Do not hold me responsible for other people's ignorance," he said quietly. He looked away, to where his sister was standing in conversation with Lady Caroline. "Nan is unusual too. I value her for it. And yes"—he lifted his chin a centimetre higher, his bearing very much a military man's—"I know her for who she is. She is not ashamed and nor am I."

Charity dug her fingernails into the palms of her hands and studied the floor as if it were a source of great fascination. "I am, though."

Unexpectedly, she felt the warmth of his fingers against her skin. His hand had gone to her face, so lightly that she was hardly aware of the touch, save for the heat.

"You should not be." His touch became firmer, persuading her to look straight at him once more. "Never apologise for who you are." He dropped his hand, and also his serious tone. "There is dancing to be done, and I will not accept an excuse," he said merrily. "Come, be my partner, if you dare to try and work through the difficulties of dancing with a one-armed man."

"It would be my pleasure," Charity said. Every word was true.

Later, she couldn't help wondering whether he would have been as kind if he had known her background—if he had known that Mr Fotheringay's wealth was built on the backs of slaves. Even had she wanted to, she could hardly have brought the conversation up at a ball, but she felt somehow as if she were deceiving him. He knew that she loved ladies and had not cavilled at that; this, however, Charity feared might be a bigger problem. If she had disliked him, it would have been one thing, but liking him, how could she hide something she knew would be important to him? It felt like cheating. She sighed, turned over in bed and tried to sleep.

CHAPTER TWENTY-SIX

"I have the nicest note from Miss Musgrove, Charity," Rebecca said next morning, looking up from her post. "She says that you mentioned I was now up to having visitors, and begs that I will allow her to visit and be introduced to the twins. She also asks that she might introduce her brother to me. I didn't realise she had a brother, but she says you have met him?"

"Yes." Charity's guilty secret came to the forefront of her mind, though in truth it had hardly been far away anyway. "I met him last night at the Carborys' ball."

"Is he nice? But Miss Musgrove is, so I am sure he must be."

Charity gave a wry grin. "That's not always the way, Becca. After all, you are nice and you got saddled with me as a sister!"

"Charity, you are dreadful!"

"Precisely my point, my dear."

Rebecca made her best attempt at a stern look. "You know that is not what I meant. But Mr Musgrove—"

"Captain Musgrove," Charity corrected her. "He's a sailor."

"Captain Musgrove, then. Is he nice?"

Charity thought of the good-tempered man who had made so little of his disability. "Yes," she said softly. "He is very nice." She saw the look on her sister's face and sighed inwardly. Rebecca had not stopped hoping that Charity might find a pleasant gentleman and settle down with him. The disastrous end to her relationship with Isobelle had made her sister even more optimistic about the possibility. Charity did not have the heart to tell her that she never would—never *could*—find a man she was prepared to marry. But sometimes it was difficult, knowing Rebecca's ambition and knowing also she could never fulfil it.

"I may ask them to come, then?"

"Becca," Charity protested, laughing, "it's your house! You may invite whomever you wish to come around."

"I know. But you would have no objection. And," Rebecca added daringly, "you would agree to be in to welcome them with me?"

Charity slid her chair back from the table and stood up. "Yes, dearest sister, I would."

The invitation for the Musgroves to visit the following day was therefore written and accepted. Charity found that she was looking forward to seeing Captain Musgrove again; Nan she was pleased to see on any occasion. There was just one small point, which grew bigger with every moment that passed. She had determined that she must tell the Captain about her brother-in-law's associations with slavery. Whether this would be an unforgivable thing from his perspective, she had yet to find out. But she recalled Nan's reaction when the news had first been discovered, and she could not feel comfortable about it. If Captain Musgrove's reaction was equally strong, how would Nan feel? Captain Musgrove was her brother; Charity was merely a friend. Would Nan still care to spend time with her if her brother's disapproval was very clearly stated? Charity was not sure.

The problem would be telling Captain Musgrove the information without Rebecca overhearing her. Someday— someday soon, Charity promised herself—she would tell

Rebecca the whole story, but not now, not yet. One thing at least she felt sure of, however: no matter how disgusted the Captain might be by his discovery about Mr Fotheringay's slaves, he would not betray the truth of the matter to Rebecca, once he understood the depth of her ignorance. No brother of Nan's could possibly consider doing such a thing.

Surprisingly, it was Rebecca who seemed more on edge about the appointment the next day. Although she had met Nan at various events—including the Abolitionist meeting she had attended—Nan had never visited the Fotheringays' house. Charity, who had seen Rebecca welcome all sorts of guests from all sorts of backgrounds, was disconcerted at first and then saddened when she discovered the two-pronged reason for her sister's agitation. Rebecca had known that Isobelle, no matter how polite, had not really warmed to her. As Isobelle was the only member of the Sisterhood who had come to the house, excepting just to pick Charity up for a function, Rebecca feared that Nan would feel likewise about her. No matter the amount of reassurance Charity gave, nor the reminders she added about Rebecca's liking for Nan on other occasions, her sister still looked anxious and unconvinced. The second reason, Charity had to guess at, but she strongly suspected that Rebecca's particular determination to do everything right for the Musgroves had to do with the idea that Charity and Captain Musgrove might make a match of it. Her one consolation was that the captain, knowing what he knew, would certainly not have any such impossible thoughts in his head—though, Charity thought ruefully, there were any number of gentlemen who had managed to avoid being bowled over by her charms without that particular knowledge!

When the unmistakeable sounds of guests arriving carried to the upstairs sitting room, however, Charity saw that Rebecca had gone quite white.

"Don't be daft, Becca!" she reproved her sister. "Anyone would think that a Royal Duke was arriving, not just some good friends." She caught Rebecca's hopeful look and shook her head. "No, dear, not *that* sort of good friend."

"You're sure?" Rebecca asked wistfully.

"Quite sure. Anyway," Charity added quickly, hearing the sound of footsteps on the stairs, "let us not speak of it quite now."

The footman announced the Musgroves, and Rebecca and Charity stood to make their curtseys. Rebecca might be shy, but she could never be anything but polite.

"It is so good of you both to come," she said, smiling. "Will you not come in and be seated? I'm sure the maid will be in shortly with the tea." Her eyes met the footman's questioningly, and he bowed slightly, taking his cue.

"It is very good of you to have us, so soon after…" Nan's gaze travelled the room, as if expecting the twins to appear by magic.

"She's glad of the company," Charity said briskly. "She has had to put up only with my company for much of the past few weeks!"

"Any face, in fact," Nan said, laughing, "would be better than none."

"No indeed. Goodness, you must think me so rude," exclaimed Rebecca, in genuine anxiety. "And Mr—Captain Musgrove too. We are delighted to see you both. Please take no notice of Charity!"

"I expect they know quite how much attention to pay to me," Charity said.

When the tea had arrived and been poured, the group separated into two parts, with Charity and Captain Musgrove talking politely about the ball a couple of nights ago, whilst Nan encouraged Rebecca to talk about herself. Charity could not help keeping one ear out for the conversation between the two ladies, a fact Captain Musgrove noticed and commented upon.

"What is the matter, Miss Bellingham? Are you concerned that Nan is going to insult your sister in some way?"

Charity looked at him indignantly. "Honestly, in some ways you are just like your sister! You were not supposed to think that I was doing anything but listening to you."

"I may be arrogant," he said dryly, "but I am not that arrogant!"

Charity had taken a sip of tea and almost choked at his response. "I'm sorry. That was rude of me. I was just making sure Rebecca was all right. She was terribly worried about whether she would find the right things to say."

"Does Nan really have a reputation for being that hard to please?" he asked. "Be assured, I will tease her about it later, if so!"

"Not at all. But Rebecca...she feels you are both so very much above us socially that she fears making a mistake, or saying the wrong thing. You must know Miss Greenaway?" The name still felt odd and difficult on Charity's tongue, most particularly when she had to make so much effort to sound natural. He nodded. "I'm afraid she made Rebecca a little aware of her position, on one or two of her visits. Unintentionally, of course. She was trying to be kind, but Rebecca could see she was trying, if you understand what I mean?"

"I do indeed," he said promptly. "Nothing serves so much to remind you that you don't belong as someone else trying to cover that very fact up. I remember when I was first made acting captain after the actual captain of my ship was taken ill. The quartermaster was so keen not to seem as if he was disrespecting my temporary position that I could think of nothing but the temporariness of it!"

Charity laughed, liking him more with every second. She could understand why Nan was so fond of him: she too would have liked to have a brother like Captain Musgrove. "That is it precisely. However, Rebecca seems to be managing quite successfully. Hush a second, or pretend to be talking to me, so I can just listen."

"Pretend to be talking to you!" Captain Musgrove shook his head. "The things you ladies ask a poor seafarer to do!"

But Charity was not listening. Both her ears were now set on overhearing the conversation between Nan and Rebecca.

"I'm afraid that I'm not clever like you and Charity, making things happen," she heard Rebecca say apologetically. "I often prefer to sit by the window with my embroidery, watching the children wriggle about on the rug. I never realised they began to move so early."

"I'm not sure you are doing so little, ma'am," Nan said. "Perhaps by the way you are raising your children, you are doing much more than we are."

"Don't call me 'ma'am'," Rebecca begged. "You call Charity by her name…well," she corrected herself, laughing, "you call her Harry. And I am her sister. Please, call me Rebecca."

The two ladies settled comfortably in for a coze, and Charity thought, not for the first time, how good Nan was about making people feel confident, able to be themselves. She took a deep breath and looked back at the captain. Much as she had been enjoying their banter, she knew she must take this opportunity to speak privately to him about what was bothering her so much. Would she lose his friendship—and more importantly Nan's? She had not realised how much she relied on Nan's support and kindness until she ran the risk of losing it. Carefully, she pulled Captain Musgrove to the window seat, as if she wanted to show him the view outside, and then looked around cautiously before beginning. She had so much she had to say, but the first imperative was that the conversation stayed private from Rebecca. Taking a deep breath, she began.

"Before we talk any further, Captain Musgrove, I think there is something I must say," she said, determined to get the words out before she lost her courage. "I know your views on slavery from your sister, and believe me, I sympathise with them. However, what you do not yet know is that my brother-in-law, Rebecca's husband, upon whom I am…." She tried not to grit her teeth as she said the final word. "…dependent…is the owner of a plantation on Tortola. In other words, a slave owner."

Much to her disconcertion, Captain Musgrove did not look surprised. "I know," he said. "My sister told me."

"Oh?" Charity was hurt by the fact that Nan had not trusted her to make her own confession. She tried to keep her feelings out of her voice, but clearly did not succeed.

Captain Musgrove smiled at her engagingly. "She said," he went on, "that she knew you would tell me yourself, but that she would not speak to me again if I upset you with my reaction.

Which I appear to have done. Miss Bellingham, please do not leave me to Nan's wrath!"

"Oh," Charity said again, but this time with very different emotions. Not only would she keep Nan's friendship, but Nan had proven how much the friendship meant to her too. Charity's heart began to sing again. "That was like her."

"I will not tell her what you thought," the captain said teasingly, "if you will not tell her that despite my best intentions, I still managed to make a mull of the occasion."

"Captain Musgrove, you—oh!" Charity said a third time, laughing.

"That's better," he said, smiling back at her. "You have such a pretty laugh."

"And you, sir, are trying to put me quite out of countenance," she retorted, flicking a quick glance over at Nan, who was still chatting comfortably with Rebecca.

"Not at all! A mere statement of fact. Now, if I were to try and put you out of countenance, I could say…" He trailed off invitingly.

"You are quite impossible," she said sternly. "I begin to believe all which is said about sailors."

He sighed and pressed his hand to his heart. "Miss Bellingham, I am hurt to the core. Must I really be accused of destroying your faith in all seafarers? It is a hard load to carry!"

"And this," Charity said, her heart lighter than it had been in some time, "is certainly not how I anticipated this conversation would transpire." She hesitated. "Rebecca, my sister, she does not know any of this," she said awkwardly. "She has been through a lot lately, and she deserves any happiness she can find. I know I must tell her, in the end, but I fear her reaction. Theirs has not been a…a happy marriage. I dread making it worse still by informing her that her husband is a slave owner."

Captain Musgrove looked serious again. "In truth," he said, "I feel less…hatred is perhaps too strong a word…less anger with slave owners than I do with those who deliberately enslave and sell others, simply for money. It is the traders whom I—well, yes, whom I hate and despise. If you had seen the conditions in which these poor people are kept during their time at sea..." He looked earnestly at Charity. Nan and Rebecca were still engrossed in their conversation. Nan had the happy knack of bringing out the best in Charity's sister, and Charity loved to see the way Rebecca was blooming with Nan's gentle encouragement. But right now, Charity turned her attention thoroughly to Captain Musgrove. She would have time aplenty with Nan, but Nan's brother's time in London was limited. Reassured that Rebecca certainly could not hear, she nodded.

"Tell me," she said quietly. "At least, tell me what you can."

"Ah, that is perceptive of you," he said. "It is truth that there are some things of which I cannot speak. Not yet, at any rate. I know I seem a frivolous character, but sometimes that is the only way to get through the sights which I have seen."

"I'm sorry."

"You have no reason to be." He took a deep breath. "Can you imagine a ship, with room down below in the hull? A hundred, perhaps more, people down there, unable to see light, barely able to move, manacled to the walls or to each other. The traders cast their bodies overboard without a second's thought if they die; sometimes, too, if they are ill and it is feared that they might spread contagion throughout the ship. British men, some of them ex-Navy sailors, running such cruel operations. Not for noble reasons, just for the money they think it will bring them. Gold over the price of a man's life—or a woman's, or a child's.

"They like to take children. They find them more malleable, easier to 'tame', as they put it. The children do not fight. They just lie there, eyes open and despairing, waiting for death or enslavement." Charity, unintentionally, had recoiled, and the movement brought his attention away from his story and back to his audience. "Forgive me. I should not speak of such things in a lady's pretty sitting room."

"On the contrary," Charity said. "It should be spoken of everywhere until this evil trade is stamped out."

"And there, you see, is the rub." Captain Musgrove looked at her, frustration clear in his face. "When we have boarded such ships, we have no power to do anything. No power to help the helpless, for by the laws of the British Empire the traders are doing no wrong."

"Then the laws must change," Charity said, chin up in defiance. "And until they do, we keep fighting. Perhaps, on the front line, you despise our silly meetings as the maunderings of ladies with nothing better to occupy our time. And how can I blame you? But we must do what we can do. No matter how hopeless," she added sadly.

"We have to believe," he said quietly, "all of us, that things can and will change. Each in our way, doing what we must to orchestrate that change. Do not think I take the women's work lightly. Every person will play their part to rid this awful trade of its power." He shook off the sombre mood. "But for now, we have said all we can. Come, let us…I was going to say 'rejoin the ladies', but I fear what your response to that might be!"

"Oh," Charity said lightly, "but I am 'Harry', one of the boys. Do not let the skirts mislead you."

They returned to Nan and Rebecca. The twins were brought down, and the rest of the conversation became child-related. Charity found it hard, looking at Captain Musgrove cooing over baby Mary, to believe that this was the same gentleman who not five minutes earlier had been telling her about the awful sights he had seen. He seemed to have put it all behind him and was once again the carefree sailor. But then, as he had said, perhaps it was all a façade—no, not that, but a coping technique. For how could one live, otherwise, with the horrors of this world?

CHAPTER TWENTY-SEVEN

"You seemed to be getting on very well with Captain Musgrove." Rebecca looked at Charity hopefully as they talked over the visit later that afternoon.

"He's a good man." But Charity knew what Rebecca was aiming at. "But no, I'm not interested in him that way, Becca."

"It's a shame," Rebecca said wistfully.

"I know. But my tastes do not run that way, and he knows it." Charity had almost wanted to love Captain Musgrove. She would have been Nan's sister indeed that way and would have had every excuse to spend her time with her dear friend. But although she and the captain had made fast friends, there was and could never be more to it than that. Absent-mindedly, she picked the dead flowers out of an arrangement on a side table, rearranging those that were left to cover the gap.

"You told him…" Rebecca broke off.

Charity looked at the dead flowers in her hand, wondering what to do with them. "No, of course I did not. But he is Nan's brother. He knows about her, and he knows about me."

"About Nan?" Rebecca sounded shocked, and Charity realised, belatedly, that she had never actually spelt out the nature of the Sisterhood into which she had been welcomed.

"Rebecca," she said gently, unsure how to phrase the information, "do you not know what the Sisterhood is?"

Rebecca was silent, and Charity turned to check that she was all right. Her sister sat quietly, hands tightly clasped in her lap.

"You mean…you are all…?" Her words trailed off.

"Yes."

"All? Even Lady Caroline?"

"I thought you knew."

"I wondered once, but it did not seem possible. I thought I must be mistaken. So many, Charity!"

"Not really, if you think of the population of the *ton* in all," Charity said.

"So," Rebecca gave a half-hearted smile. "I cannot hope for wedding bells for you, then, dearest?"

Charity kissed her forehead. "No, dear. You can't. I'm sorry."

"I am sorry too. It is a shame. I would just like to see you safe, Charity." Rebecca's embroidery had fallen to the floor; she bent to recover it.

"Safe from the deviance of the Sisterhood?" Charity flung back, angrily.

"No, dear, not that. It's just…we are women. We are dependent on our menfolk. If Mr Fotheringay insisted on you leaving the house, I could not prevent him. Mother cannot help. Even if she took you in, most of her money stops on her death. I just want you to have a settled home, to know you could never lose it."

"Oh Becca!" Charity softened immediately, dropping the dead flowers by the side of the vase, to be taken away when she left the room—if she remembered. "I'm sorry. I should have more faith in you than that."

"Well, you should, rather, you know," Rebecca agreed, smiling up at her tall sister. "So I just thought…even if it were not a marriage for love—which so few of us, after all, get—it would be the chance of a safe home, somewhere you would always belong. Captain Musgrove seems nice, and his sister is delightful. It seemed so convenient."

Charity laughed. "It would be, indeed. But I could hardly marry him for convenience, even were he to ask me!"

"I suppose not." Rebecca sighed. "So what were you talking about so fervently?"

"Slavery." Charity hesitated. Should she go on? She could not put the moment off forever. "Becca, I have something to tell you."

"To do with slavery?" Rebecca looked interested. "Has the next meeting been arranged? I believe I am well enough to attend now."

"No, no. That is, it has, but that was not what I wanted to speak about." Charity had known the subject would be difficult to broach; now that she had started, she had no idea how to continue. "Becca, it's about Fotheringay."

"Fotheringay and slavery?" Rebecca had caught an inkling of the truth. Her voice wobbled a little as she spoke.

"Yes." Charity met her sister's eye. "His money is from sugar."

"No. No, that cannot be so!"

"The West Indies. Tortola is in the Caribbean. Fotheringay has a plantation there. I hoped, once I found out where it was, that somehow it could be proved wrong, but Lady Caroline made a few discreet inquiries. There can be no doubts, I'm afraid."

"Oh." Rebecca was white and silent. "I didn't realise," she said at last.

"Nor I." Charity cast an anxious look at her sister. "I didn't know how to, when to, tell you. How could I, when you were so close to birth? Or when Fotheringay left? When the twins were so small? Then as time passed...we were so happy here, you and I and the twins. I did not know how to bring the conversation up."

"Poor Charity. You bore it all alone."

"Not quite alone," Charity said quickly. "The Sisterhood. Nan, Lady Caroline." She could not say more, could not speak about how hurt she had been by Isobelle's reaction. Not to anyone, and certainly not to Rebecca. While her sister was kind, she simply could not understand. Although Charity told herself she was over her feelings about Isobelle, it still hurt so very much. She did not like to think about it too deeply.

"Were they dreadfully angry with me?" Rebecca asked in a small voice.

Charity looked at her in surprise. "Of course not. Why?"

"For marrying him. Supporting the slave trade." Rebecca would not meet Charity's gaze. She turned her eyes downwards, as if fascinated by her clasped fingers.

"But you did not know!"

"Perhaps...perhaps I should have known. I did nothing," Rebecca cried passionately. "I knew nothing of him. My mother said 'marry him', and that is what I did. I thought it was right. Or perhaps I should say that I never thought at all."

"Becca!" Charity was shocked by her sister's response. She had known that Rebecca would be distressed by learning that her husband's fortune came in great part by slavery. But she had thought that Rebecca would be upset, maybe even angry, with Fotheringay. She had not anticipated her sister turning the blame onto herself. Charity flung herself on her knees by Rebecca's side. "Why, Becca!"

For Rebecca was crying, heart-breaking sobs wracking her body. "I never questioned anything," she sobbed. "I thought it was not a female's place to do so. Father and Mother were so angered by your challenges. I did nothing, and thought it right."

"Most people, our mother and father included, would say that was right," Charity said gently.

"But you would not."

Charity gave a soft laugh. "Am I really such a paragon that my views should be so respected? I never thought myself so!"

"But these ladies, your 'Sisterhood' of whom you speak so highly, they would think so too."

Charity bit her lip. The conversation was quickly turning in a direction she did not want to go. Back to Isobelle, her laughing, careless comment: *But Harry, why on earth should that worry you?* Yet even Isobelle was a free thinker, confident that her own views were worth as much—nay, more—than anyone else's, man or no.

"And they are great ladies, some of them," Rebecca added. "If it were known just what they are, perhaps they would not be seen so. But Becca, I never thought you would care like this. *You* are not trading in slaves, no matter what Fotheringay is doing. You cannot be held at fault. Indeed, neither truly can Fotheringay, no matter your or my opinion. He is breaking no law."

"No written law, certainly," Rebecca said, determinedly wiping the tears from her cheeks. "But a moral law, God's law, what about that?"

"The *Bible* says—" Charity began uncertainly, but Rebecca interrupted.

"The *Bible* is certainly God's word," she said. "But it is God's law written down by humans. And humans, we know, are fallible."

"And what would God say of the Sisterhood, do you think?"

Rebecca blinked away the last of her tears and looked at the upturned face of her sister, kneeling beside her.

"I do not know," she admitted. "But this much I feel sure about: there is, there must be, more sin in hatred than in love. Slavery is based in hatred. No one can love his fellow man and enslave him."

"I did not know you thought so deeply." Charity blushed. "Forgive me. That was rude."

"No, merely honest." Rebecca thought for a moment. "It is difficult to know how to put this into words," she said. "I think that this time we have had together, since my husband went abroad...For the first time, we have been alone together, without our parents, without Fotheringay. And I have listened to the things you say—and, incidentally, read many of the tracts and books you leave around—without another critical voice telling you *and* me that you are wrong. And I have heard what you say and much of it sounds right to me. But I think most of all it is because of the twins."

"I don't understand." Charity reached up and brushed the final smudge of tears from Rebecca's face. Her sister was calm now—calm and more serious, more thoughtful, than Charity had ever realised she could be.

"I have my babies. My two beautiful babies—"

"And you are such a good mother," Charity said eagerly.

"I am not sure of that. But I love them unconditionally. And I can't help wondering whether the women's movement, such as that described in Mary Wollstonecraft's book, came from a mother of boy and girl twins." Rebecca saw Charity's face and smiled at the bewilderment on it. "No, do not think me crazed, dearest. I see Mary and Patrick, such wonderful babies, and I look out over a world which values one of my beloved twins above the other. I hear people say that they are valued equally, just in different ways, but that is not what I feel, what I see. I think of how Fotheringay rejoiced over Pat while ignoring our daughter, despite the fact that in their swaddling clothes he could not tell which was which. And I try not to speak badly of them, but I cannot help thinking of the way our parents treated you, and how they would not done the same had you been the boy they craved. Even though I do not hold her responsible, I think about the way Mother believed she had the right to dictate my future in a way she would never have done had I been born male. And that is not the future I want for Mary."

"Oh Rebecca," Charity said, half-stunned by this unexpected version of her sister.

"I confess," Rebecca admitted, her eyes gleaming now with amusement rather than tears, "that I picked up *A Vindication of the Rights of Women* originally because the author's name was Mary. But when I read it, I couldn't help thinking about what she said…Goodness," she added, suddenly sobering, "how did we get to here from Fotheringay's slaves?"

"I'm sure I don't know, but I have come an awful lot further than you have! What other shocks have you got for me, dearest and most unexpected sister? To think that you have been fermenting all these thoughts and ideas inside your head without my realising a thing!"

"The question is, though, what we can do about our own situation with Fotheringay," Rebecca reminded her.

Charity got to her feet, smoothing out the wrinkles that had begun to form in her dress as she knelt. "I do not think there is anything we can do," she said seriously. "Of course, this is all new to you, whereas I have known for a while. We—I hope you do not think I have been speaking behind your back, but in meetings the Sisterhood have discussed the matter, and have got nowhere. It does make things difficult, of course. Neither you nor I can put our names down as subscribers to the Abolition movement…"

"Because?"

"It will be pointed out, quite correctly, the hypocrisy of our living on the proceeds of slavery whilst campaigning against it. I live off Fotheringay as much as you, remember, and with much less excuse."

"I see."

"It might give those opposed to Abolition the chance to criticise the movement. And," she added thoughtfully, "those opposed to women having any say on matters such as this to claim it as proof that ladies lack the logic to understand such things."

"When in fact what we lack more is independent wealth."

Charity had still not come to terms with this new, knowledgeable Rebecca. She forced herself to say calmly, "Well, yes. Which is where Lady Caroline can lead by example. She has money, a title and a strength of purpose to ignore the male critiques of her position."

"Miss Greenaway too, I imagine?" Rebecca said.

Charity felt a pain in her chest as she thought once more about Isobelle. "Well, the money is in trust with Lady Greenaway, you know," she hedged.

Rebecca smiled, following a different train of thought. "It is so funny," she said, "hearing you speak of Lady this or that, as if it were quite natural. When I think of how much Mother would have loved such friendships, and yet you have come so much closer than she ever did!"

"I found it strange myself, to begin with," Charity agreed. "Indeed, in a way I still do. But they don't treat me as their inferior, you know."

"I can't imagine you allowing them to do so," her sister said. "It is strange that you must be so underappreciated by your own family, yet those whom they would treat as superior to them see so much more in you. I know I feel shy and—and ignorant in their company, but you face them as if no such anxiety could possibly exist."

"I am not underappreciated by all of my family," Charity said, holding her hand out to Rebecca. "Although I am beginning to believe that I have been committing just that sin in reference to you."

"Oh, but I was unthinking," Rebecca said absently, taking Charity's hand but with her eyes on the small carriage clock on the mantelpiece. "Until the twins were born, I was." She got to her feet. "And it is time I went to them. Nurse says I should make them wait for my attention, but I do not see why, when both I and they get pleasure from it." She turned when she got to the door, laughing back at Charity. "I have got so very independent of thought since their birth, you know!"

CHAPTER TWENTY-EIGHT

To Charity's great relief, Rebecca did not fall apart under the shock of discovering her husband's business was underpinned by slavery. She was thoughtful, certainly, and distressed, without doubt. But her reserves of strength were much greater than Charity had imagined. Charity was beginning to realise she had been greatly underestimating her sister. Nan, when she was told, smiled.

"Good for her. There is more to Mrs Fotheringay than meets the eye. I suspected so."

"Did you?" Charity asked, much surprised. "But anyway, she has taken the news much better than I feared. And now, at least there are no secrets between us."

Nan nodded. "It is so good to have family you know you can rely on. My parents are wonderful, but they are of a different generation. We do not always see eye to eye, though I know they will love and support me in whatever I do. But my brother, well!" She smiled fondly. "He is a different matter, as I'm sure you noticed."

"Yes." Charity smiled too. "Rebecca wants me to marry him, you know."

Nan looked up. "But I thought…You said—no secrets?"

"Oh, she knows that I am not interested in gentlemen. I think, though she would not admit it, that she hopes that he, or someone, might change my mind on that front. But she wants me to have a settled home. It has not occurred to her that I might be cheating Captain Musgrove if I married him just for that reason."

"I see." Nan was thoughtful.

"Pray reassure your brother that I have no expectations from him," Charity said hastily. "Indeed, even were he to ask, I could not agree. But he is certainly the best gentleman of my acquaintance. And Rebecca clearly agrees. Having married from obligation herself, she would not wish any man upon me save the very nicest."

"He is certainly that. But a settled home? I'm not sure there's any such thing with a sailor, you know. He spends so much of the time away. We are not sure how much longer we will have him from on this furlough, you know. The moment the ship is ready to sail once more, he will be off again."

"But do they not—excuse me for the personal question—do they not object to the fact that he has…" Charity could not think of a tactful way to finish the question, but Nan knew what she meant.

"One arm?" she asked. "Certainly other men have been drafted out for such a reason. But Lord Nelson, you know, was similarly bereft, yet it was his leadership which won the Battle of Trafalgar. My brother is no quitter, and the Navy wished to keep him in post."

"That makes sense." Charity nodded. "Incidentally, I am instructed by my sister to tell you that you and he are both extremely welcome to visit again. Indeed, she would very much appreciate it if you would."

"Oh, that's nice of her!" Nan said. "Tell her we should be delighted. Just send us the invitation, and we shall be there."

But as it turned out, events were to prevent such an innocent seeming arrangement from taking place. Not a week later, Rebecca burst into the room where Charity sat playing the piano. Charity finished off the last lines of the sonata with a flourish and then looked up at her sister, smiling.

"There! How does that sound?" But the look on Rebecca's face stopped her. "Becca, what's wrong?"

Rebecca was breathing fast, her face blotchy white and grey. "I don't know how to tell you. But I know I must."

Charity got up from the piano stool, pushing it so violently away that it rocked heavily. "Tell me what? Mother? Is she—is she dead?"

"No, Mother is fine, at least I think so. Listen, Charity, you know I was out this morning?" Charity nodded impatiently. "There is a rumour that I heard about an accident, a serious one…no, not a rumour, I think. Truth. I believe it was true."

"What is it? Becca, what can it be that makes you look like this?"

Rebecca breathed out deeply, a shaky breath which trembled as it exited her body. "Charity, it's Miss Greenaway. Your Isobelle."

Charity jerked as if Rebecca had just hit her. She had not known what she was expecting Rebecca to say; all she knew was that it wasn't this.

"What? What has happened? What sort of 'accident'?"

"She…her carriage overturned. Her phaeton."

"Her phaeton?" Charity was suddenly finding it hard to breathe. She remembered Isobelle's pride in her beautiful little carriage with the matching greys, and heard again her ex-lover's confident words about her driving. "Do you mean she's…?" She couldn't frame the word.

Rebecca reached out and took Charity's hand. "Not dead, Charity. But…but injured. I think—it is not hopeful."

Charity looked down into her sister's worried face and squeezed her hand hard. "Thank you, Becca. For telling me. For…for caring."

"You're my sister," Rebecca said quietly.

They stood together for a minute or so in silence, and then Charity stepped away, drawing herself up. "I must go to her."

"But do you think…" Rebecca hesitated. "This isn't the moment for a social call. I don't mean she wouldn't want to see you, but I'm not sure what the situation may be. I believe the doctor has been round more than once already. I don't think she…"

Charity shook her head and pushed a stray strand of hair out of her face. "Not to visit, Becca. To look after her." She saw her sister's expression. "I'm good with ill people, you know that," she pressed. "It's the only time Mother ever wanted me around." Rebecca winced at this, and Charity smiled at her. "I didn't mean that badly, but you know it is true. So if Isobelle really is seriously injured, I could help."

"But her family will surely—"

"She hasn't got any," Charity interrupted. "At least, there's her mama, but her mother is an invalid herself. She won't be able to care for Isobelle. I could be of some use. Fetch and carry, whatever is needed."

Rebecca shook her head. "I still think you shouldn't…"

"I know." Charity smiled at her. "But you know I'm going to anyway. Forgive me?"

"I would forgive you anything. Charity, you know what is best, of course, but…" She trailed off at the look on Charity's face, set and determined. "Take care of yourself, dearest. That is all. Ask Wilbur to take you round, and do not worry about how long you may take. I will not need the carriage again today."

"Thank you."

Charity ran to her room to change her dress, calling for the maid as she did so. She was always a speedy dresser, but this time she must have broken all records, wriggling into her clothes with little care for the delicate materials. Finally, less than an hour after Rebecca had broken the news, the carriage drew up at the Greenaways' house.

There was a small, familiar figure on the doorstep. Charity tumbled out of the carriage in her anxiety to get to her.

"Nan!" Charity half-ran towards her, her hands held out. If she could have seen anyone at that moment, she would have wanted it to be Nan. "Have you been...Do you know...How is she?"

Nan looked tired, Charity saw, and worried. She had never seemed to adore Isobelle in the way most of the rest of the Sisterhood did, but then Nan always was more reticent. Never cold, always welcoming, but not prone to the exuberant bursts of emotion that Isobelle, Lydia, Louisa—even Charity—gave way to on occasion.

"Must you go straight in, Harry? Can you walk with me for a bit?"

"Oh, of course," Charity said readily. "Is your carriage coming, or...?" She trailed off.

"I only live on the next road, so I walk." Nan shrugged. "Perhaps I ought to bring a maid, but at my age, I don't think—"

"At your age? Nan, are you in your fifties or your twenties?"

Nan gave her an ironic glance. "As well one or the other, as far as the gentlemen are concerned. Anyone over twenty-two or –three is past their best. Not," she added, "that they showed much interest in me even then."

"Nor you in them," Charity retorted. "Come, let me ask Wilbur to drive us to the park, and we can talk to our hearts' content." She sobered quickly as she assisted her friend into the carriage. "Just tell me one thing, Nan. Is there any hope?"

"There's hope," Nan said gravely, as Charity scrambled in beside her. "But it is just that: hope."

"Tell me more whilst we walk."

The girls fell silent as Wilbur drove them to the park at the deliberate pace he felt appropriate to the young ladies' status. Shorn of the privacy Charity and Nan needed to speak of that which concerned them most, no other subject came to mind; and it was a sombre journey indeed. Finally, the vehicle drew to a halt, and Nan and Charity stepped down.

"There." Nan pointed to a pretty path edged by flowers. There was a convenient bench placed for the purpose of viewing the riot of red-yellow-orange petals—and perhaps intended also for the sharing of secrets.

"Tell me," Charity urged as they sat, the beautiful flowers meaning nothing to her in her present state of mind. "Tell me everything. Have you seen her? Have—oh, just tell me, Nan!"

"I haven't seen Isobelle herself," Nan said. "I spent a couple of hours with Lady Greenaway, though. As you know, she's severely unwell herself, and Isobelle is everything to her. I was concerned to see how she was managing."

"But Isobelle," Charity insisted. "What of her?"

Nan poked around in the gravel with one neatly shod foot. "They do not know. They do not know how much damage was done when she hit her head. You know the details of the fall?"

"That it was a carriage accident—yes."

"That is all that matters, really," Nan said. "She has broken a bone in her wrist, and a couple of her ribs, they believe. But those, however serious, are not the cause of the concern. It is the head injury which worries them. She is in and out of consciousness, as I understand it, and they are having trouble when she awakens making her rest. She seems agitated and is running a bit of a fever."

"I see." Charity blinked back the tears which were smudging the flowers into blurs in front of her eyes. "What needs to be done?"

Nan took a deep breath. "She needs constant nursing, and Lady Greenaway cannot do so herself. At the same time, she hates the thought of only a stranger being with Isobelle." She sighed. "I am no sick nurse, so I couldn't begin to take on the duties—"

"But I am," Charity interrupted. "No, truly, it is one of the few skills I possess."

Nan raised half a smile at that. "You have many talents, Harry. But…"

"But what?"

Nan hesitated. "You are a family friend. 'Just' a family friend in the eyes of the polite world. You and I and Isobelle might know differently, even Lady Greenaway, but I do not know what the *ton* would say to your nursing her."

"But you said you might have done it, had you the skills," argued Charity.

"Oh." Nan looked surprised. "But I am related to them, you know." She saw the expression on Charity's face. "Clearly you did not know. It is not a close relationship. My mother and Mr Greenaway were first cousins. I am not quite sure what relation that makes us to each other, but enough to make it easily understandable if I am present in the house."

"I see." Charity was silent, mulling over this new piece of information.

"I can see," Nan said apologetically, "that it would not be immediately obvious that Isobelle and I are related. She is"— Nan waved a hand upwards—"and I am…well, I am not."

"Don't say that," Charity said, unreasonably annoyed.

In truth, she was not certain with whom she was cross— with Nan, for her bluntness; with Isobelle, for the foolhardiness that had almost certainly led to her accident; or with herself for the strength of her surprise at their being related. In many ways, Isobelle was indeed everything Nan was not, but Charity discovered that she was not at all sure that Nan was the worse for that. The ladies sat and looked at the flowers in silence for a few moments, and then Nan roused herself again.

"You truly are a good sick nurse?" she asked.

Charity blushed, unwilling to sound boastful, but nonetheless knowing that she was indeed talented in that direction.

"My mother said so, anyway, and she was not apt to praise me."

"And I know Lady Greenaway is desperately wishing for Isobelle to have not just the best care, which is something which can easily be paid for, but from someone who knows Isobelle, knows and loves her." A little crease appeared between Nan's eyebrows. "Medical knowledge may not be all which is needed to prevent Isobelle fretting herself into fever. You know what she is like. What she needs is someone who can be with her, look after her. Someone like you."

"But I see your point," Charity sighed. "How can a mere 'friend' be given such access to a rich and beautiful lady like

Isobelle? The Sisterhood is not widely known, I know, but any breath of scandal might do more damage, both to Isobelle and to the Sisterhood as a whole, than any help my nursing might give. She might keep her health but lose her reputation."

"Something which would be much better than the other way around," Nan pointed out sensibly. "But I think we can do better than that. There must be some way to keep everything above suspicion." She gave Charity a frank, appraising look and then said calmly, "I think you must also be related to Isobelle."

"I beg your pardon?"

"It would explain such a lot, you see," Nan explained. "Why someone who—please excuse my bluntness—from a noticeably lower stratum of society than Isobelle has been taken up so fervently not only by her, but also by Lady Caroline. Cara might be a known eccentric, but her antecedents are impeccable: more, even, than Isobelle's. Yet you have managed to find your way into her circle where many others of higher birth have not. You cannot be surprised that some jealous society belles have wondered why."

"Oh." It had not once occurred to Charity that there might be ladies envious of her. "I didn't realise."

Nan gave her trademark shrug. "Nothing much has been said, nothing at all that matters. But anyway, your being related to Isobelle would go a long way to explaining everything. It might very well be a good thing all around."

"Except that I am not related to Isobelle."

"You probably are, if we look back far enough," Nan said matter-of-factly. "Most people in the *ton* are. But that is not a problem. I feel sure we can invent a background convincing enough for the majority. And if Lady Greenaway and Cara confirm the story, no one else will dare to challenge it. Now... what can that relationship be? It had best not be on my side of the family. That would add another layer of confusion which we could do without. However, Lady Greenaway's past is writ large enough for people to know a certain amount about it. So..." She sat silent for a moment, thinking. "Mr Greenaway's father was my mother's uncle. But his mother...yes, I think she came from the North, as do you, I think?"

"The Midlands," Charity said, her head spinning a little.

Nan smiled. "To most people in London, everywhere north of Leicestershire is 'the North'. I do not think we need quibble over the details. But it will make it quite convincing that you are a country cousin, as it were. Far from causing scandal, it may very well put to rest even the minor issues I've heard spoken."

"About…"

"About Isobelle's championing of you." Nan nodded. "Relations have a recognised standing; the *ton* all understand that. There may be some curiosity about how or why she paid you no attention until after your sister's marriage, but, forgive me for being so blunt, your mother's reputation might explain that. Lady Greenaway and Isobelle might well be prepared to sponsor a reserved country cousin where a lady, forgive me again, who is seen as grasping and, well, selfish might not be so welcome. And, of course," she added drily, "the fact that your brother-in-law is rich probably does not hurt your situation. Though no one could accuse Lady Greenaway or Isobelle of chasing money; nor even needing it!"

"Hardly!" Charity agreed. "But Nan…" A frown furrowed her brow. "Are you certain that it would be believed? When there has been no previous mention of any relationship?"

"Why should there have been?"

Charity kicked at the grass with a toe. "You said…there had been whispers. Why would this explanation not have been given before?"

"Because—oh, Charity, do stop doing that with your foot, you are making the most awful scuffs on your shoe! Because—"

"Sorry," Charity apologised.

"No need to apologise to me. But anyway, why should they have been told? What business of theirs was it?"

"But…" Charity could not think of the words to explain what she meant.

Nan looked at her seriously, steepling her gloved fingers. "It's very difficult to combat rumour when they are never officially said aloud. A case of 'the lady doth protest too much', you know."

"Yes, I see."

"Whereas, if you are nursing Isobelle—you are sure you can do this, that your sister won't object, by the way? Anyway, if you are sitting with her, someone will probably come out and say aloud how peculiar it is. At which point, it is very simple to disperse the explanation without an issue."

"But what if they don't believe it?"

Nan chuckled. "Can you imagine anyone telling Cara that she is a liar? It would be a brave lady, or an even braver gentleman, to do so." Charity laughed too, imagining the scene. "And if both Cara and Lady Greenaway are saying you are kin to Isobelle? Well, I do not think there will be too many doubters."

"I suppose not." Charity sat thoughtfully for a moment. "But as to that, will Lady Greenaway allow me to be with Isobelle? She knows me well enough, but it's a large leap from that to nursing Isobelle."

"If you are a good sick nurse," Nan said sombrely, "she will do whatever she can for you. Isobelle is her only daughter, her only child. Lady Greenaway would do anything and everything for her. She already lost one child before Isobelle's birth, as you know, and she clings to Isobelle the more because of it. I dare swear that if Isobelle had wanted the moon, Lady Greenaway would have done all she could to draw it down." Her eyes met Charity's. "It explains a lot about Isobelle, you know," she said. "She is like a gay butterfly, flittering where she wants, never understanding that other people have thoughts and feelings and can be hurt. She never means to hurt anyone, but she doesn't understand. How can she, when she has been so treasured and petted all her life?"

"I know."

They sat in silence, Nan looking at the blooming flowers with an almost dogged determination, Charity looking at her feet, absently noticing the scuff marks Nan had warned her about. Never mind: they were not expensive shoes. And if she were going to be sitting in a sick room half of the time, she would have no need for pristine footwear, after all. Her thoughts were ended when Nan got to her feet.

"Right," she said, "we should go. I must go back and speak to Lady Greenaway again. I will try and get to her before she has her nap, both for my own sake and for hers. May I visit to tell you what she thinks? Or would a note be better?"

"Come yourself, if you can," Charity said. "I will want to ask you all sorts of things, I know. If Lady Greenaway has any doubts, tell her that I would happily sit beside Isobelle with a nurse present also. If she is not sure whether I would be a suitable carer, I know she would nevertheless like to think that Isobelle has someone she knows beside her, even if it's only me."

"That's kind."

Charity got to her feet and smiled at Nan. "It's practical, anyway. Come, let me drop you back at the house. I won't visit now. You and Lady Greenaway need to have privacy to discuss my virtues and failings in depth. But come to me later, will you? No matter when. I will tell the footman to admit you at whatever hour you arrive. And I must talk to Rebecca, also. Thankfully, Fotheringay is out of the country and we need not concern ourselves with his opinion. Remember, I will be waiting for you to call."

CHAPTER TWENTY-NINE

Nan's call, when it came, was necessarily brief. Charity could see the weariness in her friend's face. It must have been a long and difficult day for her. Charity had already explained the situation to Rebecca and gained her sister's permission to continue with her plan, if Lady Greenaway were prepared to agree. Rebecca could not like it, but would not counter it. And with the excuse of a fabricated relationship to explain Charity's interest, there were no pressing arguments to counter against her. When Nan was shown into the room, Charity motioned for her sister to stay seated.

"Lady Greenaway agrees," Nan said, coming to the point with her usual briskness. "Indeed, she wishes me to state her overwhelming gratitude for your kindness, Harry."

"Oh, but—" Charity began, but Nan cut her off.

"I think she knows something of what happened between you and Isobelle," she said, looking questioningly at Rebecca, as if to check whether it was acceptable to speak of it. Rebecca gave the smallest of nods. "Oh, not all of it, but it has been clear to everyone that you are less often with Isobelle than previously.

Lady Greenaway is all the more grateful for your offer, in the circumstances."

"I could hardly do otherwise," Charity retorted. "Isobelle, no matter...*that* business, has done a lot for me. I do not forget that. It would be despicable indeed to take what I wanted and then refuse to give back when I saw the need."

"Many people would," Nan said. "But I will speak no more of it. Harry, Lady Greenaway has a nurse in. She may have two. But she says that if you really will spend a few hours by Isobelle's bedside each day, so that Isobelle can have someone who cares for her personally, that would be the kindest deed."

"And you?"

Nan nodded. "We may pass, like ships in the night. I hope to spend a great deal of a time with Lady Greenaway. It is a pity that it coincides with my brother's furlough, but it cannot be helped."

"No. You must give help where you see it is needed," Charity said meaningfully. Then she rose to her feet. "But I am unkind to lecture you. Nan, you're tired. You're exhausted. Go home and rest. If not for yourself, then so that you can be fitter to help Lady Greenaway."

"I will." Nan looked at Rebecca again. "Forgive this fleeting visit, Mrs Fotheringay—Rebecca," she corrected herself as Rebecca opened her mouth to protest. "But Harry is right. If I'm to be well enough to be of practical help, I must rest now. I suggest you make sure Harry does the same. Goodnight."

"Goodnight, Nan," the girls replied; and their friend was gone.

Charity soon got into the routine that Isobelle's care required. She would visit mid-morning, spending a couple of hours by Isobelle's side, before coming home. If she had no other commitments—and occasionally when she did—she would visit again in the afternoon and stay as long as she could. Sometimes she would meet Nan afterwards, as they both left, and they would drive together, or return to one or the other's houses to drink tea and chat politely with the family.

"Is it bad to say that this is my favourite part of the day?" Charity asked Nan, sitting down with relief and a cup of tea one afternoon at Nan's house. "Knowing that I have a few minutes' peace before beginning to worry about tomorrow."

"Well, I'm hardly going to be offended that you enjoy my company," Nan said, laughing. "Or is it my parents and brother whom you love to visit?"

Nan's parents were as delightful as their children. Her father had the same gentle sense of humour as Nan and her mother the tendency to make everyone feel at home within seconds of entering the house. Mrs Musgrove was sitting with them today, smiling fondly at the pair of them and allowing them to talk without too much in the way of interruption.

"Oh, your family, of course," Charity said seriously. "That is why I enjoy it when we drive together as well, you understand." She smiled at Mrs Musgrove. "I am truly grateful, ma'am, that you allow me to visit so often, though. And without much in the way of warning sometimes, I fear."

"My dear girl, you are a delight to have around," Mrs Musgrove assured her, with such clear sincerity that even Charity could not doubt it. "Both my children like you very much, and they have impeccable taste, you know."

"Mother!" Nan protested.

"Save for myself, I would have to agree with your mother," Charity told her firmly. "But goodness, isn't it nice to sit down and not to worry about what anyone else is thinking? I am so glad to be able to be with Isobelle, but although the nurse is there with me, I can't help feeling responsible when I'm beside her."

"Lady Greenaway is being marvellous, but it is understandable that she, too, frets," Nan agreed.

And Nan did look tired, Charity thought. Reassuring a lady who had already lost one child and who was herself in a parlous state of health could be no sinecure, though Nan made no complaint.

"When I think how I felt when your brother was in hospital..." Mrs Musgrove added. She said no more, and

Charity could only imagine how it must have been, knowing that her son was so badly injured.

"And yet look at him now," Nan pointed out. "We must take this as a good omen."

The good omen was certainly needed. At first, Isobelle was barely conscious; she did not know who was with her, and Charity wondered whether her presence was a waste of time. But then she realised it was not: whatever Isobelle's level of awareness, her mother was fully aware of what was happening and was comforted by Charity's presence by her daughter's bedside. For that alone, it was worthwhile.

Sometimes, too, Isobelle would stir from her heavy, drugged sleep and say a few words, or smile up at Charity before her lashes fell and she slumbered again. Charity would hold her hand and say comforting phrases, even after Isobelle seemed to have fallen asleep, just in case she could still hear and was in need of reassurance. One day, perhaps a week into her bedside vigil, she saw Isobelle open her eyes with a little more recognition than had previously been so.

"Harry? My Harry?" Isobelle's voice quavered with uncertainty.

Charity leaned over the bed so that Isobelle could see her. She took her hand. "I'm here, Isobelle. Harry's here."

In an absent sort of way, Charity realised that this was the first time she'd referred to herself as "Harry". All the Sisterhood did, of course—it was how Isobelle had introduced her, and Charity had never been able to contradict Isobelle. She liked the nickname well enough, but it was not her, not really. Her name had always been Charity. Her very existence was bound up within that word, for so many reasons. Charity sometimes thought she would have *liked* to be Harry, but she wasn't. Harry was the Sisterhood's construct, not the actual person.

Though, she thought (absent-mindedly smiling down at Isobelle and wiping her brow with the cool flannelette cloth), it might equally be said that "Charity" was her parents' construction. Could one really delineate one's own self from those who surrounded one? The 'me' and the 'not me' were perhaps not so very different.

"I'm glad you're here, Harry," Isobelle whispered. For that moment alone, Charity knew it had been worth it.

Before she went home, she made an effort to go and see Lady Greenaway, to tell her of the progress. She knew that one of the nurses had done so already, but she also knew that Lady Greenaway would like to hear it from Charity herself. To Charity's pleasure, Nan was still sitting there. She shared the information with them both and saw both faces lose the worst of their worry lines.

"She's improving. She's definitely improving," Charity said eagerly. "I do think that she will be all right, in time."

"That's such a relief off my mind," Lady Greenaway said, surreptitiously wiping a tear from the corner of her eye. "Thank you, my dear."

"I've done nothing, just sat there," Charity disclaimed.

"That is precisely what Nan says about what she's doing here. But I see things rather differently," Lady Greenaway said quietly. "Nan has been a tower of strength."

Nan looked uncomfortable at the comment. "More like a crumbling wall," she said brusquely.

For some reason, Charity was annoyed by this. She knew Nan didn't like compliments—no more did Charity herself—but in this particular case, it was too true to be glossed over like this.

"Shh!" she said, leaning over and placing a finger against Nan's lips. "Much more like a tower."

"I am grateful to you, too, though, Charity," Lady Greenaway said quietly. "Isobelle is more important to me than anyone or anything else. What you have done for her, you have done for us both."

Charity reddened. "I *like* Isobelle," she said, almost apologetically.

Lady Greenaway smiled. "I will embarrass neither of you any further with my gratitude. Now, Nan, I gather your brother is currently in town?" Nan nodded. "As you know, I am not entertaining at present. I entertain little enough at the best of times, but currently I could not consider it. But please note that family, whether old or newly created," she added, casting a twinkling glance at Charity, "are very welcome. I would be glad to see Captain Musgrove at any occasion."

"I know he will be glad to visit." Nan finished her drink and set it down on the table. "Now, ma'am, please excuse me. I promised to take John to a concert this evening, and I must have a chance to change first."

"I must go too." Charity rose. "Nan, I believe the carriage will be here. May I drop you home?"

"Of course." Nan rose as well. "I don't suppose you feel like attending the concert with us?" she added as they walked downstairs together. "I would be glad of your company, and I know John would too."

"I don't know," Charity demurred, suspecting that brother and sister would prefer to spend some time together alone.

"Please? They're playing Mozart," Nan tempted, knowing that his work was Charity's favourite.

Charity laughed. "How can I resist? I'll be delighted to come."

The evening's concert, though beautiful, was only a small comfort. Charity realised in the course of the evening that never had she felt so at home with people as she did with Nan and her brother. Of course, she adored Rebecca, but their interactions had so much to do with the childhood that Charity had hated and with the shared experiences they had been through, that there was always a hint of memories. The past bled through into the present. Somehow, with Nan, it was possible for Charity to be herself—the person she was, not the person she wanted to be, or (more perniciously still) thought that she ought to be. She could make the jokes that occurred to her, without fear of disapproval or incomprehension; she could become absorbed in the music without fearing that she was offending the people she was with; she could find an understanding friend when she needed one.

Captain Musgrove was of a similar ilk to his sister. It was a pity, thought Charity regretfully, that she really had no interest in gentlemen. It would have been so convenient, so happy, to marry him and know that she belonged to the family—that at last she had a place where she belonged. She could be with Nan every day that way. She would truly be her sister. But it was not to be, and to be fair to him, Captain Musgrove had not shown any such interest in her, either—though as he knew where her preferences lay, it was not so surprising. Once more, Charity rued the mistake which had made her take so long to realise the sort of person that Nan truly was. But she could not change the past, and the present was making itself. As long as Isobelle needed her, Charity would be there.

CHAPTER THIRTY

"It's the Abolitionist meeting this evening," Charity said, four days later. She was wan, tired by the hours with Isobelle, who had gone from strength to strength since that first moment of knowing her. The doctor had pronounced her out of danger, but she and Lady Greenaway both begged Charity to stay. It was a troublesome task, since now she was conscious, Isobelle was tetchy and difficult.

"Yes. What time does it start?" asked Rebecca.

"Seven. But I can't go, Becca. I'm so sorry to let you down."

"Of course you can't," Rebecca said maternally. "You need a quiet evening, perhaps with a novel, and then a warm bed to jump into. But I think I might go."

"Alone?"

Rebecca smiled. "I do not have much of a choice in the circumstances. I admit," she added, "that I will be a little frightened, perhaps, but I think it is important. And anyway, I know some of your friends so much better now. I need not be afraid, I think, even though I still am."

"Contradictory," Charity commented lazily.

"Not at all," said Rebecca with great dignity. "It is one thing to know that one should not be nervous, but another to feel it. You rest, Charity, and you'll feel fitter in the morning for it."

"Rebecca says you looked after her beautifully last night," Charity greeted Nan when they met at the Greenaways' house the next morning. "Wasn't it brave of her to go alone?"

"Mm. Easy person to underrate, your sister. Did she tell you about the evening?"

"A little. Thank you," she added to the footman, who took her cloak. "It sounded as if things were starting to move in terms of the gentlemen's push for legislation."

"Hmm," Nan said sceptically. "We've been here before. I'm counting no chickens yet. But I meant Mrs Fotheringay's own part in proceedings."

"I know she's said you should call her Rebecca," Charity said absently. "Becca's part? No. Why? What did she do?"

"Only asked me to take her to Cara, where she insisted on discussing her husband's situation as regards the trade."

"She did that? But she's terrified of Cara!"

"She shouldn't be, but people so often are," Nan said regretfully. "I tell Cara that it's her own fault for being so large and imposing; we little folk feel even tinier by comparison. But it's the first meeting since you told her about Fotheringay's business and where he was, and she's clearly been thinking it over in her head all this time. She'd come to the conclusion, it seems, that the best thing would be, if she dared, to lay it all out before Cara and ask what she should do next. It must have taken a good deal of courage for her to follow through."

"It would." Charity was still standing in the hallway, temporarily forgetting the servants who might be listening in. "And then not even to tell me! What did Cara say?"

"Oh, everything that was reassuring and good. She pointed out that Mrs Foth—that Rebecca could do nothing about her husband's trade interests. Even had it been a love match, even were he in this country, she'd be unlikely to persuade him to sell out. As it is, there is no chance, which is not Rebecca's fault in the slightest."

"Oh, she will be glad to have heard that. I have been telling her much the same, but she has been worrying about it. To think that she decided to face it head on and speak to Cara about it!"

"Still waters run deep," Nan said thoughtfully. "Was she always like this, I wonder, or has it come upon her since her marriage?"

They ascended the stairs together.

"No, not the marriage. Since the twins were born. One always thinks of mothers as grown-up personages. I never thought to see it happen so evidently in Rebecca, though."

"That's interesting," Nan said. "I'd like to talk to you about it more. Perhaps we can arrange to go for a walk later? I'm sure the fresh air would do us both good. But I did wonder if Rebecca had told you. It surprises me not in the least that she had not."

"You can tell me more about that, in return," said Charity. "A walk sounds wonderful. It will give me something to look forward to."

"I also."

It was to be a long morning for Charity however. Isobelle had woken fretting, and the nurse said privately to Charity that, "I couldn't do nothing with her, this morning, ma'am. All she wants is to talk to you. It's been 'Nurse, when is she coming?' for the past two hours and more."

Charity repressed a sigh. "Thank you. If you would care to have a rest, I will look after her for a little now. See if I can calm her down."

"Well, if you're quite sure…"

"Harry!" Isobelle's voice cut across their conversation. "Oh, Harry, I have wanted you."

"Well, I'm here now. Nurse said you wanted to talk to me, so I've just told her she must go and have a rest. You don't need nurse as well as me, not now you're getting better."

"I don't need nurse at all. I don't want nurse at all. Just you, Harry."

Charity nodded a dismissal to the kindly woman who had been caring for Isobelle and came and sat beside her.

"I'm here, and I'm not going anywhere for the next few hours, so you can calm down and rest now. All right?"

"Yes. Yes, I suppose so." Isobelle paused, and then the words burst out as if she was physically hurt by having kept them in so long. "Harry, I hurt you, didn't I?" Isobelle's face was white and woebegone. "With Lydia. I didn't think about it then. It seemed so little. But now…you have been so kind, even though I know I made you sad. I don't know what I did to deserve it."

"It doesn't matter. None of it matters."

Almost to her surprise, Charity realised that it was true. It really did not matter—not any more. Isobelle had…well, had turned out not to be the person Charity had imagined her to be. But that had hardly been Isobelle's fault. Certainly, she had taken Charity's adoration as her due. Everyone always had adored her, more or less, so why should Charity have been any different? Isobelle was what she was: a spoilt society beauty who nonetheless had a generosity of impulse which, whilst it might sometimes be fleeting, was still genuine while it lasted. When she had met Charity, dishevelled and distressed on her doorstep, it had been a sincere wish to help that had encouraged her to offer assistance. And help she had. Charity still now shuddered when she thought of how the day might have panned out without Isobelle's input.

"But it does." Unusually, Isobelle's eyes filled with tears. If Charity had not known for herself how very unwell Isobelle still was, that would have told her. "And even so, you came to look after me when I needed you. Can you really have been so kind after the way I let you down?"

Charity felt uncomfortable. She had not anticipated this mood of self-reproach in Isobelle. Levity or superficial gratefulness she could have dealt with, but this was beyond her.

"You helped me when I needed it," she pointed out gruffly.

"That! I did nothing."

"You did, you know. I will never forget it. But still," Charity hurried on, changing the topic as hastily as she could, "it has been no trouble to sit with you, you know. Give yourself credit for being such excellent company. Though I may change my mind on that if you continue in this vein. Come, Isobelle, stop bringing old and forgotten skeletons to light. What matters is that you are recovering nicely. Within a few days, I imagine you will be as gay and full of life as ever!"

For a moment, Charity thought that Isobelle was going to press the point, but to her relief the topic was not continued. In an evident attempt to bow to Charity's wishes, Isobelle gave a weak smile.

"Hardly a few days, Harry. Weeks, perhaps."

"And Lady Greenaway is quite well now, you know," pressed on Charity. "Nan has looked after her wonderfully."

"Oh, Nan!" Isobelle nodded. "Of course she has. You can always rely on Nan, you know."

Charity wondered why this statement made her feel unnaturally angry. It was certainly true that kind, steady Nan could be relied on. Yet somehow the way Isobelle said it, it sounded…almost insulting. As if Nan's steadiness were more of a character flaw than a virtue.

"I know," she said shortly.

"I have made you cross again," Isobelle said pathetically, and Charity gave herself a mental shake. Isobelle was very unwell still. She needed petting and looking after, not grumpiness and critical comments.

"No, you haven't," she said, softening her tone. "But Nan has been so kind, you know. Indeed, it is thanks to her that I can be here to look after you."

"I don't understand." But there was a faint sign of interest on Isobelle's face, Charity noticed with encouragement.

"It had not occurred to me that there might be difficulties in my being here," she said cheerfully. "You know me. Jump first and say 'oops' later. When I heard about…well, you know all that. But I came as soon as I could." Isobelle nodded, taking this as her due. "I met Nan on your doorstep, and we went for a quiet walk so she could tell me how you were. She was coming out as I arrived," she added in explanation. "Lady Greenaway was terribly worried about you. We all were, of course, but she most of all, for she was not able to nurse you herself. Certainly, she could afford whole hosts of nurses, but understandably she felt that this was not the same as having someone who knew and loved you by your side."

Isobelle shuddered. "I would have hated it."

"I thought at first that it would be easy," Charity said. "It seemed so obvious that I should be with you, when I knew I would be able to look after you, but Nan said—"

"Said what?"

"That people might talk. It had never occurred to me, but it seems that even before that, there had been the odd comment about the time I spent in your company. After all, you are so... so important and impressive, one of the real *ton*. Whereas I..." Charity shrugged.

"But you came anyway."

"Oh, that was Nan's doing—and Cara's, and Lady Greenaway's, but it was Nan's idea." She smiled. "It may appal you to know this, but I fear I must break the shocking news that you and I are related."

"You...What?" Isobelle looked quite bewildered, but her mood of guilt and sadness had lifted, Charity was relieved to see.

"Oh, not really," she explained. "But Nan said that the situation was different for her because she and you were some sort of cousin. And then she said...well, why should not I be a cousin too? Not the same side as her, of course, but she said your grandmother, I think..." Charity realised that she was still rather sketchy about the details. She would have to get Nan to teach her before she spoke to anyone else in the polite world about it. "Anyway, that a relation of yours had come from the North, and as I was Midlands born, it would seem quite convincing that I was from that branch of the family." Isobelle, much fascinated by the story, went to sit up, and then clutched her side with a groan. "Oh, Isobelle, I'm sorry. Are you all right?" Charity asked anxiously.

"I'm fine," Isobelle said. "I was just taken up with the story. Fancy Nan having such a romantic imagination!"

Again, Charity felt that same tingle of irritation, but she pushed it firmly away. "Well," she continued, "we needed to get Lady Greenaway's permission, of course. And Nan said that Cara would be a useful ally also. With two such leading members of the *ton* confirming the story, who would doubt it?"

"But why had this not come out before? Indeed, why had I so unkindly ignored you until recently?" Isobelle asked.

"Oh, Nan thought of that too," Charity said, choosing to ignore Isobelle's raised eyebrows. She gave a grimace. "I feel sure I should not have agreed to the next part, but I find it hard to feel very much compunction. It was my mother, you know."

"What was? Harry, I can hardly get your story straight!" Isobelle protested with a laugh.

"The reason for your previous coldness towards me. You would not, it seems, recognise my mother, who is not related to you, incidentally. I do not like to suggest any reason for this, but you may possibly be able to think of some for yourself! However, once she was safely ensconced in Bath, you felt it possible to acknowledge me—us," Charity corrected herself, "for you cannot have me without Rebecca, you know..."

"If that makes me related to Fotheringay," Isobelle protested weakly, "I will have no part of it!"

Charity grinned at the return of the Isobelle she still loved, in her own way. "You can hardly deny it now your mother has acknowledged it as true," she said. "However, the existence of Fotheringay also explains quite nicely why you and I are closer than you and Rebecca! So, to pick up where I left off, you felt finally at liberty to acknowledge our relationship and invite me to become one of your chosen acquaintances. For which," she added, "I am extremely grateful, no matter what the truth behind it may be."

Isobelle laughed, and the conversation dropped.

Charity and Nan managed, serendipitously, to meet once again on their way out of the Greenaways' house. Of course, Charity's carriage had known when to pick her up, and Charity suggested that they return to her—or rather Rebecca's—house.

"I want to speak to you alone, you know," she said seriously. "And Rebecca will understand that. I know it means keeping you from Captain Musgrove, but I hope he can accept your absence for another hour or so."

Nan grinned. "I expect he'll be glad of it! Well," she added, seeing Charity's disbelieving glance, "I don't think he will mind. Are you sure your sister would not object? It seems so terribly rude. And if I am going to tell you about her bravery last night, it seems outrageous to speak about her in her own house, but behind her back, but—"

"Trust me," Charity said mischievously, "Rebecca and I have been speaking secretly about Fotheringay almost since the moment I moved in with them."

"Charity Bellingham," Nan said severely, using her full name for perhaps the first time ever, "if ever I want to put you in bad grace with Rebecca, I shall tell her that you compared her to Fotheringay. How you could do any such thing!"

"You know what I mean." And Charity knew exactly how seriously to take Nan at such a moment.

The carriage deposited them at the Fotheringays' house ten minutes later. Charity darted inside.

"Becca? Where are you?" she called.

Rebecca appeared from the nursery, one of the babies in her arms. "Shh, dear, please. Patrick seems to have colic, or something. But he is crying without cease. Oh," she added, seeing Nan, "I am so sorry. I did not realise you had a guest. Would you both forgive me if I stayed with the babies? Nurse says I should do no such thing, but it is impossible for her to mind both children at once, and if Patrick is crying, who better to look after Mary than her mother?"

"Of course," Nan said promptly. "Goodness, has Mary grown again?"

Charity felt sure that her friend could not see any change in the baby from that distance, but she blessed Nan's tact. Rebecca smiled.

"A bit, I think. Pray excuse me."

She disappeared back into the nursery, and Charity grimaced at Nan.

"'Has she grown?' I see no difference in either of them!"

"You wouldn't. You are around them all the time! But the baby has certainly grown, I think. But come now," Nan said reprovingly, "you offered me tea, and I confess I am thirsting for a cup!"

"Are you indeed?" But Charity took pity on her friend, and led her into the drawing room. "I ordered tea when you were sweet-talking my sister. It will be here shortly. Now, whilst we wait, tell me about last night's meeting."

"Your sister was right to say that things were moving forward with the gentlemen," Nan said, once the tea and cake had been placed on the table between them. "It is said that there will be a second reading in the House of the Slave Trade Act. Of course, there was the earlier legislation last year, which banned the trade with colonies, but all a slave trader needed to do in such circumstances was claim his cargo was headed elsewhere. It did nothing, *nothing*, to stop the trade. A sop to public conscience, perhaps. That is all."

"I see."

The conversation turned first on the change in attitude in the Houses of Parliament. Slowly, the abolitionist movement seemed to be gaining ground.

"…But then," Nan said sadly, "such was the case in the late 1780s, but the French Revolution drew so much of the country's attention that it has been a mere cypher for more than a decade."

"But perhaps now is the time for change," Charity urged.

"Perhaps. I don't know. But about your sister…" Nan told Charity how Rebecca had waited until the end of the meeting before catching Lady Caroline alone. "I had seen that Mrs Fotheringay was anxious about something. I thought it was just your absence, and her awareness of being alone, but then she asked Cara if she might have a word." An explanation, and then: "It was the bravest thing, Harry, truly. She fully expected Cara to turn upon her, and rend her limb from limb. Of course, I knew, and you would have known, that no such thing would happen, but Rebecca didn't."

Charity noticed the change from the formal "Mrs Fotheringay" at the beginning of the description to the personal

"Rebecca" at the end, but she said nothing. She was so proud of her sister, and also knew—which Rebecca would not have done—that Nan knew all this not from prurient curiosity, but from a determination to stay close to Rebecca, and make sure she was not distressed. She knew better than to mention it however.

"I have something to tell you too," she said abruptly. "Isobelle talked to me today, a little. I told her of our—your—scheme, to inform the world that I was some relation."

"Really? And how did she take that?"

Charity smiled. "As you might expect Isobelle to. We talked about some other things too," she added quickly, before Nan could say anything. "About the past, and what occurred between us."

"I see." Nan's tone was guarded.

"I put her on a pedestal," Charity confessed, remembering the feeling when she had suddenly realised that she didn't blame Isobelle any more; that the hurt was now truly in the past. "It was unfair."

"Yes," agreed Nan, simply.

"I knew—almost at once when she hurt me—I knew it wasn't reasonable to feel so betrayed. She broke no promises after all. But I still felt she let me down. I didn't quite realise until now how unkind it had been to resent her for not living up to my dreams."

"Very uncomfortable things, pedestals," Nan said drily. "Gravity means that if you make any move at all, you're liable to fall off."

Taken aback by this unexpected point of view, Charity's gasp turned into a giggle.

"Nan, you are ridiculous! I don't think anyone else I know would have phrased it quite like that."

"Isn't it true? And," Nan added, more seriously, "in more than one way. I don't think any human being could stand up to the requirements of being thought without faults."

"I know. You're right," Charity sighed.

"I know that most of the Sisterhood think I'm unkind to Isobelle, for I don't pet her in the same way the others do. But

I don't see it that way. I appreciate her for who she is. And I think that although it may be nice to be so adored, it's perhaps a little terrifying also. You told me that Isobelle knows she let you down and feels bad about it. How must it feel to be put in a position where you know, or suspect, that other people's impressions of you can only go down?"

"Yes, I see," Charity said slowly.

"Isobelle knows what I think of her. She knows I love her, in my own way. And she knows above all that if she needs me, I'll be there. Shh," she said, as Charity tried to interrupt. "I haven't finished. You were going to say that any of the others are not only willing but anxious to do what they can for her. But think on this: if Isobelle does something wrong, to whom do you think she can go? Someone whose perfect ideal of her would be shattered if she told them, or someone whom she knows loves her despite her faults?"

"Nan, you're brutal."

"Am I? I don't see why."

"Because you see too clearly. To see myself reflected back at me hurts."

Nan was silent, putting a hand across the table to place it on top of Charity's. "I'm sorry," she said gently. "I was unkind then."

Charity sighed, annoyed by the feeling of tears prickling at the back of her eyes. "No, you weren't." She turned her hand over and grasped Nan's. "I can go back to Isobelle tomorrow remembering that what happened between us was as much my own fault as hers. I shouldn't have looked for a goddess to adore. I should have looked for a woman to love."

"And Isobelle is kind and loving and all those things you always thought her," Nan said, drawing her hand away slowly. "She is worth loving, after all. I think she could make you happy. I know you could make her so. Already you're doing so, by being with her every day."

"Oh, but..." Charity bit back the words. It was true that she no longer resented or felt any bitterness towards Isobelle. But to fall in love with her again? It was unthinkable. Not because Isobelle was unlovable, but because...because..."I must go to check on Rebecca," she said, standing up hastily. "I will see you tomorrow, no doubt, Nan."

"She'll be glad to see you," Nan said. "Rebecca, and Isobelle. Goodbye."

But will you be glad to see me? Charity did not, could not, say the words aloud. But a funny thing had happened as she talked to Nan. She could never fall in love with Isobelle again, because she was in love already. With Nan. With the maddening, practical, kind and funny Nan. Charity had once misjudged Nan, too, but that was different. No one could idolise Nan: she simply would not have it. But they could, perhaps, love her; if she loved back, she was the sort of lady for a happy ever after. The "forever woman", as Cara had described her. No goddess: a living, breathing, *loving* woman. But did Nan care for her? Charity was not sure.

CHAPTER THIRTY-ONE

Charity's new understanding of her feelings towards Nan lent a different colour to everything she did. She could be never-endingly patient with Isobelle, because Isobelle did not matter—not as Nan did. Isobelle, Charity finally realised, was indeed the butterfly Nan had described her as: beautiful and charming, but transient in her emotions. Even today, Isobelle seemed to have thrown off her mood of the previous day. She was complaining that nurse would not let her sit up, nor do her hair in the intricate style she preferred. Had she loved Charity? Yes, in her way. Had Charity loved her? Certainly—but perhaps not honestly; perhaps she had not seen Isobelle as she truly was.

Nan, though? The very thought of Nan made her smile. You could not misjudge Nan. If you loved Nan, Charity thought tenderly, you loved her for precisely what she was. You loved the sensible, honest soul of her. You fell in love with a woman who was intensely practical; who would always give you her truth—perhaps not *the* truth, for there so rarely was one black-or-white answer—but her truth. And Nan knew about the greys of life;

the tangled threads which made living so complicated and yet in some ways so much more worthwhile. No one knew them better. Nan was not perfect, but that was what made her Nan, what made her loveable. Not perfect, but real.

So Charity fetched and carried for Isobelle. She listened to her talk and complain and saw the way Isobelle was always looking for someone to admire her. And she was admirable, Charity thought. Not as she had first thought, but nonetheless, she was a lovely person. She could never hate Isobelle. But she could never fall in love with her, not again. And, she suspected, from the look in Isobelle's eyes, Isobelle knew it. There was no more mention of hurt, or emotions, which Charity was grateful for.

But there was one thing Charity needed to do.

It seemed silly, when she knew she was in the same building as Nan, to write a note, but it was the easiest way. It said nothing much, just that Charity wanted to meet her—for tea again at the Fotheringays' house, perhaps. Charity could think of no other thing to write. She wrote also to Rebecca, however, asking one of the Greenaways' footmen to take it, and that note was simpler. It read: *Dearest Rebecca,*

If you love me, let me speak with Nan alone. I have invited her for tea, but we need to speak in private. Forgive me? But I know you do.

Charity.

The morning passed slowly but surely. Charity tried not to look at the clock too often, but the passage of time seemed slow indeed when she had something so important to say. She left Isobelle comfortable and then met Nan on the stairs outside the room.

"Tea?" Nan asked, her voice questioning.

"Tea," Charity said in reply. It was not the time—not the place, so very much not the place, where she had lain with Isobelle so often—to speak of what was on her mind. "Rebecca is busy today," she added, an optimistic lie.

"I see. Well, I don't," Nan admitted, "but I am willing to be guided by you."

The carriage ride passed in silence, and it was only when the two ladies were alone, steaming cups in front of them, that

Charity spoke about what was most heavily on her mind. She felt her heart beating faster, and she still did not know precisely what she was going to say. All she knew was that say something, she must.

"Nan, do you hate me?" she asked abruptly, holding her teacup rather more firmly than usual in her nerves.

"Hate you?" Nan looked utterly perplexed. "Why on earth should I?"

"Well, because…you know."

"You are surely not harping back on our early misunderstanding again, Harry!" Nan's face took on a familiar expression of mischief. "But also, what sort of question is that? Do I 'hate' you? As if I might turn round and say, 'Well, actually, now that you mention it, there are one or two things about you that I dislike, one might almost say despise, in you'!"

Charity laughed reluctantly. "You are so good at pointing out the flaws in my comments, dearest Nan! Consider me thoroughly chastised!"

"I'm sorry. I can't help teasing sometimes." Nan smiled across at her friend. "Why did you choose to ask me today, of all times, though?"

Charity fidgeted, putting down the teacup without drinking from it. "It was what you were saying yesterday. About Isobelle being worthy of love."

"And you fear that you are not worthy of her love?" Nan asked gently. "Even now?"

Charity forced herself to continue. Every desperate muscle wanted to run away, but she would not do it. She would be brave.

"Not Isobelle," she said, looking straight at Nan. "You."

"I think you unworthy? Harry, you must know that is not true. I have always thought you worthy, more than worthy, of Isobelle."

Charity stood up so suddenly that the table jolted, the delicate china cups rattling in their saucers.

"Are you being intentionally dim? Do you wish to try and stop me from saying it aloud?" she demanded. "Well, it is no use. I have got this far, and I will go on. Nan, I love you. I've loved you for a while, I think, though I would not see it. Tell me no, tell me you have never thought of me in that way. Tell me anything you wish, but please, please, tell me!" She bit her lip, regretting her outburst already. "I'm sorry. I'm sorry," she said, more softly now.

"You lo...You care for me?" Nan queried shakily.

"Yes! Oh, Nan!" Charity fell on her knees beside her love's chair, looking up into the face she had grown to care for so deeply. Nan was pretty, it was true, though not beautiful like Isobelle. She did not have the gaiety of Lydia, either, or the deep knowledge Emily had of matters arcane. But she was Nan—wonderful, ridiculous, kind and funny Nan. "I shouldn't have said anything, but I could not bear to have you push me any further into Isobelle's arms. It isn't Isobelle I want. I adored her—for something she wasn't, poor girl—but I love you for who you are. I can't help it. I..." She ran out of words.

"Me?" Nan repeated again, a note of wonder in her voice.

Charity put her hands over one of Nan's, and lifted it to her face. "You," she said. "Only you."

"But I thought..." Nan stopped.

"I am not flighty," Charity said defensively. "I do not skip from one lady to the next. I know it may seem like that, but—"

"It doesn't," Nan interrupted her. She put her other hand on Charity's shoulder, looking down at her as if seeing her for the first time. "I just never thought..."

"Do you hate me now?" Charity asked, mournfully.

"Do I look like I hate you? Do I—Oh, Harry, can this be happening?"

"Shall I kiss you, to show what I mean?"

Nan's grip tightened on Charity's shoulder. "Yes."

"Do you—could you care? For me?"

And it was Nan who leaned down and pressed her lips to Charity's. "Yes," she said again.

Charity felt herself tremble under that gentlest of kisses, overcome with emotion. Nan's mouth against her own—oh, it was too good to be true. She reached for Nan again, pulling her into her arms and kissing her with more vigour. And now it was Nan who was trembling; Nan who murmured "Oh, Harry, darling," as her hands stroked Charity's back and her mouth sought Charity's lips. Nan was warm and wonderful and *right* in Charity's arms, as if she had always belonged there, had Charity only but known it. The feeling of Nan's soft, womanly body against her own almost brought Charity to tears, so perfect was it.

"You always seemed to be pushing me towards Isobelle," Charity murmured some minutes later, her arms closely entwined around Nan.

Nan laid her cheek against Charity's and said nothing for a moment as the two girls just focused on being, touching, loving. Finally, Nan said, "When you love someone, you want them to be happy, do you not?"

"I don't know," Charity said slowly.

She thought about Isobelle, of how hurt Charity had felt, seeing Isobelle in Lydia's arms. She had not cared what was best for Isobelle in that moment; she had fallen apart under the weight of her own grief, her own sense of betrayal. Had that not been love, then: was adoration so very far apart? What did Charity actually know of love, after all? Then she thought of Rebecca, and the world righted itself again. She loved Rebecca, and yes—yes, Nan was right. What mattered most was that Rebecca should be happy, not that she should be happy in the way ordained by Charity.

Rebecca was content—no, something better than content. She was rejoicing in her role as mother to the twins. Charity liked her niece and nephew well enough, but she knew that babies held little interest to her on a deeper level. She would never yearn for motherhood, nor would she have found herself so completed by it. It did not matter. Rebecca's happiness mattered. Then she thought of Nan. Dear, very much beloved Nan. She had not been sure, she had been anything but sure, that Nan cared for her in that particular way. Charity had known Nan valued her as a friend, but anything deeper than that? It had seemed impossible, somehow, that she should. But she had had to ask. Nevertheless, if Nan had turned her down, then however Charity felt about it, it would not have changed her feeling for Nan. Nor would it have prevented her wanting Nan's life to be perfect—as perfect as possible.

"Yes, though, I do," she corrected herself. "Though it would have hurt, Nan."

Nan gave a little laugh. "It did hurt, Harry. Couldn't you see it? I thought I hid my feelings very badly."

Charity drew away a little so that she could look at her love once more. "It was certainly very bad of you, dearest," she said, smiling. "I thought…I thought you wanted me for Isobelle. And for yourself, just as a friend."

"I am not that selfless," Nan murmured. She touched Charity's cheek. Neither of them could prevent themselves from this reaching out, these countless tiny gestures. "I wanted you for myself. All of you for myself, Harry. I still cannot believe that you have said such things to me. I fear waking up alone, or that you are teasing me as punishment for daring to care for you, daring to want you. I know too much I don't deserve you."

Charity kissed her. "If I teased like that, I would not deserve you." Her arms suddenly tightened around Nan. "And don't say that about yourself. You deserve much better. I know that much, if nothing else."

"And I…" But Nan broke off, giving a sudden joyful laugh, so different from when she had spoken of hurt. "And I am the luckiest woman alive, and I will not let you, nor anyone else, say otherwise. Oh, Harry!" She got to her feet, tugging Charity with her. "Look, here, out of the window. All these people going past on their own concerns, and none of them knowing that the world has changed, that everything has changed—because you love me! How can they be so silly, so blind to it all?"

Perhaps a small part of Charity had, even until now, kept something back. Perhaps a little element of doubt, of caution, had been in her mind. The thought that Nan, being who she was, had said that she loved Charity not because she did but because she liked her enough—perhaps loved her in a way—not to wish to hurt her. But this Nan—this joyful, alive, disbelieving Nan Musgrove, lit up from inside with happiness and love… Charity could not even have the smallest lingering doubt.

She looked at Nan and saw not only the lady she loved, but a lady who loved her equally, beyond everything she could ever possibly have imagined.

"I don't know whether to laugh or cry," she said unsteadily.

"I do, though," Nan returned, turning to face her. "How can I be anything but rejoicing in a moment like this?"

They held each other, kissed and held some more. Charity felt Nan's warm breath on her neck. "I love you," Nan whispered. "I didn't want to, but I do. Harry. Darling, darling, Harry. I love you so much."

"I love you. Nan," Charity said urgently. "Never think you are second best. Promise?"

"I promise," Nan said, holding Charity closer still. "I pushed you at Isobelle, even when my senses were screaming at me not to. I did everything, Harry dear, and yet you're here. Yet I have you in my arms. My darling, my love, how could I doubt you?"

"Never doubt me," Charity whispered, covering Nan in kisses. "Never, never doubt me."

CHAPTER THIRTY-TWO

The first person Charity told was Rebecca. Seeking her sister out in the nursery, with the twins, she picked up Patrick and held him close. Suddenly, having someone to cuddle, no matter how tiny, had an importance she had never realised before. Her nephew, rudely awakened from his sleep, screamed indignantly for a moment. Then, as Charity rocked him in a way which seemed (to her bewilderment) to come naturally, he turned to a minute of crying before falling asleep in her arms. Charity looked across at Rebecca—alone in the nursery, as she often tried to be.

"I've something to tell you."

"I think I can guess what it is." Rebecca lifted Mary carefully from the crib, managing not to disturb her slumber.

"You do that so well," Charity said, half-jealous.

Rebecca smiled. "They are my children. When you love someone, somehow the knowledge comes." She paused. "Which, I think, is what you want to speak to me about."

Charity looked over her sleeping baby to her sister. "Rebecca, are you psychic?" she demanded, in the soft tones her burden required.

"I got the wrong sibling, didn't I?" Rebecca said.

Charity looked down at Patrick reflexively. "What do you mean?"

"Nan, not Captain Musgrove," Rebecca said simply. "Am I right?"

Charity realised her mouth had fallen open. For a second or two, she could not speak. She reverted to her usual pacing, Patrick still in her arms.

"Do you know," Rebecca said, her eyes mischievous, "that that is precisely the way to soothe a colicky baby? I did not, until recently."

"Rebecca," Charity said warningly. Then she gave up on this fencing and melted. "Yes, it is Nan. Rebecca, how did you know? And do you really mean that you do not mind?"

"Love is love." Rebecca looked down at the little body in her arms. "The twins have taught me that, alongside so many other lessons. Would I reject Mary, if she loved another woman? Patrick, if he loved a man? They are my children. They are as they are." Her eyes met Charity. "I love you. Not in the same way, but I love you. And I love you just as you are, not as I might want you to be. And Nan—"

"Nan is wonderful," Charity said quickly, determined to cut off any criticism of her love.

"Of course." Rebecca looked surprised that Charity should have doubted it. "You must love whom you love, dearest," she said. "But forgive me. If—if it cannot be a gentleman, which is seems is true—I can only be glad it is Nan. I do not think…" she said slowly. "I do not think that she will hurt you. And that, my dear sister, is a wonderful thing. And if you love her—"

"I do."

Rebecca laughed at the vehemence of Charity's reply. "Well, then, God bless you. And whatever the *Bible* says, I believe He will."

"Becca," Charity said gratefully, "you will never cease to amaze me."

"And I'll tell you what I'll also never cease to do," Rebecca said, kissing Mary's forehead unconsciously, "and that is love you. We might..." She hesitated, holding Mary closer still to her body until the baby mewled a protest. "We might not have had the best parenting. I hope the twins will have better, if that is not too conceited of me, but I had the best sister, and no matter what she does, or whom she loves, I always shall."

Charity felt her eyes fill with tears; she clutched Patrick closer to her breast. "Becca, you...I do not have words."

"Then don't speak." Rebecca placed Mary back in the crib, took Patrick and placed him beside her. She put her arms around Charity. "Just be happy, dearest sister. Just be happy."

The Abolitionist meeting was called unexpectedly. Charity, still loyally nursing Isobelle—who looked better every day, and was now sitting up and taking an interest in the world—was otherwise bound up in Nan. Captain Musgrove had met her, and shaken her (left) hand with great fervour, saying: "I knew you were intelligent enough to see Nan for who she was. I told her so. Bless you, Harry, bless you."

Charity had told Nan that Rebecca had given her blessing, and, when Nan had looked unconvinced, made Rebecca tell her also. The Sisterhood had heard via the grapevine. Isobelle had, of course, been the first to know, and although she had looked a little sad, she had kissed Charity and wished her nothing but the best. Now she was less ill, some of the others had visited her, and news had spread, as both Charity and Nan had known it would. It was preferable: it saved them telling the same news over and over.

The meeting, therefore, had taken Charity by surprise. She cared about the slave trade—of course she did—but she had to acknowledge that it had taken a poor second place to her love affair. Rebecca had picked up the invitation first, looking at it with surprise.

"Why, Lady Caroline has invited us to a special meeting of the Abolitionists! Do you know anything about it, Charity?"

"No." Charity was equally bewildered. "You attended one only a few weeks ago, did you not?"

"Yes. Oh." Rebecca's face clouded. "I wonder if they know something about the Act."

"The what?"

"The Slave Trade Act. It was bound to go in front of the House this week."

"Oh." Charity still could not get used to Rebecca knowing about such things. "I didn't realise."

Rebecca smiled. "You have been otherwise occupied, have you not?"

Charity blushed. "Becca! But Cara does not say why the meeting has been held?"

"Read it for yourself."

Rebecca passed it to her sister, and Charity glanced through it. It was a simple enough document, stating that an extraordinary general meeting had been called and requesting all who could make it to attend that very evening.

"I see."

It seemed a long time until the evening. Rebecca busied herself with the children, but with Isobelle being so much better, Charity had little to do, and the time passed slowly. Finally, however, the time had passed and the two ladies had arrayed themselves in appropriate garments (not too special, not such that they might be accused of failing to make an effort) and been handed one by one into the carriage.

The meeting was well attended. Rebecca and Charity had to wait patiently for their carriage to reach the front of the queue.They disembarked in front of Lady Caroline's door. In the entrance hall, there was a buzz of chatter from the ladies; as far as Charity could hear, no one was certain why they had been summoned hence, but the hopes were high that the Act might have been passed.

"But we mustn't hope. Not too much," she said, as much for her own benefit as Rebecca's. "We've been here before."

"But the world moves on," Rebecca said, her eyes bright with optimism. "Oh, Charity, imagine! What if—"

"Don't!" Charity said sharply. "Don't. I can hardly bear it as it is," she explained. She caught sight of Nan, who looked almost like death. "I fear it is not good news," she murmured to Rebecca, before leaving her unceremoniously to dash to her love. "Nan," she said urgently, "do you know anything?"

"Nothing." Nan looked desolate. "I know the vote was to take place this morning, but I do not know how it went. Cara called the meeting before it happened. I've asked around, but nobody seems to know. Nobody! Oh, Harry, if this should pass…"

"I know," Charity said. The urge to put her arms around Nan was strong, but she knew she must not do so.

"I can't help but think we would have heard were it good news," Nan said. "John was waiting to hear, but he knew no more than we do when I left."

They entered Lady Caroline's large front room. Chairs—Charity could not think where Cara could possibly have acquired so many chairs—stood in rows. It seemed as if quite half of the female population of London was present. But the mood was tense. No one, it seemed, knew what had happened. When the last person was seated, there was a breathless pause. Finally, Cara herself appeared at the front. But it was possible to see from her face what had happened, before she even spoke.

"Ladies," she said—and even gruff Cara sounded emotional, Charity thought. "Ladies, today the news we have been waiting for has happened. Today—today the House of Lords has confirmed the wishes of the House of Commons. Today, not two hours ago, the results came in. The Slave Trade Act is passed. Next year, in 1807, it will become law. No British trader, no matter his market, will be allowed to work in the sale of human flesh. My friends, today a great step for Britain, for the world, was taken. Slave trading was ruled illegal." Her voice broke at that point, and she turned away for a second. But Cara was made of stern stuff, and she had herself under control in seconds.

"Ladies," she said, lifting her chin high, "when remembrance is made in the years to come, we will not be mentioned. Praise, and rightly so, will be given to the Honourable William Wilberforce for his determination in the House to bring slave trading to an end. We women will barely merit a footnote in history. All of this does not matter. The result is what matters. But ladies, remember, we were there. We were there, fighting on the side of all which is right, fighting on the side of God, to whom all humankind is important. Never forget, my friends, never forget: we helped to fight for this law and we saw it made!" Her voice rang out in triumph, her moment of emotion put far behind her. "We can be proud today, and Britain can be proud. Slavery is wrong, and our representatives in both of the Houses have acknowledged it."

Charity looked at the crowd. All around her, women were crying. Some of them were cheering as raucously as if they had been men at a sporting event. Others were nodding their agreement, or talking excitedly to their neighbours. Near the front, Miss Leigh was standing, tears running down her face in joy. She, and others like her, would still face discrimination based on the colour of her skin, but at least no one would be enslaved by Miss Leigh's own countrymen. Charity looked at Nan, who had taken her hand and was squeezing it so tightly as to be painful. She squeezed back, knowing what this meant to her love. On the other side of her, Rebecca had both hands to her mouth, staring at Lady Caroline intensely, as if were she to take her eyes away, the news might change. Charity just felt numb with disbelief. She could hear what Cara had said, but could not process it. It was as if the other woman was speaking in a foreign tongue.

The meeting broke up. Lady Caroline had said what needed to be said; there was nothing more for the ladies to discuss. Nothing—and everything. The chatter of voices was almost deafening. Rebecca stood, to make for home, and Charity grabbed Nan's arm.

"Come with us."

"You don't want me," Nan said.

"I always want you," Charity said, too quietly for anyone else to hear. "Please?"

Nan looked at Rebecca, who nodded. "I would be glad to have your company."

"Thank you."

Nan had dropped Charity's hand and was stern enough of face that anyone who had not heard the news would have thought her distraught. And so, perhaps, Charity thought, she was—but not with sadness. Good news brought its own confusion.

When they got home, Rebecca excused herself to go and see to the twins. Charity and Nan, together alone at last, looked silently at each other.

"Oh, Nan!" Charity said, looking at her love.

For practical, pragmatic Nan was in tears at the news she had wanted so desperately. Charity wrapped her arms around Nan, pulling her close against her chest.

"Is it truly...has it truly been passed?" Nan whispered, her tears dampening the front of Charity's dress. "Tell me it's true, Harry. Tell me I won't wake up and find it all a dream."

"It's true, darling."

Nan's warm body against her own. Charity felt fiercely protective, so happy...so very much in love. What she had felt for Isobelle had been adoration. Isobelle had been a goddess whom Charity had been allowed to worship. She would always care for Isobelle, even if she no longer felt that awestricken emotion. And after all, Isobelle had never asked to be placed on a pedestal. But the emotion Charity felt for Nan was different. Nan was no goddess, though Charity sometimes thought that she might be a true to life heroine. Nan was real—kind, honest and true. Someone to care for, and care about, and know yourself cared for in return. Nan might do many things, and would certainly surprise Charity over and again. She was not the simple soul so many people (Charity included, at first) took her for. She was more than that. So very much more, sang Charity's heart. To love, honour and cherish.

"The slave trade is illegal. No more people torn bodily from their homes to be sold as commodities," Nan said, her voice filled with wonder. "No more human beings being seen as mere flesh."

"No more," agreed Charity. Nan made to move away, but Charity held on tight. "Let me hold you," she begged. "I like to feel you in my arms."

"I like it too." Nan nuzzled her cheek against Charity's shoulder, looking up into her dearest friend's face. "Of course," she said at last, "it is not over. The law makes it illegal to buy or sell slaves, not to own them. For all the thousands of men, women and children who are already slaves, this makes no difference."

"It is not a perfect solution," Charity acknowledged. "But it is a start, Nan."

"Yes." Nan stood on tiptoe and kissed Charity. "I began to think it would never be so." She smiled. "I thought many things would never be so," she said quietly. "I never thought love would find me either. Today, standing here, in your arms, is it awful of me that in so many ways that means more, even, than the Act of Parliament I craved so deeply? And to have that too! I never thought this day would come."

"Well, don't cry about it, silly," Charity said, her voice more gentle than her words. She kissed Nan's forehead. "You are right. The world isn't perfect. I doubt that it ever will be. We can love each other, and the Sisterhood can rejoice in our love, but to the wider world our love must always be a secret. The sale of humans is now against the law, but until all men are free, our battle cannot be said to be won. But Nan—oh, Nan—for today, can it not be enough? Just for today?"

"For today indeed." And the smile was back on Nan's face, the joy in her voice. "And tomorrow too. And who knows, maybe for the next sennight together! Oh, Harry, I never knew I could be this happy. All my wishes, all my dreams."

"For today," Charity said, and kissed her again.

Bella Books, Inc.

Women. Books. Even Better Together.

P.O. Box 10543
Tallahassee, FL 32302

Phone: 800-729-4992
www.bellabooks.com

9 781594 935084